The
Goddess
Incarnate

Awaken

B.L. Callaghan

First published in 2020
Copyright © B.L. Callaghan, 2020
All images used under license from shutterstock.com

Published by
DarkAura Publishing
ABN 32 857 304 185

www.blcallaghan.com

For the Kindred Spirits,
The people that escape real life by
diving headfirst into books.
Okay, you got me.
I'm talking about myself.
This one is for me.
But you can read it too.

- B.L. Callaghan

Novels by B.L. Callaghan

The Goddess Incarnate series

Awaken

Wicked Darkness

The Seer's Curse

Chapter One

T he night was strangely still.

No wind blew through the wattle trees that lined my front yard, and dark clouds hid the moon and turned the sky into a patchwork of stars and darkness.

My garden, full of fragrant lavender and roses, usually a bright and cheerful sight, now an eery floral army standing to attention. What little shadows they cast off managed to come across as menacing.

"Sapphira?"

I turned from where I stood, frozen by my front door, staring at the southern cross in the sky. Under the carport of my rented house, my three friends sat in deck chairs with drinks in hand.

Fallon, with her bright smile and playful blue-green eyes, who always managed to make you laugh, flipped her long auburn hair before taking another sip of her wine. I had known Fallon since I was a child, a seemingly ageless guardian and protector. The woman never let me go without, always taking care of everything - often before even *I* knew that I needed anything as if she were psychic.

Colte, the only guy present, was always ready to party. He had an opinion to share – about anything, smiled smugly, brown eyes sparkling. Colte had just appeared at one of our get-togethers a few years ago and never left, *a friend of Fallon's* he'd said. And now mine too. He'd moved into my house a few months ago, needing a place to stay after being kicked out of his last home.

Ari, who could convince you to do just about anything, and make you think it was your idea, ran a dark hand through her shoulder-length black curls. She looked annoyed at being left with them. Again. Ari was a reluctant fourth; she'd pushed herself into my life about a year ago, a moody little firecracker. She fought with Fallon and Colte on just about everything but seemed to enjoy it immensely. Not that Ari would admit it. She often told me that she only put up with them for my sake.

I loved them all; they were the only family that I had, even if they didn't get along all of the time. Even if it felt like they were all in on some cosmic joke that they had forgotten to tell *me* about.

"Sorry, what'd I miss?" I asked, taking in their expectant stares in my direction.

"Are you okay?" Fallon asked. "You seem lost in thought."

"I'm fine." I flashed her a smile. "What were you guys talking about?"

"I was just saying that *if* there was something else out there, we would know about it," Colte continued, looking back at

Fallon. Obviously, this debate had been raging for a while."I mean surely after thousands of years-"

"I thought that we had agreed; these *beings* would have hidden all proof of existence," Fallon cut in with a frown, flipping her long auburn hair over her shoulder. "You know, to control the panic and keep the authority?"

I looked at Ari as I sat in the empty chair next to her, eyebrows raised. I sipped from the glass of Vodka that I had just poured as she rolled her blue eyes in response.

"Another debate on alien life forms?" I asked quietly, grinning. "Wasn't this *last* weekend's debate?"

"Oh no, this one's about *other* apparently fictitious creatures."Ari shook her head, sending her black curls bouncing over her dark shoulders. "The entire *paranormal world*" She let out a snort and smirked. "You know, monsters and other creatures of the night."

I choked on a mouthful of the Vodka, spluttering and gasping for air as my heart pounded loudly in my chest. Ari pat me on the back, laughing.

Colte and Fallon were watching us expectantly.

"All stories start with a shred of truth..." Ari shrugged, taking her turn in the debate when she was satisfied I wasn't dying. "But how much is twisted and changed before it's just another story to scare and entertain humanity with?"

"I'm staying out of this one."I shook my head, looking down at my glass when all eyes turned to me again.

"I guess I win by default," Colte chuckled, reaching for his packet of cigarettes. "Fourth weekend in a row!"

"Oh, no way!"Fallon groaned, folding her arms in front of her. "Come on, Saph, back me up!"

"Nope, this one is a Sapphira free zone." My voice shook, and I coughed to cover it before taking a large gulp of my drink.

I saw flashes of the past, a night not unlike this.

Only I was seven, and there was blood everywhere.

The broken bodies of my mother, my father, and my older brothers, twisted and strewn across the yard.

My two brothers had died first, a look of shock on their typically smug teenage faces. My father had tried to save them, screaming and clawing at the monster as it tore into them with talons that had reminded me of an eagle. Large jaws filled with razor-sharp teeth had taken his head, silencing him in one bite.

My mother had died trying to hide me. Her final words were a plea for me to *run*.

An inhuman scream had pierced the silence, and I was running, as if my life depended on it – and it had.

I still didn't know how I managed to get away so quickly or where the monster had gone. I knew, though, that if I had stayed still - if I hadn't run and hid from the *thing* that was chasing me, I would have been killed. Torn apart like the rest of my family.

I could no longer picture what they had looked like before that night, my memories refusing to surface. I couldn't hear their laughs, I couldn't remember a time of joy; only their pain, fear, and inevitable death.

I shook my head again, goosebumps running along my arms. What would my friends say if I told them what had happened back then? Would I become the next topic up for debate: *Is Sapphira certifiably insane?* That was not on the cards if I could help it, thank you very much.

Fallon was watching me, frowning slightly. Her blue-green eyes were full of concern. She nodded after a minute, though, seemingly content that I was okay. "Fine," She let out a long-suffering sigh and turned back to Colte. "You win by default."

My hands were shaking, the ice rattling softly against the glass. I forced a smile, still trying to shake the memory, trying to reach the happy version of myself again. What was the point in drinking with friends if you were going to be a downer? No one wanted that, not at what was supposed to be a party.

Colte clapped his hands. "As always."

Ari groaned, rolling her eyes again. "And with such poise and modesty."

"You just wish you were as awesome as me." Colte joked, running a pale hand through his short dark hair. He reached for the stereo remote, flipping through the cd tracks until he found his new victory anthem. *Good feeling* started pumping through the speakers, and Colte pumped his fist in triumph.

The smile on my face wasn't forced this time, letting out a laugh at my friend's goofy antics.

I felt a sharp pain in my head as if a thousand needles were piercing the spot behind my eyes, and I fought the urge to cry out. *What the hell?*

I'd had migraines before, but this was on a whole other level. I closed my eyes, using my free hand to rub them, hoping to ease the pressure building there. A high pitched ringing in my ears blocked out the music, and I felt a sense of terror, an impression that ran through me so quickly, and with such force that my body screamed *Danger!*

I forced my eyes open but –

Everything felt like a blur, I was staying still while the world spun by, faster and faster until I couldn't see clearly anymore. Colors twisted by – bright and light, mingling with the dull and dark, like dancers whirling across a stage.

I felt something tugging at my insides as if a part of me was being wrenched away, and suddenly I was floating. The world stopped spinning, and I could see again, but the picture was wrong.

Objects that were usually immobile were snaking across my view. I could see the air, a swirling mass of blues and whites, moving at a higher speed, and covering every space between heavier materials.

I looked down at my hands, trying to find something stationary to fix the dizziness, and gasped - the sound echoing in my ears, the ringing gone.

I was made of jade smoke – if I focused too intensely on my hands, the flesh and bones would drift apart, coming back together when I looked away. What was going on? Had I died – was this what it was like to be dead? Why was I green?

I saw my real body sink down in the chair, the glass falling from my hand and smashing as it hit the ground. I saw Fallon leaping towards me, face full of alarm. Colte was standing behind her, fear written all over his body. Ari, moving quickly to stand behind me, looking out into the night, eyes blazing an inexplicable luminous azure as she scanned the street.

I looked too, not sure what it was that I was looking for, but hoping for something that made sense in all of this.

Voices came back to me from a million miles away, muffled by the void.

"Sapphira, can you hear me? Can you speak?"

I looked back at my body from where I hovered in the air above it.

"Sapphira, fight it if you can...Just hold on," Fallon said frantically, her hands holding my face as she looked into my eyes.

I could see every minuscule detail around me– every strand of hair, the breath being released from her lips; the colors were so vivid it was almost as if they were animated. Fallon's red lipstick seemed to swim across her lips as she spoke.

"Oh God, help us..." Colte was pacing anxiously, hands behind his head in distress.

"How did they find us?" Ari whispered to herself in disbelief then, glancing back at Fallon from where she stood, said firmly, "We need help."

Fallon shook her head. "No! She isn't ready. If she sees..."

Someone was screaming - a long tormented sound. It was me – the one slumped in the chair.

Her eyes were glazed, the green in them muted, like the last bit of excess paint rinsed off a brush and washed down the drain.

"If we don't call for help, she will be dead." *Ari snarled.*

I watched as she pulled out her phone and started dialing.

I felt a sharp pressure building within my ethereal body, I tried to focus on it, feeling it expand to cover me completely. What I thought of as my soul gave another jolt, sending a wave of excruciating pain through my core, and I heard myself scream again.

"Find them, Sapphira, find the ones that are doing this...... break the connection before it's too late!" *Fallon's lips were moving, but her voice came from miles away, barely registering in my mind through the pain I felt. What was she talking about, what connection was I supposed to break?*

Then, I felt it.

Something was attaching itself to a part of me, wrapping a fluorescently shimmering thin russet cable around my soul and trying to pull it out. I followed it out from my body and into the night.

It sizzled, as if electrified, the sound getting louder the further away from my body it went.

There! *Hidden in the darkness, I saw them.*

Three figures in what looked like cloaks standing on the corner, the cable coursing off and ending within their palms.

I couldn't see their faces, they were hidden under hoods, and I felt my fear rise.

Darkness and despair... *Something whispered inside my head.*

In unison, they jerked their hands back. I screamed in agony. They were tearing away my soul.

I had to stop them; I had to stop the excruciating pain.

My hands reached towards the cable, becoming denser as they touched it. It let out a sizzling crackle, and I could feel an electrified pulse running up my arms.

"Break the line... Save yourself." *A soft voice murmured through the air around me.*

I focused my energy towards where the russet cable was curled around me, and I began to disentangle it.

The three dark figures hissed in disgust, pulling harder. "You cannot defeat us, we WILL have you."

They spoke as one, their voice cold, an impenetrable hatred, and old.

I tried to ignore them as my body shivered; I kept unwinding the cable – but quicker. I had to get it off, I had to get away. I was whimpering, a small feeble sound escaping from my lips as the pain inside me increased again.

I almost had it; I could see the line coming away from my body in long slack coils. Just a little more, and I would be free.

The figures hissed again, taking a step closer, a bright russet light exploded from their palms, and the cable that still connected us came alive. It snaked its way towards me, beginning to wrap itself around my core again, constricting me.

"Help!" I screamed as the figures laughed, the sound grating against my flesh.

Hopelessness washed over me as the voice in my head started talking again. What was the point in fighting? I had no idea what I was doing, no sense of anything. I should just let them take my soul. They would have better use of it anyway. I should just be a good little girl and let them have it...

I was about to give up completely, to stop fighting, and to stop breathing –to just stop being - when another light exploded around me.

This one wasn't coming from the figures, it was almost as if it were coming from behind me. And it seemed to be getting brighter – as if whoever it belonged to was coming closer. I marveled in the intensity of the crimson light as it enveloped me. It was beautiful, calming, and I felt myself smile faintly.

The figures hissed yet again, retreating a little. The link between us faltering for an instant.

And abruptly, someone was standing beside me.

I looked over and gasped. It was a woman. I could feel the Power flowing through her, so much Power. The cable sizzled again, trying to escape the touch of her crimson energy.

She was looking at me, her bright blue eyes shining. Her long dark hair was being fanned by a breeze that I couldn't feel. She wore a long flowing pallid cherry dress, and she had dark tribal tattoos up her arms. They seemed to dance across her skin as I watched.

"Fight this Sapphira; do not let these creatures take you." Her voice was like little bells in my head, waking me and dragging me back into myself – my floating self anyway.

I no longer felt the urge to give in. I wanted to fight. Had it been my voice telling me to give up – or was it the figures trying to gain influence?

She turned to face the dark figures, eyes glowing, as one moved forward. "You cannot have this one, Soul Eater."

"This does not concern you, Sidhe Queen," One of them said. All of the three figures lifted their hoods, revealing their faces.

They were men, but horrific scars dominated their features. The one closest to me saw me staring and smiled grotesquely, his left eye was gone, and on the left side of his mouth was a gaping hole. I could make out the bones of his jaw and what was left of the rotting muscles there. I made a whimpering sound, and the cable tightened around me.

"No Hadrian, this does not concern you." The woman said calmly, taking another step forward. The light around us burned brighter, and the figures shrunk back. "This one is marked for a different end."

"We were not informed of this..." He said slowly, suspiciously. "What end do you speak of?"

The woman shook her head, and I heard a laugh like a tinkling of tiny bells. "One that does not need your talents. I would suggest that you release her and go before the others arrive."

She moved between the men and me, causing the link between us to falter again.

"What others?" The closest one – Hadrian asked.

"The Guardians called for help. I heard the call and arrived first, but there are others on the way that will not be as lenient as I."

Hadrian's companions looked at each other with anxiety. Who were they afraid of? What could be worse than these creatures – what had the woman called them – Soul Eaters?

The cable holding me broke; I heard it snap and was thrown backward, landing on the ground. The Soul Eater's hands erupted in flames as the russet line was flung back into their palms.

"Consider this a forewarning of misfortune, if you stay and persist in this failed harvest." She told them.

The woman glanced down at me from where she stood as if I was an afterthought, and she thrust her hand towards me.

Suddenly I was flying, screaming through the windstorm carrying me away. I tried to grab onto something – anything – and stop, but there was nothing to hold.

This body was ethereal, made of jade smoke.

I was thrust back into my real body as the three Soul Eaters disappeared into nothingness.

Wake up... A melodic voice murmured through my head. *Open your eyes and breathe...*

I felt heavy, disoriented, and indisputably hungover. My arms and legs refused to obey my commands to move, my eyes wouldn't open. My chest was tight with pressure as if I wasn't breathing correctly. I was lying down on something soft – a bed? What the hell had happened to me? My mind was swirling with strange images just out of reach, taunting me. I could hear muffled voices somewhere nearby, it sounded like people were arguing, but the words didn't make sense.

"You let her drink! What were you thinking?"

"Soul Eaters... "

"Do you think it's just a coincidence?"

"Who else would have known where she was?"

I could see a crimson light in my mind, small at first and flickering like a candle until it exploded behind my eyes.

Wake up...

I knew that voice – *how* did I know that voice? Why did it sound like little musical bells? My eyes still wouldn't open. I couldn't do as the beautiful voice asked, and I started to panic.

Relax ceann álainn, you will be fine. What do you remember?

Flashes of grotesque men, fear, intense pain, and the feeling of flying coursed through my vision. A beautiful woman with dancing tattoos.

This is all just a...

Good, your mind is intact. The voice interrupted and began to fade. *Now open your eyes...*

I felt a *push* behind the words, forcing its way through the heaviness, and my eyes burst open. I sat up, gasping for air.

"...Bad dream..." I whispered, hand over my heart, the pressure on my chest easing even as my heart still thundered erratically.

I looked around, taking in the mismatched furniture, the little trinkets placed lovingly along the top of the dresser. I was in my bedroom, the curtains drawn. I could see faint sunlight sneaking in through the gaps. There were piles of clothes still folded in the armchair where I had left them and the pictures of long-gone loved ones hanging on the off-white walls.

I frowned, running a heavy hand through my long golden blonde hair. There was a sticky lump on the back of my head, and when I touched it, shockwaves of pain rippled through my nerves. My fingers came away with traces of blood. My mouth was dry, and I could smell alcohol on my breath. Had I fallen over in my drunken state? I scolded myself for drinking so much. It was never a good idea when I drank myself stupid. Like most nineteen-year-old girls, I became a clumsy fool, finding it impossible to walk without falling or running into inanimate objects.

"Never again...." I muttered, swearing a silent oath that I wouldn't touch another drop. My head throbbed as if to agree.

The arguing voices that I thought I had heard earlier had ceased when I spoke. Silence filling my house. Had I dreamt of them too? No, I could hear faint footsteps coming my way. There *was* someone else in my house. I sat up straighter under my sheets, eyes on the closed door.

The footsteps paused.

My breathing got heavier, fear rising to a lump in my throat. What if those grotesque men weren't just a bad dream? What if they were real and standing on the other side of my door?

A quiet whimpering sound escaped from my lips, my hands closed into fists around my sheets as I panicked.

There was a soft knock at the door. *Did scary things knock on doors?*

"Sapphira?" Fallon's voice, soothing from through the wood.

I sighed, relaxing. "Yeah, come in."

The door opened slowly, Fallon stepping through before closing it again. "I'm going to turn on the light." She warned me. I hissed as the light exploded, excruciating against my sore eyes. "I did warn you," Fallon said, coming to sit on the edge of the bed. "How do you feel?"

I thought about it. My head hurt, my eyes hurt... just about all of me ached. My heart still pounded, as though it knew something was wrong here.

And I was so drunk last night that I saw monstrous men trying to take my soul.

"I'm fine." I lied. "What time is it?"

"It's just after two. You've been asleep for fifteen hours." Fallon was studying me intently, her eyes piercing holes through my skin. "Are you sure you feel fine?"

I frowned. "How strange is it that I slept for fifteen hours after an alcohol bender – I mean, I fell and hit my head, right?" I paused, watching Fallon, who was still observing me closely. "That's why I'm so sore? I could have had a concussion or something."

It was Fallon's turn to frown, and unease flittered through her eyes. She opened her mouth to say something but was interrupted by a knock at the door. I jumped at the sound, my heart hammering in my chest. If it didn't calm down soon, I'd probably have a heart attack.

Fallon didn't move, her eyes still focused on me.

"Who else is here, Fallon?" I asked quietly, nervously pulling at the sheets.

"It's okay," She reassured me with a soothing smile that didn't quite reach her eyes. "Ari called a... friend."

"Fallon, a word?" came a deep, commanding masculine voice from behind the closed door. There was an accent in his voice that I couldn't place. Who the hell was in my house?

Ari - none of my friends actually - had ever invited anyone over before. Even Colte, who had moved in a while ago, had never invited anyone over. And I'd thought that they would have at least *asked* me first.

Fallon sighed, anger swimming across her expression before she stood gracefully. "I'll be right back."

"Do you mind turning off the light?" I called softly as she reached the door. "It's too damn bright in here."

The light shut off as the door clicked shut behind her. I sunk back down into my bed and closed my eyes. *At least it was dark again. That was a good start.*

"She's confused. It could be from the injuries – or it could be something else." Fallon's voice came softly. "I can sense that something isn't quite right, but I can't tell what that is yet, *Moroi*."

"We need to move quickly, the window of opportunity on this is closing rapidly." The masculine voice replied firmly. His tone suggested that he didn't like the conversation he was having. *Or maybe it was Fallon that he didn't like?* The thought surprised me for a minute. She *had* looked angry when he had asked to speak to her. "For her safety, she needs to be taken to-"

"Don't you *dare* finish that sentence!" Ari snapped. I thought that this mysterious man was her friend – isn't that what Fallon had told me? Why did she sound so angry at his words? "You cannot for one second think that I would allow her-"

My mind was foggy, and it felt as though there was something that I should be remembering. Something important – but every time I got close to knowing what that something was, it slipped away again. Like little eels swimming in murky water.

"*Allow* her?" A barked laugh from the masculine stranger, "They know that she's here – and that she's hurt. It would be better if she *wasn't* here if they came looking. At least if we move her to a Safe House, she would be better protected. The defenses are well equipped to fend off an attack. You know this."

I sighed. "You know that I can hear you, right?"

I spoke loudly, ensuring that they would hear and stop arguing, even though every word out of my mouth was like a sledgehammer against my head.

I could practically see the tension through the door. Nothing but silence answered me.

"I think if you're discussing me, I should have a say," I continued, anger and frustration continuing to rise. I could almost picture the emotions spinning like little dark-colored whirlwinds through my body.

The door flung open, and Ari stormed in.

She turned on the light, without warning. I suppressed my hiss and blinked rapidly as my eyes readjusted. She managed a tight smile in my direction as she took her seat on the bed, smoothing her jeans with dark hands.

"You let a stranger into my house?" I asked her in a hissed whisper, eyes narrowed.

The stranger in question waltzed calmly into my bedroom before Ari could answer. His bright brown eyes took in my room intently as if he were memorizing every single personal possession I had. He was tall and made of muscle, a human mountain. His skin was dark brown, an obvious hint that he hadn't been born in this country as if his accent hadn't let you in on that fact already.

"Who are you?" I asked as his eyes finally rested on me. "What are you doing in my house?"

Fallon stepped back into the room, closing the door quietly behind her. Her eyes went from Ari – who was still fuming – to the stranger. She was frowning, her lips pressed together in a thin line.

The mountain smiled. "I am Abhijay. I am here to protect you, Sapphira."

Ari snorted, rolling her eyes, but I ignored her.

"Abhijay?" I frowned at him. "Why do I need protecting?"

Abhijay opened his mouth to reply, but Ari grabbed my hand. "Maybe this should wait until you're feeling better."

I pulled my hand away from hers, anger rising again. I wanted answers, and I wanted everyone out of my bedroom. "I'm fine. And I want to know what the hell is going on!" I was yelling, my voice shaking slightly. I felt weak, as though my outburst had drained the small amount of energy I had, and my head started swimming.

"We don't have time to coddle her. She needs to be moved to a safer location." Abhijay said as if I hadn't spoken. His eyes went from staring at me to Fallon, who still stood in the doorway.

"I already told you," Ari hissed, glaring at Abhijay. "She isn't going to one of your freaking *Safe Houses*."

Their voices started to blur together as Ari and Abhijay argued. Fallon turned her eyes from me to watch them with a tired look.

There was an ache in my chest, and I closed eyes that weighed a ton. Maybe I could sleep while they sorted out whatever the hell was going on in my life. Perhaps the answers could wait. Yeah, sleep sounded good...

"We don't have another option right now."Fallon sighed. "While you two are arguing over Sapphira's wellbeing, she's about to code out."

"Shit!" Ari cursed. "Sapphira – open your eyes!"

Abhijay said something in another language that didn't sound polite, and I felt cold hands lifting me from my bed.

"The wound on her head is bleeding again," Fallon said quickly, her voice sounding a million miles away. "I can't heal this properly here. Ari, if you could get the car ready. We need to get her to the healers. And tell Colte that he should pack some of Sapphira's things – we won't be coming back here for a while." Her words were peculiar. It sounded as though she had said 'healers' instead of doctors.

"I'm so tired." I murmured, my voice sounding strange. "Let me sleep. I'll go to the doctors later."

"No, Sapphira, if you sleep now, you will probably die," Fallon told me calmly. "Open your eyes and talk to me."

I forced my eyes to open, fighting the heaviness they held. Abhijay was carrying me, the room spun with each step he took. He wasn't looking at me, although I could see the dead calm look on his face, his arms held me tightly, as if he were afraid that he would drop me.

"You're freaking me out, Fallon," I whispered. She was walking just ahead of us, and she glanced back as I spoke. She was frowning again, a worried look in her strangely beautiful eyes.

"And you are freaking me out." Her eyes flickered to Abhijay. "The wound should not be bleeding. It was already starting to heal an hour ago."

"Her blood smells strange." He replied, his grip getting tighter. "It smells *wrong*."

"What the hell are you talking about?" I had intended to sound firm, to express the anger I felt at the liberties my friends were taking. Instead, my voice was a murmur, something a tired child would have used.

I knew I was hurt. But how could these people think that I would be okay with them coming into *my* house, making decisions about *me*, *ignoring* my questions?

The warm summer air, mixed with the fragrant wattle and lavender from my garden, hit my nostrils as we reached the front door. I grimaced as pain burst through my body as he went down the two steps leading towards the carport. I whimpered as the sunlight hit my face, sending starbursts of agony through my eyes and head.

"It's okay, Saph," I heard Ari say as my eyes closed again. "Their car has tinted windows, it'll be dark in a second."

"Who?" I whispered, my mouth not letting the question come out correctly.

"Abhijay and his *friends*," Ari replied sarcastically as I was placed carefully into the back seat.

"Yeah, and its Abhijay's *friends* that'll be saving your life." Snapped a new, female voice in my ear.

"Cut it out, Leilani. Just make sure Sapphira stays breathing until we get there." Abhijay told her firmly.

"Yes, *Maharishi*..."

Except for screaming as my head exploded every time we hit a bump in the road, and someone cursing loudly each time, I don't remember much of the drive.

Actually, I don't remember much of reality over the next few days. I was in and out of consciousness for most of it, waking only to scream in pain and throw up.

I'd had hundreds of nightmares involving monsters and death while I slept. Each time I woke, Ari was there with a cold washer for my face, and a glass of putrid silver liquid she practically had to force down my throat. She'd sarcastically called it 'medicine from the Djinn.' I thought I had been delusional or still dreaming.

It wasn't that much of a stretch in imagination, really, considering everything that had happened.

I was contemplating this as I lay in an uncomfortably hard bed, my eyes closed. I could hear Ari breathing from the chair beside the bed, but I feigned sleep. I didn't want any more of the horrid silver crap. My stomach did summersaults just thinking about it.

No more throwing up for a while... It seemed to beg. My mouth agreed wholeheartedly.

Ari cleared her throat, somehow making the noise seem elegant - if that was even possible.

I concentrated on making my breathing relaxed, getting into the even rhythm of sleep.

"I know that you're awake." She said softly. "You're not snoring obnoxiously anymore."

I sighed, opening my eyes. "Please," I begged desperately, my stomach tying itself in knots. "No more of that putrid poison."

"No, no more." Ari chuckled. "You don't need any more of that putrid *medicine*."

"Thank god for that!" I said, relief flooding my voice.

I looked around. I was in a large room, the walls made from massive grey stone blocks that curved around, giving the room a circular feel, like a castle tower. There was a single, small window high on one of the curved walls that let in the sunlight, and a large chandelier hung from the roof high above my head. A steel door dominated the wall to my right – a vast, bulky monstrosity and the only exit. The bed I was in and Ari's chair were the single pieces of furniture.

Ari was watching me with calm blue eyes, her short black curls rested on her shoulders like a dark halo around her head. Her clothes were casual; jeans and a black T-Shirt. I'd never seen her in anything so laid back.

"Where are we?" I asked slowly, trying to sit up. I saw that under the sheet, I was wearing a hospital gown. And nothing else. Embarrassing.

"Take it slowly, Sapphira." She said, sitting forward in the chair. "You could still be weak."

I managed to prop myself up on my elbows and looked at her, frowning. "You know, that wasn't answering my question," I said, frustrated and on edge.

"I know."

"Are you going to answer?"

Ari sighed, sitting back in her chair. "You are at a Moroi Safe House. You have been here for three days. You were attacked by Soul Eaters and were contaminated." She was matter-of-fact, counting down the sentences on her fingers, speaking in a quick, short rhythm.

"I – *What?*" I was frowning again. I was going to get permanent creases across my forehead – I could tell.

"You were contaminated. When a Soul Eater attacks someone, they take that individual's soul, and they die. If they, for some reason, are unable to finish their harvest, the individual is infected with what we call the *wasting sickness.*"

Ari explained slowly, as if to a child. She saw my question coming before I asked it. "This sickness makes the person fall into a coma-like state in which most never survive. They are unable to heal, to acquire sustenance and eventually... just stop breathing. "

I was confused and terrified, but at least I was getting answers – even if they didn't make any sense at all.

Ari usually hated horror stories – refusing to even show up to movie nights in that genre – and typically had a better sense of humor than this.

"So, how did *I* survive?"

"You had help." Ari paused, cocking her head to one side, as if she was listening to something that only she could hear, before continuing. "And you were strong enough to fight back."

"Why was I attacked?"

Ari shook her head at me, shutting down the conversation, just as a loud metallic squeal cut through the room, and the door began to open. Abhijay, the man-mountain, entered the room, leaving the door ajar. So *he* had been real too.

His brown eyes found mine, and he smiled warmly. "You're awake. How do you feel?"

"Indian..." I blurted before I could stop myself. I felt myself blushing in embarrassment; the second the word left my mouth.

I'd never been good at talking to men, Colte being the exception, of course, But this was beyond ridiculous.

He looked surprised. "Excuse me?"

"I'm sorry, I was just trying to place your accent." I felt my cheeks burning hotter, as I tried to explain, and I avoided his gaze. "It's Indian, isn't it?"

Ari tried, unsuccessfully, to hide her snicker.

"It is," Abhijay confirmed slowly. "Why is that important?"

"Oh, it's not really, I... I just ..." I stuttered, embarrassed, sitting up properly on the bed even though I wished I could disappear into it completely. "Let me start again. We haven't been formally introduced, at least, I don't think we have."

It came out as a question, frustration tinging my tone. The last time I had spoken to him felt like a dream, and I couldn't quite recall all of the details clearly.

"I'm Abhijay, *Maharishi* of the Safe House we currently inhabit." He indulged me.

"Sapphira," I replied, throwing him a quick, grateful smile. "Ignorant and disoriented in my current locale."

"For heaven's sake... What did you want, *Moroi*?" Ari snapped.

Abhijay flinched and turned to face Ari. "I came to see if Sapphira was awake."

"And now you've seen that she is."

"What the hell is a *Moroi* anyway?" I asked, trying to distract them. I didn't need an argument between them right now, and I had seen first hand how well Ari could argue.

Two sets of eyes turned back to fix on me.

"Moroi is a type of vampire," Ari said, disgust evident in her voice.

"You're shitting me, right?" I looked between the two people in the room in disbelief. "This *is* some sort of non-humorous joke? How did she rope you into this?"

Abhijay shook his head, throwing a deadly look in Ari's direction. "No Sapphira, she tells the truth – harshly – but the truth nonetheless."

"Do you eat *people*?" I asked incredulously, my mouth running before my brain was ready. Again. *Oh shit, good one, Saph. Could you sound like any more of an idiot?* I scolded myself.

"Moroi, don't eat people, Sapphira." Abhijay said gently. To his credit, he didn't laugh.

Ari managed to turn her snigger into something resembling a cough.

"Are you one of them as well?" I asked her.

"Certainly not!" She snapped, glowering at me indignantly.

"Your friend is Nephilim," Abhijay said the word as if it burned his tongue to say it out loud, a slight shudder running over his body.

"Wait, I've heard that word before." I frowned. "Isn't Nephilim the name of half angels?"

"Well, the offspring of angels and mortals," Abhijay said. "It could also be loosely used for *Fallen Angels*."

I looked at Ari in shock. How far was she going to run with this? "You're an *angel*?"

Ari shrugged, getting to her feet, and drifted to stand below the window, face upturned to feel the sun. "I used to be."

"Are Fallon and Colte Nephilim too?"

"*Definitely* not."

My head was spinning. "Are they Moroi, like you, Abhijay?"

"Colte is a Dhampir – it means half-human, half-vampire." Abhijay quickly informed me, prepared for the question. "Fallon is one of the Djinn. Better known as - "

"That's enough." Ari cut him off angrily, spinning back to face us. Her eyes flashed a brilliant azure. The tension in the room rose another level; I could almost *see* the anger rolling off her in waves.

"She has a right to know what's going on, Ari," Abhijay said firmly. Clearly, a man that was used to being in charge. But had he ever gone up against *Ari*?

"Too much, too quickly, and it'll fry her brain." The Nephilim retorted in opposition, crossing her arms over her chest. "Time for you to go, Moroi."

This had to be a joke, a well-rehearsed one, but a joke nonetheless.

Because if what they were saying was real, and I didn't really want to believe that it was, then there really were monsters and supernatural things out there. *And my friends were counted among them!*

If it was real, maybe the images that taunted me were more than just nightmares, and perhaps I wasn't crazy after all.

How could they keep this from me?

All the years I'd known Fallon and Colte, the last year that Ari had been hanging around. *None* of them had said anything about *any* of this. Had they?

There had been debates about the existence of mythological and supernatural creatures, but that all they had been, right? Drunken discussions to fill in the weekends? Had my so-called friends being trying to clue me in? Had I been too stupid – too *afraid* to see it for what it really was?

The more that I thought about it, the more it made sense. And I was *furious*. How could I have let myself believe that they were my friends? How did I miss all of the clues – even if I didn't see the supernatural aspects - I saw and shrugged off, the deflections and the half-answers.

Fallon never seemed to age – would laugh of any questions I had about it with an excuse about a magical skin routine and impressive genes.

The fact that Ari couldn't seem to stand to be around the others for too long, and seemed to always be in an argumentative mood when they were around. How she continually vanished for weeks at a time with no explanation.

Or how Colte would always deflect questions about his family, saying that they were all sort-of dead to him and leave it at that.

"Wait!"

I wanted to scream, to rage against my alleged *friends* and the lies I'd been told. But I held it all in, choosing instead to try another tactic first.

Both Ari and Abhijay turned to look at me inquisitively.

"I'm hungry. And... and I don't want Abhijay to go just yet. I'd like to talk to him some more."

Ari glared at Abhijay as the Moroi – the *Vampire* smiled warmly at me from where he stood across the room.

I motioned to the chair that Ari had vacated, grinding my teeth as Ari huffed, storming towards the door. "I'll find you some food. This place has to have something other than O-neg in the kitchen." She paused in the entryway, turning back to throw a poisonous glare at Abhijay as he sat down. "Don't you dare sauté her brain with too much shit, Moroi, or you'll have Fallon to answer to."

As soon as the door was closed, I turned to Abhijay. "Why does she hate you?"

"She doesn't hate *me* exactly, she hates what I am. It goes against what she knows to be true and pure."

"So, being a vampire is impure and wrong?" I played along, holding the sheet against my chest, eyes wide.

"That's what Ari was taught to believe, yes."

"Why was she taught to believe that opinion?" I prodded, needing to find out all that I could. "What is it about your... kind... that is so wrong to... to Nephilim?"

Abhijay raised an eyebrow, expression telling me that I needed to think it through.

What did I know about Vampires?

The extent of my knowledge came from movies and books. I highly doubted that they were credible sources of information, but I went with it anyway.

They were supposed to be beings that relished in the night and needed the blood of the living to flourish. The living dead.

"Why would that be so offensive to an angel – fallen or not?" Abhijay countered, watching my face with an expression that hinted he had followed my train of thought.

"Because if you believe pop culture, you sound evil," I admitted.

"Exactly. In the Nephilim's eyes, we are nothing but the devil's minions – demons."

"Are you?" I paused, swallowing a lump in my throat. "Evil, I mean?"

Abhijay shook his head, his expression serious. "No, the Moroi are not demons. We are not evil in that sense. We do, however, need blood to truly prosper, so I do see how the Nephilim may think so – but we are not the threat that they believe us to be."

"So... If Ari is so against the Moroi, her enemies-"

"We are not enemies," Abhijay cut in firmly. "Ari and the Moroi have a kind of... treaty."

"Okay, but still, it seems to me like she doesn't really want to be in your company, so why is she still here?"

Abhijay's *think it through* expression was back.

I was lost, mind scrambling to make sense of everything that I had been told. I was still caught up with the *monsters are real* revelation, if I was honest with myself.

"Because *you* are here." He said, filling the awkward silence that followed as if it were the most obvious answer in existence, and he was shocked that I hadn't known it.

"But what is so special about me that would make her want to stay?" I paused for a second, truly confused this time, "Or is it a part of the 'truce' that she be here?"

"No, it is not part of the truce that makes Ari stay here. She stays to watch over you." Abhijay smiled at me. "You are special for many reasons, Sapphira, one of those being that you survived a Soul Harvest. Not many can boast that feat."

I returned his smile faintly, and then a thought jumped into my head. "Ari said that you were a *type* of Vampire. Are there different kinds?"

He sighed, folding his large hands in front of him. He studied them in silence for a time. "There are."

"What are they?" I prompted gently, not wanting him to stop talking.

The more I could get him to say, the more I would know about who the people around me genuinely were. The ones that had lied and kept so much of themselves concealed from me.

You weren't completely honest with them either. The harsh thought drifted through my mind. *Did you tell* them *the truth about what happened to your family?*

That was different, I told myself. I had a good reason to keep that hidden. I didn't want my only friends to think I was crazy. Or inventing horrific images to replace the real memories of my tragedy – as my Therapist had said.

The Therapist was wrong, though, turns out real monsters are lurking in the dark.

Abhijay didn't *seem* like a monster, but if *he* existed, what else was out there?

"There are three types of vampires." Abhijay's voice cut through my internal argument. "The Moroi – like me; the Dhampir; and the Strigoi."

I waited for him to continue, but he was silent again, still studying his hands like they held the answers to the cosmos.

"What's the difference between them?" I prodded when the silence had gone on longer than was comfortable.

He looked up at me, frowning darkly at the question. He opened his mouth like he was going to answer but thought better of it.

He exhaled slowly and turned his head towards the door. "Ari was right about not overloading you right now, Sapphira. You should take this slowly. The knowledge you seek isn't going anywhere – you have years to uncover it all."

"I'm sorry that I offended you," I said quickly as he stood to leave. "Please don't go just yet."

He sat back down reluctantly, eyes darting to the door again. "You didn't offend me, Sapphira," He said after a while. "It's just a lot of information to process – not all of it easy – for you or me."

"Because my brain will turn to mush?"

The mountainous Vampire chuckled. "Yes, because your brain will turn to mush."

"I like you," I told him with a smile. "You laugh at my lame-ass jokes."

"Well, don't tell anybody," He said in a staged whisper, wiggling his eyebrows, visibly glad about the lighter focus. "I do have a villainous reputation to uphold."

The door let out its metallic squeal and swung open. Ari's eyes took in our smiling faces, and she narrowed her eyes, clearly not overly pleased to find us acting so friendly.

She was holding a tray of food in her hands, and she stalked over to the bed. "Here, it's the best I could do. Let's just hope that it doesn't kill you." She placed the tray on my lap and stood there looking at me expectantly as I glanced down at it.

A bowl of freshly chopped fruit – strawberries, apple, pear and kiwi fruit, and a glass of water. There was also a small dish that held what looked like yogurt.

"It's fine," I told her. "I like fresh fruit."

"I must take my leave now, Sapphira," Abhijay said softly, standing. He smiled at me and bowed. Seriously, I'm not joking – he actually *bowed* at me. Like old school gallantry from an era long gone.

I blushed, speechless, and embarrassed.

Was I supposed to bow back? From the bed, and in a hospital gown? "Umm... okay." I murmured, "I'll see you later?"

He nodded, eyes sparkling. "I will return later if you wish."

"Abhijay?" I called as he turned to leave again.

His eyebrows rose in question, but he didn't speak.

"Can I call you A.J?" I hurried on as he frowned, knowing I was probably making a fool out of myself again. "It's just that 'Abhijay' is a bitch to pronounce... And all my friends have nicknames."

Ari looked shocked but turned her face away, studying a crack in one of the large grey stones of the wall.

Abhijay's lips tilted into a smile, and his eyes sparkled again. "I would be honored by the sign of favor." He made another bow in my direction, and without another word, he left.

"I wouldn't get too attached to him if I were you, Sapphira," Ari said quietly, sitting on the edge of the bed. She was watching the door with a grim expression. A.J had left it open, and I could make out an old fashioned candle-lit lamp hanging on the stone wall opposite the door.

"I'm not attached," I said quickly as she turned to look at me. "I've only just met the guy. Moroi, or whatever. I just think that he is easy to talk to."

"You don't have to justify yourself, I wasn't accusing you of anything, but I just want you to be careful. *His* kind are not exactly trustworthy, and hopefully, we won't be here for long."

"Look, he told me about how you were taught to distrust the Moroi, but I am going to make that decision for myself. I have that choice."

Ari sighed, gesturing to the food. "I think that you are making the wrong one, but let's not fight. Eat, please."

I smiled, sensing how hard that was for her. Ari had always loved to argue her point of view.

"Also," I put a strawberry in my mouth and started to chew. "He seems to be the only one that tells me the truth," I added, unable to stop myself.

"*Truth*." Ari scoffed. "When have I ever lied to you?"

"You never told me about all of this." I gestured to everything, the room, Ari, the whole world.

"Did you ever ask?" She asked calmly. "Would you have believed me?"

"If you were my friend, you could have tried." I snapped. "If this is real, it's a lot to take in, Ari."

"*If* this is real? How could you not believe your own eyes?"

"Years of therapy and fake friends, I suppose."

"Bite me, bitch. I was never fake with you – and you know it. Besides," Ari paused, head tilted to one side as she glared at me. "I told you countless times that Fallon and Colte were monsters."

"You called them *self-indulgent creatures*, not monsters." I pointed out, rolling my eyes.

"Same thing." Ari shrugged, looking bored.

"No, not the same thing. Not by a long shot."

She shrugged again, not bothering to continue our conversation.

Having been out for so long, I was starving. My anger, too, seemed to be using up more energy than usual.

Before I knew it, the entire bowl of fruit was devoured. I polished off the yogurt – even though I didn't usually eat the stuff – as Ari examined her nails.

"So, how long do I have to stay in bed – and where are my clothes?" I asked when I was done eating. "I mean, don't get me wrong, I'm grateful that I'm still alive, but hospital gowns and I just don't mix well. And I really need to stretch my legs."

Ari smirked, a knowing look in her eyes. "You can stretch your legs when you can stand unassisted."

"And my clothes?"

"Destroyed." She gestured to the chair. "There's a change of clothes in the bag under there. I don't know what exactly is in there. Colte was left to pack it for you."

"Where is Colte?" I asked, throwing back the sheet and swinging my legs over the side of the bed.

I was downright scared of what Colte would have put in the bag. My cheeks flushed at the thought of him rifling through my underwear draw.

"Gathering information," Ari answered in a bored tone, returning her attention to her perfect nails.

"What information – and from where?" I pulled the bag out from under the chair and tossed it onto the bed.

My head spun for a minute, and I fought the urge to throw up. I tried to pretend nothing was the matter as Ari watched me suspiciously, that knowing smirk making another appearance on her dark face.

"He went to find out more about the attack. Don't worry, Saph, when we know more – so will you." Fallon entered the room, smiling brightly as she spoke. "You look better."

She was wearing a blue-green dress that matched her eyes. The dress hugged her perfectly tanned and curvy body before flowing loosely over her long legs. Her long auburn hair was tied in sophisticated knots around her head. She wore a sizeable cerulean stone on a gold chain at her throat, drawing attention to her chest.

"Dizzy and confused, but no longer bleeding all over the place," Ari stated in a neutral tone, getting to her feet.

So much for hiding it from her. I thought as I unzipped the bag. There were three pairs of jeans folded neatly on top of the small pile of clothes. I pulled them out and tossed them onto the bed.

My black tunic style blouse was next, the only shirt Colte had packed apart from a tank top – also black – that was scrunched up next to a few pairs of underwear and a black bra.

My cheeks flamed again, and I turned away from the clothes with a sigh.

Fallon had taken the chair, her legs crossed and hands folded over her knees.

Ari still stood at the edge of the bed. Her voice was devoid of any emotion as she spoke. "Welcome back, Fallon. Did you get what you needed from home?"

Fallon nodded, ignoring Ari's odd behavior. "I did."

"Well, I'll leave her in your care. I'm done with babysitting duties." Ari winked at me, flashing perfect white teeth as she smiled. "See you later, Sapphira."

"You know, just because the time of acting as mortal companions is over Ari," Fallon began in a conservative voice as Ari made for the door. "Doesn't mean that all the time we spent together no longer matters. We are still friends, of a sort."

Ari stiffened, not turning around, but frozen in place for a moment, before visibly shaking herself and disappearing from sight.

Fallon sighed, turning her attention back to where I stood, dumbfounded. "So, are you going to get changed or stand there like an idiot?" She smiled at me mischievously. "I thought that you wanted to snoop around a bit?"

"That depends," I told her coolly. "Are you going to be honest with me for once?"

Fallon seemed to pause, head tilted to the side as she looked me over, eyes full of something like guilt.

I felt a warm, tingling sensation settling over me, like a calming blanket. The calm fought with my own rage and anger for a moment, before winning out and covering my skin.

"You promise to give me a chance to explain, and I'll tell you whatever you want to know." She replied.

Chapter Two

I walked beside Fallon down a long corridor made of large stone tiles, lamps lighting the way. I could hear my footsteps echoing around us as we traveled. Fallon didn't make a sound as she moved. How had I never noticed that before?

"So, tell me again where we are?"

"A Moroi Safe House, although *compound* would be a more fitting term," Fallon said lightly. "We are approximately four stories underground at the moment. This Safe House is one of the largest in the country. It has the best defense system of any of the Moroi places by far." She kept her answers short and to the point, leaving no room for misunderstandings.

"And *why* are we here?"

"We needed to move you to a more secure place. This was the only decent choice we had at the time."

"A.J told me that you were a..." I paused, trying to remember his exact words. "Djinn?"

Fallon nodded again. "I am Djinn, yes. Nice nickname by the way" She winked at me, trying to keep the tone light. "What else did he tell you?"

I told her what I remembered, starting from when I woke up, adding that not much of it made a lot of sense to me.

"What the hell was that awful silver crap anyway?" I stopped walking, turning to Fallon with a frown. "Ari said it was Djinn medicine... tasted more like poison if you ask me."

Fallon laughed. "That was a rare and powerful medicine from my people. You should be grateful that I could get some on such short notice. You'd most likely be dead if I hadn't."

"Where did you get it?"

"I told you, from my people." Fallon started walking again, nearing a bend in the corridor.

"The Djinn, right." I followed her, hurrying to catch up before she disappeared. "Fallon, why didn't we just go there if I needed the medicine so badly?"

"The Djinn were too far away. You wouldn't have made it there alive. We came here so that you could be protected while I went for more help." Fallon paused, rubbing the back of her neck, eyes closed.

"The Moroi are strong warriors Sapphira, I trusted them to keep out anyone who would harm you while I was gone." She continued softly.

"But didn't you just get back? How did the medicine get here before you - if you were the one that went to get it?"

Fallon laughed, the sound bouncing off the walls and echoing along the corridor. "I made the trip home twice while you've been here."

"But I thought you said that the Djinn were too far away-"

"It was too far for *you* to travel in the state you were in. I, on the other hand, was not bleeding like a macabre fountain, nor was I *contaminated*." Fallon paused again. I waited, mind racing to make sense of all that she was telling me.

When she spoke again, it was quietly, her tone hard. "Even if we had taken you to the *Modena Al-Djinn*, you wouldn't have been able to enter. The elders would never have allowed it. You would have died at the gates while I argued fruitlessly for them to reconsider their laws."

"Harsh." Colte's voice echoed around us, playfully. He stood leaning up against the wall next to A.J, trying to look casual. He had a lit cigarette in his hand, and he blew smoke into the air before he continued. "Couldn't you have just said 'the sick aren't allowed to enter the city, so it would have been a bad idea to go there with you'?"

He threw a lazy smile at me before turning back to Fallon, eyes worried. "I have some interesting news to share with you."

Fallon nodded, looking serious.

"Perhaps I could show you around a bit, Sapphira?" A.J offered, smiling warmly. I knew immediately that he was trying to get me away so that Colte and Fallon could talk in private. "I could introduce you to some of the other Moroi and Dhampir that helped bring you here?"

"That would be great," I told him, returning his smile before turning my attention to Colte. "But what news do you have, Colte – is it about who attacked me?"

Colte glanced at A.J and Fallon before answering slowly. "You were mentioned once or twice, yeah."

"Well, I want to hear it too," I said firmly, folding my arms over my black tank top.

Again, Colte's eyes went to the others. He looked nervous as if he was torn between spilling his guts and keeping the information from me.

This was getting old, really fast. Why did everyone think that I didn't need to know what was going on? I had a right to know who wanted me dead, to understand why they were treating me like I was fragile. How *dare* they just drop me into a world that I hadn't known had existed and not tell me anything!

My anger swirled around me, the dark vortex of emotion so strong and overpowering it seemed to fill the air all around us. *What the hell?* My rage was like a semi-solid mass that I could see clearly. The vortex faltered as I reacted with shock, collapsing in on itself and vanishing.

The others reacted similarly, surprise visible on their faces. Colte had taken a step back, dropping his cigarette.

Fallon had tensed but stayed where she was. "Calm down, Saph, that much emotion is dangerous if you can't control it." She said softly, soothingly.

"So dark for someone so young..." A.J murmured faintly, eyes wide.

I turned to him, the anger subsiding. "You can see it too?"

"Of course we can," Colte answered for him, bending to pick up the fallen cigarette. "Remind me not to piss you off again any time soon."

Hurried footsteps reverberated through the corridor, and Colte and Fallon tensed as four pissed-off looking people appeared, surrounding us.

"It's alright," A.J told them calmly.

"What the hell was that?" One of them asked, dark eyes regarding us suspiciously. He was tall and slender, dark skin seeming to vibrate with Power. He wore blue jeans and a tight white T-shirt. He folded his arms over his chest, frowning.

"Our guest just got a little upset. Return to your post, Saul."

"A little upset?" Saul exclaimed incredulously, "I felt that surge from the communication room. I thought the Strigoi had-"

"I said it was fine, return to your post." A.J cut in. His tone was commanding, leaving no room to argue, and Saul stiffened.

"Yes, *Maharishi*... My apologies." Saul bowed to A.J before motioning the others to go. He turned and moved fluidly back the way he came.

"Sorry, I didn't mean to cause problems for you, A.J," I said softly.

He waved my apology away. "It's alright, Sapphira, no harm done. Fallon, perhaps I could get one of my people to teach Sapphira how to control her emotions a bit better?"

Colte and Fallon shared a glance before Fallon nodded. "I think that might be a good idea... if you're up for it, Saph?"

"How did I do that anyway – I mean, why are my emotions like... almost solid?" I should have been furious that they were deferring to Fallon about me, but I was still in shock at what I had done.

"Because you are coming into your Power – and you *are* extremely powerful. It is not surprising that emotions that strong take on solidity. You will be able to use them as weapons once you have mastered how." Fallon answered carefully, watching my face for a reaction.

"I'm sorry... did you just say that I was coming into my *powers*? What powers?"

"We believe that you are the *Incarnate*." A.J said softly, a tone almost like awe filling his voice.

"The *what*?" I was getting dizzy again, my head starting to pound. What the hell were they talking about? I didn't have powers – I wasn't like them, I couldn't be. I was human, plain and simple. Like my parents and my brothers... wasn't I?

I'd moved beyond the idea of this being a prank. Now, it was all beginning to feel like a movie. A horror movie, where the pretty little human finds out they are actually one of the monsters. Here's hoping that the pretty little ex-human doesn't kill everyone.

"You know, the insanely powerful Goddess of Reincarnation?" Colte said lightly, unaware of my internal ramblings, wagging his eyebrows in my direction.

I shook my head, "You're insane. What Goddess of Reincarnation?"

"You've been known by many names over the years," A.J answered.

"Yeah – you know; Isis, Arianrhod, Persephone, Rhiannon... you were even one of the Tulku at one point in history." Colte shrugged, cutting in. "You tend to get around a bit – culturally, that is."

The stone walls began to dance around me, and my stomach was doing summersaults. The food I had eaten earlier threatened to make a re-appearance. This was too much.

I couldn't keep up as hard as I tried. I hated that this was supposed to be about my life – or was that *lives*? – and most of all, I hated that everyone else knew so much, and I knew nothing.

"That's enough." Fallon snapped as Colte opened his mouth to say something else crazy. "Are you feeling alright, Sapphira- you look pale."

"I... I'm fine," I murmured, head spinning and energy depleted. "I just need some air."

My legs gave out, and I started to fall. Fallon caught me before I hit the floor.

"Easy, just relax." She soothed, "Abhijay, let's get her up to ground level."

I closed my eyes and tried to breathe. *Relax...* I told myself. *Just breathe and calm down. No more losing consciousness for a while, okay?*

My head felt like it was packed full of cotton balls, competent thought was impossible. I lost all sense of direction, words echoing, and faces blurring together.

"She can't go outside – not like this. What if someone sees her?" Colte's voice swam around my head.

"Shut it, Colte, there are enough Moroi here to keep her safe. She needs the air – would you keep her inside like this?"

I felt A.J's strong arms picking me up, and then I was leaning into his chest, breathing in his scent. *He smells like rain...* I thought dreamily and giggled.

"What's funny?" He whispered, tensing, his chest vibrating as he spoke.

"You know A.J, this is becoming a habit. You carrying me around," I told him, my voice millions of miles away, and opening my eyes to look up at him as I cuddled into his body.

He smiled but said nothing as we made our way out of the labyrinth that was the Moroi Safe House.

Outside, the sun was shining, and a light breeze caressed my face. A.J gently set me down on a patch of soft green grass.

How could the Moroi be in the daylight? I thought groggily. *Didn't Vampires burn in the sun?*

"Myth," A.J whispered as he stood back, the smell of rain fading. He laughed at the look on my face when I realized I'd spoken out loud.

I turned away to hide my mortification and breathe in the fresh air. I counted my breaths, ignoring everyone, and when my head cleared, I took in the scenery.

There was a forest of gigantic trees grouped not far from the building – which looked like a deceptively small and abandoned farmhouse from the outside. I assumed what I had thought of as towers inside, were masquerading as the small silos that edged the house. To a passerby, the Safe House would look like an almost dilapidated farm. How clever of the Moroi to hide in plain sight like that.

We were in the middle of freaking nowhere, I made a mental note to ask someone where the hell we were. How far from my home town could we have traveled to get here?

I was glad that I could breathe fresh air and just chill for a minute, though. All of the information I had received was still making my head spin. I took a few deep, calming breaths while the others stood behind me in silence. I could sense an anxious vibe coming off of them and could almost feel their eyes burning holes in the back of my head.

"I'm fine, really. You can stop staring at me any time now." I said calmly, watching the grass dance slowly in the breeze.

"I will go and tell the guards to double the watch on the perimeter while you're out here. Excuse me." A.J said with a bow and was gone.

"I'll just wander away and… admire the trees for a bit." Colte threw a salute at Fallon and winked at me before, he too, was gone.

Fallon moved to sit beside me. I turned my attention to watching the breeze dance with the leaves of the gum trees nearby. It had always been a soothing method for me, and I'd definitely needed calming.

Every time one of my friends came too close, or I thought about all the lies they had told me, my anger threatened to take over. I had to force it down, work extra hard to look calm and in control. I knew that if they knew how I really felt, they wouldn't tell me a goddamn thing. I refused to live in ignorance again.

But now it seemed that they were right, too much information at once would make my brain shut down with skepticism and an inability to process.

"We're just worried about you, Saph. Not many people have survived an attack from Hadrian and his lot." Fallon said gently, mistaking my reaction for worry about my health and safety. "And because you are so… well… *rare*… we have no way of knowing for sure if you've made a full recovery. We have nothing else to base this on."

"You're wrong, you know," I said with determination, turning to face the Djinn. "About me. I'm not this *Goddess Incarnate* or whatever."

Fallon raised an eyebrow. "How do you know?"

"Gods and Goddess' don't have souls – well, that's what the books all say. And I do – I saw it myself when Hadrian attacked me."

"How do you know it was a soul that you saw?"

"It just *feels* right, saying that it was my soul," I told her truthfully and then frowned. "What else could it have been? Does Hadrian normally try and harvest anything else from people?"

"*Power* has the same feel to it sometimes. So does life essence. But no, Hadrian and the other Soul Eaters normally just go for souls. They personally have no use for anything else. There have been times when other beings have done deals with the Soul Eaters, though. Make a good enough deal, and they will harvest just about anything."

"Who would deal with them?"

"Any being in our world that is corrupt enough to want more Power – like the Strigoi. Why so many questions about this?" Fallon wanted to know.

"Curious, I guess," I answered. "Turns out, I know absolutely nothing about the world. There are things out there that I never knew existed – and you all think that I'm one of them. I might as well learn all I can."

"I'm happy to answer all of your questions, Saph, but take it a bit slower okay?" Fallon said, taking my hand in hers. "I don't want to overload you. It is a lot to take in after all."

I didn't believe that I was who they were telling me I was. But if I just went with it, for now, I would be able to get more answers.

"Hey," I said, a thought springing to mind. "If I am this high and mighty Goddess, why worry so much? I mean, Goddess' are immortal, right? As in *they don't die*?"

Fallon sighed, a small, patient smile playing at her lips. "No, unfortunately. Didn't you ever pay attention in school?"

I shrugged, a quick rise and fall of my shoulders. "Too busy skipping classes to pay attention, I guess."

"Gods and Goddess' die – they're just a hell of a lot harder to kill. But with you, you are the Goddess of Reincarnation. You keep coming back in different bodies in different places all over the world. Once you reach the full potential of your Power, you will be near impossible to harm – until then, though, you're as mortal as anyone else."

"So, if I die, just wait for the next time I come back."

"You can sometimes go hundreds of years between lives though – no one ever knows for sure how long you will be gone. And you are hard to find after the initial burst of energy that is your 'birth' because your Power goes dormant until about now. Until your magic matures, you are basically human. Many of your reincarnations have been killed off before we've gotten to you in the past."

"Killed off?"

Fallon nodded, looking me over slowly as if to make sure I wasn't going to explode from the insanity she was sprouting. "You are a great prize to both sides, Sapphira, but more often than not, your incarnates chose the side of light over dark – and once you chose, it was impossible to turn you from that path. Darkness would rather kill you and wait for your next life than allow you to come into full Power against them."

"Wow."

"I know."

We sat in silence for a while, staring at the trees.

The bombshells of the day swirled around my mind, fighting with my preconceived thoughts of the world, trying to gain footholds.

I tried to understand what my friends had done, I tried to see *their* side. But all I saw was their betrayal and lack of trust in me to be okay with the truth.

"How many incarnates has there been?" I asked, trying to calm the rage that had started to rise again.

"More than I remember. There is a Djinn historian that has them all recorded, though." Fallon told me distractedly, still staring out at the trees.

"So why do you think that this is who I really am?" The question seemed to surprise her. "What do you mean?"

I took another deep breath, feeling the sweet air fill my lungs. "What made you think that I was the *Incarnate*?"

It was Fallon's turn to sigh. "Are you're sure you're ready for more just now?"

"I'm fine." I nodded, not sure who I was trying to convince more.

"When you were born, there was a huge surge of Power. So much that it was felt on the other side of the world. Every being that holds Power felt it like a bolt of electricity running across the air. It sent the darkness into a craze. Everyone wanted to find you, but it was me that did. Your mother in this life was a mortal woman, which is rare in itself. Your father had Seer blood, but it was so watered down, he had no power. Your other incarnates were usually born into a body that already had stronger defenses than mortals. I... convinced your family to move you – to *anywhere* that was as far from where you were born as possible. I hid any traces of you as best I could, and went to Abhijay and my people for help protecting you. They formed a treaty for your protection, and the 'Guardians' were formed – a group of Moroi, Djinn, Dhampir, and Nephilim. We watched over you from a distance, ensuring that your family had every comfort while shielding you against whatever darkness came your way. Years passed until, somehow, the Strigoi and their allies discovered where you were."

Fallon paused, squeezing my hand, waiting for my thoughts to catch up to what she had just said.

"So... it really happened?" I asked breathlessly. My heart was pounding, and my body was stiff. "My family were really torn apart by a monster?"

"I'm sorry."

"How did they get past you?"

"I think I was...distracted, but it shouldn't have been enough for them to sneak under my radar."Fallon shook her head, frowning into the distance, lost in the memory and self-blame. "I honestly don't know, though."

"So... after... how did you find me again? I mean, I remember *now* that it was you who found me cowering in that alley."

"I've known you since you were born Sapphira, I could find you anywhere. But that time, I was already looking. I'd found your family, and could sense your fear."

"Well, that's not at all creepy..."

Fallon smiled, turning to face me again. "I know, but the Djinn – and a few other beings, like the Moroi, can sense a presence they are accustomed to quite easily."

"Sorry to intrude" Came a deep voice from behind us. "But I wanted to come and say hello."

I startled. These damned creatures should wear bells around their necks. Fallon's face lit up as she stood, turning to the newcomer. "Hello, Aryk."

"Hello, Fallon."

I stood, and as they embraced each other, I took in Aryk. He was the same height as Fallon, with tanned skin, and his eyes were a sapphire blue. His entire stunningly flawless face lit up when he smiled, eyes sparkling. He was wearing a cerulean shirt under a black suit that added to his immaculately perfect appearance.

"What are you doing here?"

Aryk frowned. "You weren't told that I was coming?"

Fallon shook her head, stepping out of the embrace. "No, I've been kind of preoccupied."

"Of course," Aryk said, turning to me and giving me the full effect of his dazzling smile, running a hand through his short dark hair. "Sapphira, what an honor it is to meet you at last. Although, my wife has told me absolutely nothing about you. I have had to lower myself to listening to the court gossip for reports."

I gaped, looking like a complete idiot, I'm sure. "Your wife?"

Aryk laughed, a captivating sound, taking Fallon's hand in his. "I see that she has not told you of me – shame on you, Princess! You know how I love to be the center of attention at all times."

"*Princess?*"

"Yes, Sapphira dear, didn't my wife tell you that she was Djinn royalty?" He shook his finger at Fallon as if reprimanding her. "Keeping secrets, Princess?"

Fallon was glaring at Aryk, eyes blazing. "That's enough, Aryk. We have had more important things to discuss than my lineage."

"Sorry, Love." He said, looking anything but. "Your Father requested that I join you in your cause. Your mother agreed, thinking that almost nineteen years of unremitting separation from your loved one was long enough. And that, my darling Fallon is why I am here."

"Um..." I started lamely, taking a few steps back towards the building. "I think that I might go back inside and find A.J. He said that he would have someone teach me some stuff."

"Alright, if you feel up to it, Saph," Fallon said, making to follow me.

"No, it's okay, Fallon. Stay here and catch up with Aryk. I'm sure I can make it from here to the door without anyone trying to kill me."

"One can only hope." Aryk joked, earning another glare from Fallon. He held his hands out as if to say *what?*

I turned and made for the door as Colte seemingly appeared out of nowhere, heading towards me, his customary I'm-so-bored face on. "Hey Saph, what's up? Done with breathing in the salubrious air? "

He looked back to where Fallon and Aryk stood, quietly talking to one another, faces lit up. "Oh, I see the love birds have been reunited."

He winked at me, and grinning shrewdly, he asked, "Making a hasty retreat before they start sucking face?"

"I heard that, Dhampir!" Fallon called.

Colte laughed, falling into step beside me as we continued walking. "You were supposed to. Why don't you get a room? There are plenty here, you know!" He called over his shoulder.

The further I walked from Fallon, the lighter the calming blanket over me became. I could feel my anger and hurt swirling inside of me again, searching for a target.

Inside, Colte turned to me. "Where to, *Goddess*?"

"Don't call me that," I said firmly, slapping him on the arm. "Why didn't you tell me about all of this?"

Seeing Colte acting like everything was fine – as if nothing had changed between us, was making me mad. And upset.

Colte had been a constant in my life for a while. Someone that I had shared my hopes and dreams with – had treated as a brother and trusted completely.

"I'm just a lowly Dhampir." He answered, tone despondent. "I was ordered not to."

"Since when do you do as your told?" I sneered. "I thought that we had a real friendship, Colte."

Colte shrugged, his head down. "I tried Saph. So many times. I argued that you had a right to know, that we were wrong for keeping all of this from you. I got into a ton of trouble for trying." He shuddered, lost in the memory. "But, you have to understand that, in our world, I'm a nobody. I have no choice but to follow the orders of my superiors."

"Was it all an act – just a job for you?" I wanted to know.

"At the beginning, it was just another protection detail posting, but then I got to know you." Colte fidgeted with his sleeve, unable to meet my eye as we stood there. "Then, it was all real."

"How can I believe you?" I snapped. "You started our friendship under orders and pretense. You lied to me!"

"You are my *friend* Saph, the best friend that I've ever had. I promise you, *that* was real for me."

I'd never seen him so dejected - the party boy was gone wholly and utterly. I tried not to feel sorry for him, to stay angry. He just seemed to *genuinely remorseful*.

I couldn't do this without a friend, I determined. It was too much to deal with alone.

"Okay, I'll believe you." I sighed, running a hand through my hair. "I'm not sure I *trust* you, but no more lies, Colte. Friends don't do that. We'll have to start again, build up a real friendship – not one you've been told to make."

His eyes lit up in gratitude as he finally looked at me. "I can work with that." He nodded, smiling tentatively.

We shook hands, marking the promise made between us.

"Now, where to?" He asked, bumping my shoulder with his. "Training? Food? T.V.?"

"I'm just going to head back to my room... I'm tired." It wasn't exactly a lie. I *was* tired.

"Sure thing *Incarnate*, I'll walk you."

I slapped him again. "Don't call me *that* either."

He laughed, rubbing his arm. "Okay, okay... don't attack me. Jeez, I *do* need functionality in my limbs, you know."

"I didn't hit you that hard. I probably didn't even leave a mark you sook."

He snickered. "You're right. The big bad Sapphira hits like a little girl – who would have known?"

"Did you just say 'big'?" I paused, mouth open in mock-horror. "Oh my god, did you just call me *fat*?"

Colte's step faltered for an instant. "Um... no, I – "

"Relax." I laughed, rolling my eyes. "I didn't know how easy you half-vamps were to tease."

"Oh, ha-ha... so *very funny*. Remind me to laugh next time."

I smiled despite myself, unable to completely resist relaxing into the rhythms of friendship.

"What?" Colte asked softly, taking in my smile.

"I needed that. Thank you."

"Well... you're welcome... but why exactly are you thanking me?"

"You helped me relax. I feel better." I told him, looking around. I bit my bottom lip. I may have felt better, but I was horribly lost.

"I'll walk with you to your room, shall I?" Colte asked knowingly. He held his arm out like the gentleman from an old movie escorting a lady. "This place is like a labyrinth to those who don't know the way around."

"And again, I thank you. You've been just what I needed today, Colte." I took his arm, resting my head on his shoulder.

"Again, you're welcome."

We walked in companionable silence all the way to my room, passing not a soul along the way.

"I thought A.J said that there were guards here?" I wondered out loud.

"There are – hundreds of them. They're just not needed this far in. But you are safe here, Sapphira, I promise."

We had reached the door to my room, and we stopped.

"You're room, my Lady." Colte bowed, gesturing the door. I laughed. "Why, Thank you, kind Sir."

Colte grinned and winked. "Any time."

I opened my mouth to ask if he wanted to stay and hang out like we used to, trying to regain some semblance of normalcy. Deciding to try to begin building trust again. But he cocked his head to one side, listening. All I could hear was silence, but his face was pretty intense.

"Do you need me to tuck you in?" He asked after a minute, the grin back in place. He ushered me into the room, remaining in the doorway.

"No, I'll manage." I told him. "What was that?"

"What was what?"

"What did you hear just then?"

"Oh, some of the guards and I have a bet on the game. It's almost over, and it sounds as if I'm about to be a few hundred bucks richer."

I so didn't believe him for a second.

"Well," He said, trying hard to sound nonchalant "I'll leave you to your rest. See ya, Saph."

He closed the steel door and was gone before I could protest.

I sighed and went to sit on the bed, crossing my legs.

"Left out of the loop once again..." I murmured.

Colte had probably been summoned to some top-secret meeting about me. Fallon and Ari too. Frustration, hurt, and anger rose, and I could see the dark vortex spiraling through my body and out around me. I scowled at the door.

It was becoming all too clear that everyone knew more about me and my life than I did – and they were going through a great deal of trouble to keep it that way. Colte had lied to me again – and after he had only just promised that he wouldn't! What information had he been talking about earlier? Why weren't they telling me? I didn't really appreciate them babying me all of the time either. I was capable of hearing the truth – of handling myself. I didn't need others to make decisions for me. *And I definitely did NOT need to be locked in a bloody tower while they did it!*

I watched, fascinated as the vortex grew until it consumed half of the room.

*Let it go, let it erupt through the safe house, let it destroy everything it could. Let them know your fury...*The thought caused a strange sense of sinister exhilaration. I could do it, the power was *right there*, begging to be released. It would feel so good to let it go...

The door burst open, Fallon charging into the room. She skidded to a halt just out of reach of the power that still spiraled furiously.

"*Stop!*" she cried, her blue-green eyes wide and strangely illuminated. I thought that I could see a golden aura shimmering around her body as she held up her hands, testing the edge of my power. She didn't actually touch the vortex, but I could feel her energy gently *pushing* at it. Shimmering around the edges, covering it like a shield, and directing it back towards me.

"You're projecting for miles – anyone sensitive towards power will feel you. You're like a beacon right now – and trust me, Sapphira, you don't want that." Her voice sounded so reasonable, so soothing. The blanket was back, covering me with tranquillity. I began to calm down.

"Just relax – take a deep breath. It's okay, that's it, Saph..." She edged closer to the bed as the vortex slowly receded, seeping back down inside of me. What had I been thinking?

Would I really have released all of my hate onto my friends – would I really have hurt them?

As the last bit of my anger returned home, I collapsed on the hard mattress, all of my energy gone.

Fallon was there, stroking my hair, looking down at me with her power still flowing.

"Shh..." she whispered serenely. "Just sleep now. You're okay..."

I closed eyes that weighed a ton and listened to Fallon whisper soothing words in my ear. And then there was nothing.

I dreamed of faeries.

A beautiful Queen telling me that I was being used. That my friend was controlling me with her magic.

"You're better than this, *Ceann álainn*." She told me, her smile bright. "Stop thinking like a human, and become who I – who *we all* – need you to be."

Chapter Three

I woke to the faint sounds of screaming and metal hitting metal. It was pitch black, and I sat up in bed. There was a sudden added weight on the mattress as if someone had slid on beside me. A cold hand clamped down over my mouth, and I struggled to get away from them.

"Be still." A female voice ordered. "Do not make a sound. We are here to protect you."

"I can't see!" I whispered furiously as the hand was taken away.

"Quiet!" The voice came again, an exasperated hiss in my ear.

I sat quietly, wondering who it was that was ordering me into silence, listening as the sounds of fighting continued. What was going on out there? It sounded as though there was a struggle going on, with actual swords – but that couldn't be true, could it? Who used swords anymore? I wondered if anyone I knew was out there fighting – were they getting hurt – or worse, were they dead?

"Ils sont Presque là..." A male voice whispered tensely through the darkness. I couldn't understand a word of what had been said. Were they speaking French? "Se préparent au combat..." The voice continued, oblivious to my lack of understanding.

"Okay, remember what the *Maharishi* said." The female voice answered quietly, her voice deceptively calm. She slid off the bed, and I heard a gun click as it was loaded. Well, at least they had more modern weapons.

A deep inhuman growl, from just outside my room, sent shivers down my spine. Steel squealed as something like nails raked along the door.

"Vârcolac..." Someone hissed in horror.

The voice was vaguely familiar. It was the guard from the hall earlier – what had A.J called him? Saul. "Where the hell did they find a freaking *werewolf*?"

The thing on the other side of the door let out a howl, freezing my blood. *Oh my god, I'm going to die...* I thought in panic.

I whimpered softly, and the... *werewolf*... growled again. *I'm gonna die, it's all over, I'm dead...* It became a repetitive mantra in my thoughts as I shook in fear on the bed.

There was a loud thud, and the door groaned as the creature hit it, trying to get in.

"That won't hold it for long," Saul said, stating the obvious.

"Just be ready to keep it off of her. Hold it back until reinforcements arrive. She cannot be harmed." The woman told him. There was a slight tremble in her voice as she spoke.

"*If* they arrive..." Saul said softly. "Leilani, for all we know, they could all be dead."

"Shut up and do your job, Saul." Leilani snapped, though she was probably thinking the same thing. I know *I* was.

The door thudded again and then gave in. It came down swiftly, falling noisily to the ground and letting in, not only the light from the corridor but the werewolf as well. The creature was like terror incarnate. It was a horrific cross between wolf and human. Standing on two legs, it was taller than any of the three people standing between *it* and where *I* cowered, and it was all trembling muscle. Fur covered almost every inch of the body, and massive razor-like teeth lined the mouth, saliva dripping down its muzzle as it panted.

Its blood-red eyes took in the room with one quick glance before it growled low in its throat and leaped towards me.

I screamed, shrinking back – trying to disappear.

The man who had spoken in French stepped in front of the beast, a large gleaming sword held in his right hand. He lunged at the oncoming werewolf, barely managing to slice it across the face as it changed direction at the last minute. It skidded along the floor, on all fours, and turned to face its attacker with a vicious snarl.

Saul wasn't moving from where he stood by the chair next to my bed. He held a dangerous-looking bow loosely in his left hand, a quiver full of arrows strung to his back. His eyes were wide, and his lips were moving without sound.

"Allez laid, dansons." The swordman hissed, bringing my attention back to the fight. His stance said that he was ready for another round with death. He held out his sword, a single drop of blood falling from the tip.

"Denni..." Leilani said softly, taking a tentative step towards him.

The werewolf growled, eyes darting between the two.

Leilani held a gun towards the beast and pulled the trigger as it pounced at her instead.

Again, Denni managed to step between the werewolf and its target. He moved so fast, almost a blur. This time, the beast kept coming, taking Denni to the ground. His sword clattered to the floor as he dropped it, leaving him defenseless. The werewolf tore at his face, blood spurting from massive gouges in his flesh.

It happened so fast that Denni didn't have time to make a sound. Leilani's face was a mixture of anger and heartbreak as she screamed, pulling the trigger again and again. The bullets hit the beast in the back of the head, the noise echoing around the room, deafening me for a minute.

I watched, frozen in place as the wolf turned on Leilani. Grabbing her by the leg with its teeth and dragging her to the ground.

The gun, out of bullets now, was useless. Screaming and swearing, she kicked wildly at it with her free foot as it shook its head, trying to tear the leg from her body. One of the kicks struck the wolf in the nose, it yelped in pain and released her, taking a few steps backward. The beast shook its massive head and growled.

It began to slowly advance again, blood-red eyes full of what could only be described as pure hatred. It gnashed its teeth, biting at the air between them as it came closer.

"Saul, shoot it!" She screamed desperately, "For god's sake – shoot the fucking thing!"

The werewolf jumped at Leilani again but fell short as a broad arrow pierced its chest.

Saul took a step closer to the beast, moving to stand between it and Leilani as she dragged herself towards the bed, blood leaving a bright trail behind her. He nocked another arrow into the bow and loosed it into the werewolf's throat as it opened its mouth to howl. The noise stopped abruptly as the beast collapsed to the ground, not moving.

"Oh my god, oh my god..." I whimpered, pulling my knees into my chest and rocking. "This isn't real; it's just a dream..."

"Yeah, a real fucking nightmare." Saul hissed sarcastically, and moved closer to the werewolf, kicking it hard in the gut. Thankfully, it didn't move. "I think it's dead."

Leilani dragged herself over to where Denni lay, unmoving. "Please don't be dead, please, Denni." She whispered sobbing.

Tears streamed unchecked as she ran her shaking hands over his chest, eyes on his ruined face. "Come on, baby, open your eyes, and let me know that you're okay." She turned to glare at Saul. "What the fuck were you doing? How could you freeze like that?"

"I..." Saul looked away. "I don't know, I'm sorry."

Footsteps resonated down the corridor, getting louder by the second.

Saul nocked another arrow, the tip gleaming silver in the light. He moved so that he stood directly between me and the door. Leilani picked up Denni's sword and held it in front of her, from where she sat on the floor beside her lover's body. Both were facing the door, bodies tense, waiting for whatever was coming.

"*Shit*... the door's gone." Colte's voice, sounding panicked.

Leilani let the sword fall back to the floor at her side, and Saul relaxed the bow, replacing the arrow in the quiver at his back as Colte skidded to halt in the doorway.

"Oh, crap." He said fervently, taking in the scene before him.

A.J, bloodied from fighting, appeared beside him. "Colte, help Saul take Leilani and Denni to the infirmary, and tell Fallon that she is needed here, quickly."

"Yes, *Maharishi*." He said, striding quickly into the room and picking up Leilani as if she weighed nothing.

She groaned in pain, gripping her leg that was barely still attached to her body. Saul gently lifted Denni, blood instantly staining his white shirt. Without a word, he left.

My eyes went to the pool of blood on the floor, and then to the werewolf's limp body.

"I can't believe they had a Vârcolac – *here* – in Australia. Aren't they only found in Albania?" Colte asked as he headed for the door. "Plus, I thought that they were extremely sporadic – and *vicious*... how the hell did the Strigoi get one to fight for them?"

"We can discuss this later, Dhampir, for now, do as I have instructed," A.J told him firmly.

"Yes, of course, *Maharishi*, apologies." Colte, too, left without another word.

I was still breathing heavily, my pulse racing. I realized that I was still rocking, making small noises. I couldn't take my eyes off of the werewolf and all of the blood.

"Sapphira."

I jumped, turning towards the voice. A.J remained in the doorway, tired eyes on me. "Sapphira, may I enter?"

I nodded slowly and watched A.J stride towards me. I tensed as he sat at the foot of the bed, and he froze.

"You're sitting in blood," I whispered.

He looked down, taking in the blood-spattered sheets. "I'm sorry that the Vârcolac reached you here, Sapphira. My guards were not quick enough to stop it."

"Did... did any of your people die?"

A.J nodded sadly, his eyes returning to my face. "Unfortunately, yes. Many lost their lives tonight."

"Was it the Strigoi?"

Again, a nod.

"Were they here for me?"

"I believe so. Their numbers were... surprising."

"What do you mean?"

"There are the occasional scouting parties that the Strigoi elders send to scope out our defenses. Tonight was more like a front line attack. I believe that they felt your... energy... earlier and thought that they could take you from us."

Aryk's voice floated across the room. "And now that they have found you, they will keep trying." I turned and watched him saunter through the mess. His clothes were still immaculate as if he had just stepped out of the cover of a men's fashion magazine. "Who knows what else they will send in their attempts? The Strigoi don't like to lose."

"Where is Fallon, Aryk?" A.J asked tersely.

"On her way." He sat in the chair beside the bed, glancing over at the werewolf in distaste. "It's not dead, you know, just unconscious."

I froze, glancing at it in fear, and a small whimper escaped my lips. A.J stood, taking a few steps forward and picked up Denni's sword. He raised it over his head and brought it down quickly. The blade sliced through the werewolf's neck, detaching its head. Blood splattered all over the bed, and me.

Aryk chuckled. "And now, the beast is slain."

I gagged as the smell of fresh blood, and other flowing bodily fluids reached my nose for the first time. My body shook, and I found myself unable to breathe correctly. I could taste the bile that rose in my throat, tears stinging my eyes.

"Oh god..." I groaned, starting to rock again. "Please don't be sick," I whispered over and over, squeezing my eyes shut and trying to forget what I would see if I opened them again.

Aryk chuckled but said nothing as I kept up the mantra.

"Sapphira," Fallon's voice said softly in my ear. I jumped, eyes darting open. "Are you hurt?"

She knelt at the side of the bloodied bed, inches from me. I noticed then that, this whole time, no one had touched me –

not to comfort or to punish me for all of this death. It was almost as if they didn't want to come near me. Like they blamed me. I really couldn't fault them – I didn't want to be near me either. Her eyes filled with sympathy as if she had heard my thoughts, and she slowly reached her hand over to mine.

Tears ran along my cheeks, my lip quivering. "I'm so sorry."

Fallon squeezed my hand. "For *what* Saph?"

"This is all my fault. They died because of me." I sobbed, putting my head on my knees to hide my face.

Fallon climbed onto the bed next to me, wrapping me in her arms. "It's okay Sapphira, the Moroi knew what they were getting into when they agreed to help protect you."

"That doesn't make this right, Fallon," I argued quietly, eyes begging her to understand. "The Strigoi attacked here tonight because of what I did. If I had just-"

"You can't think like that, honey. You don't know if it was truly because of you." Fallon cut in, reverting to the voice she had used when I was younger and in need of mothering. She stroked my hair as she spoke. *Hair that was probably soaked in blood...* I thought. I pictured my long golden-blonde hair drenched with blood, and whimpered as bile rose to my throat again. "I'm going to be sick..."

I threw up all over the bottom of the bed, Fallon holding back my hair. The sickly sweet smell of vomit laced with fruit and yogurt smothered my nose, adding to the smell of death, and I vomited again. A.J had to move before it ended up all over him. Aryk sat, unperturbed in the chair.

"Are the wards up?" A.J asked as I emptied my stomach.

"Yes," Fallon answered calmly. "We are protected by Djinn magic until tomorrow evening. I'm sorry, Abhijay. That was the best that I could do."

"Thank you, Fallon, I appreciate whatever I can get."

"I need to get out of here," I groaned, struggling off of the bed. "I can't be here..."

"You're in shock," Fallon stepped up beside me. "Let's go get you cleaned up."

A.J nodded. "I must go and oversee my people." He bowed and was gone.

Aryk smoothly got to his feet. "I will accompany you." I managed a glance at Fallon, noticing that she was pristine, not a hair out of place. Her beautiful dress was spotless. How had she managed to stay clean? I glanced down at myself and wished I hadn't. I was covered in Vârcolac blood and my own vomit. I felt sick again but fought the urge to gag. "Please, get me out of here," I begged Fallon miserably.

She smiled sympathetically and took my hand. "Let's go."

She led me quickly through the corridor, having to step over bodies in the more congested parts. I tried not to scream as I saw the corpses of not only the fallen Moroi but the monstrous Strigoi, as well.

They had a roughly human shape. But their skin was leathery and almost translucent. There was no hair on the parts of the bodies that I could see, but nails like claws protruded from their fingers, and teeth that would make a shark envious dominated their mouths—so many teeth. My legs gave out from under me, Fallon scooping me up before I hit the ground.

"Almost there, Saph." She told me gently. "We're almost there..."

But the calm and quiet darkness of unconsciousness claimed me before I could breathe in air that didn't smell of death.

I was sitting on a park bench, watching the sunset over a beautiful clear lake.

I didn't know what lake it was, or how I had gotten there, but I was calm, at peace. There was no other noise, but the faint rustling of leaves as a breeze blew through the towering trees behind me. This place was stunning, and you couldn't help but be relaxed.

"You are making a habit out of blacking out my Ceann álainn..." A melodic voice chimed, causing me to jump. *"It is making you look weak. Is that what you want?"*

An overpowering sense of Déjà-vu took hold as a crimson light appeared in the air around me, small at first and flickering like a candle until it exploded before my eyes. And suddenly she was there.

She was standing at the edge of the lake, her back to me. She was wearing the same long flowing pallid cherry dress as the first time I had seen her, and the dark tribal tattoos up her arms danced across her skin as she turned to face me, bright blue eyes sparkling. Beautiful as ever, she approached the bench, sitting beside me. Her long dark hair moved gently in the breeze.

"I don't mean to," I said softly, turning my attention back to the sunset. "Who are you anyway?"

"I am Kamilla, a Queen of the Sidhe."

"As in Faeries?"

Kamilla nodded, smiling softly.

"Okay," I said in a disbelieving tone. Was she nuts?

"It isn't too hard to believe, is it Sapphira, after everything else you have witnessed this past week?"

I shook my head, thinking about it. I finally gave a little shrug. "No, I guess not."

Kamilla laughed, turning her gaze to the clear water of the lake. She didn't say anything more, letting a companionable silence fill the air around us.

"Where are we?" I asked curiously.

"This is the lake not far from my home." The woman said, turning to me again.

"*Am I really here?*"

Kamilla raised an eyebrow in my direction.

"*I mean, am I physically here, or is this some sort of dream?*"

"*You are dreaming.*"

"*So, this isn't real?*"

"*It is a real place. But all of this is being projected into your mind as you sleep.*"

"*Why?*"

"*So that we may talk privately.*" *She stated as if it were obvious, and I was foolish.*

"*Oh.*"

The Sidhe Queen sighed, taking in my confused look. "*You have never had a true-dream before?*"

I shook my head. "*Nope, can't say that I have.*"

"*Well, it doesn't really matter. We can ponder the magic of true-dreams later. For now, I wish to talk to you about something else.*"

"*What did you want to discuss?*"

"*Why, you, of course.*" *She flashed a dazzling smile at me.*

I frowned. "*What about me?*"

"*Do you remember the incident with the Soul Eaters, dear?*"

"*How could I forget?*"

She patted my hand. "*Of course. But do you recall how you escaped them?*"

"*A woman...*" *I paused, my eyes growing wide as it all came rushing back with crystal-clear lucidity.* "*It was you? You helped me.*"

She nodded, smiling again.

"*And then I heard your voice telling me to wake up.*"

"*You are correct, Ceann álainn.*"

"*What is it that you keep calling me?*" *I asked quickly, changing the subject for a moment, trying to give myself time to process.* "*I don't understand it.*"

"*It is Irish for 'beautiful one.'*" *Kamilla smiled.* "*You do know how beautiful you are, don't you?*"

I shook my head, frowning again – another frown line added to the collection. Was she expecting me to brag? "I know I'm not like ugly. But my looks don't define who I am, so it doesn't really matter to me." I offered up lamely.

Kamilla chuckled. "Long golden blonde hair, perfect unblemished pale skin with a natural rosy blush in all the right places, very kissable lips, large green eyes, and a seductive curvy figure... No, my dear, you are definitely not ugly. You may not care about looks, but to some, they matter a great deal. But back to the important conversation. I'm glad that you remember that it was I who saved you, as now I want to make sure that you understand something."

"Understand what?"

"You owe me a favor."

My pulse quickened at the tone in her voice as she spoke. The way she said favor sounded more as though it meant debt.

"What do you want?" I asked, my mouth going dry. I remembered something I had read once. Before I knew that the Sidhe really existed. It said it was always a bad idea to get into a position where you owed a Faerie.

Kamilla smiled, eyes gleaming. "Nothing yet, dear. I just wanted to make sure that you were aware of the situation between us."

"But you didn't have to help me. I mean," I added, seeing her raise an eyebrow. "Don't get me wrong, I'm glad that you did, but I didn't ask for your help."

"But you did ask for help, Sapphira. You screamed for it, begged so loudly into the universe. I heard you and obliged."

"And now I owe you for it."

"Correct."

"So, what now?"

Kamilla got to her feet. "You will wake up. Go about your life, and when I call, you will come to pay your debt. Try and stay alive until then, could you?"

Without waiting for a response, she vanished into thin air.

"Wait!" I cried. "How do I get out of here?"

"Simply wake up..." Her voice whispered through the air.

I opened my eyes, taking a deep breath, and instantly wished that I hadn't. The air smelled thick, stale, and my eyes ached.

"Welcome back." Colte's voice echoed around me. "How do you feel?"

I was in another stone room, this one had no windows, and a dense layer of dust covered every surface. A lamp hanging from the roof illuminated the space, the light flickering occasionally.

Colte sat on a couch along one of the circular walls, opposite the bed that I was lying on. He had a clean pair of jeans and a tight white shirt on – identical to the ones that Saul had been wearing earlier.

I sat up, swinging my legs off the bed and stormed over to him. He stood as I approached, the grin that had been on his face faltering as he took in my dark expression and clenched fists. Dust stirred as I walked, rising into the air around us.

"You promised me!" I yelled, throwing my fist towards him, hitting him squarely in the jaw. "You promised that it was safe!"

His eyes held a shocked expression, but he didn't fend off my blows as I continued to hit him, my fists moving to his chest.

"You lied to me, Colte, and now people are dead!" I was sobbing, tears streaming down my cheeks as I collapsed into him.

I could still see the blood, the mangled bodies. I could hear the cries of terror as people fought for their lives, and others lost them. I could still smell the death that had settled over the compound, would probably never get it out of my nose. It was a smell so foul and distinctive that I would always remember it.

His arms came around me as he helped me gently to the ground. "I'm sorry Saph, I'm so sorry."

I shook my head. "No, it's not enough," I said, still sobbing.

"I know, but I didn't know that you would just... *explode* like that. I didn't know that your emotional power would awaken so strongly. I didn't know that the Strigoi were close enough – or organized enough to attack the way they did."

I turned to him, eyes blazing, anger stirring within me. *His* eyes were full of regret, sadness at what had happened filled him. He had probably lost people he knew and cared about. *It wasn't his fault,* I thought to myself, *It was mine.*

I took a calming breath, counting in my head. I didn't want to lose control of it again, I had done enough harm the first time.

"I'm sorry I hit you," I said softly, after a few minutes of awkward silence had passed.

He flashed a bright smile, though it didn't quite reach his sad eyes. "At least you're not still hitting like a girl."

I smiled, getting to my feet, and wiping off the dust that clung to my clothes. "How's the face?"

He rubbed his jaw, where I had hit him. "I'll live."

"It's bruising already," I told him, watching as he too, stood and dusted himself off. "You should probably ice it."

He shrugged. "It'll be gone in a few hours – the upside to being a half-breed vampire. I heal small things super fast."

"So how long was I out this time?"

Colte shrugged, "Only a few hours."

"Are we still...?"

"At the Safe House? Yeah, A.J suggested that I stay with you while they finish the cleanup... " He paused before continuing. "Saph, while you were out, you were talking... do you remember what you were dreaming about?"

"What did I say?" I looked at him in surprise.

His voice had held a hint of an emotion that I couldn't place, his eyes suddenly looking everywhere but me. "Umm... I'd rather you answered my question first... because what I heard didn't sound too good, Saph."

"Did anyone else hear me?" I asked curiously. Why was Colte acting so strangely?

He shook his head slowly, finally turning his gaze on me. His eyes were worried, a little scared. "No. I was the only one here when you started. Please, Saph, tell me what you were dreaming."

I sighed, frowning at him. "I was sitting by a lake watching the sunset and a woman named..." I paused, trying to remember. "Kamilla appeared. We talked a bit – why, what did I say? And why do you look terrified of a dream?"

"Bloody hell..." Colte whispered, running shaking hands through his hair. He started pacing, mumbling under his breath. "Fallon's gonna go berserk... Ari will probably kill me...we're fucked..."

"Colte!" I snapped, "Talk to me!"

He was at my side in an instant, hand on my elbow, staring at me. "That was no dream Saph, tell me quickly – tell me everything she said to you."

So I told him everything.

"Oh fuck, not good..." He murmured when I had finished. He started pacing again. "I had hoped that I had heard you wrong... I hoped that you were just dreaming – the truth is so much worse." He paused, tensing, eyes wide with fear. "I have to tell Fallon."

"For god's sake, Colte – what are you freaking about, Kamilla didn't threaten me, and in fact, she's saved my life. Why would Fallon go berserk over that? Wouldn't she want to thank-"

"No! You never thank a Sidhe – that puts you in debt." He cut in quickly. He continued his nervous pacing."Tell me you only owe her one debt? You didn't thank her, did you?"

I shook my head, frowning at Colte as if he were nuts. "No, it must have slipped my mind."

He sighed in relief. "Well, at least that's one good thing about this whole mess."

"Colte, please stop pacing- you're making me dizzy watching you."

"Sorry." He froze in place, eyes closed in concentration. His lips were moving, but no noise came out.

"What are you doing now?" I asked.

"Asking Fallon to please join us – quickly."

"You can do that?"

He nodded, tapping his temple with a finger. "Thought-speech."

"And she can hear you from wherever she is?"

"Yes, I can." Fallon's voice echoed around the room. I spun around to see her materialize out of thin air, a faint golden aura around her. She had changed since I had seen her last. Her long auburn hair hung loosely down her back, and she wore an elegant black dress that flaunted both her legs and chest. It seemed now that my friends didn't have to act human around me; they were relishing in their abilities – using them around me as often as possible.

"Wow." I was a little breathless. "That's cool."

She smiled brightly at me before turning to Colte, who had frozen again. "Is this important Colte, I was in the middle of something..."

"Umm... well..." He stuttered nervously. "I think you should know..."

"I spoke with Kamilla... a few times, actually." I stepped in, cutting off the fumbling mess that was Colte. "And now he's kind of freaking out about it."

Fallon's head snapped back to me, blue-green eyes flashing. "You *what?*"

"Well, it wasn't like I had a choice. She saved my life once, and I couldn't help the dream I had."

"What are you talking about?"

I told Fallon everything I knew about Kamilla, which wasn't much. And everything that had happened, both in the dream visit and when she saved me from the Soul Eaters.

"Why didn't you tell me this sooner?" She asked when I had finished.

"I didn't really remember anything about her the first time, and I haven't really had much of a chance to tell you anything lately."

"This is going to cause problems for us," Fallon said stiffly to Colte as if I hadn't spoken. "Abhijay and the other guardians need to be informed."

Colte nodded, leaving the room quickly through a wooden door that I hadn't noticed before.

"Look, I'm sorry that I didn't mention it, but there is a shit load of things that you have kept from me, *Princess.*" I snapped at Fallon, anger boiling inside of me. The Vortex whirred, wanting to be released. "And I am so over being left out of the loop about things that I should know."

Fallon's eyes flashed, her anger almost as evident as mine. "I have done nothing but try and protect you from the day that you were born, Sapphira, a duty that has almost cost me everything. I kept things from you for your own protection."

"I can protect myself."

"Oh, *yes.* You made that obvious when you faced down that Vârcolac and an entire army of Strigoi – oh wait... *that wasn't you.* You sat cowering on a bed while hundreds of us lost our lives for *you.* If you think that you can do better on your own, I will show you the way out. I'm sure that we would all live longer without you around."

I froze, shocked, and hurt by her words. The vortex subsided. "Fine." I said softly, "I'll go."

I walked towards the door, not looking at my friend as I passed. She stood, frozen, not looking at me.

I had reached the door when her voice reached me.

"Saph, wait."

I didn't stop, I didn't want her to see the tears that were escaping from my eyes, or know that my heart was breaking. I had wondered if our relationship had been real, and now I knew how she really felt. I hated her right then, hated that my whole life had been one big lie – an inconvenience for the people in it. I didn't stop until I found my way outside, the moonlight illuminating the grounds. I still didn't know where I was, or how far from a town the Safe House was.

"Damn it!" I sobbed, crossing my arms over my chest as I shivered. My feet began to move again, carrying me in the direction of the trees. The night was quiet, the air cold. Where was I going to go?

I knew that I couldn't go home, and I couldn't stay here, but where else could I try? I didn't have any other family or friends that I could turn to. I had no money or clothes with me. What was I going to do?

A slight rustle from the tree in front of me made me stop. *Was there someone there? Something hiding in the shadows?*

An image entered my mind – a creature covered in fur, blood-red eyes, and sharp blade-like teeth.

My heart was pounding, and I tried to keep the scream that was bubbling up inside of me from coming out.

A figure dropped to the ground, silently landing on their feet. "Where are you going?"

It was Saul. He walked over to me, eyes burning holes through my skin. He was all in black, a tiny earpiece in his right ear. *Crap*, I thought, my nerves relaxing slowly. *So much for getting away unnoticed.*

"I'm just walking, getting some air." I lied, hurriedly wiping at the tears on my cheeks. "It clears my head."

He frowned. "Was this little outing sanctioned by anyone?"

I fought to keep my anger under control. "I hadn't realized that I was a prisoner here, Saul."

He blinked slowly as if weighing up my words. "You are not."

"So, I'm free to make a decision for myself, yes?" I held my head high, daring him to disagree.

Inside, I was terrified. How the hell was I supposed to get by him – before he blabbed to anyone?

I decided that I'd try the *Goddess* card – everyone seemed to believe it anyway, why not see if it could help me?

He nodded. " Here, everyone's movements are monitored – especially after an attack. It does not mean that you are a prisoner, *Goddess*. It is merely for protection. Sorry if I have offended."

"And did you monitor my movements just now?"

"*Goddess*?"

I motioned to the earpiece. "Have you told anyone that you have seen me?"

He shook his head. "Not yet."

"Good. Keep it that way."

"I'm sorry, but I report to the *Maharishi* of this Safe House, not to you."

I sighed. I was going to lose my cool soon. "I'm just taking a walk, and right under your post. Surely I am protected enough?"

"But if we are attacked again – "

"Have you ever been attacked twice- this close together?"

Saul shook his head. "Not as far as I know."

"There, see?" I smiled at him. "I'll be fine."

Saul opened his mouth to protest further, but another voice cut him off.

"Let her go." Aryk appeared through the trees, beautiful eyes focused on me. He leaned up against a trunk not too far from us, arms folded over his chest. "The *Goddess* wishes to walk, let her."

"But – "

"If anyone queries it, *Moroi*, tell them that I cleared it."

Saul sighed, beaten. "Of course, Highness." He disappeared up his tree again.

"Thank you," I said to Aryk.

"Don't mention it." He waved me away. "Would you like some company on your *walk*?"

I shook my head. "Thanks though, but I just need to be alone in my thoughts for a while."

He gestured to my left with a finger, as if to say *go that way*, gave me a wink, and vanished.

I shrugged to myself. *Left is as good a direction as any*, I thought. *Mainly because I had no idea where I was heading anyway.* I turned and began walking to the left, wondering how many more guards were hidden out in the darkness. Would I be stopped every few meters? Turns out I needn't have worried.

Chapter Four

I walked for what seemed like hours, frozen stiff, but not seeing a single soul. Eventually, I hit the road, and I wondered if anyone at the Safe House was looking for me yet, or if Fallon had told them not to bother. And why had Aryk – Fallon's *husband* helped me?

I was freezing, and I wished that I had grabbed my bag – or a jacket. I had no money, no ID, no food or water, and I was beginning to freak out. What had seemed like a good idea, was turning out to be a terrible one. I'd probably freeze to death before sunrise.

"God, could you have screwed up any more Sapphira?" I snapped at myself as I walked along the road in the dark. I could smell Eucalyptus from the trees, hear the crunching of gravel under my feet. Fog curled around everything, dancing with the breeze.

"Well, you could be dead, that would be somewhat worse, wouldn't you agree?" Ari's voice purred from right beside me. I jumped, letting out a girly squeal. My heart was racing, and it wouldn't have surprised me if she could hear it.

Ari was walking by my right side, between me and the road, almost invisible in her black clothes. Her face was turned to me, her blue eyes sparkling mischievously. She was grinning.

"Jesus Christ, Ari!" I cried breathlessly, holding a hand to my chest. "You scared the shit out of me!"

She kept grinning, perfectly white teeth gleaming in the dark. "I know."

"How did you know where I was?"

"I'm Nephilim." She shrugged as if that answered everything. "More importantly, what are *you* doing out here... *alone*?"

"I... I couldn't stay there." I told her, filling her in on what she had missed.

"Huh, interesting..." She muttered when I had finished.

We walked in silence for a while, my footsteps echoing through the night. Ari didn't make a sound; I had to keep looking over to make sure that she was still there.

It must have been a supernatural thing – the silence. I thought. Fallon could do it too.

Ari had always been like this. She could fill the room with her presence, the star of the show, or she could be a shadow, quiet, and moody. The night that I had met her, Ari saved me from the advances of a drunk guy on the dancefloor of my favorite club. She yelled at him so harshly, I thought that he would start crying. Ari had taken my arm, dragging me to the bathroom.

"Us girls need to stick together." She'd told me when I thanked her, flashing a wicked smile.

But that was all part of the larger plan, I realized. She'd been there to watch over me, just like Fallon and Colte.

"So, your plan was to run away – to where, and for what purpose?" she finally asked, pulling me out of my memories.

"I don't know," I stated lamely. "I actually didn't think that far ahead."

Ari nodded, eyes on the road in front of her. "Decisions made in angry haste will always fail."

"Jeez, way to be reassuring Ari."

"Sorry, Saph," She laughed. "But its true... this plan of yours – or lack of one - sucks."

"Yeah, it does." I agreed, shivering again. "Did you come to take me back?"

"Not if you don't want to return."

"So, what now?"

"Now, we find somewhere warm – preferably somewhere with food."

"And what then?"

"And then you can rest before we make any other plans. You need to recharge your batteries before we do anything else. There is a half-decent town not far from here; we should be able to get a room there until tomorrow."

"What if someone comes looking for me there?"

"I hid your tracks. No one will find you until you want to be found."

I remembered something that Fallon had told me about being able to sense a presence that you were familiar with. "What about Fallon? Won't she be able to sense me?"

"She's as worn out as you are, so she won't be up to much of anything until tomorrow," Ari said calmly. "Besides,

Nephilim are usually great at hiding things from other creatures."

And strangely, with that puzzling comment, the night was slowly looking up.

"Saph, get up," Ari called from the bathroom of the dingy hotel room.

"I'm up." I groaned, putting the pillow over my head to block out her voice. My body was stiff from sleeping on the crappy bed. The shower had been making so much noise, I didn't know how anyone was expected to sleep through Ari using it just now.

The bathroom door opened, the light illuminating the small room.

Ari's head poked through, her short black curls dripping with water. "You might want to get in the shower while there is still a bit of hot water left." She advised. "We'll have to get moving soon. Check out was like forty-five minutes ago – I had to pay for another night just to let you sleep in."

I groaned again, throwing the pillow at her. "Seriously? What time is it?"

"It's almost three pm. Now, unless you want to be found and dragged back to the Safe House, I'd get a move on."

I crawled out of bed, cursing under my breath.

"I thought you had a treaty with the Moroi... wouldn't that mean that you have to hand me over?" I asked her as I entered the tiny bathroom.

Ari shrugged. "My treaty with them was that I would help keep you safe. You're safe with me, and you don't want to go back there. I'm fulfilling both *your* wishes *and* theirs at the same time."

I looked at Ari, drying her hair with a towel. She was watching me through the dirty mirror.

"Does it really work that way?" I asked her dubiously.

Again, she shrugged. "What can they do? I'm not exactly breaking any laws." She paused. "And besides, I'd rather listen to the *Goddess Incarnate* than to some Vampire or Djinn."

"Do you believe that I'm the incarnate too? Doesn't that go against the whole 'there is only one true god' thing you angels have?"

Ari turned to me, leaning her thin frame up against the sink. Her eyes were serious as she looked me over. "You really should hurry Sapphira, I found a dress that will hopefully fit you until we can find something better." She threw her towel onto the floor and stalked out of the bathroom.

I followed her. "Ari, please talk to me. I have no idea what's going on, and no one at the Safe House would really give me any information about what was happening *right now*. I just want some answers. I didn't mean to offend you or anything."

"We leave in ten minutes." She said tightly, her back to me.

I sighed. *You just couldn't help yourself, could you?* I thought as I turned on the deafening shower taps. *You just have to insult everybody...*

Five minutes later, I wrapped my freezing body in the last dry towel, Ari had been right about there not being much hot water left, and turned to the mirror.

The person staring back at me looked like a stranger. Her pink lips were shivering from the cold, and her bright green eyes were wide under thick dark lashes. Her pink cheeks were standing out more than usual against her pale skin. Long, wet golden blonde hair clung to her face, along her shoulders, and came to rest at the base of her back.

"Who are you?" I whispered. This person was not me, I didn't have emotions that could become a physical entity, and I didn't know Vampires, Djinn, and Nephilim. I had never survived a werewolf – or Skin Walker – attack. Those things had never happened to plain old Sapphira – so who the hell was the girl standing in front of me?

"Saph, hurry up," Ari called, knocking on the bathroom door. "We have to go."

I turned to the dress that Ari had 'acquired' and sighed. It was a short, tight-fitting red nightmare. "Yeah, I'm coming – give me a sec."

I pulled the scrap of material over my head and struggled into it before looking into the mirror again. The dress accentuated my curvy figure like a second skin. I groaned, pulling at the bottom of the material. It barely covered the top half of my thighs! "I can't wear this Ari – It's a bloody shirt!" I cried in horror.

"Oh, for shit's sake – I'm coming in!" Ari huffed, opening the door. She took one look at me and covered her mouth with a hand, eyes sparkling with laughter.

"Don't you dare laugh at me!" I snapped. "Where the hell did you get this thing- Hookers'R'us?!"

"You look... great." She said with a grin, fighting the urge to break into laughter. "Very... *sexy*."

I glared at her, hands on my hips. "You will have to find something else. I'm not leaving this bathroom until I'm fully clothed."

She shook her head. "Sorry, Saph. No time." She took a step closer, grinning broadly. "But, we can use a different mode of transport if you like?"

She offered me her hand. "It'll get us to where we need to go a lot faster than a car, but brunch will have to wait I'm afraid."

I frowned at her, taking her hand. "What are you – "

The minute my hand touched hers, I felt a zap of electricity, and suddenly I was spinning. The bathroom vanished, colors whooshing around my head, and Ari's grinning face was a blur in front of my eyes. My stomach was doing summersaults, and I felt like I was going to be sick.

"Oh god, I'm gonna, hurl!" I gasped when the world stopped spinning. I fell to my knees and gagged. I was more than likely flashing anyone standing behind me, but at that moment, I didn't care.

Ari laughed, her feet appearing beside me. "And that, my dear friend, is why food had to wait."

I glared up at her. "Not cool – you could have warned me."

"And miss that reaction?" She motioned down at me. "No way!"

I shakily got to my feet, pulling at the bottom of the 'dress' self consciously, and looked around.

It was dark, thousands of stars shimmering brightly in the sky. *What the?* I thought, confused. *It had been the middle of the day just a few minutes ago! Where had the sun gone?*

We were standing in a cobblestone street, at the base of a set of pale stairs, and we were surrounded by white buildings; more than a few had lights on. I could smell the salt in the air and hear the ocean, but I couldn't see it.

"Where are we, Ari?"

"Thira." She said, starting to climb the stairs. "Come on, I'll race you to the top – trust me, you'll want to be up there for the sunrise."

"Where the hell is Thira?" I called hurrying to catch up. Ari's laugh echoed back to me.

I finally caught up as Ari reached the top of the stairs, breathless, and more than a little grumpy until I saw the view.

"Holy shit," I breathed. "It's beautiful!"

The sun had just started to come up over the ocean, illuminating the bay – and the cliffs of the islands around us – with pale colors of pink and blue.

Soon, the sun would rise higher, and the colors would darken to oranges and reds before the crystal clear ocean waters cast a breathtaking blue across the bay. *This place is paradise!* I thought happily. We were standing in a village of white houses and breathtaking villas that perched on the edge of a cliff. I could see blue domes on some of the roofs, and the ruins of a castle-type building behind us.

"That's part of Oia Castle." Ari murmured, following my gaze.

"Oia Castle..." I repeated softly, taking her outstretched hand and following her towards the entrance of a large white estate – presumably another part of the castle. "Ari, where exactly is Thira on the map?"

"Well, you'd know this island by another name." She said, glancing over her shoulder. "Santorini."

"Santorini?" I paused, my steps faltering as I tried to think back to geography class. "As in *Santorini, Greece*?"

"Yep." She paused, turning to me and holding her arms out to her sides in greeting, eyes sparkling. "Welcome to the Greek Islands."

"So we've been here for six days now, what's the plan?" I asked, glancing over at Ari as she walked beside me. She wore her short black curls pulled back in a complicated-looking bun, a bikini top, and a short sarong wrapped around her body. She, like me, was barefoot.

Water from the Aegean Sea lapped at my feet, and I could taste salt when I licked my lips. The sunlight was reflected back to me through the clear blue ocean waters as we made our way along the rocky beach, the cliffs of Oia looming above us to the right. The breeze gently blew at my hair, and the long sundress that I wore.

"The plan was for you to rejuvenate in peace." She said calmly, breathing in deeply. She had her eyes closed, a look of pure joy on her face. "I just love it here. So relaxing, don't you think?"

I nodded in agreement, casting my eyes back out over the water, my attention caught by the volcano in the distance. It was the eruption of that volcano, in the distant past, that led people to believe that Santorini was a part of Atlantis.

"I could just stay here forever..." Ari breathed, dragging my attention back from daydreaming.

"But *I* can't. I need to-"

"To what? Go back and face the mess you ran away from?" Her tone was soft, numbing the harshness of her words.

I looked at her, hurt. "Fallon sent me away just as much as I ran."

She shrugged. "Fallon was weakened from putting up the shields around the Safe House. She was probably just consumed by the emotional train wreck you were throwing out."

I stopped, frowning at the Nephilim in disbelief.

"What? You didn't know that the Djinn react to the power around them if they're worn out?" She asked. "Besides, Fallon has been locked onto you since the night your family died, like you have some sort of magical tag. Your emotions probably register before hers do at this point."

I pictured myself like a whale, tagged by scientists, swimming through life, and unaware that every move I made was monitored and recorded. A flash of betrayal and outrage threatened to take over. *How dare she?*

I shook my head, pushing those feelings down, trying to focus on the rest of what Ari had revealed.

Could that have been why Fallon had been so angry? Was she really just consumed by *my* emotional outburst?

"Why didn't you say something when I was telling you what had happened?"

"I'm not perfect..." Again, a shrug. "And I thought that you needed some time out."

"I have to go back, Ari. I have to fix this whole mess. I have to talk to her!"

"I thought you might say that." She regarded me thoughtfully. "First, you need to learn to control yourself. It'll be no good going back like you are now."

I frowned. "So, who's going to teach me?"

"I am." It was a male voice, a whisper in the breeze around us.

I spun, trying to locate the source. There was no one on the beach except Ari and me. "Who...?" I glanced at Ari in confusion.

She was smiling brightly. "You can show yourself, Hunter, before Sapphira has a heart attack."

A pale flickering emerald green light appeared to Ari's left, and Hunter materialized. He was tall and skinny, with pale skin that made his long dark hair and green eyes stand out. He had pale lips that broke into a grin as he bowed, and was as light as Ari was dark – like yin and yang standing side by side.

"Hunter, at your service." His eyes sparkled with mirth as he spoke.

"Hunter is a brother of mine, a Nephilim. He will teach you how to control your emotional energies." Ari informed me, before turning to her 'brother'. "And that is *all* you will be doing here."

Hunter winked at Ari. "Of course, sister."

I sighed, closing my eyes and started counting, a strategy my therapist had taught me.

One... I will not be mad, just think calming thoughts...

Two...I'm sure she meant to tell me...

Three...Ari knew how infuriating it was for me to be kept in the dark...

Four...

"I see what you mean, Sister." Hunter's voice broke through my thoughts. "No control in this one."

My eyes snapped open, the vortex rising inside of me. Ari was watching me closely, a sober expression in her eyes. Hunter, on the other hand, had a goofy grin on his face.

"Not telling you about this was the fastest way to get a reaction," Ari explained patiently. "And we didn't have time to take it slow. I'm sorry that I didn't tell you Saph, but believe me when I say that this will truly be worthwhile. Hunter will help you to get control of yourself quick enough to get back to Fallon and the others before they do anything stupid."

"Like try and find you here." Hunter added, throwing a meaningful look at Ari.

"Why would that be stupid?" I asked curiously.

Ari smirked, but it was Hunter that answered.

"This island is off-limits to a lot of... *species*. They will be able to locate you if they are close enough, but the minute they try and step foot on the island *poof!*" He made an explosive gesture with his hands. "Nothing left but a cloud of smoke and a bit of ash."

"But why would they try and come here if they knew..." I trailed off, seeing the looks on the faces of both Nephilim. "Oh my god, *they don't know*? How do they not know about this?"

"Angel's secret." Hunter shrugged, nonchalant. "Back when we... *fell*... we needed a place free from all of the *others*." He made 'others' sound like a dirty word. What was it with the Nephilim and their high and mighty routine?

"So how can *I* be here then?" I asked, glancing between them. "I'm not Nephilim."

"No, you're not," Ari stated plainly. "But you're not one of *them* either."

"*Them* being Moroi and Djinn, right?"

"Among other things, yes." She turned to Hunter, eyes narrowed. "You have three days, brother. Work a miracle."

He nodded, eyes sparkling with the challenge. "Yes, Sister."

Ari turned to me then, taking a step closer. "Work hard at this, Sapphira. You need to be able to control yourself – and learn how to use what you have to your advantage. I'll be back in three days. Make me proud." She smiled and vanished, leaving me alone on the beach with Hunter.

"So..." He started, rubbing his palms together, goofy grin on his face. "Are you ready to get pissed off?"

Chapter Five

B lood dripped from my fingertips, landing in a pool at my feet.

"Please," I begged softly, my eyes screwed shut. "No more. Just stop."

My head was pounding, and I felt like I was going to be sick. My legs were getting weaker, threatening to collapse any minute. And *he* continued to throw what he had ludicrously nicknamed 'emotion-daggers' at me.

"No, no stopping. Focus, Sapphira!" Hunter's firm voice grated against my skull. "You are not weak, so stop acting like it. You can do this. Just *shield*."

I hated him. And his relentlessly nasty teaching methods.

For almost three days, he had been tormenting me with what he called *training*. Forcing me to do things that no sane person should have been able to do, and all the while, he kept that stupid grin on his pale face, kept making jokes and laughing at my pathetic attempts to do as he asked.

How did he expect me to be good at this? Up until recently, I had believed that I was human, I thought that magic belonged in movies and books. It felt unnatural to me – not second nature like Hunter told me it should.

I opened my eyes, glaring at him in his spot across the room. "I *am* weak – I'm *tired*. It's been *three days* Hunter. I need to rest – and to eat!" I snapped.

I felt the anger inside me rising tentatively as if it were asking if it was needed. I let it grow, relishing in the feeling. The vortex solidified in front of me, a wall of magic made from emotion.

It was so easy to hand over all control to it, to take a back seat and let the anger and rage drive. They were my strongest emotions, after all, the vortex quickest to manifest when using my emotional magic.

"That's it, Saph. Remember to concentrate and feed all of that rage into something that you can use."

"I've had enough!" I screamed, releasing everything I had and directing it straight at him. It hit him square in the chest, sending him flying backward, thrown off his feet and into the wall behind him.

I collapsed to the floor, fighting to breathe – to stay conscious. I felt empty, like a big part of me was missing. *It's across the room, smashing the cocky Nephilim bastard into the concrete wall...*I thought to myself.

I had kept nothing for myself – no strength left to keep me up. I used so much energy just to do the *basics* of magic.

If this had been a *real* fight, I would have just left myself utterly defenseless, and the next blow aimed at me would be the last thing I ever felt. Or so Hunter had informed me each time we got to this stage over the previous few days.

"Fantastic!" Hunter was laughing as he got to his feet, his grin firmly in place. "Although, now you're dead. You need to remember to keep a reserve for yourself at all times. How many times have I told you this?"

"Shut up!" I hissed, raising my bloodied hands to cover my ears. I didn't want to hear his voice anymore. I didn't want him to *exist* anymore. I groaned and blocked him out, closing my eyes and tried to picture myself somewhere *far* away from him.

I didn't want to practice burying my emotions or calling them up to create a shield. I didn't want to know that I could use them to influence people around me – or that I could shape them into weapons to harm or even kill others.

I just wanted to sleep, to close my eyes and drift into a peaceful nothingness for a while. I wanted to relax, to be by myself and do nothing. And eat – after three days of not eating – anything even remotely edible would be like heaven in my mouth.

I felt myself filling up again as I lay there deep in thought. And knew, from one of Hunter's many lengthy lectures, that my anger was returning home, burrowing back down within me until it was needed again.

He appeared beside me, totally unscathed by my attack. "You did well Sapphira, just try and recall all that I have said in the future. I think that will be enough for now. Here, let's get you to the bath." He reached down, grabbing my arms and hauling me to my feet. The room spun, and I groaned.

At least he was giving me a break, I thought with surprise. I was dead on my feet because of him, but he was *finally* letting me rest.

"I hate you," I told him as he helped me to the giant bath.

It was filled with icy water, and I wondered how he had managed it. For days, since Ari had left me with him, he had not been out of my sight.

"I know you do." He laughed, helping me to sit on the edge of the enormous tub. "Are you able to do the rest yourself?"

I narrowed my eyes at him. He sighed, and I noticed the smile was gone. "I didn't mean anything by the comment Saph, and I know that you think I pushed you too hard, that I was harsh and uncaring towards you these past few days. But don't you think it's better that you learned this way, instead of in the middle of a real fight?"

I snorted, still glaring at him. "I'm covered in blood, starving and too weak to move on my own. How is that not cruel?"

"You were always perfectly safe," Hunter stated, taking a step away. "And if you had not been fully capable of pulling off any of the tests that I had for you, we would have stopped. I knew that you *could* do it all – Ari knew it too, or she wouldn't have told me to come. Besides, all we did was learn a little hand-to-hand combat and beginner's magic-wielding. *Children* know this stuff."

I ignored him, choosing not to take offense at his barb, and dipped my fingers into the water, gasping as my body reacted with shock from the cold.

"I'll leave you to soak your body in there for a while. Take your time, and when you're done, I'll have food fetched for you." He was gone before I had even taken another breath, the door closing behind him.

I slowly removed the tattered remains of the sundress from my aching body. It was soaking in my blood and made a wet splattering sound as it hit the floor. I swung my legs over the edge of the bath and lowered myself into the glacial water. Attempting not to make a sound as my body tried to adjust to the temperature. Still, I couldn't stop my teeth from chattering.

Ever so slowly, my muscles started to numb, the aching easing off. I closed my eyes, relaxing completely, letting my mind wander.

I must have drifted off, because when Hunter knocked on the door, I jumped, sending a wave of ice water onto the floor.

"Sapphira, are you alright in there?" He called.

I sighed. "I'm fine."

"Did you hear a word I said just now?"

"What?"

"I asked you if you were getting out anytime soon. I don't want you to fall asleep in there. It would be unpleasant for both of us if you were to drown."

"I'm getting out now," I said gruffly, standing and reaching for the towel. The bathwater was a pale pink color, and I knew that it was my blood that colored it. I dried myself carefully, inspecting my body as I did.

There were cuts and bruises all over me, the handiwork of the Nephilim that was outside the bathroom door. I avoided the mirror, not wanting to see how bad my face looked, dropping the wet towel, and reaching for a new one. I wrapped it around myself, sighing as I realized that I had no clothes.

"Hunter, I need something to wear," I called, embarrassed.

"Oh... right." He called back. "There is a dressing gown in the bedroom – I'll just go and get it."

I stood in nothing but the towel, cursing under my breath for a few seconds before he knocked on the door again. I opened it a crack, putting my hand through the small space, and Hunter placed the long white gown in it.

"This will do for now. You just put it on and come out and eat, I'll go and find you something more... appropriate. What size should I be looking for?"

I told him as I pulled the dressing gown around me.

"I'll be back soon," Hunter said and vanished.

I sighed and opened the door.

The vast hotel room was empty as I tentatively walked towards the smell of hot food. All signs of our *training* had vanished. More magic?

Hunter had ordered a meal from the hotel restaurant while I had been in the bath. My mouth watered as I sat at the table in front of it. There was a large plate of fresh fish and salad, a small bowl of steaming chips and gravy, and a large jug of soft drink. I dug in, ravenous after three days of not eating, and what seemed like a blink of an eye later, there wasn't much left.

Hunter returned as I finished off the jug of soft drink, an arm full of clothes in his hands.

He eyed the table. "Feel better now?" He asked, turning to me.

I nodded. "I'll feel even better after a few weeks of uninterrupted sleep."

He smiled, shaking his head. "Sorry, Saph, the best I can give you is a few hours."

He handed me a pile of clothes. "This is all I could find at this time of night."

"What time *is* it?" I asked, curious, and put out all at once.

Time had become an unfamiliar concept in the world of Hunter's crazy training.

"It's after ten, and don't sound too sad, Saph. Tomorrow Ari will return. I have taught you all that she has asked – but she'll want to be sure." He warned, sitting down in the chair across from mine. "Now, go get some rest, will you?"

I had hoped that our training was over, but the way he was talking didn't sound too promising.

I stood, taking the pile of clothes and heading for the bedroom.

I heard Hunter chuckle as I locked the door behind me.

I had learned that the Nephilim didn't *need* to sleep. But that didn't mean that I trusted Hunter to stay out of the room.

I wanted this time to actually sleep, not to defend against another attack- or something more problematic. It wasn't as if he had tried anything improper. He had left no time for anything but training, but I wasn't taking any chances.

"Goodnight, Sapphira." He called, laughter in his voice, "Rest well."

I was asleep before I hit the pillow, every noise, thought, and worry fading into blissful nothingness.

"Get up quickly." Hunter's voice, an urgent hiss in my ear, "You need to prepare yourself."

I opened my eyes, heart pounding, feeling the urgency Hunter was projecting at me. What was with everyone interrupting my sleep? Couldn't a girl have a full night's sleep without an emergency ruining it? "What's wrong?"

He was kneeling beside the bed, eyes on the closed door. "She's here – and she's mega pissed."

"Who?"

"I've never seen my sister this mad." Hunter glanced at me, ignoring the question, his eyes wide. "Saph, you have to *do something.*"

My heart slowed, and I frowned at Hunter in disapproval. "Is this a test? Because if it is, you could have let me sleep a bit longer – and not scared the shit out of me!"

"Sapphira, please!" Hunter said hurriedly. "Calm her down a bit before she tries to kill us, would you?"

"Why is she so mad?" I whispered, turning my eyes to the door.

I couldn't hear anything, but that didn't mean that there wasn't an aggravated Nephilim out there.

"I don't know, just use your energy to take some of her anger away. Then we might be able to safely ask her what the problem is." He was getting impatient, but his eyes were growing wider by the minute. *Impatient* and *freaked... What a combination!* I thought.

I sighed again, getting to my feet. I slowly padded towards the door, ears open for any sound.

I sent out a probe, searching for any other emotions within the walls of the large hotel room. I could feel Hunter's worry, and my annoyance, but nothing else jumped out at me.

I turned from the door, looking back at Hunter. "How the hell did you get in here anyway – the door was locked."

"It still is." Ari's sharp voice came from behind it, making me jump. "Open it now, Sapphira. Or I'll knock it down."

I could suddenly feel her anger in the air as if a shield had been dropped, pulsating energy that heated my skin as it touched me.

"Damn," I whispered, angry at myself. "I forgot to look for shields..."

"A rookie mistake," Hunter mumbled from the far side of the bed.

I glared at him, watching as he gestured towards the door, a meaningful look on his face.

I closed my eyes, imagining Ari's anger as a solid black ball.

Mine... I thought, reaching out invisible hands to take it for myself. I pulled it into me, adding it to my own pit of black anger and hate.

"Awesome, Saph, you did it!" Hunter praised "Now, shield like a bitch because Ari will probably-"

He was cut off as the door burst open, wood shattering into tiny pieces that splintered through the air. I threw up a mental shield, picturing it expanding to cover my whole body as Ari stalked into the room. She was no longer angry, I had eaten all of her anger, but she was still annoyed, still dangerous.

I summoned some of the calmness I held within me and gently let it go. It glided towards Ari, sinking into her skin.

She glanced at me, her eyes looking me up and down before she turned on Hunter. I flicked my fingers out towards him, my shield expanding to cover him as well.

Ari lifted an arm, a strange azure light appearing in her palm. She closed her hand around the light as it flickered like a flame, before flinging it at Hunter. It hit my shield, sending shockwaves back to me.

Ari paused, turning back to face me.

Hunter was grinning broadly, watching me as well.

"What the hell is going on?" I asked, a little breathless.

I was beginning to run out of the small amount of energy that I had left, and I could still feel the aftershocks of Ari's attack rippling through my shield. Hopefully, this strange situation sorted itself out soon, or I'd probably pass out trying to keep the shield up.

Ari blinked slowly, her hands normal again. "You can drop it now." Her voice was perfectly calm, her blue eyes sparkling with delight and something like pride.

I didn't need to be told twice, and I sighed with relief as I sat on the bed. I was exhausted, but both Ari and Hunter were smiling like I had done the impossible.

"What the hell was that all about?" I demanded weakly. "I was gonna pass out!"

Hunter took the few steps that separated him from Ari, and they embraced. It wasn't a sensitive hug, more like a congratulatory one.

"Thank you, Hunter." Ari said softly, ignoring my question.

"My pleasure, Sister. It was fun to be put to work again."

"Um, Hello?" I called, waving my hand in the air in front of me weakly. "Can you hear me?"

Hunter chuckled, turning to me. "Ari wanted to test you in a situation that was unexpected – but totally safe. That was your demonstration of what you have learned under my instruction."

I grunted, folding my arms in front of my chest, raising my eyebrows at Ari. "You couldn't have just asked what I had learned; you had to give me a freaking heart attack? I thought you'd gone nuts!"

She shrugged. "The best way to show me what you can do is by actually *doing* it."

Hunter smirked. "You owe me a hundred dollars, by the way. I won."

"What are you talking about?" I asked, glancing between the two Nephilim.

"I bet Hunter that you wouldn't throw your shield out wide enough to include him too. I thought that you hated him enough after what he had put you through to let him burn."

"I do hate him," I said, glaring at the Nephilim in question, still smirking from his spot next to Ari. "But I couldn't let him get hurt. It wouldn't have been right."

Ari turned to Hunter. "I sense that she didn't like your teaching methods, Brother."

Hunter shrugged, pulling an innocent face. "I just don't see it, what's not to like?"

"Um, the torture part, maybe?" I threw a pillow at him. "Or the withholding food and sleep part?"

"You're alive, are you not?" Hunter asked, smiling softly. "And in one piece?"

"Barely." I muttered, getting to my feet. I needed a drink of water, my mouth was dry, and my head was starting to pound again.

"Then, my job is done." Hunter said as I made my way to the kitchen, pouring myself some water from the tap.

They had followed me, all joking gone, and eyes serious again.

"You're late, by the way," I muttered, glaring at Ari. "You told me that you would be back in three days... it's been almost four."

"I had Nephilim things to do." She just shrugged, a smirk on her face, before turning to Hunter. "Thanks again. I'll see you soon."

"Of course, Sister. I'll see you soon." He threw a wink at me. "It was a pleasure, Sapphira."

I toasted him with my glass, downing the water quickly, watching as he smiled his goofy grin and vanished.

"God, I wish you people would stop doing that." I said, putting my now empty glass on the sink.

"Why?" Ari asked, sitting down at the table.

Hunter had cleared away after I had gone to bed earlier, the mess from dinner completely gone.

"Because it's not fair." I half-joked, "You're all making me jealous."

Ari smiled in response, tapping her fingers on the surface of the table. She crossed her legs, the long black skirt she was wearing, draping across the chair and down to the floor. She had stunning black and red high heels on her feet, a red halter neck top clinging to her chest. Her dark curls were loose along her shoulders, and her blue eyes gleamed with silent laughter.

"Well, if you are truly the *Goddess*, Sapphira," She said slowly, watching my face as I sat across the table from her.

"You will come into a lot more power than just the one you have now."

"What other powers does the *Goddess* have?" I asked curiously. "I mean, in the past. What else could she do?"

Ari shrugged, continuing her tapping. "She could do many different things. But I'm not going to tell you all of them just now; one of the ways that we will know if you are really *Her* is to see what else *you* can do."

"And how will we know?" I asked, leaning forward, "When will we know either way if I am who everyone thinks I am?"

"Patience Saph, you still have over a year before you come into full power. Anything could happen in that amount of time."

"And that doesn't sound ominous or anything." I muttered, rolling my eyes.

Ari laughed. "You did well today, Saph." She said quietly, filling the silence that had formed in the air around us. "I'm... proud of you. I know that Hunter's methods are a bit...well, medieval, to say the least. But you really kicked some ass there."

I rolled my eyes, waving away the compliment. "I'm covered in cuts and bruises and can hardly stand up I'm that tired. I wasn't that great. Speaking of being tired– can I go back to bed now?"

Ari shook her head. "No, I'm sorry, Sapphira, but we need to be going. I know that Hunter acquired more clothes for you last night, so maybe just change, and we can head off."

"And where, may I ask, are we going now?"

"Australia," Ari said softly, getting to her feet. "I'm taking you home."

I ended up on my knees again, gagging as the world spun,

Ari was standing beside me, chuckling. How did the Nephilim get used to traveling that way without losing their breakfast?

"Ugh, I don't think I'll ever get used to that," I complained, holding out my hand for Ari to pull me to my feet. "Isn't there an easier way?"

"That *was* the easiest way." She informed me with a grin.

"Why don't *you* feel sick?"

"I've been doing it for millennia, and besides, it's only the passenger that gets queasy."

"Oh. Lucky me." I groaned, glancing around at our new destination. "Um, Ari?"

"Yes?"

"Why are we in the middle of a crowded shopping center? I thought that you were taking me home?"

I started to panic, frozen in place, and thinking that someone would have just seen two young women suddenly appear out of thin air. I looked at the faces of the people closest to us, waiting to see the panic in their eyes, fear maybe, but saw nothing out of the ordinary. We were standing between the entrances to a supermarket on our right and a bakery on our left. People made their way across the passageway, going about their business, not even noticing us.

"Don't worry, Saph, they can't see us – or hear us," Ari said, grabbing my hand and walking us into the supermarket. She grabbed a trolley and steered us around the blissfully, unaware people. "They can't see the trolley either." She said, taking in my expression. Ari started throwing random things into the trolley, humming under her breath as she went.

"What are we doing?"

"We can't go back to the Safe House without... *gifts*. It would break some kind of silly Moroi code. So we are here to fill a trolley with all kinds of crap that could be considered useful to them out there in nowhere land."

"We're going to steal?" I asked, horrified. "Can you do that, Ari?"

She shrugged. "I can do pretty much anything I want – free will and all that crap."

"But isn't stealing a sin?"

She sighed, turning to face me. "You have to stop thinking that I'm some sort of heavenly angel, Sapphira. I'm not. I am Fallen – which means I'm pretty much just a powerful human, as tasteless as that is to say. So you need to realize that I can do anything that you can do, and not worry about sin and heavenly retribution and all that. I am stuck down here for eternity. There is no chance of me returning home. So yeah, I can steal; I can drink and gamble, I can have sex and commit murder. I can do anything."

I gaped at her, shocked. "Oh, I... I didn't realize. I'm sorry."

She shrugged, turning back to the shelves. "Now, you know."

"Can I... Can I ask how – well... why are you a Fallen?"

"No." She shook her head, her shoulders stiff, voice firm.

We made our way through the isles in silence, Ari filling the trolley while I studied the oblivious people around me. They all looked so *normal*, going about their day completely unaware of me and my problems. I envied them – and I wished that my life was more like theirs.

"Time to go." Ari's voice cut through my daydream, making me jump in surprise. The trolley was full, and Ari steered it out of the supermarket, muttering under her breath. I followed silently, glancing around nervously, and waiting for someone to catch us.

"I told you, they can't see us," Ari said, not looking at me. "Stop worrying."

"How do we get it to the Safe House?" I asked when we were through the outer doors of the shopping center.

"The same way we got here. Or, if that doesn't appeal to you, we could wait until someone picks up your energy and comes to claim you." Ari answered, glancing over at me, eyebrows raised, smirk firmly in place. "So which will it be?"

I sighed, holding out my hand for her to take. "Let's just get it over with."

The minute my hand touched hers, I felt a zap of electricity, and I was spinning. The shopping center vanished, colors whooshing around my head. My stomach was doing summersaults, and I felt like I was going to be sick... *Yeah, this never gets old.*

Again, I landed on my knees, gasping for air, and trying not to gag. I heard an alarm going off somewhere nearby as I struggled to my feet. Ari was standing beside me, leaning up against her trolley casually, and examining her nails.

We were in a large stone room, a bed, and one little chair, the only furniture. There was a small window high on one of the curved walls that let in the sunlight, and a large steel door leaning up against the wall, hinges broken.

"This was my room!" I exclaimed, recognizing it.

I was glad that someone had cleaned the blood off of everything. If they hadn't, I would probably have been throwing up – or passing out at that moment.

"You might want to start explaining yourself about now," Ari said calmly, motioning to the door. "Seven agitated Moroi are about to appear and start shooting otherwise."

"*What?*"

Ari sighed. "Ari and Sapphira request an audience with the *Maharishi* of this Safe House."

"Request Granted." A male voice replied, and the body that the voice belonged to appeared in the doorway. It was Abhijay, the *Maharishi* himself, followed by six Moroi guards. Each one was as tall and as muscular as their boss.

A.J was wearing a black suit, which made him look like sex on legs. His brown eyes were smoldering as he took in Ari and me. *The Moroi do like to look good...*

"What can I do for you?" he asked formally.

"We wish to take advantage of the Moroi hospitality that this Safe House is so famous for." Ari sneered.

"And if I were to refuse?" Came the grave reply.

What the hell was going on? Why was A.J acting so formal? And why was Ari back to acting like a bitch?

"If you were to refuse, which is well within your rights as *Maharishi*, Sapphira and I would be forced to try our luck elsewhere. But, who knows where the *Goddess Incarnate* would be safe from all of those that wish harm upon her."

"She was offered our hospitality once before," A.J said his voice like stone. "And that did not pan out so well, did it Sapphira?" he turned hard eyes on me, his lips pursed in annoyance. I shook my head, opening my mouth to apologize.

"The *Goddess Incarnate* does not apologize for her behavior. Your Safe House proved to be lacking in the security measures required for her safety." Ari snapped before I could speak.

"So why did you return?"

Again, Ari answered for me. "She has decided to give the Moroi another chance."

A.J bowed formally, eyes avoiding me altogether. "We are honored by your trust in us, Goddess."

"Sapphira also brings a gift for you, *Maharishi*." Ari added, motioning to the full trolley at her side.

A.J nodded, not even glancing at it. "Your gift has been accepted. You are both welcome here."

"Wait!" I called as he turned to leave.

He froze his back to me. "Yes, *Goddess*?"

"Is... is Fallon here?"

"She is, *Goddess*. Do you wish to speak with her?" He turned his head slightly so that he could look in my direction.

I nodded. "If she has the time, that would be great."

"Fallon will make time, Sapphira. You have requested her presence, so she must come." Ari said firmly. "Isn't that right, Abhijay?"

A.J nodded. "That is correct. Is there anything else, *Goddess*?"

"Um... No... At least, I don't think so..." I stuttered, flustered with all of the formality.

"Very well." A.J left, the guards trailing after him, and silence filling the room.

I took a seat on the bed, running a hand through my hair.

"What the hell was that?" I asked, turning to Ari as she moved to sit in the chair.

"You had to return as the *Goddess Incarnate*, not just as Sapphira. This way, you cannot be blamed for anything that has happened here in the past, and they will have no choice but to do as you say."

"But – "

"That includes telling you everything that you want to know. When you want to know it." Ari added quickly, her eyebrows raised, waiting for me to catch on.

"How clever." Sneered a new voice from the hall.

I spun to face the beautiful stranger as he stalked into the room. He was tall and slim – but I could see muscle definition under his silk shirt. He had light skin and long black hair, but the feature that drew my breath was his *golden eyes*... Like no kidding, his eyes were *gold*!

"*I* thought it was clever," Ari replied calmly, looking the stranger up and down with her usual expression of distaste. "What do you want, Sidhe?"

I tried to hide my gasp of shock. Was he Sidhe? What was he doing here? Had Queen Kamilla sent him to collect me?

Even though I was filled with dread at his presence, I couldn't help but keep looking at him, wishing that he would never leave. He was breathtaking.

"My Queen sent me to guard the *Goddess*. And to remain close to her, until that time when she calls on Sapphira to pay her debt."

I loved the way his lips moved, so sensuously, his words brushing against my skin like a lover's caress.

"And if the Goddess were to refuse your presence?"

As if I would! I wanted him with me always! I thought, suppressing a sigh. *God, he was stunning!*

The stranger shook his head, smiling tightly. "She cannot."

"The Goddess can do as she pleases." Ari snapped. "She cannot be dictated to by anyone."

"Technically, she isn't the true *Goddess* until she comes into full power. And my Queen has every right to send me to Sapphira's side until she has repaid the debt."

"Damn the Fae," Ari muttered, glaring at the Sidhe stranger. "I had hoped that you lot had forgotten how that worked."

"We forget nothing, Nephilim."

Ari sighed, turning to me. "Looks like you're stuck with him, Saph. Just try not to stare at him for too long, his kind have some freaky powers."

"What?" I snapped out of my little trance, my heart racing.

"You know... crazy attractive faeries that enchant you to follow them into their world, never to return?"

"You're kidding, right?" I asked wide-eyed.

Is that why I had been so fixated with his looks? Was he using some sort of enchantment on me? The Sidhe laughed, a sound like deep bells ringing. *What was with the Sidhe and bells?*

"Not exactly." He answered. "There is some truth to what she says, although you need not fear Sapphira, I am not here right now to enchant you in any way whatsoever."

"Then why..." I paused, blushing. I was about to ask why I found him so attractive but thought the better of it.

"Why what, Saph?" Ari prodded, curiosity all over her face.

"Nothing, never mind." I hurried, waving away the conversation.

"So, what are we to call you?" Ari asked casually, turning back to the Sidhe. "If we are to be stuck with you, I guess we had better know your name."

"You can call me Raine." He replied just as casually.

"Raine, huh?" Ari cocked her head to one side. "Is that a nickname?"

"You know it is." He replied with a grin. "Did you think that I would so easily give my real name to you, Nephilim?"

"Why not?" I asked lamely.

"A Faerie never gives out their real name." Raine said slowly, eyeing me strangely, "Names hold power."

I looked back at him, a blank expression on my face.

"If he were to tell us his real name, we could make him do anything we wanted. Including shoving something iron through his flesh while he burned," Ari told me patiently, a merciless smile on her lips. "He would have no choice but to obey."

"Oh."

"So, you may call me Raine." He made a small bow. "I'm at your service until my Queen tells me otherwise."

"How convenient for us." Ari exclaimed sarcastically.

"He arrived just before you did." Fallon said dryly from the doorway, looking at Ari, her face expressionless.

I jumped, still not used to people appearing out of nowhere all of the time. *At least I didn't squeal this time though...*I thought to myself, slowing my racing heart. *That has to be a step up!*

Fallon was wearing a sophisticated black and white dress that hugged her hips and chest, ending just above her knees. She had extremely high heels on her feet, making her look a lot taller than she already was. Her auburn hair was up in the same kind complicated bun I had seen her wear a week ago.

She turned to me, eyes guarded. "You wanted to see me, *Goddess*?"

"Um... yeah, I..." I turned to Ari and Raine. "Could you excuse us for a minute?"

Raine nodded respectfully, murmuring something that sounded like "As you wish, *Goddess*..."

Ari shrugged as if to say *whatever,* and they both left the room. Fallon let them pass before slowly entering. She sat on the edge of the bed, her hands folded in her lap.

"Fallon, I wanted to apologize." I began slowly, awkwardly. "I-"

"There is no need, *Goddess*." Fallon cut in quickly. "You have done nothing to apologize for."

"Please, not you too." I groaned in dismay. "I'm the same person that I used to be Fallon, the one that you were friends with – at least I hope that part was real... God, I'm doing this all wrong!" I looked over at Fallon. She was sitting still, carefully respectful eyes on me. "I mean that... I consider you one of my best friends, and I really don't want you to be all... *formal* with me. I just want to go back to the relationship that we had before all of this happened." I gestured around the room as I spoke. "I'd like to be told about a lot more, of course, but I want us to be friends again. And I'm sorry about what happened the last time that we spoke. I didn't realize what had really happened until Ari told me days later." I'd been pacing in front of the bed, but paused, spinning to face Fallon, who still hadn't moved. "Can you forgive me, Fallon?" I asked, my eyes pleading.

"You shouldn't have left, Sapphira." She said softly, eyes sad. "You had me so worried. We couldn't locate you. I thought that something terrible had happened until Ari finally told us that you were safe."

"I know!" I cried, "I wasn't thinking, and my anger was so strong. But I know how to control it now, and I promise - "

"No!" Fallon said quickly, holding out a hand to stop me. "Don't promise anything! When it comes to magical beings, Saph, especially Djinn or Faerie, never promise... It's dangerous. I probably should have told you that... and a lot of other things evidently."

I nodded hurriedly, beginning to smile, hopefully. "So, are we friends again?"

"I guess so. I mean, who else is gonna get me killed while I'm trying to protect them?" Fallon shrugged. "Or drive me crazy with a million questions a minute?"

I laughed, a grateful, relieved sound.

She smiled at me. "So, where have you been anyway?"

"Oh, well, I was with Ari and her brother."

Fallon raised an eyebrow. "Ari's brother? Another Nephilim?"

I nodded. "Hunter. He taught me how to control my emotional energies."

"At least your time away wasn't for nothing, I guess. But Saph, next time, could you please tell me before you vanish?"

"But I *didn't* just vanish."

"No one had seen you since you left me."

"That's not exactly true," I said slowly, frowning. "Saul and Aryk saw me."

"Really?" Fallon's voice had dropped a few degrees.

I nodded. "Saul was on duty in the trees, he stopped me and asked what I was doing, and then Aryk appeared and told him to let me be. He kind of... showed me which way to go to get away from the Safe House."

Fallon's eyes narrowed, anger whirling around her. "Did he now?"

"He didn't tell you?"

She shook her head. "No, he did not. If you'll excuse me, I need to go have a little chat with my husband."

Crap! I thought as she left the room quickly. I had just got Aryk into trouble – but why had he kept his involvement a secret? What did he hope to gain from it?

Ari and Raine were back. The moody Nephilim took the chair, crossing her legs and examining her nails with a bored expression, the Sidhe leaning casually against the wall underneath the only window.

I sighed, sitting on the bed and running my hands through my hair. "I just create drama everywhere I go..." I murmured softly.

Ari snorted. "It goes with the job."

"Well, I never wanted this job!" I snapped, keeping my voice low.

"I know, but you have it." Ari looked at me, eyes drilling holes through my skin. "So, you need to deal with it."

"Nice pep talk." Raine commented dryly, folding his arms over his chest, looking like he was posing for the cover of a men's fashion magazine.

"Shut up, Faerie-boy, no one asked you." Ari said sweetly, flipping him a nasty gesture with her finger.

"Stop it – both of you." I yawned. "And could you, like, disappear for a few hours while I sleep?"

"I'll stay here... quietly, and you can guard the door." Ari told Raine, who nodded and made his way purposely toward the steel door.

"What, no arguments?" Ari prodded sarcastically. "Your Queen didn't order you to keep her in your sights at all times?"

"I have already told you... Queen Kamilla ordered me to remain close until Sapphira can repay her debt."

"Oh, for god's sake, quit it, will you please?" I snapped, punching the pillows as I laid down. "I'm too tired for this crap. You can provoke each other tomorrow, but let me sleep for a while first, okay?"

They didn't make another sound, thankfully, and I made myself comfortable in the bed. I closed my eyes and blissfully waited for sleep to come and carry me away, hoping that this time I wouldn't be woken up with some sort of disaster.

Chapter Six

I opened my eyes to the sound of whispered conversation, my mind groggily trying to catch what was being said.

I had no idea how long I had been asleep, but my body was telling me it wasn't long enough. I was facing the wall, my back to whoever was in the room. I could feel a swirl of strong emotion coming from them, and I didn't move from where I was, feeling that most of it were meant for me.

"I just wanted her to know..."

"I will tell her, Leilani." Fallon's voice cut in softly. "The Goddess will know that Denni, a Dhampir warrior that bravely fought to protect her – who was injured in the battle with a Vârcolac – still lives."

"He'll likely not be a Warrior anymore Fallon; his face is... he can't..." Leilani's voice broke.

"I know, but he will want for nothing for the rest of his days. He will still be an honored member of this Safe House, Leilani."

Sobs escaped from the woman, and I felt Fallon reach out with her power to comfort her.

"It is an opportunity that not many Dhampirs get – a second chance. He can still be with the one he loves – can still contribute to his clan – even after this horrendous attack. How many others can say the same?"

I was frozen, my heart breaking as I listened.

"Thank you, I... I have to go." Leilani sniffed after awhile. "I need to get back..."

"I will tell her." Fallon promised again as Leilani's footsteps receded, and the door closed.

I sat up in the bed, turning to face Fallon as I did.

She was standing in the middle of the room, shoulders slumped.

"Don't." She said sadly. "Don't apologize."

I frowned, drawing my knees up to my chin under the sheet, hugging my arms around them.

"But – "

"Sapphira, you cannot apologize for every bad thing that happens around you. You cannot keep feeling so responsible for every little incident, or it will drive you mad." She finally turned to face me, her eyes drained. "It is honorable that you feel it, but nevertheless, a burden that the likes of us have to bear quietly."

"Why?"

Fallon sighed, moving gracefully to sit on the bed beside me, the floor-length gold dress flowing magically along her skin, as if it were made of water. "Truthfully, it is tiring, and 'sorry' does not comfort those who have lost so much so easily. Nothing we can say will. Warriors and their loved ones know that death or severe injury is a strong possibility – and it is futile to try and unburden them their grief and anger."

"So what do I do?"

"No one can answer that but you. What you do at times like these – how your people react – all depend on the kind of leader you are." She patted my knee, a tired smile on her lips that didn't reach her eyes.

"I never wanted to be a leader, Fallon."

"Either did I, but we were both born into leadership. We have no choice."

"The last time that I saw Leilani, her leg was..."

"Dhampir heal extremely fast Saph, they can heal almost anything. Denni's wounds were too severe. He is lucky to even be alive." She added, sensing my next question before I asked it.

We lapsed into silence for a while, each lost in our own thoughts.

"I didn't mean to cause problems between you and Aryk," I spoke into the quiet as Fallon absentmindedly plaited small parts of her long auburn hair. "I should never have said -"

"I'm glad that you *did* tell me Saph, what he did was imprudent. You could have been lost to us, and Aryk would have been at fault. He should have never let you leave like that, and not try and stop you – or tell anyone afterward."

"Did you talk to him about it?"

She nodded. "He said that he had no idea that you would leave the safety of the compound. He thought that you just needed some privacy to think things over."

"Do you believe him?" I asked carefully, prompted by her tone of voice.

Fallon looked at me, her expression blank. "He has never given me any reason to doubt his word in the past, and as you are here in one piece, I guess I have no reason to start now." Her voice was clipped, her body taut.

"I didn't mean to offend you, Fallon," I began softly, leaning closer to my friend. "I only meant..."

"It's okay, Sapphira, really. It's just been a long few days. On top of everything else, his appearance – and the reason for it - was a shock, that's all." She smiled, lying down beside me, her left hand holding up her head as she gazed up at me. "It's just strange having the husband that I haven't seen in almost nineteen years around again."

"I bet." I winked. "I can see that he would be... distracting."

Fallon grinned, slapping my arm playfully.

"Are Djinn princesses allowed to hit a Goddess?" I asked, feigning injury as I rubbed my arm.

"A Djinn Princess can do whatever the hell she likes." Came the indignant reply—the voice of royalty.

"Will you tell me what your life was like before all of ... this" I waved my hand around, motioning our surroundings, "I see... frilly ball gowns and fancy tea parties."

Fallon raised her eyebrows at me, a smile creeping over her lips. "Oh yes, that was it exactly. Every day was just one eighteenth-century ball after another. We Djinn are an indulgent bunch that way."

"Seriously though Fallon, it's like I know nothing about your real-life... Who were you before you met me? What did you have to give up keeping me safe?"

"It wasn't like that at all Saph, I didn't have to give up anything that couldn't wait for my return – or come to me wherever I was. Keeping you safe was – and still is – more important than my duties as a Princess. As long as the King and Queen are alive and well, the Djinn don't really *need* me. I was more for looks than anything else."

"Now, that isn't entirely true, Princess." Aryk's voice floated over us. "You are much more than just a pretty face to your people."

"Listening in on private conversations, Prince Aryk?" Colte admonished good-naturedly from the doorway as I jumped in surprise, "How beneath you!"

"Completely unintentional, I assure you." Aryk stated with an elegant shrug, stepping into the room.

He bowed low, looking as perfect as ever in another suit that looked like it could have come straight from Giorgio Armani himself.

"I came to apologize. First to you, Goddess, for the trouble that my actions have caused, I truly did not wish for you to be placed in any danger. And to you as well Princess, my actions were beyond irresponsible. I do hope that you can both forgive me."

"Yeah, what he said." Colte added, lighting up a cigarette. He leaned up against the door frame, blowing a puff of smoke into the room.

"I accept your apology, Prince Aryk." Fallon said, getting to her feet in one fluid motion, and stepping into his arms.

Aryk grinned, kissing her forehead gently. "Thank you, Dearest."

"What she said." I nodded, grinning. "And Colte, surely I've told you before that those things will kill you, right?"

"Nah," he said, slapping his chest. "Another Dhampir plus side - I'm impervious to lung cancer."

I groaned, rolling my eyes, a smile on my lips. "Is there *anything* that will kill you?"

I realized too late that it was in bad taste, considering what had happened. I opened my mouth to apologize, but Colte, seeing my discomfort, feigned a wounded expression, holding a hand over his heart. "Do you really want me dead?"

I pretended to think about it, grateful for his attempt to pass over my insensitive mistake, and then shrugged, tilting my head to one side teasingly. "Hmm, who else would I find to annoy me like you do?"

He smirked. "No one can do it as well as me, that's for sure. I've had *years* to refine my skills. But there was one other reason that we dropped by..." Colte continued, glancing from me to Aryk and Fallon, who were still standing in their embrace in the center of the room.

"Oh?" Fallon inquired. "And what reason would that be?"

"Akil and Amin are at the compound boundary. They are requesting an audience with 'the one that holds power'" Colte air quoted the last few words, rolling his eyes.

Fallon frowned. "What did Abhijay say?"

"He told them to wait where they were while their request was deliberated," Aryk told her. "But he didn't tell them who it was that they were waiting for."

As one, they all turned to stare at me, contemplating looks on their faces.

"Umm... who are they exactly? And what would they want to talk to me about?"

"Amin and Akil are the leaders of the local Lycanthrope packs. They would have felt the power rush from the other day." Colte said disapprovingly, putting out his cigarette and flicking the butt into a nearby bin. "It's just like the Lycanthropes to come sniffing around after all of the action."

"What are Lycanthropes?"

"Shapeshifters," Fallon answered neutrally. "More precisely, they are beings that can turn into animals."

"Are they good or bad?"

"Generally, they're whatever pays better," Colte spoke up again. "They're like mercenaries for hire."

"Well, that's a little unfair," Aryk told him. "Most Lycanthrope packs are very cultured and pleasant to deal with.

They run their kingdoms – so to speak – much the same as the Moroi do. They can turn quite nasty when their pack is in danger, true, but not all are the goons that you make them out to be. Only a handful of packs across the globe have turned rogue like that."

Colte shrugged. "You'd know more about it than me."

Aryk nodded, answering tightly. "It is part of my duties as Prince of the Djinn to know these things."

"Will you tell A.J that I will be there to discuss this with him in a few moments?" I asked Colte, throwing back the sheet and stepping off the bed before any insults or arguments broke out. "I'll just change first..."

Colte nodded and left.

I began rummaging around, searching for something respectable to wear. The clothes that Colte had packed were magically sitting in my bag beside the bed. What do you wear for your first meeting with Lycanthrope leaders anyway?

Aryk bowed to both Fallon and me and then departed as well.

Once we were alone, I turned back to Fallon. "What should I do? Do you think it's safe for me to talk to them? What could they want from me?" I was panicking. A week ago, I hadn't known that Djinn, vampires, faeries, and fallen angels existed in real life – and now I had to add shapeshifters to the mix?

Well, why not one more preternatural breed? A voice whispered in my head. *Why not just start assuming that all of the things that go bump in the night are real?*

"I think that, if you decided to allow them an audience Saph, you would be safe enough surrounded by some Moroi guards. I believe that the Sidhe is still skulking around here somewhere as well."

I had forgotten all about Raine! Where had he disappeared to? And Ari as well! The last I had seen of them, they were taunting each other while I tried to sleep. Had Fallon taken over – is that why they were gone? And why she was here with Leilani when I woke? I had to remember to ask Fallon where Denni was, and if I could go see him. And what was I going to say to him? Could I tell him that I was grateful for all that he had done to protect me, and not sound conceited and insensitive to his suffering?

"If Akil and Amin wanted to do you harm, they would not have requested an audience with you here." Fallon continued, oblivious to my inner dialogue. "I am unsure of what their reason behind this meeting is, if I had to take a guess, I would suggest curiosity, perhaps? Maybe they just want to see what new power is in their territory?" She paused, thinking.

I hardly even flinched as a beautiful Grecian style jade formal gown appeared on the bed beside me. "Try that one. And I'll fix your hair when it's on," Fallon said distractedly, pausing before continuing with her original train of thought. "Or it could be that these two packs have finally decided which side they are on. I really don't know Sapphira, but I believe that you would gain more insight if you were to ask Abhijay. He knows these two better than I do."

I managed to pull the dress on over my jeans and tank top while she spoke, wiggling the jeans off before struggling with the top – and not flashing inappropriately. Yay me!

Fallon fixed the dress so that it sat correctly before running her fingers through my long blonde hair, beginning a sophisticated braid. "I also think, Saph, that you should be respectful and encouraging with Abhijay when it comes to decision-making in his Safe House. He needs to be involved in the decisions regarding his home and his people. Even though you are the *Incarnate*, you are still just a guest here. I know that Ari negotiated your return to the compound, but it is you that holds power. You need to be in control of how it is wielded at others."

"That sounds an awful lot like a reprimand, Princess." Raine's voice snapped.

I jumped, spinning around to face him in all his stunning grandeur, my heart pounding. Fallon hadn't moved, other than to release my hair from her fingers when I turned.

"Oh my god, does no one knock anymore?!"

He shrugged his beautiful shoulders, theatrically leaning closer and knocking on the doorframe. "If you wanted privacy, perhaps you should have closed the door?" he suggested, entering the room and taking a seat in the chair.

I was getting more and more breathless the longer I watched him.

"Does your Queen let you enter her chambers unannounced, Raine?" Fallon asked calmly, her voice snapping me out of my daze.

"Of course she does not. But Sapphira Dawn is not my Queen."

"Did your Queen not tell you that you are here to serve Sapphira as you serve her?"

"Until that time when Queen Kamilla calls me back, yes."

"Then, from this moment until the moment that you return to the Sidhe Queen, you will treat the *Incarnate* as if she is your Queen. Or perhaps you would like to tell Kamilla why you are not following her orders as she has described them?"

Raine's golden eyes turned cold as he looked Fallon over. He got slowly to his feet, eyes not leaving Fallon. "Of course, Princess, you are correct in reminding me of my duties. I apologize to you, *Goddess*, for my encroachment in conduct." The Sidhe turned to me, his face thawing slightly. "I assure you that it will not happen again. I shall await your orders at a respectful distance." He retreated to the hall, softly closing the door behind him.

I glanced at Fallon, who was smiling at me. "Now, to conjure up the perfect shoes for that dress…"

We met up with A.J in the surveillance room a few minutes later. He stood in front of a massive screen showing the compound from hundreds of different angles.

He looked away from the screen at the sound of my heels entering the room. Fallon still managing to walk without a sound, even in her stilettos.

He seemed to freeze momentarily as he took in the sight of me.

"*Goddess*, you look spectacular." He complimented me, recovering and bowing formally.

"Thank you, A.J." I blushed.

Fallon moved further into the room, her eyes focused on two figures standing inoffensively on the screen. "How long have they been standing there, Abhijay?" She asked the Moroi, glancing over her shoulder at him.

"About fifteen minutes now." He answered, turning back to the screen as well. "They appeared and requested an audience. I sent word to you both immediately."

Fallon nodded, leaning in closer. "They don't look armed – I'm assuming that your guards searched them?"

A.J shook his head. "They didn't need to. Both Akil and Amin came here in animal form. They only changed back after clothes had been supplied to them. There was nowhere to conceal any weapons."

Fallon nodded as if this was an everyday occurrence. Who knew, it probably was in their world.

I was struggling to keep up with the conversation – had A.J really just said that they had to have clothes supplied? Did that mean that they had been *naked* when they changed form?

"Did they say anything else?" Fallon asked, her eyes not leaving the screen.

A.J shook his head again. "No, nothing else was said; only what I have told you."

"What do you want to do, Goddess?" Fallon asked, turning to look at me, blank-faced.

"A.J, you know these two men. What do you think their reasoning behind coming here is? Do you think that it would be safe to agree to their request?" I asked the Moroi, watching as he turned to face me in surprise.

"You're asking my advice, Goddess?"

I nodded. "I am. You're the master of this compound, and I am here under your protection. It would be unwise of me to ignore your council here."

Fallon nodded behind Abhijay's back, smiling her approval.

"I believe that they are just curious about the power that they felt. They may be just checking to make sure that their Pack's are safe – that you don't pose a threat to them. They could be here to ensure that you are not here to wipe them out."

"That has happened in the past?" I interrupted, shocked.

Who would want to wipe out an entire pack?

"There have been others around the world that boasted success in such a task," Abhijay confirmed. "Men, women, and children all slaughtered."

"Why? Who would do such a thing?"

Abhijay shrugged. "Many beings believe that Lycanthropes are too great a risk to their safety to allow them to populate their territories."

"So, they kill them all?" I was outraged. "Do you think that too Abhijay?"

Abhijay shook his head, calm against my anger. "If I thought the way many others did Goddess, the packs belonging to Akil and Amin would not exist here."

I frowned. "And if you did think that way, you would have no qualms in destroying the lives of women and children?"

"If my belief was that they posed a threat to my people, I would do what was necessary to keep them safe. But I do not believe the Lycanthrope race a threat to the Moroi."

"What can you tell me about Amin and Akil?" I asked, changing the subject. I needed to keep focused on the issue at hand and not linger on the negative.

I took a few calming breaths, swallowing my anger. *It would be a bad idea to let it out now*, I reminded myself. *Remember what Hunter taught you...*

"Akil is the Alpha– or King of the local Wolf pack – they are nothing like the Vârcolac," A.J added quickly, seeing my expression. "Akil is the taller of the two men you see on the screen. He has a somewhat fiery personality and is very argumentative. Amin is the King of the Taipan group; he is a quiet type of man and is extremely intelligent. Both men are cunning in their own way, so if I were dealing with them, I would be cautious about what I said, and what they were up to."

"How are there wolves in Australia?" I asked, curious. "Taipan, I understand. We have those naturally here. But wolves?"

"The Lycanthrope community is spread across the world, not only where their natural animal is found," A.J answered matter-of-factly. "There are many different exotic species of Lycanthrope in Australia. I know that Akil's wolves' ancestors are from Europe, but they migrated here a few generations ago for more land. Akil once told me that in his homeland, different Packs were constantly fighting for territory. Many Packs were on the verge of being wiped out because of it."

I nodded slowly, trying to take the information in. "So when I speak to them, do I call them by name – or is there a specific title? I have no idea of the protocol here..."

Abhijay seemed impressed by my question. "What you call them and how you act depends on how you see them. If you believe that they are superior to you, you would call Akil 'Alpha', and Amin 'King Amin.' If you see them as equals, it would just be by name, or 'Highness' if you wish to be polite. If they are lower than you, you wouldn't name them at all."

"What do you call them when you speak?"

"They are treated as my equals. I call them by name only. But you, Goddess, are higher than us all. I cannot counsel you in how you greet them – if you do meet them, it will have to be your choice and yours alone."

I was getting nervous. What if I did this all wrong? What if I damaged the relationship that A.J had built with them? Would Abhijay kill them if he thought that they were a threat to our safety?

"Where would be the easiest place to defend while we did this?"

"Possibly inside – if it went badly, the Lycanthropes would have less room to maneuver, and we would have the upper hand. It gives us many more places for you to retreat to while we fought to calm them, more places for my guards to ambush them if they followed you. Meeting them inside also gives Fallon the chance to scope out their intentions as they pass through her shields. I don't believe, however, that things would get anywhere near that bad during your audience with Akil and Amin."

I looked to Fallon, who had turned back to the screens while we had been talking. "You can do that?"

She nodded, returning her gaze to me. "I can. But if you wanted me to do that, you would have to invite them in soon, my shields are due to drop any minute."

I nodded. "Okay, A.J, let's do this."

He bowed. "As you wish, Goddess. Allow me to escort you to our audience hall. I can give our guards their posts along the way."

I nodded again.

Abhijay turned to a guard standing by the door to the security room, who had been silently standing at attention since I had entered. "Tell our guests that they will be received in the Hall Alayla."

The guard, a pretty brunette woman with brown eyes and dark skin, was almost the same height as Abhijay and had similar facial features. How had I not noticed the similarities before? Were they related?

"Of course, *Maharishi*." She bowed and retreated down the hall.

I walked with A.J, my arm in his. "Can we still be friends?"

"If you wish it." The Moroi squeezed my arm gently.

"I do, A.J," I confirmed, smiling at him. "And you should know, I hate being so formal with my friends."

"Then, it will be relaxed between us when possible, *Goddess*."

"Sapphira – or Saph." I corrected him, smiling again as he bowed his head in acknowledgment. "After this, will you tell me more about your people?"

"Of course, it would be an honor, Sapphira."

Fallon stood on the left of where I sat, eyes closed in concentration.

I took in my surroundings as I waited for her to scope out our guest's intentions. The hall was about the size of a basketball court, with massive white stone pillars and marble steps leading up to the dais where I sat. There were no windows along the walls, but over half of the roof was stained glass, letting a rainbow of color dance around the room.

I glanced at Abhijay, who stood beside the chair on my right.

He smiled down at me reassuringly, his hands clasped behind his back.

"This place is beautiful." I told him a little breathless.

"Thank you, Goddess. My daughter designed it."

"Alayla?" I guessed, glancing at the woman who was standing not too far away.

Abhijay smiled lovingly at her. "Yes, that's her."

Alayla glanced up at us, smiling briefly before turning her attention back to the entrance to the Hall.

"She is the light of my life," Abhijay told me conspiratorially. "But my little War Goddess does not like me bragging too loudly."

I smiled at him. "War Goddess?"

Abhijay nodded. "That is what her name means. Even from an early age, Alayla has shown great skills in battle strategy. She has her mother's temper too."

"I sense nothing that suggests that they mean any harm." Fallon said suddenly, turning to face me just as I was about to ask Abhijay about Alayla's mother.

Her blue-green eyes were still glowing, an effect using her magic gave off. "I feel that they are a little anxious to see what your view on the Lycanthrope population is, but more than anything, they're just curious about what you are."

I nodded, butterflies making tornados in my stomach. "Okay."

Abhijay motioned for the guard closest to the door to open it, and seconds later, the two Lycanthropes entered.

"Welcome, Akil, and Amin." Abhijay greeted them when they had reached the base of the dais, bowing politely to him. "May I introduce Princess Fallon of the Djinn?"

"Greetings, Princess." They bowed to her in unison.

Fallon nodded politely.

"And this is Sapphira, the *Goddess Incarnate*." Abhijay continued.

Both Akil and Amin startled, glancing at each other quickly before bowing low to the ground. "Greetings, *Goddess*."

I smiled, clasping my hands together on my lap in an attempt to stop them from shaking. *Please don't mess this up!* I begged myself.

Before I could speak, Abhijay stepped forward, gesturing to a guard who disappeared in a blur of movement. Moments later, the guard – carrying two chairs – reappeared, offering the seats to our guests. They sat, seemingly grateful for the chance.

"I understand that you have requested an audience?" I asked my voice surprisingly steady despite my nervousness.

Again, the two men glanced at each other before speaking. "We came to offer our greetings to the newest power holder within this territory. That was, however, before we knew that it was the beautiful Djinn Princess and the *Goddess* herself."

The man that spoke was tall and thin, with light brown hair and what looked like grey eyes set in a pale face. He was – if I had to hazard a guess – around forty years old. This must have been Akil, the Alpha of the Wolves.

"And now that you know who we are?"

It was Amin that answered, running a hand through his short blonde hair. His green eyes flickered from me to Fallon and back again. "Had we known that we would be in the presence of royalty, we would have come bearing the customary gifts."

I fought the urge to glance at Fallon. Were they supposed to bring gifts? What was I supposed to say to that?

"I'm sure we can forgo that tradition this once." I told them with a smile, hoping that it was the correct thing to say.

"We thank your understanding, Goddess." Amin said, bowing again.

I nodded.

"How did you both fair with the Strigoi attack?" A.J asked.

I was shocked, had the Strigoi really attacked the Lycanthropes as well as us? Why? And how did A.J know this?

"Luckily, not too many of our peoples suffered at their hands this time. We were able to get most of our women and children away before the attack got too intense." Amin replied grimly. "And your people Abhijay? How did they fair? Akil tells me that his people sensed the presence of a Vârcolac?"

A.J nodded. "Yes, the Strigoi attacked here with a strong force – stronger than many of the previous attacks. We lost many good warriors but prevailed in the end. There was a Vârcolac among their ranks, but unfortunately, it was killed during the struggle."

A surge of anger erupted into the air, my power picking it up from where I sat. It was coming from the Alpha Wolf, Akil. His face showed no sign of emotion, however, and no one else in the room seemed to notice anything. Outwardly, he looked as calm as Amin did.

"I am... sorry to hear that." Amin said slowly.

A.J nodded his thanks to the Taipan King.

"It has been a long time since we have been blessed with your presence in these parts, Princess." Amin continued, turning to Fallon. "I hope that nothing too serious has kept you away?"

Fallon smiled, the warmth not quite reaching her eyes. "Indeed, it has been too long, Highness. But I don't believe that we have ever officially met before today?"

Amin nodded. "That is true, the last time you visited my domain, I was not the one ruling it. We have never officially met, but I remember your aura. I have been told many stories about the grace and compassion you held towards our kind."

Akil, still silent, remained bursting with anger. What was his problem anyway? He caught me looking at him, and his eyes were cold as he forced a smile that looked more like a sneer.

"Do you know how rare a Vârcolac from a pure bloodline is, *Goddess*?" his harsh words cut through my skin like knives, his tone almost contemptuous. "Like the one that was killed senselessly here?"

Amin tensed from his chair beside the Alpha Wolf, a small sigh escaping his lips, his eyes closed. The guards in the room inched closer to us, hands on their weapons, and I froze in my chair.

Is *this* what he was so mad about? Did he blame *me* for the death of the monster that had tried to kill me - the same beast that had ruined Denni's face when he had tried to protect me?

My own anger rose from its place inside of me, like searing water bubbling over the side of a pot. I let it grow, enjoying the feeling. "I am not aware of the exact number of Vârcolac bloodlines – pure or not, no. I didn't think to stop and ask it while it was trying to kill me and - everyone around me." I raised an eyebrow in questioning, "Is there something in particular that you wish to accuse me of? Or is it that you simply take offense to my apparent lack of knowledge on Wolf pedigree?"

It seemed as if everyone in the room suddenly held their breath. It was so still that you could have heard a pin drop. Akil snarled, getting to his feet. The guards were inches away from him in seconds, weapons out.

"Perhaps you should think about what you say or do next, Akil. The *Goddess* might take offense." A male guard advised in a light voice. It was Raine, the handsome Sidhe sent to babysit me by his Queen, Kamilla. *Where had he sprung from?* I had asked him to wait outside, assured that A.J, Fallon, and the other Moroi and Dhampir's were enough to guard me. A.J had thought it a good idea – why did the Lycanthropes need to know that there were Sidhe here anyway? And whenever he was around, I got distracted – of course, I kept this to myself.

But it looked as though Raine had other ideas.

He stood in front of Akil, blocking his view of where I sat, hands clasped together behind his back. Amin held his hands out in front of him, a gesture of peace, as he too got to his feet.

"Please forgive the Alpha, Goddess. He is very... passionate... about his people's genealogy. I assure you that he does not blame you for the death of the Vârcolac that made an attempt on your life, nor does he wish you any bad will. He only needs a minute to calm down – if you would allow it – before we continue?"

I nodded, burying my own anger.

"Perhaps I will accompany you both for some fresh air." A.J agreed, lightly stepping down the three steps of the dais and coming to a halt beside Raine.

He placed a hand on his shoulder, making him take a step back. "Thank you, Raine. I believe the Goddess is safe. You can return to your post."

Raine looked to the Moroi with barely concealed aversion. "Of course, *Maharishi*, as you wish."

A.J gestured for the two Lycanthropes to follow him and led them out of the hall.

Raine turned to me, eyes sparkling with suppressed anger, and bowed.

How could I not notice how his presence made my heart beat faster, how I felt the urge to be closer to him?

I fought to remain where I was, to calm my heart rate, and keep a neutral expression on my face.

"I would prefer to stay close to you, Goddess. But I can see that you do not have the same wish. I will wait for you outside. If you happen to need me before we meet, just call my name, and I will be by your side in an instant."

Oh, if only he knew!

He vanished into thin air before I could take a breath to reply.

The moment he was gone, though, the strange feelings I felt towards him disintegrated. Were they just a reaction to the Sidhe magic – like Ari had warned me? How could I find out for sure – without looking foolish?

Fallon, who had been quiet for a while, sighed, turning to face me. "Well, this could be going better."

"That's the understatement of the century," I said dryly, standing and stretching my legs. "I have no idea what I'm doing here, Fallon. Any advice you can give me at this point could only make things better."

Fallon shook her head. "You have to forge a relationship with these two on your own. I would only suggest that you be cautious and not burn the bridge between you too far. You could need their help at some point in the near future."

It was my turn to sigh. I had messed this up – big time. How had I let that happen so quickly – and without even realizing it? And why had everyone seemed so assured that I would do this right?

I was only a nineteen-year-old girl! I had been thrust into a world that didn't make sense, that shouldn't even have existed, and had been expected to immediately know the correct politics?

"What could happen that I would need their help?" I asked the Djinn Princess with a frown. "I mean, if I can fix what I've just done, that is?"

"War for one," Fallon replied, taking the seat that I had just vacated. "It never hurts to have powerful allies."

"War with who?"

Fallon shrugged a graceful gesture on her. If I had done that, I would have looked like an uncoordinated idiot. "You have a year before you come into your full powers. The Strigoi have already made an attempt on you, the Soul Eaters have tried as well – and at the most heavily defended Moroi Safe Houses in the country no less. There are many other groups out there that would rather see you dead than leave your choice to chance."

"You mean the choice of 'am I good or evil'?"

Fallon nodded. "The *Goddess Incarnate* has been killed for a lot less in the past, Sapphira."

"So, you're saying that I need to apologize?"

"The *Goddess* doesn't need to apologize for anything." Fallon reminded me, getting to her feet. "You merely need to decide if you want the Lycanthrope community to be allies or enemies."

"I think that Akil would rather be enemies..." I muttered, retaking my seat.

"Then, change his mind."

"How?"

"Up to you." Fallon smiled as I groaned. "But if it were me, I would find something that I had – or could get – that would make an alliance between us worth his while."

A.J, Amin, and Akil returned at this moment, denying me the opportunity to ask Fallon what that could be.

A.J returned to his spot beside me, and the Lycanthropes stood in front of the chairs they had previously occupied.

"I apologize for my outburst, Goddess. I am aware that my behavior warrants permanent exile from your sight if you were to wish it." Akil bowed before me, practically lying on the floor to beg my forgiveness.

I glanced at A.J for a hint on the correct response, but he too was watching the Alpha Wolf prostrate himself with something like surprise on his face. "I... do not wish for your exile, Akil. I accept your apology."

"Perhaps we could start over?" He asked, smiling at me as he straightened.

I nodded once. "I don't see why not."

"Thank you, Goddess. Your indulgence is heartening."

Amin, visibly relaxing, stepped forward. "Goddess, may I ask a question of you?"

Again, I nodded. Inside, my heart was racing.

What could he want to ask? Would I know the correct answer? Would my answer get us all in trouble?

His eyes were wary, and I could see the muscles in his neck tensing. *He* was nervous? "Where do you stand on the Lycanthrope issue?"

"In what respect are you asking?" I replied, frowning slightly. Was he asking me if I hated them like so many other beings in their world did? Did he wonder if I would kill the women and children of his Pack? Did he genuinely believe that I would be capable of something like that?

"I guess I am asking if you believe us to be the vermin of the preternatural community."

"And why would I think that?" I answered calmly, "I barely know you. How am I supposed to have formed an opinion of your kind in the last few minutes?"

"I guess that is true, Goddess. Thank you for your honesty. If there is anything that my people can do to help you formulate your opinion of us, we are at your service until you say otherwise." Amin bowed, smiling politely.

"And what of my people, Goddess?" Akil asked, face carefully blank. "Will you judge my people based on what you have seen of me?"

I shook my head. "No group of people should be judged based on one. I do not know your people or your culture. I harbor no unpleasant thoughts against them."

Akil frowned, eyes darkening. "I was hoping that you would think differently." He growled.

In a blur of movement, he was on the dais, inches from my face.

"Akil – No!" Amin cried, his voice sounding miles away.

Time seemed to be going by in slow motion.

I could see A.J and Fallon reaching out to me, but I knew that Akil would have attacked before they could reach me, he was that fast. I saw the look of pure hatred in his black eyes before his face vanished from my eyesight, and a sharp pain ripped through my stomach.

I heard low guttural growling and flesh-tearing, as the pain intensified. I tried to move, but Akil was pinning me into the chair.

A flash of golden light hit him, causing him to howl in pain and turn away from me. Blood dripped from his lips, and he bared bloodied teeth to his attacker.

It was Fallon, blue-green eyes glowing, a golden aura surrounding her body. She stood tall, her auburn hair blowing in a non-existent breeze. She looked beautiful – and scary.

"You think you can stop me, Djinn?" Akil snarled "You are nothing!"

He leaped towards her, but Fallon held her hands out in front of her, a golden force field appearing between Akil and herself.

The Alpha Wolf hit it, reverberating off like it was a solid wall. Akil landed in a crouch, using his momentum to spin himself around and leap towards her again.

A.J intercepted, grabbing the frenzied man around the waist, and slamming him to the ground. The marble beneath him fractured, the sound echoing off the stone walls. Three other guards were there in a nanosecond, pinning him so that he couldn't move.

Akil struggled against them, but it was futile.

I sunk lower into the chair, my body beginning to go numb. I noticed that Amin was surrounded by pissed off looking guards, all holding guns pointed at him, but he had his arms up in surrender and a horrified look on his face as he watched the events unfolding around him.

And then another face was in front of me, his golden eyes angry as he took in the sight of me.

"Why didn't you call?" He growled, removing his shirt and bunching it in his fist. "I could have protected you!"

The Sidhe pressed his shirt to my stomach, and I groaned as my vision swam. His hands came away covered in my blood as he worked to remove his belt. *Why was he doing that?* I wondered groggily. *And why was he so mad? It wasn't my fault that a crazy wolf-man attacked me!*

My blood ended up smeared across his abdomen, and the top of his pants, as Raine quickly tied the belt around my stomach. Ensuring that his shirt continued to apply pressure to the wound there.

"Queen Kamilla is going to kill *me* if you can't stay alive!" He hissed, wrapping his arms around me and gently lifting me up.

I cried out in pain as the movement tore at the edges of the wound. I wanted to tell him to put me down, to stop whining and leave me alone. I tried to tell him that I hadn't asked for his help because I didn't want it – I didn't want any of this stupid life. But my lips wouldn't obey my commands to speak, there was barely enough air to breathe, let alone voice my thoughts.

I did notice, however, that his charms were not affecting me. Was it because I was injured? Or did he just not worry about turning them on?

Fallon's magical, golden light flickered across my vision. I couldn't see exactly what she was doing, but from Akil's deafening pain-filled shrieks, I guessed that I didn't want to know.

"I am so sorry, Goddess." Amin's voice came as a whisper in my ear as Raine carried me away from it all. "I did not mean for any of this to happen."

I managed a nod, my world spinning before I closed my eyes to finally give in to the darkness.

"Stay awake, Goddess. For both our sakes, just stay..."

Everything went black before I could tell Raine to shut up.

Chapter Seven

"... Is she okay?"

"...dead?"

"Stay with us..."

"...healers – now!"

"... not strong enough..."

"...is she contaminated?"

"...war with the wolves..."

"...requested a meeting... not her father..."

"...dead since the Strigoi attack....skin removed...."

"...Skin Walker?"

"...working with the Strigoi..."

"...believe her?"

Voices swam in and out of my mind, broken pieces of conversations in the far off distance. Nothing I managed to hear made any sense in my heavy head. I felt as though I was drugged, unable to feel much of anything; I couldn't open my eyes or speak at all. I tried to remember what had happened, but my mind, in all of its drug-induced genius, blocked it out.

I drifted in this state for a while until a strange pressure began building in the middle of my body, erupting into agonizing pain.

An inhuman scream pierced my ears, an unnerving sound amidst the silence before I realized that it was me. I was the one screaming.

My eyes snapped open as hands pushed my thrashing body back onto the bed. The world was spinning and faces blurred across my vision, making it impossible to recognize anything.

"Be still, Sapphira!" An unknown voice ordered sternly, "You are tearing your stitches out!"

A needle was shoved into my arm, a slight sting. I felt myself sinking down into the emptiness of unconsciousness again, my body too tired to fight it.

"She has been infected with the wolf strain of Lycanthropy, but it has been... mutated somehow."

"What does this mean? Will she turn?"

"I'm not completely sure."

"... My fault...Tired, wasn't quick enough..."

"...can't blame yourself..."

"Welcome back." A deep voice murmured from somewhere nearby. The voice was familiar, but I couldn't place it.

I was lying on my back, eyes closed, and my body tight and aching. How had they known that I was awake?

"You stopped snoring and groaning awhile ago." The voice answered as if reading my thoughts.

I slowly opened my eyes, fully expecting them to explode from the brightness. The artificial lights dimmed immediately as if they sensed my irritation. I sent out a silent thank you to whoever controlled them, sighing in relief when my corneas didn't burn to a crisp like they felt they were going to.

I glanced around the room, frowning when I didn't recognize it.

"Where am I?" I asked, turning my attention to the man sitting in a chair beside me, feet up on the edge of my bed. As usual, he was wearing an immaculate and expensive-looking suit with a cerulean shirt – similar to the one he was wearing when I first met him.

He ran a tanned hand through his short dark hair, flashing me a captivating smile that made his eyes sparkle and lit up his flawless face.

I frowned again. "What are you doing here?"

"Well... I've been sitting here, without so much as a book to read, for hours. And *that's* the thanks I get?"He feigned insult. "Where's the '*I'm so grateful to you, Prince Aryk*'?"

"That's not what I meant..." I grumbled, glancing down at myself for the first time.

My arms were covered with tubes that seemed to be pumping me full of various liquids. I tried moving my feet to find that they were restrained. "What is all this?"

Aryk shot me a look, something dark crossing his eyes before he flashed me another one of his dazzling smiles. "That, my dear, is what has kept you alive these past few weeks."

"Weeks?" I repeated disbelievingly.

"Yes. You've been out for exactly three weeks, four days, eight hours and..." He paused, glancing down at his watch dramatically. "Thirty-seven minutes."

"Shit."

Aryk chuckled.

"Was it really that bad?"

He nodded. "If you hadn't received help from the best healers in the Lycan..." He paused, frowning. "Well, let's just say that you would have been toast."

"Lycan... You mean Lycanthrope?" I asked incredulously, heart pounding. "Why would I need a Lycanthrope doctor?"

"You were bitten." Aryk replied as if that answered everything.

"So?"

He sighed, taking his feet off the bed and leaning closer. "You really know nothing, don't you?"

I was getting angry. Was he really *insulting* me right now? "Are you going to enlighten me, or be a pain in the as-"

"Okay, okay." He cut me off with a smirk, holding his hands up in mock surrender.

"When someone is bitten or scratched by a Lycanthrope, they become... infected with the 'disease.' More often than not, they... become one."

I think my heart stopped beating just then. Was he telling me that because Akil attacked me, that when he bit into my flesh, he infected me and now I was going to become a *Wolf*? I shook my head. "No, that can't be true. You're just messing with my head. Where's Fallon?"

Aryk looked at me with something like pity in his eyes. "I swear to you that I am telling the truth. I can see how it might be confusing for you, but I am not lying."

"Explain it to me then – tell me everything that happened from the time I was bitten," I demanded. It felt as though the world had stopped spinning. After all the shit that sprung itself on me already, now I had to deal with *this* too?

"Akil attacked you. Fallon caught him in a force field of her energy. The Sidhe appeared and took you to a safer place. Abhijay and Fallon questioned Amin – he seemed to know nothing about why Akil had suddenly gone crazy. Akil was sentenced to death, the Moroi finished him off. We all thought that you were dead, your wounds were remarkable – in a morbid sense," He added, seeing my expression. "Fallon put you in a magically induced coma to stop you from deteriorating too quickly. Akil's daughter, Freyja, requested an audience with Abhijay – quite brave of her, I have to admit, considering what had just happened. Turns out, Akil – the one that attacked you – was not the real Alpha Wolf. He was killed in the Strigoi attack by a Skinwalker who, disgusting as it may sound, took his skin and turned into him. He posed as Akil to get close enough to kill you. Are you with me still?"

My mouth was open in shock and disbelief. How could Aryk sit there and tell me this twisted movie plot with barely a hint of emotion? I had a million questions running through my head, and I wanted to ask them all. What the hell was a Skin Walker? How could no one have noticed the difference before it was too late? *How* had the Skin Walker been killed?

"What else did Freyja say?" Was the question I asked instead.

"She just told us about her father. And then when we told her what the Skin Walker had done, she was mortified. She swore that the Wolves didn't have any part in the imposter's plans. She begged for mercy towards the wolves and offered you a place in the 'hospital' that the Lycanthropes run for their community. You have been here ever since."

"So... am I one of them now – a wolf?"

Aryk shrugged. "I'm just your babysitter. All of the 'sensitive information' regarding you is told directly to my wife. You may want to ask her."

"Then where is she?"

Again, he shrugged. "Could be anywhere."

"Could you *be* any more ambiguous?" I retorted, glaring at him.

"Perhaps."

I rolled my eyes, trying to sit up. If he wouldn't tell me where Fallon was, I'd just have to go looking by myself.

"I wouldn't do that if I were you." He warned seconds before an alarm went off. "Oh, look. You've done it now...You're supposed to be lying still, and not pulling all those out." He added as I started ripping out all of the tubes.

"I don't care." I told him, finishing one arm and moving on to the next.

"The healers won't take too kindly to you doing that." Aryk warned again, just as the door burst open, and three bodybuilders rushed in. Well, that's what the men looked like, solid walls of muscles. "Stop what you're doing." One of them ordered angrily. "And lie back down."

"Umm... No?" I told him firmly, finally freeing myself from the last tube. The restraints on my legs would be harder. They were cold metal, and I couldn't see how I was going to get them undone without a key. Or gnawing off my legs, which, I reminded myself, wouldn't exactly be the best option as I may need them later. "I think I've had enough of lying down, thanks anyway."

Everyone in the room looked shocked for a second before Aryk laughed, and two of the bodybuilders dived to pin me to the bed.

"What the hell!" I protested furiously. "Get off of me!"

"Relax, Saph." Fallon's calm voice projected across the room. "The Doctors are just trying to help."

She had just entered the room, her sympathetic eyes on me. She looked as perfect as ever in a little black cocktail dress that showed off her long legs and killer heels. Her long auburn hair was done in a braid that almost reached the middle of her back.

"Doctors?" I hissed, throwing poisonous glares at the men in question. Two still had hold of me, trapping me to the bed despite my efforts to wiggle free, while the other one tried to reattach the tubes to my arms.

"Yes," Fallon said, moving to stand beside her husband. "They are just trying to keep you safe."

"Safe from what?" I demanded, turning my glare on my friend.

"From other newly changed Wolves, and from yourself. Just relax, let the doctor's put the tubes back in, and I'll explain everything, okay?"

"*Other?*" I asked, picking up on what Fallon seemed to be hinting at. "So I *am* one of them now? And why would I need protecting from myself?"

My anger, mixed with fear, wrapped itself around me like a cloak. My skin seemed to shimmer in the dim light. The two 'doctors' that had been holding me down flinched away from where they touched me, eyes wide.

"Please, Saph. Calm down."

"*Stop telling me what to do!*" I screamed, a wall of shimmering jade power standing to attention around me.

One of the doctors tried to breach it with a hand, trying to continue placing the tubes back into me. The minute he touched my power, his arm began to smoke and burn. He shrieked in pain, pulling the blackened appendage away and falling to the floor to nurse it against his vast chest.

Aryk slowly stood, eyes focused on me, mouth set in a grim line. "What have you *done*, Sapphira? He was only trying to *help* you."

Fallon, who had moved to the still shrieking doctor's side, called up her power to try and heal him. "Stay still," She told him gently as he tried to pull away. "I think I can fix this."

"I told you to stop touching me." I growled, causing the energy to flare and sizzle around me.

"Again, I say; *he was only trying to help you!*" Aryk hissed, eyes flashing. "Is that how you repay people who try and aid you?"

Everyone in the room, Fallon included, looked at me with reproach. My anger subsided, guilt taking its place, and the wall of power shrinking in on its self until it had vanished.

"I... I'm sorry. I don't know what came over me." I said lamely.

What *had* I been doing? I knew deep down that they were only trying to help, but I just didn't like feeling helpless – and something inside of me hadn't liked being tied down.

Aryk threw his hands up in anger, storming out of the room, mumbling under his breath.

"Help me carry him to the showers," Fallon said to the closest doctor. "We need to get his arm under cold water."

"It could be the beast." The third doctor said softly, eyes scrutinizing me. "She's gaining *its* emotions on top of her own."

Fallon froze, halfway through lifting the wounded man off the floor. Doctor number two had to take his colleague's weight, or he would have fallen to the floor again. The uninjured doctor slowly led his co-worker out of the room, heading to the showers to gain relief from the injuries that I had caused.

"Already?" Fallon asked, eyes wide. "But it's only been-"

"It's strong, probably an Alpha. They mature faster than subs do." He explained. "But I can't know for sure yet...I'm waiting on more results to come back."

My heart was pounding hard in my chest, my breaths coming out erratically. "So it's true then. I am a wolf."

"Not exactly, no." The doctor said slowly. "The strain of Lycanthropy that you caught is mutated. I think it's because the man who gave it to you was not a real Wolf. He was only wearing the Alpha's skin. We don't know how much of him was passed onto you."

"What does that even mean?" I asked miserably.

"Well, this has never happened before, so we have nothing to compare it to, but we think that you have gained some of the Lycanthrope abilities, but not all of them." The doctor said, slowly approaching me, his hands out where I could see them.

"I'm just going to untie your legs." He added, seeing me tense.

I nodded, resisting the urge to growl at him. "So you think that I have gained a... 'beast'?"

It was his turn to nod. "In a sense, yes. I believe – and the tests that I have done are confirming this so far – that you have gained the parts of us that are animal. You have already shown signs of fear and anger at being contained against your will. The tests have shown that you have gained strength from it as well."

He pulled a key from his coat as he talked, leaning in closer to my legs to unlock the metal restraints.

When he was done, I pulled my feet up, rubbing my ankles with my hands. "You will probably cultivate better stamina, eyesight, hearing, and taste." He paused, looking at my face nervously before continuing. "And with the increased sense of taste, you will probably experience strange... cravings. This is all perfectly natural to the new Lycanthrope."

"What strange cravings?" I asked, frowning.

Please don't say raw meat and blood! I begged silently. *This is not a horror movie; I will not eat still wriggling food!* My stomach convulsed at the thought.

"And a different way of thinking in times of danger too..." He continued as if I hadn't spoken. "It will be almost like another voice in your head, telling you what it thinks you need to do. That's your beast's instincts kicking in."

"What cravings?" I repeated slowly.

The doctor paused, looking at me with a serious expression. "Fewer greens and more meat – cooked less than you're used to?"

"Ugh, I think I'm gonna hurl..." I moaned.

"Will she shift?" Fallon asked, frowning.

The doctor shrugged. "I'm not sure. As I said, we have nothing to compare this to."

"As far as I know, there hasn't been an incarnate of the *Goddess* that could catch Lycanthropy before..." She murmured, more to herself than to either of us. "What could this mean?"

"That I'm not the Goddess after all?" I offered up, earning myself a glare from the Princess.

"She could have you there, Fallon." Ari's voice whispered through the air as she appeared, sitting on the edge of my bed.

"Where have you been?" Fallon all but snapped at the Nephilim. "I have been trying to call you for days!"

Ari shrugged, flipping her shoulder-length black curls in disinterest. "I've been busy."

"Doing what? We've had an emergency here, and you've been nowhere to be found!"

Ari flashed Fallon a dark look. "It's none of your business, *Djinn*. And besides, when did I become your lap dog?" She winked at me. "No pun intended, Saph."

I could feel the waves of anger washing off Fallon as she glared at Ari. "May I remind you that you are a part of this guardianship and that you have a duty to protect Sapphira just as much as I do?"

"And what a fine job you've done so far, Princess." Ari smirked, waving her hand out towards me. Her tone was condescending as she continued, "You've managed to turn the poor girl into a talking fleabag."

"Shut up, Ari." I muttered, rubbing the back of my neck and trying to ease the tension there. "I've had enough. Will you both just vanish and leave me alone?" Both women looked at me as if I had just sprouted a second head.

"What?" I snapped, throwing my hands up angrily and glaring at them, "Am I not entitled to some alone time after everything?"

"We will go, but you may not be alone just yet, Saph," Fallon said calmly, ignoring the dirty look I threw her way. "Raine will stand guard – just in case."

"Just in case what? Just in case the *Goddess turns* – or there is another attempt on her life?" Ari asked, her eyebrows arched and a small smirk on her lips. "I said shut up, Ari." I groaned.

I'd had enough of the conversation, of having to think about what they all thought I was. Of worrying that I was now so far from human that even *I* couldn't pretend anymore.

"Jesus – it's like I'm talking to myself here..."

"Raine, your presence is requested." Fallon called softly, continuing to ignore me and my outbursts.

The Sidhe appeared in the doorway, annoyingly sexy as ever, even in the crumpled suit he wore.

"You called?" He sneered in his arrogant way, mockingly bowing towards Fallon.

"Sapphira is awake and in need of a guard." Fallon told him, sending a disapproving look his way.

Raine turned his eyes to where I sat, huddled on the bed.

Something unidentifiable flashed across his face before he shook himself and stepped closer, his expression a blank mask.

"It will be done."

"Come, Princess. We need to talk." Ari said snidely, heading for the hall without looking back.

Fallon managed a smile in my direction. "I'll be back soon."

I shrugged, working hard to curb my annoyance. "Take your time."

She closed the door softly behind her, and I was left alone with the Sidhe.

"So..." Raine spoke into the silence. "How do you feel?"

"Seriously?" I glared at him, annoyance running through me in waves. "You really want to have this conversation with me right now?"

Raine chuckled. "No, not really. But there is a conversation we *do* need to have – while there is at least a facade of privacy."

He gestured to a surveillance camera nestled into the corner above the door. How had I not seen that before? Was it normal for hospitals to have cameras in patient's rooms?

He sat in the chair beside the bed, his back to the camera. "I know what you are, little *bailitheoir draíochta,* and it isn't what everyone else seems to think you are."

"What?" I asked, shocked. "What do you mean? How do you know I'm not a Lycanthrope – the doctor said..."

"They were wrong." Raine interrupted smoothly. "You are in a *Lycanthrope hospital*, were bitten by something wearing an Alpha skin. Of course they're going to see signs of their own kind in you, but they're misguided – pulling at straws really. They have not come across anything like you in a very long time, almost beyond memory actually." He paused, seemingly lost in thought. Silence surrounded the room, a heavy blanket against my growing impatience. Raine shook himself, visibly relaxing before continuing, "There are other things in our world with heightened speed, stamina, and agility. And who in their right mind *likes* being tied down – outside of the bedroom, of course?"

"Were you eavesdropping before?" I accused, ignoring his kinky comment with difficulty. "You seem to know everything that the Doctor said to me."

He shrugged. "It's what I'm good at."

"So what do you think that I am?" I humored the Sidhe.

What other seemingly make-believe life form could I be accused of being?

"Oh no, I'm not giving that gem up for nothing."He shook his head, eyes sparkling.

"What do you want?"

Raine chuckled again. "Nothing yet, we need to speak with my Queen first. She needs to be updated about... recent events."

"What does she have to do with it, and..." I asked, suspiciously, heart dropping at the thought of seeing Kamilla again. "What do you mean 'we'?"

"Surely, you would want to ask the Queen yourself?" Raine asked, his eyes sparkling as a small smirk drew up the right side of his perfect face.

Last time, she told me that I owed her for saving my life. Then she sent Raine to watch over me, to ensure I stayed alive until I could repay the debt. And I had the sudden feeling that he acted as a spy for her, informing the Sidhe Queen of what the Djinn Princess, the Moroi at the safe house, and the supposed *Goddess Incarnate* were up to.

"No way," I said forcefully, shaking my head. "I'm not having anything to do with her. She isn't *my* Queen."

"My, my... Is that how you speak about the woman that saved your life?" Queen Kamilla's voice echoed through my head, making me jump.

"Greetings, My Queen." Raine said softly.

"Wait, you can hear her?" I asked, "I thought she was in my head?"

Raine chuckled again from his seat. "She is. But yes, I can hear her."

"*Because I wish it so.*" Kamilla's voice whispered her voice like little bells. "*What is it you need to discuss, Raine?*"

"She was bitten, Your Grace. By a Skin Walker in the guise of a Lycanthropic wolf."

"*And?*"

"I don't believe that she is the one they think she is."

"*Why?*"

"The strain I was infected with mutated into something new." I joined in, wanting to speed the meeting along—the less time I had to have Kamilla's voice in my head, the better. And hopefully, we could get this meeting over with *before* Fallon returned.

"But I'm not going to be one of them..." I added with determination. If there was another way, I was going to find it – I *had* to find it!

"*Who are you trying to convince, Sapphira?*" The Queen asked. "*Why would it be a bad thing for you to be a Lycanthrope?*"

"Are you kidding me? I mean, don't get me wrong I have nothing against them, but this isn't the life that I want for myself."

"*And what if I told you that you could not have a choice in the matter?*"

"You can't take away my right to choose."

"*But the choice you speak of is taken away from thousands in the world every day. What makes you any better than them?*"

"Where are you going with this?" I snapped, tired of the voice in my head. "Just tell me what you want me to say and get the hell out of my head. I'm tired."

Raine was staring at me, a disapproving frown covering his face. "Be mindful that you speak to the Queen, Sapphira. Show your respect."

"Again, I say; she is not *my* Queen."

"But a Queen nonetheless." Raine reminded me harshly. "And you need to treat her as such."

"I am *done* being told what to do, how to *speak*, and where to *stay!*" I snapped, getting to my feet and ignoring the dizziness that settled over me. "If you have a problem with that, *get the fuck away from me!*"

"*Now, now, Sapphira.*" Kamilla reproached gently in my head. "*My Raine was merely suggesting a few... manners would be nice. There is no need for angry remarks.*"

"Oh, bite me." I hissed, folding my arms over my chest angrily.

"*We shall ignore her until she finds her manners, Raine. Continue with your report.*"

"As you wish, My Queen..." Raine said, closing his golden eyes.

Kamilla's voice no longer whispered through my head, her presence all but vanished from my senses, but I could tell that she was still talking to Raine. I could see his lips moving, his eyes fluttering beneath closed lids as if he was watching his Queen pace in front of him.

I sighed, feeling foolish standing beside my bed in a hospital gown. Where was going to storm off to in my tantrum? Why were my emotions so hard to keep a handle of? And when was I going to wake up from this crappy nightmare and go back to my normal life? The one where nothing supernatural existed, and I was just an ordinary nineteen-year-old girl? I was beyond tired of going along with everything that I was told. Who would really believe that there were goddesses, angels, faeries, and vampires – let alone were-animals – in the world? Who in their right mind would believe that emotions could be shaped into visible weapons? *I have imagined things this whole time – since my family was killed all those years ago.* I thought to myself, rubbing at the goosebumps on my arms. *I am certifiably insane...and the level of insanity just keeps on rising!*

I glanced over at Raine, surprised to find him staring at me intently, golden eyes pinched at the corners.

"You are not insane, Sapphira" he told me decisively, frowning as if I were a puzzle that he couldn't comprehend. "Why do so many of your thoughts lead you to that conclusion?"

How had he known what I was thinking – how long had he been listening in on my thoughts? I opened my mouth to protest, taken over by the sudden compulsion to make *someone* understand that this couldn't really be happening. That this world couldn't possibly exist, but Raine's sigh stopped me.

"There are millions of humans that dream of having the gifts that you have – millions more in our world that would kill to take them from you. And yet you still fight the truth even after everything that you have experienced already."

"You don't understand!" I cried, frustrated. I sank back onto the bed.

"Then make us understand." The Queen's voice whispered, floating through the air between Raine and me.

I could see a faint trickle of her crimson power surrounding us, acting as a magical bridge between the Sidhe and myself. I wondered if Fallon were to walk into the room at that moment what she would have seen. What would her reaction have been if she knew that I was conversing with the Sidhe Queen in private again?

"I don't have time for this..." I muttered. "Can you just tell me what you think is happening to me?"

"I could, but not for free."

"What do you want?" I sighed.

Why did every answer have to come at a price?

"Another favor..."

"Another debt you mean."

"If you prefer..."

"Are you ever going to tell me what I have to do to repay them?"

"*All in good time, my Ceann álainn. These things cannot be rushed.*"

Raine placed a warm hand over mine, his golden gaze on my face. I tried to remember what Colte and Fallon had told me about making deals with the Faerie. But, for some reason, the conversation eluded me. I gave a mental shrug, any doubts I had slowly slipping away. "Fine, tell me what I am." I demanded.

"*You will pay the price for this knowledge?*"

"I will."

"*First, there is a test you must complete. This will leave no doubt as to the validity of what I tell you. Raine will help you, but Sapphira you must not tell anyone what you are doing – no one must know of our deal, do you agree to my terms?*"

"I already have." I snapped my impatience and frustration swirling around my body like a cloak. "Just tell me what you want me to do."

Chapter Eight

I hated my life. Or whatever the hell this last year had been. Nightmare. Yeah, it was definitely a nightmare.

It had been three months since I made the worst deal of my pitiful life, and I had regretted it every second after the words left my mouth. The 'test' set before me was impossible to complete. Not without losing what remained of myself.

I hadn't turned furry, didn't feel as though anything inside me had changed. Raine reassured me that it meant I wasn't a Lycanthrope after all. He said it was further proof that his

Queen was right – that all of this was worth it. I was honestly just glad that I didn't have to add shapeshifting to my list of impossible things I could do. Although, after all of the drama at the hospital, it kind of felt like a cosmic cop-out. All that stress and panic for nothing.

I could feel the tension and fear building within me, the closer it came to fulfilling the test, and I was struggling to keep it contained and hidden. Raine had been a constant presence at my side, helping me to prepare. Without his reassurance and guidance, I would have given up already.

He kept the others at a distance without much explanation, to the chagrin of Ari, Fallon, and Colte.

I helped build the wall between us, choosing not to listen to their attempts to close the distance. It killed me, watching my friends struggle between giving me the space I asked for and keeping me close.

Even though I felt myself drifting away from them, knowing that it was for the best, I had pestered Raine for a break from our secret training. For a last chance to spend time with my friends before I ruined everything, and probably died in the process.

"You have to play it safe right now, we cannot afford to have any of them breathing down your neck again." He had told me. "I know you feel guilty and alone right now, but it is better this way. I'm here for you. I understand what you are going through. You can talk to me."

"It's more than that, though, Raine." I had argued. "These people – *my friends* – have always been with me. I feel like a part of myself is missing being apart from them like this. Even after everything that has happened."

Lunch in the mess hall was all he would agree to.

Now, he sat to my left, close enough that his knee bumped mine. He reached for another bunch of grapes from the platter in front of us.

"Does your boyfriend ever blink?" Ari asked, popping a berry in her mouth and glaring at Raine from her spot across the table. "Or bathe?"

"Stop it," I told her for what felt like the millionth time today. "Raine isn't my boyfriend."

She'd taken it upon herself to taunt and belittle him every chance she got since we had left the hospital and returned to the compound. Raine, to his credit, had ignored her completely.

"He might as well be," Colte muttered, "He acts like one."

"A clingy one," Ari smirked in agreement. " Does he follow you to the bathroom too?"

Fallon hid her grin behind her glass, taking a sip of the wine inside, eyes flashing her amusement.

Colte pretended to gag. "Gross."

"Aaand, I'm done." I declared exasperated, pushing against the table as I got to my feet.

Ari rolled her eyes and kept eating.

"Come on, Saph." Fallon sighed. "They were just trying to get a rise out of him. You don't have to go. Raine doesn't seem bothered by it."

"I miss hanging out like we used to," Colte admitted. "You remember those days, don't you?"

"I don't remember her ever being this grouchy." Ari pouted. "Boys kill your chill, Saph."

"Whatever. I'm tired of this, and you're giving me a headache. See you later."

I didn't bother glancing Raine's way. I knew that he would follow. Instead, I turned my back on my friends and walked out of the room.

Fallon called out, but I didn't stop. And she didn't come after me. None of them did.

I walked in silence for a while, wandering aimlessly through the passages, listening to the echo of my footsteps.

Raine, the sneaky fae, walked like my shadow. His steps were silent and, had he not still been munching on grapes like an animal, I could have forgotten that he was there at all. He was content to leave me to my thoughts, intent on filling his stomach, I suppose.

I was fighting with my emotions more and more as my power grew, and it was getting harder to keep them all bottled deep down inside of me. So much of my energy was used just holding them, filling that space inside, feeling them build. I was constantly distracted, missing conversations happening around me as I fought the battle within myself.

All the while, those damned emotions grew, swirling around, pressure building to cause physical pain within me. I had lost count of the migraines, aching bones, and muscles. The cramps and nausea that had left me hiding in my room. I felt like I was going to be torn apart if I didn't release it all soon.

My breath came shallow and brisker as I struggled.

Too much. It was all too much.

I stopped walking, feeling a panic attack coming on. My heart beat faster in my chest, skin going clammy.

"Relax," Raine ordered softly. "Don't lose control."

"I can't do this. I can't pretend anymore. I need to let this *out!*"

Raine shook his head, throwing the remaining grapes on the floor, and took me into his arms. "You can do this. Don't lose control. Just breathe." He ordered again. His touch shocked my system, the feeling of his hands on me, the smell of him filling my nose as I breathed in. Again and again.

"What are you doing?" I asked, calmer already.

How could you not love being this close to him? He was safe. And strong. And he smelled so damned good!

"Giving you a hug." He replied, laughter and warmth filling his voice. "Have you never been hugged?"

"N..not by you, I haven't. Not like this." I blushed, thinking of the things we *had* done. It had been intimate, but never this impulsive. And never where people could have happened upon us.

His body tensed, seemingly coming to the same conclusion. "I suppose not. Are you calm?"

I nodded, and he released me, face bland and gold eyes looking anywhere but at me. "Good."

"Raine, *why* did you hug me just now?"

He sighed, running a hand through his black hair, and continuing along the passage at a fast pace.

I had to run to catch up.

"You were about to lose yourself. It would have ruined everything."

"So… you *hugged* me?"

"It worked, didn't it?" He asked playfully. "It took your mind off your panic. Would you have preferred I let you loose?"

I smirked, all but skipping circles around him. "I don't think that was why you did it."

"Oh," A raised eyebrow as he faced me. "Tell me then, why did I hold you?"

"Hugs, make everything better!" I stated matter of factly.

Raine snorted. "Okay, *Goddess*. If you say so."

"I do say so, and don't call me that."

"Your wish, my command."

"Or that."

We'd spent so much time together lately that I thought of him as a friend. Actually, *more* than a friend if I was honest. I had done things with Raine that I never had – or would – with my friends. Moody like Ari, dedicated like Fallon, and as amusing as Colte. That was Raine for you, all of my buddies rolled into one hot fae body. He never let anyone else see those things in him, though. To everyone else, he was an unapproachable, detached guard, and nothing more. If he would only open up to the others, they'd see how great he was, and ease off.

I'd been staring absently in the general direction of his rear as we walked, so didn't stop when he did. He stood firm as, like a child, I ran into the back of him.

Raine had led us back to my room. Or, *our* room, I suppose. Not that he ever *slept* there. Did he sleep at all?

"Distraction works for many things," He informed me, holding the door open, and flashing a brilliant smile. "Battle, pain relief, monotony, girls about to have a tantrum and kill everyone around her…"

"Shut up, faerie boy."

"Relax, Sapphira. You'll need your strength for what comes next."

My stomach dropped. *Way to ruin the mood.*

"I still don't understand why you think you're so weak and helpless," He added from his place by the door, watching as I moved to the bed. "Why won't you accept the power you hold?"

"It's not who I am, who I want to be," I admitted. I sat on the edge of the bed, hands on my stomach. "I'm not sure I can do this part, Raine."

"You don't have a choice. You made the deal, and there is no backing out." His tone was firm, leaving no room for argument. His eyes held a softer, more understanding look. I sighed, laying down, and stared at the roof, tracing the cracks in my mind.

I heard the door close and lock. And then seconds later, the mattress drooped as Raine sat down beside me. "I understand that this is hard for you, I do." He murmured, placing a light kiss on my brow. "But Sapphira, sometimes we need to think of the many over the few."

I closed my eyes, taking a deep breath. "It's harder when the 'few' are your only friends, Raine."

"It is." He agreed sadly, "But it'll all be over soon."

"I'm glad you're here, Raine," I whispered. "I couldn't do this without you."

"I know." He told me with a melancholic smile, "Relax your mind, and let's get this done."

I felt my mind and body begin to loosen up to the sound of Raine humming a fae lullaby, his hand caressing my cheek. I sensed his magic slipping into my skin, like a gentle warmth caressing my very soul. "Walk with me, Sapphira. I will guide you where you need to go."

I felt myself sink through the bonds of reality and enter the *Other*.

I had been here before, many times in the last few months, but the thrill of it had yet to wear thin. Colors were more vivid and fluid, and sounds were more intense in here. Blues and greens were the most predominant. Happy, calm tones.

There was no painful emotion, no weighty expectations. No fighting or death, no walls closing in on me. Just careless joy, freedom, and peace. I could easily get lost in the *Other*, and never want to leave.

My body was jade smoke, reminding me of my encounter with the Soul Eaters. Minus the terror and almost losing my soul, of course. Raine had explained that the experience you had in the *Other* depended on the guide you were with.

Soul Eaters worked in horror and death. Raine did not.

"The *Other* is a real place, but not everyone can travel here." He had explained on our first visit together. "Each guide projects what they want to experience and, like a magnetic mirror, the *Other* is drawn to, responds, and reflects it back at them."

"You make it sound like a sentient being."

"It is, in a way."Raine had confirmed. "It was created with raw magic by ancient fae – long before humans existed."

I felt the thread that bound me to Raine give a little tug, guiding me out of my memories, and to the waiting fae.

"Ready?" He asked, gold eyes blazing with glee and anticipation.

I smiled, all misgivings vanished. *How could you be worried when he looked at you like that?*

"I could stay here forever." I sighed happily. "We could. No one would ever find us, Raine."

The faerie shook his head, smiling wide. "As pleasant as that would be," He winked, "We have a job to do, Sapphira."

Right, work first. Pleasure later. "Let's do this, then."

I took his waiting hand, solidifying at the point of contact, and followed him further into paradise - to create a little chaos.

"Remember what we practiced." Raine reminded me as we neared our destination. "They can't see or hear you, but some of them may be able to sense you. Be quick, be thorough. Be strong."

I laughed, filled with delight, thanks to the *Other*, and the feeling of his hand in mine. Raine's answering smile almost curled my toes. "Get to it!"

I could see the swirling mass of colors in front of us, and knew that in the real world, we had just entered a training room within the compound.

Each colored swirl represented a person – or being – since technically, none of them were human. Each swirl, or *thread* really, was made up of four smaller fibers, wound tightly together, and held life essence, the soul, power, and memory for every living thing on earth.

Raine had taught me how to differentiate each fiber within a thread, based on shades of the color.

Today, I was going to collect the brightest fibers from each of the threads in this room. And I was going to hide them within myself for later.

A twinge of doubt and revulsion wormed its way into my mind as I thought about my task. But, before I could fully grasp it, Raine squeezed my hand, and a wave of peace washed it away.

It was okay, I could take the fibers, and no one would be hurt. I wasn't taking away life essence or souls today, it really was fine.

Raine gave me an encouraging nudge, and I got to work.

It was easy, taking power from others. Easier than anything I had done with my abilities so far.

Find the thread.

Cut the fiber.

Absorb the thread.

Over and over, more and more. I moved fast, vaguely aware of Raine coaxing me on, encouraging me to *hurry*. I didn't speak, intent on my work.

Find the thread.

Cut the fiber.

Absorb the thread.

When there were no more bright fibers left on any of the threads in my sight, I turned to Raine. His smile was like the sun, his golden eyes sparkling with triumph. Raine hoisted me into his arms and spun me around. "You've done it!"

I giggled with delight at his exuberance, relishing in the moment of victory.

The *Other* shuddered around us, causing Raine to frown, putting me down and looking away from me.

I hated it right then, that sentient being, for taking away my sun.

My joy, and the peace that had covered me dissipated, replaced with anger, fear, and hate. I could see that all of the swirling colors, the *beings* that I had stolen from, had slowed their movements, had become sluggish, and just *sad*. They were duller, too. Now that I had taken the brightest parts of them all. What did that really mean for them? Who were they now that they had no power?

"We need to go – *now*!" Raine hissed, grabbing my wrist and dragging me away.

"What's wrong?" I asked, gasping at the pressure he held me with.

"They know something is amiss. The Djinn and the Nephilim are heading this way." He picked up speed, racing away from our crime scene. "They cannot find us here!"

"You're hurting me, Raine," I complained, attempting to pull away from him.

"Move!" He yelled, tightening his grip and yanking me forward. I was definitely going to have bruises.

"Where are we going?" I cried, feeling him begin to panic – mine rising to join his. "Pull us out!"

"I can't, not here." He snapped. "We're too close. Shut up and *run*."

The colors the *Other* projected at us began to change from blues and greens to reds and oranges. The softness of the space we occupied began to sharpen too. Making any sort of movement became harder - as if the *Other* was trying to slow me down or keep me in place to be caught.

Raine swore, spinning to face me, and snarled as he watched me stumble as the ground beneath my feet lurched. He swooped me into his arms and kept running.

If I had thought he was fast before, I was dead wrong. He must have been holding back so that I could keep up. Now, he *flew* through the *Other*, keeping just ahead of the dangerous shifting colors.

Raine's thread, still connected to mine, wrapped itself around us and seemed to sizzle against me.

Mine flared in response, but Raine was too busy to notice.

"Almost there." He muttered.

I ran my hands over the spot where our threads connected, marveling at the feel of them. Ethereal and beautiful, yet solid under my touch. The tingling sensation that the threads pulsated through my body when I touched them was ecstasy, the rush addictive.

The power within me stretched, wanting to be used. *Just a little taste,* it begged.

I felt something slimy and cold sink into my hands, and let go of the threads as if I had been burned. *What the hell was that?* I wondered, a little repulsed.

"There!" Raine hooted, oblivious to what I had done, what I had *taken.* "Hold on and stay quiet." He warned. "This might hurt."

He punched through the walls of the *Other,* and we fell back into our real bodies. I inhaled sharply, eyes springing open, every part of me in absolute agony.

Raine's hand covered my mouth before I could cry out. "Quietly now, Sapphira." He whispered, head tilted to one side as he listened.

There was a commotion in the distance, people screaming in fear and confusion. *I had caused that.*

Revulsion hit me like a punch in the stomach. Raine smirked at the look in my eyes and removed his hand from my mouth.

I sat up on the bed as he moved away. "Raine," I started, but he cut me off.

"We need to leave." He stated coldly. "Now."

I had been delusional when I told myself I could be forgiven for this, that they would understand my motives. How could I have been so *wrong*?

"I need to make sure they're alright."

"Stupid idea."

"Can I just – "

"No."

"Let me say goodbye, at least!"

Raine laughed harshly. "No."

I had no choice but to go with him. After what I'd just done, I couldn't stay here. I'd be killed, I knew that. But it was a shock to hear him speak so hard-heartedly, to see him indifferent to my suffering – to the pain of those I had stolen from.

Raine held out a hand, beckoning me to his side.

I got off the bed and went to him. "Where are we going to go?"

"As far away as we can get."

"That's not an answer, Raine."

He shrugged.

"I hate this," I told him as he took me into his arms again. "They'll never forgive me. I don't think *I* will ever forgive me."

"I don't care." Raine replied as we vanished into thin air.

We reappeared in a woodland forest.

I much preferred this style of travel. It was painless. I didn't get dizzy - or feel as though my insides wanted to become my outsides as I did with Ari. Was it as instantaneous too?

The second that we had emerged, Raine let me go. I reeled at the swiftness of it, missing his touch on my skin instantly, struggling to keep my feet.

"Where are we?" I asked, looking around curiously.

"Ireland."

"*Where* in Ireland?" I pressed.

"Home."

"A little more information would be nice, don't you think, Raine?"

He shrugged. "Probably."

"What is your problem?" I demanded, anger pushing its way through me, swirling in the air around me like armor. "After what I've just done for you and your Queen, I think that I deserve – "

"I don't care what you think you deserve, and this was as much for *you* as it was for my Queen," Raine snapped, stepping closer to me, eyes blazing. "We both had jobs to do. They're done. End of story."

"Come now, *mealladh*. Is that how we treat guests?"

Her voice was just as beautiful in person, I thought.

Kamilla, Queen of the Sidhe, stepped away from the trees and approached.

"Apologies, my Queen." He bowed low, smirking.

She barely glanced her bright blue eyes in his direction, though, intent on running them over me instead.

Kamilla's long, dark hair was fashioned in an intricate braid on top of her head, held there by a crown constructed from twigs and leaves. The dress she wore matched the color of the leaves throughout the forest and flowed like grass in a breeze as she moved. The hem kissed the ground, rustling quietly. Two slits opened up along her legs, stopping inches from becoming scandalous. The material hugged her hips and wound itself in strips around her torso and breasts like a snake. The tribal tattoos that covered her arms, intricate Celtic knots, symbols, and vines, danced across her skin as if they were alive.

"How have you fared, Sapphira?" She asked, smiling. She had seen me checking her out, and I could tell that she enjoyed the attention. Raine usually liked it when I did that, too, I remembered. Even though he tried to hide it. "Did you succeed in your task?"

"I-"

"Sapphira!"

Fallon's voice. *Close.*

Raine was instantly on alert, scanning the trees, a deadly-looking dagger in hand. *Where the hell had he pulled that from?*

Kamilla stiffened, frowning in annoyance. "Perhaps we had best have this conversation inside." She said.

The Sidhe Queen turned, walking quickly back into the forest, not waiting to see if I followed. I suppose she knew that I had no choice, as Raine nudged me after her.

"Sapphira, where are you?" Colte called, further away.

"*Goddess,* please!" Abhijay, this time. "Come out!"

They had found me, and so quickly! A million thoughts rushed through my head. Did they know what I had done? Were they here to kill me? What could I possibly say to them?

Nothing, I realized, my heart breaking a little more. There was nothing that I could ever say to make my friends understand. *I* didn't even know how I had been able to make such a selfish and evil decision. Or how it had been so easy to do so at the time. I may have regretted the decision almost immediately, but I hadn't hesitated to make it in the first place. No, I couldn't go back to them now, even if I wanted to. I could never face my friends again.

I heard myself sobbing quietly as I was walked through the forest, branches leaning low to hit and scratch at my face and arms. Sorrow emanated around me, a purple so deep it could have been black.

"Give her to me, Sidhe filth."

Raine laughed as the Queen swirled around, eyes narrowed.

Ari stepped into existence, barely a foot away, between the Queen, and Raine and I. Her eyes were scorching as she glared at Raine. Her clothes were bloody, and her shoes were gone, But a bright aura surrounded her, pulsating with unbridled power—wrath in a human-shaped form.

"I think you'll find that she wants to be here, *Nephilim*," Kamilla commented calmly. "You traveled all this way for nothing."

Fallon, Colte, and Abhijay crashed through the trees, as disheveled and bloody as Ari, coming to a halt at the Queen's words. They turned incredulous looks my way, waiting for my contradiction. I swallowed the lump in my throat, unable to look them in the eyes. I kept my mouth firmly shut. Confusion hurt, and suspicion replaced their disbelief.

"I don't care what you say, she's leaving with us, now." Ari snarled, taking a step closer.

Raine was at my back, anticipation thick in the air around him. "Take another step, and you won't be going anywhere ever again."

"Resorting to threats, Faerie?" Ari crooned. "Are you that pathetic?"

"It's no threat, Nephilim," Raine answered smugly. "Merely a warning. You're in the boundaries of the Sidhe barrow, the *Banríon Cruach*. Make a move against the wishes of the Queen, and the magic here will obliterate you."

Ari, who was about to do just that, froze. "Well, shit."

"Goddess," A.J tried "You mustn't know what has happened, it is not safe for you here. Come back to your friends."

Raine snorted.

"Is… is everyone okay?" I asked, terrified of the answer. Already recognizing, by the state of the people in front of me, that bad things had happened. Something that had ended in death.

"No." The Moroi shook his head sadly. " No, they're not."

Fallon had been staring at me, trying to get my attention. "Saph, why did you leave?"

I shook my head miserably, eyes on the ground in front of me. "I can't say, not yet."

"Talk to us, what's going on?" Colte pleaded. "Help us understand."

"You should go," I mumbled hopelessly.

"This isn't you. Tell me what's going on!"

"I'm fine." I lied.

"Sapphira is here of her own free will. She is under my protection as a guest." The Queen stated, waving her hands at the group as if shooing away children. "You have no justifiable reason to be in my territory uninvited any longer."

"Sapphira!" Ari snapped. "Be smart. Come with us."

I shook my head again. "Just go."

The ground beneath us rumbled, the trees creaking and swaying menacingly. A blast of strong wind pushed at my friends, forcing them away as surely as I was trying to do.

"The Queen has spoken." Raine intoned arrogantly. "You will leave these lands immediately, or die."

A legion of Fae appeared around us, intimidating in their leather armor, with blades and bows at the ready. Hostile eyes stared at my friends as they began to back up. These men - these Fae soldiers - would have no qualms in killing any of them.

"Please, come with us." Fallon begged over the wind.

Something inside of me broke, seeing my friend so desperate, and knowing it was my fault. Knowing, too, that things would never be the same. "No." I turned my back on her pleading eyes and walked towards the Queen.

Chapter Nine

T he *Banríon Cruach*, Queen Kamilla's kingdom, was incredibly beautiful. Even in my emotional state, I could appreciate that.

After the forest, there was a green grassy meadow.

The dirt mound in the center of the glade was the official entrance to the palace. Magic allowed us to enter, and we stepped into a majestic stone hall.

Blooming vines crept up and spanned the length of the stones, giving the whole place the feeling of being alive, of *shifting*.

Tapestries, encrusted with gems and crystals, hung from the ceiling far above our heads and swayed gently in the florally fragrant breeze. Sconces lined the walls; the magic flame flickering within them created both light and warmth.

Fae of all types bustled about, stopping only to bow or curtsy to their Queen, nod a greeting to Raine, or to gawk at me.

I was doing my share of staring, too. I had never seen anything like them before. My brain had trouble processing the strangeness of the fae before me. Horns and antlers, fur and scales, wings, and animal bits where I was used to seeing human parts, all kinds of colors and patterns in place of skin and hair.

The fashion was just as foreign, leaves, flowers, and scant amounts of cloth – if they were wearing anything at all.

Kamilla didn't stop, though, barely even acknowledging her people at all. She led us into her throne room, another magnificently indulgent space. Sentries stood at attention, evenly spaced throughout, ensuring that any threat made against their Queen, would not succeed. Raine halted me at the base of the dais as Kamilla ascended and sat on her throne.

"Now, where were we?"

"Your guest was about to tell you about her task, my Queen." Raine reminded her, bowing.

"Ah, yes," Kamilla smiled. "Of course."

She gestured to me to continue.

"Well…. I…"

"Quickly now, out with it."

"I did as you asked," I said, "I spent this whole time stealing power from all sorts of beings. No one noticed until today."

"Why today?"

"It was the biggest group, and they were Moroi. I suppose their power is more integrated within their thread than the others?"

"You could be right." Kamilla frowned thoughtfully. "Moroi power *is* based in the darkness of death. Taking it from them would more than likely see them cease to be any more than human."

"Something I'm sure would be noticed instantly," Raine added. "Humans in a Moroi stronghold would definitely cause a... commotion – a feeding frenzy perhaps?"

"Interesting." Kamilla agreed and *smiled*.

I felt like I was going to pass out. Again, I wondered what the hell I had done. Why I had agreed to do this. Is that why my friends had been covered in blood?

I was struggling to breathe, arms around my stomach, trying to stop myself from being sick all over the perfectly polished floor.

"What else did you collect?"

Her voice came from a distance, muffled by my pounding heartbeat and the ringing in my ears.

"You will answer," Raine said, nudging my back. "Now."

"Why are you acting this way?" I heard myself ask weakly. "Why are you so *cruel*?"

Raine frowned, eyes narrowed. "What did you say?"

Kamilla laughed in delighted surprise. "Well, well. It looks as though our little *bailitheoir draíochta* has sampled some of you too, *mealladh*."

Raine snarled at me, hands closed into fists. I felt his magic close the distance between us, looking for what I had taken.

I stood, frozen in place, too scared to move. I wouldn't get far anyway, not with the guards everywhere. I didn't even think I'd be able to find my way out of Faerie again if I had the chance.

"Your compulsion doesn't work on her anymore, Raine." Kamilla clicked her tongue and shook her head. "What use is a deceiver, if the target sees through the magic and charm?"

Raine snarled at me again, taking a step closer.

I braced myself for an attack. The look in his eyes was a promise of violence and pain.

Kamilla chuckled. "Do not fear, Raine. I don't need her to fall for your tricks anymore. Tell me instead, what else did she get?"

He glared at me one last time before turning back to his Queen. "Lycanthrope, Skinwalker, Djinn, Nephilim, Seer, and Siren. Although Moroi is the only one she fully *took*. The rest were sampled, not stolen."

"Still, impressive. Can she tap into them yet?"

"Not intentionally."

"Good work, Raine." The Queen praised. "Give her to your brother. Let us see what *he* can get out of her."

I was swimming in a murky ocean, being tossed around by tempestuous currents. They had tricked me, I realized. *Used* me. And, like the naïve fool that I was, I had fallen for it hook, line, and sinker. *He didn't care about me.*

These past few months had been a lie, a means to an end. But for what? The power I had taken was inside of me. As far as I knew, there was no way to get it out again – unless Raine had lied about *that* too.

"Wait!" I cried out, as Raine grabbed my arm to lead me away. "You haven't fulfilled your end of the deal!"

"I never specified when *exactly* I would tell you, only that I would." The Queen smiled coldly. "And, if you can recall, after you pay the *debt*, not after the *test*."

Raine dragged me away, the Queen laughing as I hurled curses her way between gasping sobs.

I didn't know how long I had been here, only that I was drowning in unyielding darkness and self-pity – or was that *hate?*

I'd had enough time to replay the last few months in my head, cursing my own stupidity.

Raine had fooled me so completely, even the warnings from my friends hadn't made me see it.

I understood now that he had used his magic to influence me. Every time I had second-guessed the plan or started to stray from the task, Raine had pulled me back in – with sweet words from his forked tongue, and by *touching* me. All so that his power could flow through my body and set me on *his* path again.

He'd kept my friends away, creating rifts between us, isolating me, and making himself out to be all I needed.

And I had let him.

Raine had laughed, about how simple it had been, as he dragged me here.

"Pathetic really," He had sneered. "You were so desperate, all I had to do was smile, and you dropped your only allies like hot coals. I held your hand, and you invited me into your bed. It was so straightforward to deceive you, *extraordinarily* easy to manipulate and twist you to my will. You hadn't even felt my magic. Or wondered why you were okay with the things you were doing. Until it was too late."

"Screw you!" I had screamed.

Raine laughed, the sound like ice. "Haven't we been there, done that?"

My skin crawled, remembering all the times we had been together – all the things I had done to please him. All of the things I had done *because* of him.

Blood pumped in my ears so loud, I had almost missed his parting words.

"No," He hissed in my ear. "There are some things that even I wouldn't do."

He'd thrown me into the dark closet of a room, locked the door, and left. I'd been alone, curled up on the floor, in darkness, ever since.

Raine's brother had yet to make an appearance, and I shuddered to think of what would happen when he did.

Turns out, it was worse than anything I could ever have imagined.

Raine had dragged me from my closet and introduced me to Darragh, my new, most detested person.

Darragh, Raine's psychotic older brother.

He had the same good looks as Raine – long black hair, gold eyes, slender but muscled physique, and that *damned* smile. The smile that lit up the room, shining bright like the sun.

How I hated it. I hated *them*.

The minute I had been hauled into the room, I felt Darragh's magic shroud mine. I felt hopeless and submissive.

Right then, I knew that I would probably die here.

They had caught up on court gossip while chaining me to the wall, in what Darragh called his *motivation room*, ignoring my pleading and cursing.

Raine had left after that, telling his brother to get to work.

Thanks to Darragh, I knew what it felt like to drown, to be hanged, and to be burned alive. Along with his personal favorite, being stabbed with poisoned blades and arrows.

I also knew how it felt to be brought back from the brink of death, and the feeling of bones and organs knitting themselves back together, in agonizingly slow motion.

Even when I lost consciousness, or managed to fall asleep, Darragh invaded my dreams to torture me there too. He'd replay the 'games' of the day in whatever dream location I had fallen into.

He was a thorough healer, relishing in both tearing the body apart, and putting everything back exactly where it was supposed to be. He had spent hundreds of years learning his games. Or so he had told me conversationally one day, while we waited for the latest poison to leave my system.

My throat was hoarse from all the screaming. My vision was gone, taken by magic, and my ears were ringing so loudly; I couldn't hear anything else.

At least, at that moment, I was alone.

Darragh had blinded me and told me to enjoy my brief reprieve.

"I've got such plans for us today." He had informed me excitedly. "Such *wondrous* plans!"

He'd left not long after that.

I didn't know if it was day or night, there were no windows in the motivation room, and he came and went at random times. He seemed to find pleasure in the fact that I was clueless.

And now, blind too.

I tried to sleep, not knowing when I would get another chance. Not that I cared about anything in particular anymore.

I could die at any moment, and there was nothing I could do to change that. I wasn't sure that I even wanted to.

I must have dozed off because the next thing I knew, fingers were prodding my cheek.

"I have a treat for you today." Darragh crooned. "You get to choose our next game!" His breath was in my ears, the ringing gone. "I've got two exceptional friends that I want to introduce you to. I can't decide who you should meet first, so I thought that you could choose for yourself." He laughed gleefully. "Aren't you lucky!"

I whimpered, having met many of his 'friends' already.

"Will you choose the *Picana* or the *Maiden*, I wonder." He continued. "Oh! I almost forgot the most exciting part!"

He began unfastening the chains holding me up, chatting away as he did. "We are going to have a visitor today! One of your old friends!"

What?!

I think I was hyperventilating.

How had Darragh gotten his hands on one of my friends? *Who was it?*

I could feel tears running down my dirty face as Darragh released me. I fell to the floor, scraping my hands and knees on the rough stone.

I didn't care if he hurt me anymore, but one of my friends?

What are you going to do about it, you can't even stand up on your own – you can't see!

Darragh grabbed a fist full of my hair and dragged me across the floor. I could feel the skin on my legs tearing into strips on the rough stone as I tried to find my feet, but Darragh didn't slow down enough to allow me to stand.

"So, who are we playing with today?" He asked, "*Picana* or *Maiden*?" Darragh came to a halt, yanking me up to face him. "I suppose you want your sight back, too?"

I could feel his breath on my face, his hands around my throat, my feet dangling just above the floor.

"How else are you going to see your friend again?"

Suddenly, my eyes were burning, and I was trying to scream - and find enough air to breathe around his fingers, squeezing my throat. Darragh was laughing in my face. So, that fucking smile was the first thing I saw when my vision came back.

He threw me to the floor, and I gasped for air.

"*Picana* or *Maiden*?" He asked again.

I shook my head, trying to crawl away unsuccessfully.

"No?" Darragh asked, incredulous.

He kicked me in the stomach.

"You have to choose one, we need to play!"

Another kick.

"Perhaps we should let your friend decide."

Kick.

"I'm sure he won't have any reservations about choosing."

Kick.

He? Was it *Colte?*

I was sobbing helplessly, lying prone on the floor while Darragh beat the living shit out of me.

If he had Colte, if he *hurt* him, I would be completely broken. I'd known Colte for over half of my life. He had been an almost constant smiling face at my side. He knew how to cheer me up, make me feel important. He could make me see the world in a way that made sense. Colte was always there when I needed him, was on my side – no matter what. Even after all of the lies and half-truths, I loved him. He was a brother to replace the ones that I had lost—a playful, loyal brother.

The door creaked open, and my heart stopped. I squeezed my eyes shut, not wanting to see.

Darragh laughed, stepping on my back and pinning me to the floor. "I don't think she wants to see you."

"That breaks my heart."

I knew that sneering voice, I could never forget it. But I was happy that it wasn't Colte.

My friend was safe. *He wasn't here.* No one I cared about was here. That thought alone gave me the most wondrous sense of relief.

But then Raine opened his mouth again and ruined everything.

"I've missed her so much." He blew me a kiss, and I gagged.

"Come, brother," Darragh invited. "Let's play!"

"With pleasure," Raine replied.

In the end, they couldn't get me to decide what form of torture I would be receiving. So it was to be both.

Darragh started with the *Maiden*, a locked box with sharp spikes on the inside.

I was forced inside the box, screaming and begging.

The Fae didn't listen, they seemed to enjoy my anguish.

The lid was closed slowly, Darragh wishing to see my expressions for as long as possible.

I watched the spikes as they were lowered down. Closer and closer.

I knew that it was going to hurt. How could it not, those spikes were going to skewer me.

The more the lid closed, the closer they came, and the darker it got.

I felt the moment the spikes made contact along my body. Softly at first, barely a whisper of connection. Sitting on top of my skin.

And then, pressure. As the sharp points pushed against my resistant flesh.

But my skin never had a chance of winning out.

Agony. Spikes were puncturing the skin, digging deeper. I could feel them slicing into muscle, and pushing through to reach the organs below. Blood, tears, and other fluids leaked from everywhere, they mixed together and pooled in the bottom of the box.

Gasping for air through the pain, drowning as my lungs filled with blood. Every minuscule movement I made causing the spikes to tear me apart more.

Digging deeper, wounds getting wider.

More blood. More pain. Less air. Less thought.

I wasn't acquainted with the *Maiden* for long. At least, I don't think that I was. What felt like an eternity to me, was probably only a few minutes. Who could note the passing of time as they died?

When I stopped screaming, probably because I'd passed out from pain and blood loss, I was introduced to the *Picana*.

Raine and Darragh had pulled me out of the *Maiden* and returned me to the wall when I woke to the first shock.

My thigh was on fire.

"My *Picana* is pretty much an early version of the cattle prod or stun gun, except, I have made a few *adjustments*." Darragh gloated, showing it off. "Instead of two short prongs at the end of the wand, which makes contact with the skin to release the charge, this little guy is spiked."

"Fascinating," Raine commented. "Tell her how it works."

"Well, I know how much you like my sharp friends, so you'll *really* like this! The spikes are inserted *through* the skin, either through already opened wounds, or you could create new ones!" Darragh was beaming, as enthusiastic as a kid in an ice-cream shop. "Then, the charge goes off, bouncing off each of the spikes, and *frying* anything it touches."

"Did you hear that, Sapphira?" Raine asked, taking the weapon back from his brother. "All so your organs can be introduced to the shock – up close and personal."

He leaned in to whisper in my ear. "I bet you'll smell like barbeque before we're done. And so close to dinner time. Isn't Darragh thoughtful?"

Raine ordered his brother to lower the magical restraints in the room, and almost instantly, I felt some of my anger return. I didn't feel quite as despondent or compliant either.

They'd healed all of my old wounds while I was out. Or numbed them, as I couldn't feel pain anywhere but my thigh.

Looking at the anticipation on the faces in front of me, and the way Raine held the *Picana*. I knew that was about to change.

"I must admit, Pet." Raine stated conspiratorially, "I'm not here just for fun. Our Queen sent me to find some answers to questions she has about you, now that Darragh has had some time to play."

"Not… my… Queen." I rasped, unable to keep my mouth shut.

"There she is." Raine's smile was predatory. "I thought Darragh had broken your spirit. I'm glad that he failed, it's more interesting this way."

I didn't see it coming, too intent on his stupid face to watch his hands. The spikes punched through my abdomen, Raine putting a great deal of force behind his blow.

The shock was excruciating, akin to being burned alive from the inside. He pulled the *Picana* out as quickly as he had forced it in.

"First thing I'd like you to do." Raine continued calmly, "Is sing a siren-song."

I shook my head. "Can't."

"Make me fall in love with you, the way you loved me." He taunted. "The way I *made* you love me."

"Never... loved... you."

"Come now, Pet." He held a hand to his heart. "Words hurt, you know."

"Screw... you!"

Raine chuckled, but Darragh looked bored. He preferred physical pain over the emotional sort. "Fine, we'll skip the siren-song. Perhaps you can show me another trick?" He twirled the *Picana* around absentmindedly, narrowing his eyes at my face as he thought. "How about this. Create a forcefield around yourself, as the Djinn did around the compound, and I won't shock you..." A pause as he looked me over, contemplating. He pointed the spikes at my throat. "Here."

A smirk. "I'll even count down for you, ready?"

I shook my head, tears welling in my eyes.

"Ten."

I didn't want to be shocked again. Darragh's piece of shit toy would probably rip my head off.

"Nine."

But I couldn't do what he was asking of me.

I didn't know how to access the powers I had taken.

I didn't know how they worked.

"Eight."

"I can't do it!" I scraped out. "I don't know how!"

Darragh actually yawned.

"Seven."

Raine's golden eyes watched my face, waiting for a sign that I was complying with his wishes.

I guess he was going to be disappointed.

And I would just be dead.

"Six"

I shut my eyes, trying to escape into a happy memory, before the pain, and death occurred.

"Five."

I definitely didn't want the last thing I saw to be Raine's smug face. Or his brother's.

Instead of happy memories, though, I found something better waiting for me. *Much* better.

An old friend. An emotion I'd sorely missed.

"Four."

I let myself sink deeper, reaching for it.

Even if it didn't work, even if I still died, I couldn't go out without trying *something*.

Raine's voice barely a whisper now.

"Three."

I had to move faster, time was nearly up.

There!

I felt it wrap around my consciousness like a comforting hug, even as it grew in strength.

"Two."

I pulled it up, opening my eyes to see both of the fae in front of me watching the *Picana* make its way towards my throat, as if in slow motion.

"One."

I *pushed* my little surprise out, as hard as I could.

And laughed as my tormentors went flying backward, crashing into the *Maiden* on the far wall, and crumbled to the ground.

The *second* that both fae were unconscious, and their power no longer held me in check, I felt my own power rise.

Like a tidal wave, it crashed over me, healing the wounds in my abdomen and thigh, and making me feel refreshed and full of energy. It even repaired my ruined clothing.

So much power.

I gave myself over to it, giving it the reigns while I hid like a child behind her mothers' skirts.

I felt *invincible*, even shackled to the wall. I was *strong*, and I wouldn't allow anyone to hurt me again. I pulled hard on the chains around my arms and smiled as they snapped like twigs. The ones on my legs were next.

When I was free, I made my way over to the unconscious Fae, picking up the *Picana* from where it had landed, along the way. Raine and I needed to have a little… chat.

And then, it was Darragh's turn to scream.

I took everything from him.

And then, I made him beg. And scream.

Raine was powerless to help his brother.

I made him watch.

When I was done, what was left of Darragh burned.

"You're going to get me out of here," I whispered, cupping Raine's cheek in my hand. "And you're going to do it quietly."

When my power had returned, I found that I had more control over it than I ever had before, I *understood* it.

Not just mine, but the stolen power too.

It flowed through me like a river, dancing with what was already there, merging – *fusing* – into something new.

Raine had wanted to see if I could use it, he had wanted a siren-song.

So I sang one for him.

The blank look on his face, the lack of his usual smirk, gave me immense pleasure. I had him under my control, he was mine to do with as I wished.

That thought should have repulsed me. It *would* have not that long ago, but now I couldn't think of anything more enjoyable. Not after everything that the bastard had put me through.

I pushed down my emotions, and the majority of memories of my time here, needing a clear head for my plan. "Take me out of the *Banríon Cruach,* and return me home."

For what I hoped was the last time, Raine took me into his arms, cloaking us both with his magic, and we vanished.

I felt it calling out, calling to the small part of it that was inside of me. The piece that I had taken in the *Other.*

I could sense how his magic made teleportation possible, along with all of the other amazing things it could do, and buried that information for later.

We reappeared in the forest at the edge of the *Banríon Cruach.*

"What are you doing?" I snapped, pushing away from Raine. "This isn't where I said to go!"

"You must walk out of the Queen's domain." He replied. "No one can use magic to exit."

I snarled at him. "Then walk!"

I followed behind Raine as he led me through the forest, listening to a strange hum from in front of us.

"What is that?"

"It's the boundary." He answered, continuing to walk towards it.

"Why didn't I hear it on the way in?"

"My magic was still blinding you to the truth. You couldn't hear it, because I didn't want you to."

I scanned the trees for any hidden threats, any Fae waiting to stop us, but saw nothing.

"Where is everyone?" I wondered.

This seemed too easy.

"No one knows what you have done yet," Raine answered. "There is no one looking for you."

"Will we be able to cross this without raising the alarm?"

"Yes."

We crossed the barrier, and I sighed in relief. I was out!

He held out his arms, waiting for me to go to him. "Shall we go?"

I shuddered, remembering how many times he had made this same gesture in the past, always making *me* go to *him*.

It had always been a sign of dominance– and I had never noticed how *weak* and beneath him I had been, had allowed him to make me.

But now I saw it, and I wouldn't allow it anymore.

I shook my head. I didn't need him anymore, I didn't *want* him anymore.

"Come here, Raine." I smiled, the siren-song wrapping tighter around his mind. The smile that lit up his face was one of pure joy as he closed the distance between us.

"I want your heart," I told him.

"You have it." He replied quickly, eager to please. "All of it." He got to his knees, hand on his chest. "It will only ever be yours."

I summoned a blade, *his* blade, from nothingness, the tip dripping with poison, and held it out to him. His eyes flashed with confusion.

"I want to see it." I purred. "Give it to me."

His blade was in his hand instantly, the tip pointed at his rib cage. And yet, he paused. The last sense of himself – self-preservation if I had to guess – kept him from pushing it in.

"Go on," I encouraged, the siren-song like a vice on his mind. "You want to make me happy, don't you?"

"Of course."

"There is nothing in the world that would make me happier than this," I told him, nodding to the blade. "You know what to do."

That's all it took.

He didn't cry out as the blade entered his chest, nor when the poison began circulating. I knew the torture that particular poison inflicted. I knew, too, that Raine was in pure agony as it burned through his veins. And yet, he made no sound at all. Too focused on carving out his own heart.

He didn't quite manage to cut it out entirely before the poison paralyzed him, and he fell to the ground at my feet. Still, he'd done much better than Darragh had before I had taken everything from him.

But, as Raine lay dying, I knelt on the forest floor at his side. And, humming a Fae lullaby that I had heard once, I took everything from *him* too.

Chapter Ten

E verything I owned was gone, my house was nothing
but rubble. Police tape cordoned off the property, but
there was nothing left.

Rage and despair battled to take dominance of my mind as
I stood in what was left of my garden. I didn't care about my
clothes or material belongings, but all of my pictures were
gone. The only things I had left of my family. How long would
it be before I couldn't remember what they had looked like?

I could feel a lingering power throughout the debris, like a scent trail, made by the creatures who were responsible, but it was weak.

This had happened weeks ago. *Why had they done this?* I pondered as I drifted away from what *had* been, the last normal part of my life. *What was there to gain?*

The streets were quiet as I walked, lost in thought, the sun setting on the horizon.

I knew that I should have gone back to the compound, back to my friends. But I couldn't face them. Not yet.

Surely by now, Kamilla had discovered what was left of Darragh and Raine, and that I was gone. She'd probably have people out looking for me. I needed to figure out how to remove the debts I owed, even if that meant coming up with a plan to kill a Fae Queen. All before she found me.

"Escape," A male voice asked from behind me. "Or release?"

I spun to see a familiar Nephilim leaning his tall and skinny self against a street light, little more than three feet away, pale lips grinning.

The light did nothing for his already fair skin, but made his dark hair shine and green eyes sparkle. He wore simple jeans and a maroon hoodie with white joggers. I'd never seen him look so... human.

"Hello, Hunter." I purred. "What brings you off your island?"

"You do." He answered, straightening, eyes running me up and down inquisitively. "*Everyone* is looking for you."

I shrugged. "I can't help that I'm popular."

Hunter laughed. "Of course you can't. Everyone loves you."

I winked at him. "You've spent time with me, you know how loveable I am."

"I do." He frowned. "How did you end up here?"

"I escaped the *Banríon Cruach*, and went home – or to what's left of it anyway."

"Ah." Hunter nodded. "I looked for you there too, a few days ago. What a mess."

"It doesn't matter anymore."

"Still, I'm sorry."

I smiled my thanks.

"How did you escape?"

I shrugged again. "Killed a few faeries, and walked out."

"That easy, huh?"

"That easy," I confirmed quietly. Still not believing it fully myself.

Hunter closed the gap between us but didn't make contact. "What happened in there?"

"The usual stuff, Hunter," I stated in an armored tone, shaking my head, and turning away. "Torture and terror."

"I've heard of the kind of cruelty the Fae dabble in, Sapphira. How did you survive it?"

"Who said I did?"

"*I* did," Hunter told me, falling into step at my side, as I started walking again.

"You're still standing. Still making jokes. You survived when even *Nephilim* often don't."

I remained quiet, counting the steps I took in my head. *What was I supposed to say to that?*

Hunter seemed focused on the silence too.

"Why were you looking for me here?" I finally asked. "Why not in Ireland, or at the compound?"

Hunter's steps faltered a little, but he was quick to correct them. "Others are watching the entrances to the Fae lands. I don't know how they missed you there." He paused, glancing at my face before continuing. "The Moroi compound is no more."

I stopped, whirling to face him. "*What?*"

Hunter stopped too, and nodded in confirmation, keeping his face neutral. "After you left with the Fae, which may I add, everyone thinks you were *coerced* into." He raised an eyebrow in question, sighing when I shook my head.

"Something turned half of the Moroi and Dhampir in there human. From what I hear, it was… *messy*. And, to make it all that much worse, the Strigoi attacked again. Even with their already decimated numbers, the Moroi prevailed, but the compound was destroyed."

I swallowed the lump in my throat, not meeting his eyes.

"Those that were left, when it was all over, are out looking for a way to get *you* back."

"I can't go back to them," I told him sadly. "Not after what I did."

Hunter cocked his head to the side, taking in my posture. "What did you do, Sapphira?" He asked slowly.

"It's my fault they're all dead."

"How?"

"I didn't realize that Raine was… using me. I didn't understand what it would do, not really."

"What *what* would do?"

"I didn't know that he was using his power to control me, to make it seem as though what he was making me do was all so *reasonable*, so *harmless*."

"Sapphira," Hunter prodded, grabbing my arms and making me look at him. "What did you do?"

"I killed them all."

"What?"

"I took their power, and it turned them human." I went on, shrugging off his touch. "It's my fault they all died."

"You… took *their power*?" Hunter looked stunned. "How did you do that?"

"Raine took me into the *Other* and showed me how."

"No previous *Goddess Incarnate* was able to do that," Hunter told me, frowning. "I can't recall *anything* on earth that can."

"So what, I'm an alien?" I joked weakly, rubbing my arms where he had touched me.

"No." His response was thoughtful, his eyes calculating. "I don't know *what* you are."

"That Fae bitch told me *she* knew what I was."

"What did she say regarding it?"

"She held it above my head, dangling the information like a carrot. I was supposed to fulfill a debt for it. But," I admitted, angry at myself, "I didn't get the chance to push her about it before I left."

"You *did* survive it, Sapphira. You made it out."

"I know," I whispered. "And I won't let anyone hurt me like that again."

I shivered, pushing down the memories that threatened to spill out. I wasn't ready to deal with those yet.

"Where were you going just now?" Hunter asked, apparently picking up on my inner struggles. "If you weren't going back to the Moroi and your friends, I mean?"

"I don't know."

"Ah, no plans, then?"

"Not for where I was going, no." I admitted, "I *was* thinking I needed to find out how to kill a Faerie Queen, though."

Hunter snorted. "Well, how about a trip to the beach?"

I was grateful that he knew when to change the subject. He knew how far he could push me before I crumbled. Training with me all those months ago had taught him that.

"Can I still get there?" I asked an eyebrow raised, remembering what he had said the last time I was on Santorini. "Or will I explode?"

He waggled his eyebrows suggestively. "Why don't we find out?"

"Well, you look like you need a tan," I smirked at him, "So let's go cavort in the sun and surf."

"Stick with me, little thief," He nudged me playfully. " I'll get you there."

I had almost forgotten what *travel-a-la-Nephilim* felt like.

Hunter's howling laughter only made it worse.

"I think I hate you again, Hunter." I groaned, head between my knees. "That was *awful*."

"Nah, you love me. That's why you came on holiday with me."

I rolled my eyes, not that he could see them.

"It's interesting," He said conversationally while I pulled myself together. "I think I can sense a little Nephilim in you."

"Yeah, sorry about that." I brushed myself off, standing straight. "I sampled a tiny bit of Ari."

"As if we need *more* of her running around."

"How are you okay with this?" I asked curiously.

"Oh, I'm not." He stated, looking around casually. "But as long as you leave all of me *in* me, we'll be fine."

"Deal." We shook on it.

I didn't think that I had any intention of stealing from anyone else ever again. "Now, can you get me to a shower, and maybe some clean clothes?"

"Right this way, ma'am."

I followed him up the winding stairs, and into a stunning Villa perched on the edge of the cliff that overlooked the bay.

"Welcome to my home," Hunter said, pointing towards the back of the villa. "Shower's that way."

"Thanks." I hurried off, looking forward to washing away the last few days.

"Take your time, I'll get us some lunch!" He called after me.

"And some clothes!" I called back.

"I swear, all I ever do is find clothes for you!"

"Then, you should be good at it."

"Go shower, little thief." Hunter laughed. "You're stinking up my house."

His shower was *ridiculous*, taking up most of the bathroom. I stood leaning my back against the closed door, staring, and mouth open in awe.

Bright white tiles covered the floor and the wall holding the faucets and showerheads – of which there were many. The side 'walls' were glass from floor to ceiling, with one end entirely open for the rest of the room. A giant, decadent walk-in shower fit for a god. Or, a fallen angel, I suppose.

I ripped my clothes off, throwing them on the floor and walked in.

I had to play around with the faucets for a few minutes, trying to figure them all out—two for temperature, one for pressure, and three for different perfumed soaps. There were multiple shower heads on the roof, too, I noticed.

Extravagant to the max, but absolutely *worth* it.

It was heavenly, like standing beneath a waterfall fed by a hot spring. Pretty sure that I lived here now. Right here, in Hunter's shower.

I ended up sitting on the floor, letting the water stream over my back, knees to my chest.

It's time… A voice said softly in my head, *You need to face it.*

I hugged my knees tighter, curling into a ball. I didn't want to face what had happened. I was happy to keep letting anger and denial run the show, confining the memories deep down.

But, I knew, that suppressing every bad memory was a terrible coping mechanism. I had tried that when my family died – and it never worked, not really.

So, I took the reins back, and as I let the hot water from the shower wash over me, I let go.

Hunter found me like that, hours later, long after the water had turned icy.

He didn't say a word as he wrapped me in a towel, scooped me up, and carried me to the couch, carefully keeping skin contact to a minimum.

My nakedness didn't seem to bother him either, he didn't even comment in it, which I was thankful for.

He stood behind the couch at my back, and brushed my hair, keeping the silence comforting somehow. I hugged the towel around me tighter, barely taking in the details of the room, too focused on my pain.

When he was done with my hair, Hunter placed a pile of clothes on the coffee table in front of me and excused himself.

I was alone in the villa of a Nephilim, in one of the most beautiful places on earth, and yet in my mind, it wasn't real – I was still in Faerie – chained to a stone wall, dying.

The power within me swirled encouragingly, waiting to be acknowledged and explored.

I knew, from the memories I had stolen from Darragh and Raine, what each power was, and how they were used. Still, the knowledge on its own wasn't enough to ensure that I could use them effectively. *Knowing* and *doing* were two separate things.

I knew, from my own memories, that I would not have survived had it not been for the magic I now possessed. Knew, too, that the trauma I had been subjected to had changed me forever. I was a different person now, the old Sapphira gone.

I wasn't sure if that was a good thing or not.

I was stronger now, had a better understanding of the world I lived in – and everything in it - knew how cruel and heartless it could be. I had seen extraordinary things – things of beauty and wonder. I had seen kindness and loyalty, fear, horror, and hate.

But I had lost everything that I had held dear in the process – my house, my friends. Lost, too, my innocence and sense of self.

I had done things that I had thought I would never be capable of. I had survived torture, had in turned *tortured*. I had betrayed my friends, had been used by a man I had given myself to.

I had killed – not to save others, but for revenge.

What was my life to be like now, when so many people wanted me for their own purposes? Everyone I had ever met had tried to use me for something – there had always been a hidden agenda. To keep me alive, to make me a weapon, or just to kill me – it didn't matter. Was I just a pawn in their game, an expendable soldier in their war?

I had decided, back in Darragh's *motivation room*, that I was never going to let anyone hurt me again. Now, sitting on Hunter's couch, I vowed to never let anyone *use* me again either.

I got dressed slowly, holding the towel around myself awkwardly while I slipped into the underwear Hunter had found. The black sweatpants and t-shirt next.

"Want to talk about it?" Came his voice from the balcony.

I jumped, spinning around. "Were you watching me get dressed?"

"I carried you naked from the shower, remember?" Hunter stepped inside, face carefully blank. "You don't have anything I haven't seen before, Sapphira."

"That's not the point!"

"It's alright, little thief, I don't think of you *that* way." He chuckled. "You're more like a little puppy, a sad, little, power stealing puppy."

"Hunter!" I couldn't stop the smile that tugged at my lips.

"I brought you comfort food – to go with your comfort clothes." He announced, waving his hand towards the balcony. "Are you hungry?"

I couldn't remember the last time that I had eaten – or even felt hungry.

I had dreamed of food – long banquet tables full of all my favorites – while I was with Darragh. But the Fae had made sure that even my dreams were tainted. The food turned to ash in my mouth, was rotten or often poisoned, and caused severe pain and vomiting. My waking hours saw Darragh denying all forms of sustenance.

The sun had begun to set, I noticed as I stepped onto the balcony, Hunter on my heels. Visual proof of the time that had passed while I worked through my issues in the shower.

As beautiful as the view was, though, the dining table in the center of the balcony was what took my breath away.

It was piled high with a plethora of deliciousness; cakes, Ice-cream, fruits, and nuts, pasta, and meat dishes, salads, and sides. There were pitchers of wine and beer, water, and juices.

Hunter made himself comfortable, sitting at the head of the table and pouring a glass of wine. "I didn't know what you would want, so I got a little bit of everything." He said, noticing me staring. "Please, sit."He gestured to the empty seat across from him. "Eat."

I did as he asked, and lost myself in the motion of eating my fill. Which, was probably enough to feed an entire family, if I was going to be honest.

Hunter picked at his plate and sipped his wine in silence, watching me glutton myself. His eyes followed the progress of the fork each time it carried a mouthful to my face.

"That's really offputting," I said, pointing my fork at him, my mouth full of mashed potato.

"I'm sure it is." Hunter agreed seriously. "But how can I not watch the spectacle you're putting on? I don't think I have ever seen anyone eat as much – or as fast as you are."

"Shut up," I said, narrowing my eyes at him.

He smiled, hands raised in surrender.

After a few more minutes, I was done. I'd probably be sick, but it would be worth it.

"So…" Hunter said, tapping his fingers on the table, eyes on my face again. "I have a confession to make."

I froze. *Here we go…*

He saw my panicked expression. "Nothing bad, Sapphira, I promise."

"Then what is it, Hunter?" I asked, folding my arms over my chest.

"I spoke to Ari while you were in the shower – "

"What?"

" – and she is going to meet us in Greece with Fallon when you're done eating."

"*What?*"

"Ari is my sister, Sapphira. She was my commander for millennia. I had to tell her you were here, and that you were safe."

"You had no right to go behind my back, Hunter." I snapped, getting to my feet.

"Ari and Fallon are your *friends*, little thief, and were worried about you."

"I'm not ready, you *knew* that."

"They can help you," Hunter replied, "If you let them."

"No."

"Did you know, little thief, that Kamilla only became Queen after her father was killed in battle?" Hunter said conversationally, following me back inside the villa. I hadn't even sensed him leave his seat. "A battle against the Djinn?" He added.

I sighed, coming to a stop beside the couch. My wet towel was still on the floor. "Did you tell them everything?"

"Yes."

"I trusted you." I closed my eyes, head bowed. I could feel Hunter freeze behind me as I spoke. "I don't know why I bothered. This was supposed to be an escape."

"What's the point in escaping?" He asked softly. "Your problems don't vanish just because you run from them."

"I know."

"You wanted space, somewhere to go. I gave it to you. You wanted information. I found someone that can give that to you too."

"I know," I repeated, sighing and turning to face him. "It's just…things seem to move so *fast*. It's like I'm always moving from one place to the next. I never feel rested or settled. I feel off-balance, lost – like I don't belong. I really wanted to just stay here and catch my breath before I jumped back in."

"Understandable," Hunter said. "But you have friends to help you. Friends that care about you – *worry* about you. I don't know if I could have lasted this long without my friends – my *family*. They have my back, no matter what. You have that too, you know. All you need to do is let them in."

"Were they mad?"

"About?"

"Everything."

"Why don't you ask them?"

"What if they hate me," I asked, tears in my eyes, "After I tell them what I've done?"

"What if they don't?" Hunter countered.

"I hate you." I sniffed, wiping my face.

"No, you don't, I'm adorable."

"Shut up, idiot."

"Come on, let's go face your friends together."

Chapter Eleven

A thens was a sight to behold. Breathtaking in its beauty and energy.

Well, I'm sure it would have been if I *could* breathe – or see clearly. I was too busy misplacing my dinner over the cobblestones.

"Damn you, Hunter," I grunted, on my knees, between heaves.

"You're centuries too late for that." He laughed, holding my hair back.

"You couldn't have told me not to eat so much?" I elbowed him in the shins. "You knew this would happen!"

"I did." He admitted. "Maybe I needed a laugh. And this *is hilarious*."

"Hate... you."

"Oh, little thief, one of these days, I might believe you." He purred, patting me on the back. "Watch the shoes!" Hunter let go of my hair, jumping out of reach as I threw up again. "Rude."

I was laughing uncontrollably, still on my hands and knees over a pile of my own vomit, when Ari and Fallon appeared.

They wore similar outfits – knee-length black dresses and heels. Fallon's long auburn hair was loose, swaying across her back in the breeze. Ari's black curls were pulled back in an intricate updo.

"Shit." I struggled to my feet, wiping my mouth with the back of my hand. "Hey."

"Hello, Sapphira," Ari replied, nose screwed up. "You stink."

Fallon's eyes searched my face with concern. "It's good to see you."

"Is it?"

"Of course it is," She said, stepping closer. "We were so worried about you."

"Can we move to a more *appealing* space, please?" Ari cut in. "I need fresh air."

Hunter chuckled, passing me a handkerchief. "I know a spot. This way."

He led the way through bustling little streets, and into a small courtyard covered with fairy lights. There was a little café there, the strong smell of coffee permeating from within.

"Lyra makes the best coffee in all of Athens," Hunter whispered, seeing the eager look on my face.

He winked. "Don't tell her I said that, though."

"Lyra has already heard, you sycophant!" Called an old lady sitting at one of the tables in the courtyard, "You will get no free coffee today, Hunter."

There was no way she could have heard him from that distance.

I glanced at Hunter, eyes wide. Hunter was watching me, grinning like a fool. "She loves me."

I rolled my eyes. "You think everyone loves you."

"Because to think otherwise would hurt my ego."

He all but skipped happily over to the old woman, dragging me with him.

Fallon and Ari walked with more dignity, watching the way Hunter and I interacted curiously. Well, Fallon was curious and maybe a little anxious. Ari was exasperated with her brother's childish antics more than anything.

"Lyra, this is-" Hunter began when we had reached her.

"I know who this is," Lyra cut him off with a wave of her ancient hand, "Hello, Sapphira."

"Uh, hi, Lyra," I said slowly. *How did she know who I was?*

"I'm a seer." She stated calmly.

Oh.

Lyra nodded her greetings to Ari and Fallon, then turned her attention back to Hunter. "I sent everyone away when I saw you coming. You have the place to yourself."

"Thank you, Lyra. I appreciate it."

"I am aware." She struggled out of her seat, and Hunter helped her inside."You will cover the mislaid cost for the night."

"Of course." He agreed without hesitation.

The seer patted his hand, smiling. "You know where everything is, serve yourself and your friends."

Hunter hurried off to the counter, and I could hear him rustling around back there.

That pleasant coffee smell increased, and my mouth began to water. I freaking *loved* coffee.

I took in the café; wooden tables and chairs with colorful cloth table coverings filled the floor. There were lots of little windows along the front wall, old black and white photographs covering the others. The countertop was one solid piece of polished wood, ancient and well worn. There was no register or modern technology of any sort to be seen from where I stood. Even the lights were old – flickering candles on each table, along the counter, and in sconces on the walls.

I turned back to Lyra, feeling her attention on me. She was regarding me with a solemn expression, reaching out to take my hand, pulling me closer with more strength than I had thought possible.

She leaned in, forcing me to bend down to meet her. "Before you leave here, come and find me." She murmured. "I have something for you."

I nodded, "Sure, I can do that."

Lyra smiled sadly, letting me go. She turned away, gesturing to the biggest table in her café. "You can have your talk here. If you break anything, you will pay for it."

Fallon and Ari took the seats Lyra offered for them.

I remained standing. Without Hunter's playfulness keeping me occupied, I was a bundle of nerves.

"*Sit.*" Lyra insisted firmly.

I sat.

"Good. I will take my leave now, but remember what I told you." She told me, and, without waiting for a reply, she hobbled away. "Do not break anything in my café, Hunter," Lyra warned loudly, not turning around as she exited through a door in the back. "Or I will ban you from this place, and remember to lock up when you leave!"

"You got it, Love!" He called back.

With no more distractions, I turned to face the music.

Ari and Fallon regarded me in silence.

I guess I was going first.

"I'm sorry." I forced out, trying to calm my racing heart and keep my power in check. "More sorry than I could ever say."

"For which part?" Ari snarled, "Causing the complete destruction of your biggest allies or running away?"

"Ari." Fallon warned softly.

"No, she's right," I told them. "Both of those things, and more."

"Will you tell us everything that happened?" Fallon asked carefully. "Hunter told Ari what he knew, but I'd like to hear it all from you. Help us understand."

I nodded. "I'll do my best."

I launched into it quickly, letting my story tell itself, trying not to focus on any *one* part of it too much.

At some point, Hunter rejoined us with the coffee, handing it out, and sitting in the last remaining chair without a word.

When I was done, I buried myself in the now lukewarm coffee cup, unable to look at the three people around the table.

"Saph," Fallon started. "What you did..."

I glanced up, expecting to see hatred, or repulsion in their faces. Instead, even Ari looked horrified.

"What you did at the compound was not your fault. You were compelled by Raine's Fae magic." Fallon's voice was soft, emotional. "You have nothing to be ashamed of."

I waited to hear Ari's scoff or objection, but she remained silent. Hunter did too. I had told him some of it, but this was his first time hearing the story in agonizingly full detail.

"I *am* ashamed though," I stated finally, "If I had just-"

"Just *what*?" Ari cut in, visibly shaking herself. "How could you have done anything against compulsion? I should have killed him the moment he appeared at the compound..." She broke off, shaking her head, eyes angry.

"The Fae had us all fooled by the end." Fallon continued. "None of us liked him being so close to you, watching helplessly while he isolated you, but none of us thought that he was sent to do *that*. We thought they had turned allies. The Sidhe kept their motives close to the chest."

Hunter was thrumming his fingers on the side of his mug, deep in thought. How were they just brushing this off?

"As for your time in the *Banríon Cruach,* what you did was for your survival. *Any* of us would have done the same."

"No," Ari cut in, glancing at Fallon and shaking her head sadly. "Even the Nephilim do not make it out of that place." She turned back to face me again, letting me see the emotion swirling across her face. Sadness, wonder, fear, and anger, relief, and pride. "I'm glad that you killed them."

"And you heard nothing else about what they thought you were, if not the *Goddess Incarnate*?" Fallon asked.

I shook my head. "No."

"The Great Library!" Hunter blurted, slamming his cup onto the table and jumping to his feet.

"What about it?" Ari asked insipidly.

Fallon and I looked at each other in confusion, but Hunter continued, bouncing on the balls of his feet excitedly. "There are accounts in there as far back as *The Fall*. There must be something in there to explain what Saph is!"

Ari looked thoughtful, contemplating the possibility Hunter had provided. "You're right. It's worth a look."

Her brother smirked. "Not just good looks after all."

Ari rolled her eyes, groaning. "Whatever you say."

"How is Colte?" I asked, ashamed that I hadn't asked about him earlier.

Fallon and Ari shared a glance, and my heart stopped. I knew what they were going to say before they'd even looked back at me.

"Saph, I'm sorry," Fallon said gently. "Colte is dead."

The café was already spinning.

Colte is dead…

He couldn't be *dead*. I had seen him in the forest - he had looked okay – dirty and tired, but okay.

It was just a bad joke, that's all. Colte – my funny, opinionated, party-loving Dhampir friend couldn't *really* be dead. "How?"

"He was on a scouting mission in Scotland," Fallon's voice sounded distorted as if I was underwater. "His group was ambushed outside of the Unseelie mound, *Rìoghachd na fala*, and they were all killed."

No.

"Sapphira, this wasn't your fault either," Fallon said, sensing where my head was going.

"How is it not my fault?" I snapped, glaring at her, my rage abruptly swirled around me, the dark vortex of emotion so strong and overpowering it seemed to fill the air all around us. "None of this would have happened if I had been smarter. *My friend is dead* because I was too stupid to see that I was being used. Colte is dead because I didn't listen and ran away. He is dead because he had to go and look for me!"

"Oh, cut it out!" Ari snapped, eyes blazing. "Colte was following orders from his *Maharishi*. His people are sent on missions like this all of the time. If it hadn't have been at the *Rìoghachd na fala*, it would have been somewhere similar eventually. Stop making out that every bad thing that happens in the world is your fault, and *tone down your fucking tantrum.* You're acting like a spoilt child."

"Ouch," Hunter muttered in disapproval.

"Am I supposed to be heartless and cruel like you?" I snapped back. "Am I supposed to revel in the pain and suffering of others, like Darragh and Raine? How can you sit there and lecture me when you have the emotional capacity of a slug?"

"Sapphira!" Fallon exclaimed in shock.

"That is enough, all of you." Lyra's ancient voice demanded from the back of the café. She clapped her hands together, and my rage vanished. Just like that, I was eerily calm. I didn't know how she did that. It wasn't magic that a Seer had. "You will stop this nonsense at once, and focus on the problem at hand."

"Which problem is that, Love?" Hunter asked, proceeding to help her into the seat he had vacated earlier.

Lyra sat down, eyeing us all with dissatisfaction. "I have seen that you must face a great enemy. Only *together* can you defeat them. There are many working as one, but topple the *right* one, and the rest will fall. It will not be easy, and there are many more heartbreaks along the way, but you *mustn't give up.* You have to succeed. For us all."

Lyra pointed a finger at Ari. "Go to the Great Library, there is something of use for you there. Start at the beginning."

Her eyes slid to Fallon, and she frowned. "Go *home.* You will be greatly needed in the coming days."

Fallon opened her mouth to protest or question, but Lyra wasn't finished.

"Hunter, take Sapphira back to your island. Study the *stories of Amyntas* and train with her. She will need to know how to fight with more than just her collected magic."

Hunter bowed to the old woman as if she had just made a royal decree.

"Sapphira, you must listen, and learn all that you can – from Hunter, *and* from the memories you took from others. Only when you know all that they *did*, will you stand a chance to stop what they will *do*."

Finished now, Lyra nodded to herself and stood. "I'm going to bed now, I suggest you all get moving too."

Hunter stepped up to help her, but Lyra shook her head, patting his arm. "Sapphira will walk with me."

Hunter looked surprised but backed away.

I got to my feet and made my way around the table to her. She took my offered arm, and we walked towards the door in the back room.

"Don't forget to lock up." She called back to Hunter.

"Of course, goodnight Lyra."

The old Seer was quiet while we walked, her grip on my arm tender. I wondered, not for the first time, who she really was, and all of the things that she had seen with her magic throughout her life. Why did she order us to do the things she did – what had she seen about *me*? How had she met Hunter, and why was he so indulgent around her? Why did it feel that every time she spoke, you had to shut up and pay attention – even if it didn't make any sense at all?

"I see many versions of the past, present, and future," Lyra told me smoothly. "That's what a Seer does. We can see into secret places, and follow the actions of a person we choose. We can guide the world to safety or ruin with our words."

She stopped at the door, turning to face me. Her eyes reached into my very soul as she stared. I'm not sure she liked everything that she saw there. "You stole some of that ability, and now must use it to help bring peace, before the world falls to ruin."

I swallowed heavily.

Lyra opened the door, still staring at me. "Come, I have something for you."

I followed her into the dark beyond the opening, feeling as though I were falling into nothingness.

"What is this place?" I asked in wonder.

The room was deceptively large – an entire house the size of Hunter's villa on Thira.

Except, where Hunter's villa was full of modern comforts, Lyra's house looked like it belonged in a time long past.

"My home."

"But *how* is this possible?"

"Magic." Here, Lyra seemed younger, more agile. She walked with a grace she hadn't possessed in her café. The seer motioned me forward, towards the couch in her living room. "I can give you answers to three questions." She told me as I sat down. "And a gift."

Lyra took a seat in an armchair beside a fireplace that crackled softly. A little cat slept peacefully in front of it, purring.

"Think carefully before asking, and make them count," Lyra added.

I sat quietly, thinking. What were the three things that I wanted to know? What would help me the most?

"Am I really the *Goddess Incarnate*?" I finally asked.

Why *not* ask it? I thought. *It was a question that had caused so much pain and death. And stirred everyone up to the boiling point.* If I could find out now, instead of waiting for my magic to settle, it would save so much time and effort. Maybe I could go back to some semblance of an ordinary life.

"Only through you will the *Goddess* return," Lyra stated, smiling gently at her cat as it woke, stretching and rubbing its body against her leg.

"Definitely not the answer I was hoping for."

The cat jumped onto her lap, and Lyra stroked it absentmindedly. "The truth is rarely easy to hear." She agreed.

"How do I kill Kamilla?"

"*You* cannot. The Fae Queen still has a part to play, and that part must be played out in full."

"Worst possible answer." I groaned. "I was hoping she would die before she caused any more trouble."

"Everything dies eventually," Lyra shrugged. "Even Fae Queens."

"Will I find a way to get out of the debts I owe her?"

"Not in any way that is easy, or without great risk to plans already in motion." She shook her head sadly. "Those plans are as important as what you must do. They cannot fail either, or more than this world will fall. And *that* is the worst part of all."

We sat in silence for a while, Lyra patting her cat, while I stared into the fire.

"My gift for you is on the mantle." Lyra's voice brought me out of my daze. "And before you say you don't need a gift, know that it is an insult to refuse it."

I stood, making way to the fireplace, while Lyra watched in anticipation. I felt as if I was being tested, but for what?

Sitting on top of the solid wooden mantle was a beautiful silver charm bracelet. I picked it up, taking a closer look. Twelve silver charms dangled around a delicate silver chain; little wings, an apple, a crown, a sword, a heart, a conch shell, a rosebud, a harp, a crescent moon, a mountain, the sun, and a star.

"It's stunning," I told her. "Thank you."

"The charms are infused with generations of my family's seer magic." She told me with a triumphant smile.

"Oh," I stuttered. "That's amazing. But... why would you give it to me?"

"Because you can see it."

"Of course I can see it," I replied, confused. I waved the bracelet in the air in front of me. "It's right here, in my hand."

"It is." She agreed, laughing. "One of the requirements of owning that bracelet is having the ability to see past the charms. No one except seers from my bloodline, and Hunter to a degree, can see – or sense it."

"But I'm not part of your bloodline, am I?"

"Says who?" Lyra shooed her cat off her lap and stood up, coming to stand in front of me. "My family is vast. It's branches reach all over the world. Who is to say that you don't have my blood in you somewhere?" She took the bracelet from my hand

and clasped it onto my wrist. "Your mother was human, but your father?" Lyra asked, "Do you know where his bloodline sprung from?"

I shook my head. "I don't remember much about them."

The Seer smiled knowingly, "No one can see or sense this bracelet outside of my bloodline." She repeated.

"You mean, I am of your bloodline?" I asked, eyes wide. "We... We're *family*?"

"Distantly. Only worth noting in the sense that the bracelet showed itself to you."

"What would you have done if I didn't see it sitting there?"

Lyra chuckled. "There are many other things on the mantle, Sapphira."

I glanced back at it, seeing nothing. I told the woman in front of me as much.

"You only see the item meant for you, that doesn't mean there is nothing else there."

She ran her fingers over the ornaments lovingly. "These charms have gotten me through a lot in my long life. You'll need to convince them to talk to you if you want to be able to use them in the future."

I frowned, not understanding.

"Each charm has its own essence, it's own unique ability. My family didn't make it easy to use, so *convince them* that you are worth the effort. Now go, Hunter is getting restless."

She ushered me towards the door that led back to her café.

"How did you meet Hunter?" I asked curiously. "He seems pretty smitten by you."

Lyra laughed, a hand on the doorknob. "And so he should, he was my husband, once."

The seer pushed me through the door.

"Good luck, Sapphira. You'll need all you can get."

And with that, Lyra shut the door in my face, leaving me in stunned silence.

I found the Nephilim in the courtyard, staring up at the stars. He flashed me a smile as I approached. "Let me lock up, and we can go."

I nodded, watching as he pulled a key from his pocket and locked the café door.

"Where are the others?" I asked him as he made his way back to my side.

"They've gone. Lyra gave them lots to do." He shrugged. "They said to say bye, though."

Oh.

"Ari will check in when she can, and Fallon told me to remind you that if you need her, just leave Thira and call."

"I don't have a phone. Or remember her number." I told him, confused.

"No, not with a *phone*," He laughed. "With your *power*."

"Of course." I rolled my eyes. "I keep forgetting that I'm magic."

Hunter's eyes fell to my wrist, to the bracelet there. His expression turned serious. "Lyra gave that to you?"

I nodded. "She did."

"I gave her that charm when we first met." He ran his finger across the little wings charm, a sad smile on his face. "She told me that there were other charms on it, but I could only ever see this one."

"How long were you married?"

"It doesn't matter." Hunter pulled his hand away, turning his back on it, on me. "Let's just go."

I moved to step into his arms, preparing my stomach for the trip. But Hunter shook his head.

"That charm will allow you to enter Thira unharmed. All you have to do is visualize the Villa and will yourself there."

And, without waiting for confirmation that I had understood, Hunter vanished.

It took more attempts than I cared to admit, but eventually, I made it back to the Villa, just as the sun began to rise.

I reappeared, smashing face-first into the glass shower wall. Which, Hunter just happened to be occupying at the time.

He let out a girlish squeal and tried to cover himself, as I lay dazed on the floor, blood running from my nose.

"What are you *doing*?" He hissed. "Get out!"

As my vision cleared, and the bathroom came into focus, I couldn't help the laugh that exploded from my lips. I hadn't meant to crash *into* the shower, but I'd made it back on my own!

The Nephilim *in* the shower was also not part of the plan. His high pitched squeal, soaped-up body, and hands desperately trying to cover *everything* at once *was* pretty funny, though.

And had he been *singing*?

Hunter's pale skin reddened. "Seriously, *get out!*"

Hunter emerged sometime later, finding me rummaging through the kitchen cupboards.

He was wearing black dress pants and a royal blue shirt. Better than the soap bubbles, for sure.

I opened my mouth to apologize, but he shook his head.

"We are never going to speak of it."

I nodded in agreement, turning back to my search of the cupboards. "Do you have *any* food here?"

"You ate it all." He informed me. "And then deposited it all over the streets of Athens."

I shut the cupboard door, turning to face him again with a sigh. "Thanks for reminding me."

"We need to start working," Hunter said, changing the subject, and tapping his fingers on the center island absently. "Lyra didn't say how long we have before things get bad, but I doubt that we can take our time here."

I agreed, but had no idea where to begin, the seer had been vague.

"I'm going to get started on the *stories of Amyntas*. I'll be gone for a few days, at least. I thought that perhaps you would prefer to stay here," He raised an eyebrow. "And learn what you can from the memories you pilfered recently?"

"It's as good a place as any to start." I shrugged. "Can we stock the kitchen before you go?"

Hunter snapped his fingers, grinning. "Your wish is granted."

"Haha, you're funny," I remarked dryly.

He looked at the cupboard meaningfully but said nothing.

"Where are you going, exactly?" I asked. "I've never even heard of *the stories of Amyntas.*"

"Amyntas was the name of several Greek Kings and military men. I've never heard of a specific text named *the stories of Amyntas*, so I'm not sure which one, or *what* precisely I'm supposed to be looking for," Hunter sighed. "But there are a lot of ancient texts around all of them, so I suppose I'll have to read them all and see what stands out. I'll start in Pella, at the Archaeological Museum there. "

"Maybe you'll get lucky and find an expert curator that can point you in the right direction?"

He crossed his fingers but didn't look too convinced.

"Well?" I prodded. "Shopping trip first?"

"If you can't find anything to eat in *this* kitchen, you're not hungry," Hunter smirked, wagging his eyebrows.

"Seriously, take a look." He added as I just stared at him.

I rolled my eyes, turning back to the cupboard - that I *knew* was empty. "This is a lame joke, Hunter," I informed him. "I thought you were funnier than – *oh*!"

The cupboard *had* been empty, only minutes before. Now it was stocked almost to bursting. All of my favorite foods were there. The fridge, too, I discovered, was full.

"Funny, loveable, *and* a provider." Hunter sighed, watching me flitting around, opening and closing everything in his kitchen. "I'm *such* a catch."

He blew me a kiss in answer to the rude gesture I made with one of my fingers. "See you in a few days."

And then I was alone.

Food first, I decided, and then… a trip down memory lane into hell.

It really *was* hell in there.

The Fae brothers were evil to their core, but also a mine of information and secrets about their kind.

I'd spent two whole days digging through their memories, skirting around any that included *my* time in the *Banríon Cruach*.

Ari had checked in earlier, needing a break from digging through the archives of the Great Library. Which I'd learned, was a massive building hidden somewhere in Asia. It was filled with stone tablets, scrolls, and books, written by Nephilim historians throughout their time on earth, which was from like, *day one*.

She'd agreed to go with me back to Athens, so I could practice using the magic I had taken from the Fae. And, since Thira was protected against it, we had to journey out of the shielded zone.

Ari had watched from a safe distance and laughed at my pathetic attempts to master it, one of Lyra's famous coffees in her hands.

I was determined, though, having gained all of the knowledge I needed from the memories. All I had to do was convince my mind it was natural to be able to use the magic properly. It fought against it, trying to apply human logic. It cried out that magic wasn't supposed to be real, that it was impossible. My magic fought back, though, *needing* to be released.

By the time I had exhausted myself, Ari had grown bored.

"There's one more power I'd like to try," I had said awkwardly. "But I need your help."

"You are NOT trying that on me!" She hissed when I'd told her what it was. "No fucking way."

"How do you suggest I learn it then?" I asked, my palms up in surrender, "Don't you think it would come in handy one day?"

"How *handy* did you think it was when it was used against *you*?" Ari had narrowed her eyes, crossing her arms in front of herself. "Find someone else to turn into a mindless drone."

She'd left not long after that, returning to the archives.

I'd gone to visit Lyra, hoping to talk with her, but the little café had been packed full of customers.

I'd left without even going in.

Now, I was back in the Villa, cooking up a storm and dancing along to the radio, trying to block out what I had decided to do next. Alcohol would have been preferable, but Hunter's kitchen seemed to have everything but that.

So, a whole bunch of my favorite comfort foods was on the way; blueberry muffins, spaghetti bolognese, and chocolate mousse. All for *after* I'd finished my work, of course, I'd learned my lesson about eating *before*.

I'd been over everything in Darragh's memories – most of Raine's too.

It was like speed reading, or skimming through until something interesting caught your eye. I had imagined little filing cabinets, each drawer labeled for different pages of information. There were drawers for things like how the magic within the *Banríon Cruach* worked, what the political and social dynamics were within the Fae. Drawers, too, for the many *types* of Fae, and the different kinds of magic the brothers had come across.

The only vital memories I hadn't sorted through were the ones that included me.

Today was going to be spent seeing the worst parts of my life, so far, through the eyes of the people responsible.

After I'd cleaned the kitchen, the muffins cooling on the counter, mousse in the fridge, and pasta keeping warm in the oven, I couldn't find anything else to distract me. It was time.

I settled myself on the lounge room floor, back against the couch, and took some calming breaths.

I started with Raine, cringing at how he saw me at the beginning. Pathetic, weak, and naïve. Admittedly, I had to agree. Every time past me had looked at him, it was with pitiful puppy-dog eyes.

I had hung on every word he'd said, happy to believe the lies that, looking back, were so obvious. It was embarrassing and infuriating to hear his thoughts and inner monologue, to feel his revulsion every time we touched. I was so overwhelmingly glad to learn that we had never actually had sex, Raine had merely used his magic to make me *think* that we had. Another tactic to keep me close to him, to keep my mind off what he was really doing. I saw the truth in his actions – how his kindness and understanding had been a game, magic that Raine had placed in my head. The words he *spoke* and the ones that I *heard* were often different. *You disgust me* turned into *I'm falling in love with you.*

I saw how Kamilla and Raine had played me, had kept in contact, and plotted to get what they wanted. Saw, too, how *little* magic he had needed to expend to keep me in his thrall. I had been such an easy, *stupid* target. I hadn't sensed his magic at all, being too untrained and *new.*

I watched myself in the *motivation room*, strung to the wall, clothes in tatters, and eyes glazed.

I felt Raine's indifference at seeing me that way. He really didn't care about me at all.

And then, the shock he felt when I overpowered him, the disbelief that I had managed to do anything but die. And how hard it had been to accept that he had underestimated me.

I saw with horror, the look on my face as I tortured his brother, the spite and exultance he saw there.

And then, his revulsion transformed entirely.

I sang my first siren-song, and all of that hate turned to love and adoration. I saw how intoxicating I was to him, how incredibly beautiful. I felt his overwhelming need to please me, to do whatever I asked of him, he was so desperate for my attention. All of the things that had made Raine his own vanished absolutely.

And then, I saw myself tell him to put the blade through his heart, to cut it out and give it to me.

I saw the lack of remorse in my eyes as I watched, the raw pleasure that appeared as he fell, the indifference as his eyes closed, and he took his last breath.

I came back to myself, shaking.

Hunter was sitting on the coffee table, face inches from mine. I yelped, slapping him across the cheek before his features became clear.

"Shit, sorry!" I gasped, "I didn't know it was you!"

The Nephilim laughed, rubbing the spot my hand had connected with. "My fault."

I got to my feet, stretching. "Did you find anything useful in Pella?"

"I don't know." Hunter shrugged. "I'm not sure what I'm supposed to be looking for."

"Do you think Lyra will answer some questions, give us a few hints, maybe?"

"Probably not. I think it goes against some sort of Seer code to give straight answers." Hunter smiled, only half-joking. "But I guess there's no harm in asking."

"I could use some of her amazing coffee," I admitted, returning the smile. "It's been a long few days."

"Really?" Hunter asked, standing to follow me as I made my way to the kitchen. "It looked like you were sleeping sitting up."

"If only," I replied, opening the fridge. "I don't think I'll ever be able to sleep properly again."

"Oh?"

I grabbed the chocolate mousse, chilled after spending the last few hours in the fridge. "Yeah, I've re-lived Raine's whole life – and most of Darragh's too. Those bastards were a piece of work, let me tell you."

"I can imagine." Hunter raised an eyebrow. "Are you alright?"

I nodded. "I'll be fine. I have mousse."

"Ambrosia for the soul." Hunter smiled. "Is there enough to share?"

I nodded again. "I plan on sharing with Lyra."

"I meant me."

"I know. If you want some, you'll have to come along."

"I'm there." Hunter turned and began walking away. "Let me change first, and then we can go."

He paused in the doorway to what I assumed was his bedroom. "Where have you been sleeping, Sapphira?"

"On the couch, why?"

"You know, there *is* a guest room with a perfectly good bed, right?"

"No, I *didn't* know that," I replied slowly. "*You* never told me, and I never snooped." I shrugged at his raised eyebrows. "Been a little busy."

"Right, well. Now you know." He disappeared into his room, door clicking closed behind him.

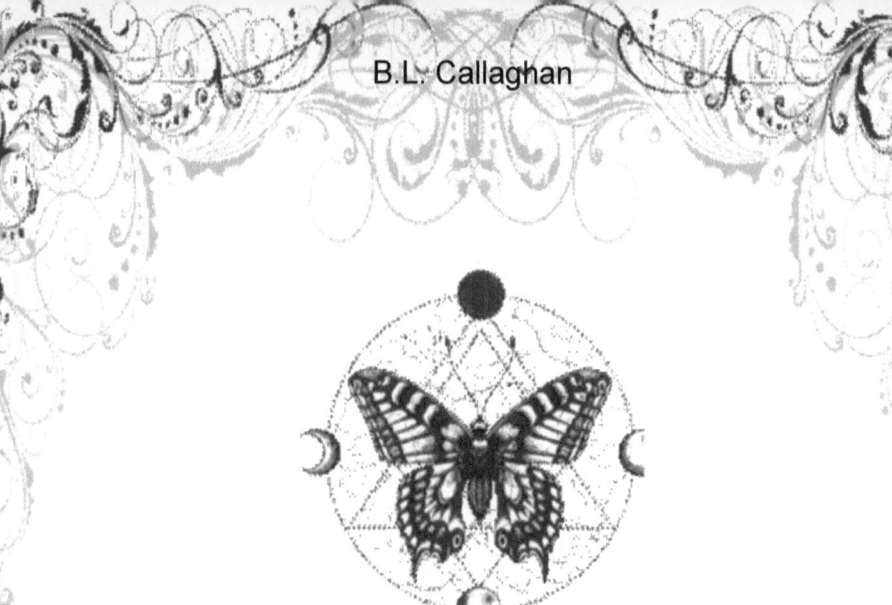

Chapter Twelve

T he café was quiet when we appeared in the courtyard, not a soul around. Was it closed today?

I'd never heard the place so quiet. So devoid of the usual hustle and bustle of this part of Athens.

Hunter frowned, his steps hurried as he made his way inside. I followed on his heels, juggling the dishes of mousse and muffins in my arms.

Inside, were signs of a struggle – of utter chaos.

Tables and chairs were strewn across the floor, broken glasses scattered around. The candles were all out, shrouding the scene in almost-darkness, the pictures that usually covered the walls were smashed and torn.

"Lyra!" Hunter called out, panic in his voice. "Where are you, Love?"

He dashed across the café, heading to the door that led to the Seer's private living space.

I followed, carefully stepping over the mess.

"Lyra!"

Her door was splintered, hanging off the hinges.

My heart dropped. I knew what we would find inside.

The dishes in my arms crashed to the floor as Hunter sobbed.

Lyra was in her armchair, the one by the fire, her little cat on her lap, just like the last time that I had been in here.

Only, this time, the fire was out, the little cat hissing at us furiously.

And Lyra was dead.

The noise that came out of Hunter was one of pure desolation and mourning. He knelt in front of Lyra, oblivious in his pain, as the cat peppered him with bites and scratches.

I was frozen by the door, unable to get any closer. Whether by my own shock, or Hunter's will, I was barred from Lyra's home.

Lyra was dead.

Her throat had been sliced open, blood covering the front of her body from neck to stomach. Her eyes were wide, seeing nothing. Not anymore.

From where I stood, I could see that the blood hadn't dried yet, the vivid red liquid glistening, even in the low light.

The café had been empty – I hadn't sensed anyone else inside when we had arrived. Had we only just missed Lyra's killer?

The cat gave up its attack, realizing that Hunter wasn't there to hurt its mistress. It turned back to Lyra, wailing in a pain that matched Hunter's.

"Hunter," I called softly when the noise had stopped, both creatures mourning in silence.

He didn't move, seemingly deaf to everything around him.

"Hunter, please," I tried again. "What can I do?"

He shook his head slowly, as if in a daze. "Get out."

"But – "

"I said, *get out!*"

I retreated, stepping back into the disarray of the café.

He needed time to say goodbye, to process. The Seer had meant the world to Hunter, anyone could see that.

For Lyra to be taken like this when he had been so close. It must have been tearing him up inside. Who could have done this? *Why* would they have done it? I had no answers, but Ari and Hunter would know more than I did. I'd ensure that we found whoever had murdered her, and make them pay.

In the meantime, I could tidy up Lyra's cherished café. She would have hated to see it in such a mess.

Warm tears streamed down my face as I began returning tables and chairs to their rightful places—tears for Lyra, *and* for Hunter.

I heard him sobbing, murmuring to Lyra's body.

I wanted to be able to help him - to comfort him in some way. I knew how it felt to lose someone you loved. Knew too, that there were no easy or quick fixes.

"I wish Ari was here," I whispered. "And Fallon. They'd know what to do."

When the table and chairs were done, I found a trash bag behind the counter and began picking up the broken picture frames. The shattered glass joined the wooden frames in the bag, and then I carefully placed the photos in a pile, the top one grabbing my eye.

The carefree woman in the picture took my breath away. Eyes sparkling, smile big, and full of joy, young Lyra had been stunning.

"What the hell happened here?" Ari stepped into the café, eyes wide.

"Ari!" I exclaimed, but she was already walking towards the back room.

She had perfect timing, as usual. I didn't know how she did it. She disappeared into Lyra's home, voice low as she spoke to her brother. I expected Hunter to kick her out too, but she didn't return. I was glad that she had come and hoped that it was a comfort to Hunter.

I went back to tidying up with gusto. Lyra had liked everything clean, tidy, and in its place. I couldn't stop what had happened to her, couldn't bring her back, but I *could* give her this. I lost myself in my work, not noticing the passing of time or the heavy silence that had fallen around me.

The crunching sound, as someone stood on broken glass, had me turning towards the front door. I expected to see the police, or even Fallon, standing there.

Instead, my blood ran cold at who – or *what* – stood there.

I had seen them before, but their appearance still made me cringe as they lifted their hoods, beaming their horrid smiles. They looked like men, but I knew better this time. Horrific scars dominated their features, one was worse than his two companions.

His left eye was gone, and on the left side of his mouth was a gaping hole. I could make out the bones of his jaw and what was left of the rotting muscles there, which seemed to have decayed more in the months since I had last seen him.

"Hadrian!"

"Hello, Sapphira." He grated out. *It must have been difficult to speak with half of a voicebox.* "I've been waiting for you."

"What are you doing here?" I snarled, rage replacing my fear. *How dare they come here now!*

"Working." His eyes slid past me, towards the back room. "The Seer's strength was... unexpected."

"*You* killed Lyra?" I asked, eyes wide with shock and horror. "*Why?*"

"She had something we needed."

I balled my hands into fists, nails biting into my palms, teeth gritted. *Where were Ari and Hunter?* I wondered. *Surely, they could hear us out here. Surely they would come.*

"What," I asked, trying to stall until help arrived. "Could Lyra have had that you needed?"

"You." Hadrian smiled, taking a step closer, his companions doing the same. "She knew where you were."

"You killed *Lyra*," I gasped. "Just to find *me?*"

"I have been tracing your location since our last meeting was interrupted."

Memories of that encounter flashed through my head, and I shuddered.

"I lost you for a while," The Soul Eater confessed. "And then you kept popping up in Athens. I followed your friends here, knowing you would come back. And, here you are."

"You bastard."

Hadrian inclined his head, agreeing. "I do what I have to, to get the job done."

"I won't let you take my soul," I growled. I felt for my anger, the almost solid wall springing into place around me. My hands were forming the little daggers Hunter had taught me. I threw them at the Soul Eaters with as much force as I could muster.

Hadrian's laugh was like rocks being ground together as the daggers disintegrated before making contact.

"I don't want your soul."

"Then, what *do* you want?" I spat, the wall morphing into a vortex, building in strength and speed. I tried to conjure more daggers, intent on killing the creatures in front of me. This time, I would make them stronger, aim them at the Soul Eater's heads and throats.

"Come with me, and find out."

It was my turn to laugh. "I'm not going anywhere with you."

"Then, the Seer's soul will be lost."

"What did you just say?" My magic faltered.

Hadrian held out a rotting hand, and a small golden light appeared in his palm.

Lyra's soul!

"I suggest a trade." He said. "Your friend's soul, for you."

I could feel her essence there, could almost hear her telling me not to be a fool, to *listen closer.*

How many times had I been a fool in the past? I wanted to ask her. *What was one more time… for a friend?*

I wanted to kill Hadrian and his companions for what they had done. But how do you kill a Soul Eater – a creature that survived even as their bodies rotted away around them? My magic seemed to have no effect on them. The Fae's memories that I held within me had no answer either.

"I don't understand what you would want with me. How can I make this bargain blindly?"

Hadrian shrugged under his hood. "That is not my problem. You either accept my trade and allow the Seer's soul peace in the afterlife, or, you don't, and the soul becomes sustenance for my kind."

Gross. Unacceptable. Over my dead body, which, if I was honest, was probably how this was going to go down. Better to ask questions, gather information and clarity, so I could make an informed decision – or until help could arrive.

"Where would you be taking me – and would I be safe there, or do you plan on treating me like you treated my friend?"

"To my realm. I will not harm you unnecessarily, nor will any of my kind."

"Swear that no one will touch me, or restrain me in *any* way, that goes for magic too," I added quickly. "And I'll go with you."

"You will not be able to leave my realm without my permission. No visitor can." Hadrian informed me solemnly.

"Will you let me leave?"

"Perhaps."

His companions were getting restless, Hadrian too.

"You will not be harmed, or restrained unnecessarily, You will not leave my realm without my permission, but the option will be there. The Seer's soul will remain intact if you journey with me now. I swear it."

It was the best deal that I was going to get, and it looked like fate had decided that Ari and Hunter wouldn't be coming to my rescue.

At least, I thought to myself, it would not be anything like my time in the Banríon Cruach.

It could be a hell of a lot worse. Another voice argued.

I had survived Faerie, I could survive this too. For Lyra, and for Hunter. I sighed. I could tell this was going to bite me in the ass, but I couldn't deny the last remnant of Lyra a chance at peace.

"Fine, I'll go with you," I told him through gritted teeth. "Give me the soul."

I thought about the last time I had spoken to Lyra, the things she had told me I had to do. I thought about Hunter, Ari, and Fallon - and hoped that they would get their tasks done.

I thought about what Lyra had said was coming, and my part to play in it. Had she seen *this* coming?

Lyra's soul felt warm in my palm.

"I'm sorry, Lyra," I whispered. "I hope you find peace."

I didn't know what had happened between Hunter and Lyra in the end, didn't know what the afterlife was like, but I could give them one last chance to be together. If that is what they chose.

I ran my finger over the little angel wings charm on the bracelet at my wrist.

"I gave her that charm when we first met..." Hunter had said.

"Each charm has its own essence, it's own unique ability..." Lyra's voice floated through my memories.

"We must leave now," Hadrian announced, bringing my attention back to him. "Come."

His companions turned, making strange gestures in the air, a shimmering patch of darkness appearing through the front door of the café.

They stepped aside, waiting for Hadrian, who was watching me expectantly.

I wanted to find Ari and Hunter, to see Fallon again before I left.

But, as I removed the charm from the bracelet that Lyra had gifted me, and set her golden light within it, I didn't even call out to say goodbye. For Hunter and Lyra, I said nothing. I just left the charm on the counter for the Nephilim to find.

And went with the Soul Eaters into the darkness.

Chapter Thirteen

M y footsteps echoed through the ancient passage as I ran, my breath coming fast and uneven – broken by the sobs escaping my lips. My vision was blurred by the tears that flowed from my eyes, staining my cheeks pink as they mixed with blood.

Not much further, *A voice urged in my head.* Keep going. You're almost there...

"*I can't!*" *I gasped hopelessly, a hand clutching my side as if to stop the pain.* "*I won't make it!*"

You can. I know you can do this, *The voice coaxed gently.* Don't give up just yet.

My foot caught on an uneven bit of stone, and I fell to the ground.

Get up – he's right behind you!

Hands grabbed me from behind, pulling me violently up, my body pressed against another.

I screamed as a blade was shoved into my stomach, the pain making the world spin.

"Did you really think that you could escape me?" *My assailant hissed, his hot breath on my neck.*

My legs gave out, but the strong hands holding me didn't let me fall.

His grip tightened, a hand encircling my waist, the other around my throat. "You belong to me. There is no escape."

Don't listen to him, he lies! *The voice in my head whispered urgently.* You have to keep going!

I could feel my blood draining out of my body, my clothes soaked in it - could hear it dripping onto the floor at our feet.

"I can't..." I murmured weakly. "Not strong enough..."

"I know, you're pathetic."

The world went black to the sound of my attacker laughing.

"That was one hell of a clusterfu-"

"Don't even finish that sentence!" I growled, throwing the ghost-like creature in front of me a glare as I came out of her mind control. Her nightmare. "Just...*Don't*."

"Well, it was," She laughed, the sound whispering around me like an icy breeze. "Is it possible that you're getting worse?"

"I made it further than yesterday, Mora." I reminded her with a frown. "And the day before."

"*Did* you, though?" She smiled, tilting her head to one side. "Distance counts for nothing if the fear and self-doubt drag you down."

I shook my head, counting to ten in my head. I wouldn't lose my temper over nothing.

"You reverted back to the pathetic, human mind frame you had when you arrived here. It made it easy to defeat you, just like all of the times before."

I shot her another glare but didn't argue.

There was no point. I knew Mora was right, even if I didn't want to admit it out loud. I'd let my memories overpower me. I'd been lost in them, and in doing so, I had failed Mora's test. Again.

"You hadn't fought back or even tried to gain the upper hand today. *And where was your magic?*"

I felt like a chastised child. I shrank under the intense black eyes that stared her reproach straight into my soul.

"You're not pathetic, or human. You'll never succeed here if you don't recognize that. Own it and *stop wasting my time.*" Mora waved me away, a dismissal. "Come back tomorrow and try again."

I sighed, leaving the Night hag to her work.

Stepping out of the training center was still a shock to the system. Inside, the walls were solid, made of stone. There were modern lights, amenities, and equipment. You could be forgiven in thinking that you were in a gym somewhere on Earth.

Outside, however, was a different story.

The *City of Darkness* was a patchwork of history. There were stone temples reminiscent of ancient Egypt, towering skyscrapers from modern New York, marketplaces open to the sky, and mud and brick stores and houses. All surrounded by swirling darkness and sound-eating silence. The only consistent light came from the energy of the creatures that lived here, surrounding them like an aura.

The inhabitants were stranger still, and it was hard not to stare, even after being here for what seemed like years. Night hags, Soul Eaters, Necromancers and their creatures, Ghosts, and so many more terrifying things called the *City of Darkness* home. It was where nightmares were born.

I thought back to when I had first arrived.

Hadrian, the ruler of the city and a Soul Eater, had bought me here after I traded myself for the soul of a friend.

A friend that *he* had killed.

I'd stumbled through the doorway his companions had created, fear rising as I took in the creatures waiting in the hall for their King's return.

The Soul Eater had barked orders and sent them all scurrying before turning to face me.

He handed me a golden pendant, which had liquified at my touch, and sunk into my skin.

I turned horrified eyes to him in question as I felt the liquid swirling around inside my wrist.

"That is my mark, a sign to all that you are a guest here. And as such, are under my protection and bound by my rules."

I'd heard similar words before, in another realm with equally monstrous creatures, and it hadn't worked out well. I'd been tossed into a torture chamber and expected to die. I'd escaped, but things had been dire for a while.

I was skeptical of his kindness, waiting for the penny to drop. I didn't trust him. How could I, after he had killed Lyra just to get to me?

"You are free to travel throughout my city, but cannot leave it." He continued, gesturing me to follow him.

He led me through the palace and into a massive apartment suite. It was stunningly beautiful – surprisingly so, considering where we were. At least it wasn't the dungeon, but still, it made no sense to me.

"These are your quarters. If you need anything, tell the servants."

"Why am I here?" I asked, turning my attention back to the King. "You said if I came with you, you'd tell me what all of this was about."

Hadrian had smiled his grotesque smile. "Rest now, or explore if you wish. We will talk again tomorrow."

"Give me something Hadrian," I called after him as he walked away. "Please."

"I never wanted your soul." He said softly, not turning back around. "The Sidhe set the whole encounter up to get close to you."

And with that, he was gone.

That had been weeks ago *if* I had worked out how time functioned here.

I'd spent most of that time exploring, too scared to stay in the suite Hadrian had gifted me - scared that the doors would be locked, and I'd be trapped inside. Only returning to eat, the palace the only place I had found so far that had food that wasn't horrifying or inedible. Or still alive.

I'd put my friends and all of the trouble back home out of my mind. I don't know why it had been so easy to do so, but I'd written it off as cowardice. I hadn't wanted to deal with it – to be what they all wanted me to be.

So far, I hadn't found myself in any trouble here. Neither had I received all of the answers I was after.

It had been a nice change of pace, though, no expectations or feelings of regret.

Hadrian had been scarce, too busy ruling his domain, I suppose. He had, however, told me that he would help with 'all of that' eventually, then he'd introduced me to Mora and set her to training me. Every single day.

So not that much had changed from my time on Thira, really. Although Hunter's version of training was friendlier than Mora's. If you could believe that.

Hunter's training had left me bloody, exhausted, and starving. But I'd accomplished something after all of that. I'd learned how to use my emotions as physical weapons.

Mora's training, on the other hand, was impossibly difficult. It was all mental. The Night Hag was trying to teach me control. How to face my fears, and still get things done. How to cope in a crisis; no more freezing and losing control – or not being able to access my magic.

I don't know why Hadrian and Mora bothered. I sucked at it.

But, I *had* been practicing with my own magic while I mapped his realm. It was more accessible now than it had been before. Not only did I *understand* it better, but my body also responded and reacted better too.

As I walked along the cobblestone street, heading back to the palace, I tried not to gawk at the child skipping along beside me. She was grinning, large green eyes sparkling with mischief.

She was also extraordinarily translucent and very, very dead.

Her tattered pink dress was flowing around her reminiscent of the water she had drowned in.

"Powerful lady is requested by the King. Must go to the Palace immediately." Her little fingers pointed at me, and then the palace up ahead.

"Are you sure?" I asked the girl-ghost, who nodded solemnly, her mischievous smile gone.

"Important. Have been searching all day."

Message delivered, she vanished.

Maybe Hadrian was finally going to tell me what all of this was about.

I closed my eyes, picturing the suite. I willed myself to be *there* instead of *here*, on the street. I felt myself dissipate, my magic conveying me through space and putting me back together, appearing inside the suite inside the palace.

In a matter of seconds, I had successfully transported myself halfway across the city. Painlessly and without much effort.

"You're getting better at that." Hadrian's second-in-command stated from where she stood at my door. "At least it seems you aren't in agony this time."

Valdis was a Necromancer. A human-looking demon of reanimation. What better second could a King of Nightmares have than a woman who could control the dead?

I snorted, rolling my eyes and smiling at her.

She looked to be in her twenties, but I could sense that she was *much* older. Her long black hair fell below her waist, her dark skin, quick to smile blood-red lips, and large brown eyes – along with her supermodel physique drew you in and made you want to love her. That is until you see her work her magic with the dead. And then, she was terrifying. So were her creatures.

She was usually a fan of wearing leather. Leather that *she* had made, from the skin of things she had killed herself.

Today though, she was wearing a long silver dress. The material rippled around her body like liquid mercury and accentuated her feminine beauty.

"It seems *all* of your magic is coming to you easier." She prodded, eyebrows raised. "Almost as if your time here is doing you good."

"I was summoned, Valdis?"

"Ah, yes. I'm supposed to warn you before we get there." She stepped into my room and closed the door behind her. "An old enemy of yours is here, and we need to play a little game."

I liked Valdis, her companionship had been a real blessing in all of this. I had joined her for meals every day, chatting and getting to know her. Valdis was one of the only beings in this realm that ate *ordinary* food. Her humor and openness had been refreshing too. But my heart still dropped at her words.

I knew the kind of games she liked to play.

"No," I hissed, glaring at the Necromancer. *"No freaking way!"*

Valdis was grinning, the dress held out in front of her. "It isn't that bad."

"It's hideous!" I pointed an angry finger at the dress in question. "There is no possible way I could even walk in that thing, let alone fight in it!"

The dress was some sort of red ballgown made from what looked like silk or satin. It had a low back and *miles* of skirt and train. I hadn't even touched it, and I just *knew* that it was heavy and that I would drown in it.

"Who says you have to fight?" Valdis smirked. "It's a formal greeting, not a battle."

"You've just told me who was here, how could this not end in a fight?" I shot back, arms crossed over my chest. "Why can't I just wear what I've got on now?"

Valdis laughed. "You will insult the entirety of Hadrian's realm if you attend such a formal event in *sweatpants*."

"Then I'll just stay here, in my room."

"You can't do that either. The King has requested that you attend – to help us play this game. You cannot refuse him."

"Screw his game." I snapped. "I'm not doing this."

"It's just a damned dress, Sapphira." Valdis was losing patience, her eyes flashing. "Put it on, and let us go play."

She had to help me in the end.

The gown was massive. And as heavy as I had thought it would be. When I was finally dressed, Valdis sat in an armchair, setting a few of her creatures to doing my hair and makeup.

I tried not to flinch as the rotting bodies flitted around, curling strands of hair and adding blush to my cheeks.

"In this game, you are to play as a creature from Hadrian's realm. And, no matter what happens, you must not break character." Valdis informed me. "You must keep your magic locked away, it cannot be sensed by those in the room."

"So, you want me to hide in plain sight."

"Exactly!"

"Why?"

"Hadrian's visitor mustn't see through our trick."

"Why?" I repeated.

"Because she mustn't know that we are not under her power," Valdis answered, getting to her feet and coming to stand before me. "Because she mustn't know that you are here as a guest. And, she mustn't know that we plan on destroying her influence here altogether."

She grabbed my arms, eyes narrowed. "You must play this game perfectly, *or we all die.*"

Kamilla, Queen of the Sidhe, was here.

The evil bitch sat on Hadrian's throne, smiling as his people bowed and scraped at her feet.

She wore a dress made from golden armor, hair pinned in a braid atop her head.

As Valdis and I entered the room, her creatures rambling in around us, Kamilla and her guards looked us over.

"Ah, *there* she is."

I hated the sound of her voice, the fake sweetness within it. She was the reason that so many bad things had happened.

Kamilla had set up my first encounter with the Soul Eaters so that she could play the hero. It had been her way of making me trust her, to force me into doing as she wished. She had sent Raine to me, told him to use his powers to control and twist me – to drive a wedge between my friends and me.

Kamilla had ordered the attack on Colte and the Dhampirs – had allied with the Strigoi against the Moroi, feeding them information Raine had gathered at the compound.

"You've kept me waiting, Valdis." Hadrian's gravelly voice called coldly from beside the Queen, dragging me out of my memories. He wore a navy blue suit that hid most of his decaying body. He almost looked handsome – if you didn't look too closely at his face. But the way he held himself left no mistaking his power, or his place on the throne here.

"My sincere apologies," Valdis swept into a curtsy, her creatures, myself included, followed suit. "Your messenger only just found me."

The Queen waved her hand in dismissal, eyes roaming the new arrivals. "I was told that you hold something that belongs to me."

Valdis dropped into another curtsy, remaining low this time. I followed her again, feeling those around us do the same. "If I do, it is without my knowledge, my Queen. I mean no disrespect."

"No harm was done." The tone Kamilla used said otherwise. "If you return her immediately, there will be no reprisal."

"Perhaps, if my Queen can tell me who it is she is after, I can correct this mistake and return them."

"The one called Sapphira Dawn, so-called *Goddess Incarnate*."

I willed my body to remain still, to keep in character.

She won't recognize me, Valdis changed your appearance. I told myself. *Stay calm.*

"I was unaware that she was claimed," Valdis said solemnly. "Of course, she is yours." The necromancer made a gesture with her arm, and one of her creatures shuffled forward.

Valdis had created it to look like me, and I'd infused some of my magic into it, so it *felt* like me too. I didn't know what, precisely, she had made it from, but I had to admit it was a good likeness.

Kamilla's eyes lit up when she saw it, stepping off the dais to get a closer look. "What have you done to her?"

"I apologize, my Queen," Valdis shifted nervously. "She was dead when I found her. Her body was filled with poison. I reanimated her, not knowing who she really was."

The Queen looked over the fake me, "This bitch killed two of my favorite men and escaped the *Banríon Cruach*. I wanted to take my time to kill her. It looks as though my Darragh did it for me."

She looked to Valdis, sounding anything but upset. "And her magic?"

"This is all that remains."

"Where is the rest?"

"I chased off a Fae. Perhaps he siphoned it?" Valdis said. "I swear my Queen, this is all I know."

Kamilla had her by the throat before she could even finish speaking. "You lie!"

"No, my Queen, I swear I speak the truth!"

"Perhaps there are still those in your court that dispute your rule, Kamilla," Hadrian said, coming closer. "What a fine weapon the *Goddess Incarnate* would be."

She whirled on him, Valdis still in her vice-like grip.

"Do you threaten me?" She hissed, eyes burning. Her guards surrounded them, hands twitching by their weapons. Hadrian's people didn't move. In fact, they seemed unarmed and unworried.

"Of course not, my Queen," Hadrian assured her. "It is not *we* that threaten. We have never challenged your right to reign supreme."

Valdis was quickly losing air, her gasps slowing down as she slipped closer to unconsciousness.

"If your majesty might consider letting my Second go," Hadrian smiled, "Before her creatures are set loose, we can finish this."

He waved his hand in the direction that the fake me stood.

Kamilla hissed in Valdis' face before releasing her. "Where was this *Fae*?"

Valdis got to her feet, hands clenched at her side. Deep red marks from the Queen's fingers wrapped around her throat, and blood welling where her nails had broken the skin, dominated the Necromancer's neck. A necklace of pain.

"Last saw it in Athens, standing over her body." Valdis gasped out. "Only a few days ago."

"Do you need assistance from my realm to find them?" Hadrian asked calmly, taking the Queen's attention from his Second.

Kamilla's eyes flashed. "Of course not." She stormed to the fake me, grabbed its head, and took the small amount of my magic that was there. "Keep her," Kamilla sneered at Valdis. "She's of no use to me now."

"You mean it, Majesty?" Valdis said, eyes wide with gratitude. "You're giving me all claim over the *Goddess Incarnate*?"

Kamilla laughed coldly, waving a hand in dismissal.

"If you want what is left of her, I release all claim."

"Thank you, my Queen." Valdis gushed. "Your magnificence and generosity-"

"Whatever." Kamilla cut her off, turning to Hadrian. "This visit is over."

Hadrian bowed to empty air, the Queen and her people vanishing at her words.

As he raised himself from the bow, he started laughing, his people following suit. "And *that* is how you outwit a Pretender Queen."

"Quickest visit ever made." Valdis agreed.

I frowned. "What exactly did you accomplish there?"

"You owe her nothing anymore." Valdis smiled, removing the concealment around me, waiting for me to catch on.

"You mean the debts?"

She nodded. "She released you to me, thinking that you were of no use to her anymore. All she ever wanted from you was your magic – a power that she now believes is inside one of her own people."

"She'll tear her kingdom apart looking for it," Hadrian said. "It will be a slaughter. But she isn't looking here anymore. Sapphira, you're dead as far as she knows."

"I thought you would have been happier," Valdis frowned at me. "Why do you look as if we've killed your puppy?"

"She gave my debts to you. *You* own me."

Valdis laughed, brown eyes sparkling with mischief. "And that's a bad thing?"

I nodded, shaking. "You *own* me," I repeated, willing her to understand. "I don't want to be owned by anyone but myself."

"Valdis," Hadrian said calmly. "Release her."

"I, Valdis, Second in command to King Hadrian, release you, Sapphira Dawn," She intoned. "From any and all debts owed."

"That's it?"

"What did you expect?"

"I don't know," I shrugged. "I thought... maybe I'd feel different."

Valdis hugged me, smiling brightly. "Sorry to disappoint you, my friend, but that's all there is to it. You're free."

"Now, Sapphira," Hadrian said. "I think it's time that we had our little chat."

I sat in Hadrian's private dining room, the King of the realm, and his Second, seated across the table from me. I don't know why he even had one, I'd never seen him eat food before. Only souls. And you didn't really need to be sitting at a dining table to do that.

"I want you to help me free my people."

"I'm sorry, *what?*"

Valdis was rubbing her neck, eyes closed. The marks left by Kamilla were still there, still raw, and it had to be killing her, the pain.

"I bought you here so that you could train with Mora, and to pull yourself together. I knew that Valdis and I could release you from the Queen's clutches. In return, I want *you* to help remove her from the picture altogether."

I shook my head in disbelief. "*How?*"

"Your power is expansive. You can do a great many things."

"I know that, but what is it exactly that you expect me to do, Hadrian?" I frowned, smoothing the bodice on the stupid red dress I still wore. "I'm not the one that can kill her, Lyra told me that."

"Ah, yes. The Seer." Hadrian sighed. "She had some exciting things to say before she died."

He pulled a glass orb from thin air and held it out to me. "Would you like to hear it?"

Before I could answer, he smashed the orb into the table, glass shattering.

"She will be the one to bring all our people together. She is the one to lead the charge against the Pretender. Only with her help, can all of the worlds be safe. She doubts her magic and her strength. She will need her friends and allies – much more as the time comes closer.

Sacrifices are never easy, but the ones that she faces will destroy her if she faces them alone."

Tears sprang to my eyes as Lyra's voice echoes through the room, having been contained within the orb. Free, now that the glass was broken.

Valdis and Hadrian watched me silently from their seats.

"Sapphira, don't leave your friends and allies to fight your battles. You must trust in yourself. Take all I told you in my home, and use it. Don't forget what bloodline you spring from. All you need to do is ask them for help."

I started at my name, surprise, and sadness, causing the tears to fall silently down my cheeks.

"And Hadrian, old friend. Do not mourn what you must do next. I have seen this moment coming for many years. My time has come, but yours is just beginning."

Her voice faded into nothing, the Soul Eater and the Necromancer sat, staring at me in silence.

She knew! Lyra knew that Hadrian was going to kill her. They had been friends! And he had done it anyway.

"How could you have killed her, your *friend*?" I demanded, wiping tears from my face.

"The Seer's strength was... unexpected." He had told me.

"She was my friend," Hadrian agreed. "She also told me that it was a necessary action. As was the tourniquet that was placed on you upon your arrival here."

"The what?"

"Have you not noticed," Hadrian asked carefully. "That you're not drowning in regret, or sadness at all that has happened to you this year?"

"You took away my emotions?"

"No, we didn't take them away," Valdis replied, braiding her hair absently. "We took the edge off, letting them drip back in slowly so that you could function efficiently."

"I'm... not okay with that," I said slowly, frowning and trying to get a grip on what they had done.

"Why?" Valdis asked, surprised.

"You took away my chance to deal with it all in my own time," I told her, trying to understand it myself, trying not to sound like my therapist either. "Pain, fear, and anguish are supposed to be *felt*, to be *acknowledged*. You can't heal and grow without walking through them."

"You did walk through them," Valdis argued. "Efficiently, and without falling apart. You just didn't notice."

"It's not the same."

"I don't think that you have *ever* fully been in control of your emotions. Ours wasn't the only magical influence you had on you." Valdis said, frowning. "Someone else had been limiting and changing them – and for a long time."

"Wouldn't I have noticed that?" I asked, definitely not believing her. Who would have done something like that, and *why*?

Valdis shook her head, shrugging her shoulders. "It was embedded deep, and with you being kept in the dark for so long, any manipulations would probably have felt normal. As though you just suddenly decided it wasn't worth being angry in the middle of an argument. Or you stopped crying and felt happy like..." She snapped her fingers, a sharp, quick sound. "*that.*"

"Why would someone do that?" I muttered, my mind already pinpointing moments in the past that had felt like that. It had to have been Fallon. I remembered the feeling of a calming blanket settling over my skin, of anger and rage, suddenly vanishing. Recalled, too, my therapist's insistence that I had never adequately dealt with the emotional consequences from the death of my family. Had Fallon stopped me from completely feeling it? Is that the reason I hadn't fallen into a gibbering heap yet – even after all of this?

"It can be useful," Valdis told me. "A warrior coming home from the horrors of a battle that can siphon their emotions at their own pace. They could function the way they did before without PTSD – and still work through the issues war presents. Or a woman who had lost a husband but still needs to care for her young ones without falling apart. The tourniquet can help her achieve that."

Hadrian had been watching me, head cocked to one side. It was like he could see my inner turmoil, the battle my thoughts were fighting on the ethical dilemma that they had presented. "Do you feel functional, and like yourself?" He asked, "Can you recall all that has happened and not fall apart?"

I nodded slowly. "It still hurts, but I can still function. I don't feel as though I'm being controlled or swayed by emotion or magic. But that could be your influence."

He shook his head. "The tourniquet has dissipated. There was nothing else for it to limit the flow of. Everything you feel within yourself now is *yours*."

"You worked through your issues. All of them." Valdis added.

I sighed, shaking my head. "I don't think we are going to see this in the same way. It's done, so let's just move on."

They nodded their agreement.

"If you want me to help you, we need a plan," I told them. "And I have conditions."

"Of course." The King smiled, gesturing for me to continue. "Let's hear it."

"First, I want to be able to leave. I need to know what my friends have learned."

"As long as you have my mark within you, and you mean my people no harm, you may come and go as you please."

My wrist tingled, the mark adjusting to the amendments.

"Anything else?"

"I don't want you or any of your people to use magic on me without my consent."

"Agreed."

"I don't want anything kept from me anymore. We need to work together candidly for this to have a chance."

Hadrian nodded his agreement.

"What do you get out of all this?" I asked him. "Why do you want your Queen dead?"

"I get freedom for my people. I get to rule in my realm without having to answer her beck and call."

"Kamilla isn't the real Queen, not of our people. She tricked and schemed her way to both Sidhe High-thrones." Valdis added, eyes flashing with a wave of old anger.

I was confused. I'd seen the memories of both Raine and Darragh, I knew that Kamilla was the Queen.

"I don't understand," I admitted.

"Kamilla was born in the Unseelie court – the dark court. She was not close to the throne, having many older brothers with immense power. So, she managed to marry the Prince of the Seelie court – the light." Valdis informed me.

"Unions like that were rare, but not unheard of." Hadrian continued the story. "The royals from the High-thrones are obsessed with power, and Kamilla had it. But, after she married the prince and moved courts, tragedy struck. Her father, the King of the Unseelie, died in some little battle between the Fae and the Djinn. Her brothers squabbled over who would succeed him. The war that raged saw millions of us killed. Finally, one brother was left. He took the throne, and all seemed well. But then, the Queen of the Seelie died similarly. Kamilla and the Prince ascended the throne and were to rule together." Hadrian paused.

"Let me guess; the new King died too?"

"He did. Both new Kings did, in fact. Kamilla attempted to merge the thrones, ruling them both on her own."

"She managed it though," I said, I'd *seen* it.

"Not without another bloody battle. Many were horrified at the thought of the Seelie and Unseelie becoming one. She rules them through fear, and is always searching for the power she thinks will hold them. "

"Raine and Darragh helped her."

"Those two bastards loved to deal in pain and deceit. They did anything the Queen asked of them. I'm glad that you took them down." Valdis shuddered. "I've spent some time with them, and wish I'd had a chance to repay the favor."

"Sorry I took that from you." I smiled.

Valdis snorted. "Now that her pets are dead, the last remaining highborn Royal Fae are beginning to rise against her again."

"And you want me to what, fight in your war?"

"It's not just our war, Sapphira," Hadrian said softly. "The whole world burns if the Fae go into battle. All beings that hold power are drawn in. It spills over into the human lands, and mortals will not survive it."

"Who takes the high-thrones when she dies?"

"Princess Lileas is the lawful Queen of the Seelie Sidhe, and Prince Cillian is the rightful King of the Unseelie."

"And why can't they just take their thrones from her?"

"They're young and need more allies. Right now, they're in hiding. Kamilla has been hunting their families for decades. They're the last ones left. If she finds them, it's all over."

"I'll help you, as much as I can," I told them. "but I need to see what my friends have managed while I've been here. They might have learned something that can help us all."

Hadrian nodded. "You can't tell anyone that we are not under Kamilla's thrall. We can't risk the wrong people finding out. Keep that to yourself while you are gone."

I agreed and readied myself to leave.

"One last thing, Sapphira," Hadrian said, getting to his feet. "Valdis will be close by – not as a guard, as hidden help. She won't interfere unless you ask her to, no matter what you find yourself getting into. She has other tasks to complete for me there, so call out to her if she is needed."

I glanced at the Necromancer, and she smiled back, lifting a hand to her ear like a little phone. *Call me!* She mouthed as I vanished.

Chapter Fourteen

S omething was wrong.

I should have landed in Athens, should have been able to move. Instead, I was in darkness, arms and legs bound.

"Are you awake, Love?" Crooned a voice I thought – hoped – I'd never hear again. "Are you ready to play?"

No, no, no, what the hell? He was dead. I'd killed him. How could he be here? *Where* was here?

I forced my eyes to open; something had caked them closed. Blood, I remembered. It was dried blood. I gasped at the sight before me. *No, it can't be!* Had it all been a dream, my mind's attempt at escape?

Raine stood in front of me, smiling his stupid smile. Darragh stood behind him, fiddling with one of his toys. I was in the *motivation room* in the *Banríon Cruach*, still chained to the wall.

Blood hammered through my head, panic, and despair rising. I hadn't made it out at all; *I had never even left.*

"Where were you just now, Love?" My eyes returned to the Fae as he spoke. "That vision took you for quite a while. Tell me what you saw."

Vision? I kept my mouth firmly shut, willing my mind to make sense of what was happening.

"Or perhaps, Darragh's *Picana* needs to say hello again." Raine continued smugly, his utter confidence in his control imbuing the air between us.

It wasn't a dream; it was a vision.

Something clicked into place, a shift in my comprehension so sudden, time seemed to stand still for a moment. *My Seer magic!*

I'd seen a version of the future—a premonition showing me how to survive this place, how to get out.

I knew what I had to do next, and this time, it would be real. I wouldn't fail; it wasn't even an option.

I started singing my siren-song, softly at first, while digging down into myself, pulling up whatever magic I could grasp through the smothering effects of Darragh's power. The song's strength was growing as I gained confidence. I watched, relief and determination driving me on, as the Fae's eyes widened in shock.

Immobilizing Raine, keeping him from touching me – preventing his power from affecting me – was easy, he was frozen in disbelief anyway.

Oh, yes. I thought darkly. *You've underestimated me for the last time.*

I pushed Darragh harder, knowing that it was *his* magic that I needed to destroy first. I needed to knock his out, so mine could come through.

I felt joy as Darragh's magic – the magic that stifled my own – fell away. It had been so heavy, weighing me down, that its absence made me feel as though I was soaring. My rage returned, a familiar and comforting friend, swirling through me and out into the room.

I laced my will through the Fae's, binding them to me as I liberated myself from the chains in the wall.

When I was free, the two males on their knees at my feet, and entirely under my control, I reached out with my magic, searching.

There!

Dark, feminine energy that felt like death mixed with wicked delight. My power called to the one I had found, feeling confusion and worry pushing back. But, they came anyway, appearing in the room behind the Fae.

Her long black hair was braided and hung down her back, blood-red lip curled in disdain. Large brown eyes focused on my face disinterestedly. A mask she often wore to hide her fear.

She wore freshly made red leather armor, the sigil of her realm scorched into the breast.

"Who are you?" She asked coldly, dark arms crossed against her chest. "Why did you call me?"

"My name is Sapphira, and I'm going to be your King's ally," I replied, smiling slyly. "I have a request– and a gift for you."

She took in the Fae, kneeling and blankly waiting for my commands. Shock flashed through her eyes, quickly hidden and replaced with interest and anticipation.

"I need to contact my friends before bad things happen. Get me to Athens *quickly* and *undetected*, and they," I motioned to the men at my feet, "are yours."

"This is some gift," A raised eyebrow in my direction. "What makes you think I want it?"

"You told me once. In a vision."

She sniggered.

"We're going to be friends," I continued, smirking confidently. "I've *seen* it."

"With games like this," Valdis' replying grin was full of wicked pleasure. "Yes, I think we are."

Athens, under the stars, had to be my most favorite place. Lyra's café, and her incredible coffee, helped make it so. I sat in the little courtyard in front of her shop, sipping at the cup of pure bliss, staring at the stars.

Valdis had dropped me near here, before returning to the *City of Darkness* to update her King and relay my request for a meeting.

I was trying to keep my mind off all that had happened, afraid that if I focused on it too much, I'd fall apart. Now that I'd taken back the reigns from my rage, I was flinching at random noises, and jumping at shadows. I felt haunted but was doing all I could to ignore it. I pushed all of the fear and anxiety down as far as I could, focusing instead on the breeze that swayed through the hem of the ankle-length maroon dress I wore. I listened to the sounds of water splashing softly in the fountain, smelled the coffee wafting through the air. I made myself take deep, soothing breaths, tried to keep my heart from racing.

I felt the friendly presence long before she spoke, almost as though she had intentionally waited for me to notice her, not willing to startle me.

"If I had known that coffee was all that was needed to lure you out," Came the familiar female voice from the doorway, "I would have done it sooner."

"Only *your* coffee could have done it." I agreed, smiling at the old Seer as she walked over and sat beside me, wiping her hands on the apron she wore. "But surely you could have *seen* that?"

"Perhaps. But the visions can be difficult to interpret sometimes."

"Visions suck," I muttered in consensus, deftly braiding my hair to keep it from my face. "I don't know how you keep yourself straight."

"Decades of experience." She laughed, patting my hand fondly. She smelled of coffee beans and chocolate. "Welcome back, Sapphira."

"Hi, Lyra." I grinned, genuinely glad to see her.

"I take it you had your first vision then?" She asked, ancient and knowing eyes scanning my face.

I bobbed my head, frowning now. "Do you know what I saw?"

"Do you want me to?" She replied, eyebrows raised and a mischievous grin on her lips. "I can teach you how to share them if you'd like?"

Lyra waited for me to impart my approval and then took my cheeks in her hands, resting our foreheads together. "Close your eyes, and send it to me. *Show* me what you saw." She whispered.

Her skin felt warm and welcoming, a tickle of her golden energy wrapping around my mind like a hug.

"Like replaying a tv show?" I asked, searching for clarification, to put it into words I could relate to quickly.

"As you say."

I did as she asked, *feeling* rather than *seeing* the images playing out, moving from my mind into hers—my jade magic mingling with her gold one. When it finished, Lyra let me go, both her magic and her grip on my face. She sat back in her chair, frowning as she processed what I had given her.

"That was…" She struggled to find words, still reeling.

"Disturbing?" I offered quietly.

"*Enlightening.*" She corrected firmly. "There were many distressing events in there, but many more that gave crucial information."

"I can change events in them, right?" I frowned, worried eyes taking her in. "By doing things differently this time?"

Lyra smiled knowingly and a little sad, nodding slowly. "Some things can always be changed. But others must remain as they are. Some events will always find a way to come into being, no matter what you do to change it."

"I *think* that I've changed so much already," I told her softly, worry lacing my words. "I hope it was enough."

"You've discovered a few truths about your enemies, and made strong allies. What more can you hope to do?"

"Keep all of my friends alive," I told her, taking her hand in mine. "I hated that you sacrificed yourself, you know."

"What sacrifice?" Lyra laughed, squeezing my hand gently. "I'm still standing, Sapphira."

"Make sure you stay that way, Love." Came a new voice. He appeared at the edge of the courtyard, out of sight of the bustling Athenians around us. They would all be getting ready to head home for the night, leaving the city to the tourists.

He wandered over to our table, a look of calm plastered over his face. I could feel the tumultuous concern bubbling beneath the façade, though. So could Lyra.

"Oh, hush, Hunter." She admonished the Nephilim as he took a seat beside her. "Don't be such a worrywart."

"Your friends are on the way, Sapphira." He told me, after smiling sheepishly at Lyra. "They were comforted to hear that you were alright."

"All of them?" I asked, fearing the answer. I knew that I had been too late to prevent the destruction at the compound, but had I been too late to stop Colte from going to the Unseelie mound?

"All of them," Hunter confirmed, brushing off a speck of dirt from the navy blue suit he wore. "The Moroi and your Dhampir had not yet left for the *Rìoghachd na fala.*"

I sighed in relief, a heaviness in my heart melting away—one less disaster on my hands.

"Now, care to fill me in on what's going on here?" Hunter added, glancing from our faces to our joined hands. "You two seem pretty chummy."

"Would you like me to catch you up, sýzygos?" Lyra let me go, holding her hands out to him, an invitation. "I know how you hate to be left out."

It was fascinating to watch the exchange from the outside, seeing the intimate pose, the way their magic played off of each other. The contrast between Lyra's serene, aging face against Hunter's shocked, eternally youthful one somehow complimentary.

"Holy *hell*, that was intense!" He exclaimed when they broke apart. "*Now*, I know why you would never show me yours, Lyra."

Lyra folded her hands in her lap, calm against the incredulity Hunter threw off in waves.

"You've been on a *journey*, little thief." He told me, eyes wide, and adopting the nickname from his vision-self. "Well, kind of."

"It still feels real," I told them, digging my nails into my thighs. "It's so vivid in my mind."

"Of course it is, all true visions are," Lyra told me. "Any good Seer worth their salt would tell you that."

I felt their presence before I saw them, felt the sudden desire to leave gently cast into the minds of the humans around us.

My friends had come.

Fallon, Ari, Colte, and Abhijay appeared, into the emptying courtyard.

Colte was wearing what I had come to assume was a uniform – white shirt and black pants – many of the Dhampir I had met at the compound in Australia had worn the same.

Abhijay looked remarkably upscale as always in a dark, fitted suit, and Fallon wore one to match. Ari was in a slinky little blue dress, more of her dark skin on display than was hidden.

They watched me as they approached our table, with varying degrees of relief and concern spread across their faces.

I stood to greet them, smiling uncertainly. The *real* last time we'd been together was… in the woods in Ireland? They didn't know what had happened after that – my time with the Fae, the real reason for it.

"Are you alright?" Fallon asked, drawing me into a hug. "I was so worried!"

"I'm fine, really," I assured her, returning the embrace. My eyes met Colte's over Fallon's shoulder and started watering. I was so intensely relieved to see him alive. He grinned, throwing me a mock-salute.

"I'm glad that you are all okay too."

"Care to explain yourself?" Ari cut in, glaring at me.

It used to be that I thought she was adamantly uncaring to almost everyone. Now I could see that she worried about a small few, myself included, so much it hurt. She used her temper to mask what she saw as human, and therefore worthless, emotions.

"I've learned a few new tricks," I mimicked one of her famous smirks, stepping out of Fallon's arms. "How about I *show* you instead?"

Sharing my vision with so many people was exhausting. So was my constant begging for forgiveness, and adamant refusal to be treated formally.

Sitting back in my chair, elbows on the table and hands holding my head, I groaned.

Lyra patted me softly on the back, chuckling. "It takes a bit to get used to," She told me kindly.

I ended up with a killer headache and a vow that, if any of my friends ever called me *Goddess* to my face again, I'd explode.

I realized that I had forgiven them for keeping things from me, how could I not after I had done the same thing? *Their* decisions had kept me safe – *mine* had destroyed countless lives.

"Is your daughter okay, A.J?" I asked the Moroi as I rubbed my temples. He had followed the others closer to the table, dragging chairs to join us. "Did she make it out?"

"She did." He confirmed a grateful smile in my direction. "Alayla is leading the rest of my people in the clean-up effort as we speak."

"I'm glad," I told him honestly.

"There was a lot of new information in your vision, Sapphira," Fallon said, adjusting her suit pants as she crossed her legs. "How sure are you that it is all still true?"

I knew what she meant. A lot had changed already. Colte was still alive, Lyra too. But what had altering those two events affected? "I honestly don't have a solid answer for you," I admitted. "It *feels* right in saying that you all need to follow Lyra's vision – and I need to get to Hadrian's realm. Kamilla needs to be dealt with. And right now, I still owe her those debts."

"Will you repeat your vision, Lyra, please?" Fallon asked, bowing her head at the Seer in reverence.

Lyra nodded, sighing. "I can repeat the parts that still feel relevant. But the future Sapphira saw may have changed the need for much of it."

Lyra closed her eyes, head bowed. Silence filled the courtyard as we waited for the Seer to gather herself. I could feel her pulling the pieces of the vision together, each person having their own path. It was like sorting through a box full of puzzle fragments, looking for the middle parts without knowing the finished picture. All while blindfolded to everything around you.

Finally, Lyra lifted her head, eyes focused with intent. "I have seen that you must face a great enemy. Only *together* can you defeat them. There are many working as one, but topple the *right* one, and the rest will fall. It will not be easy, but you *mustn't give up.* You have to succeed. For us all." Lyra pointed a finger at Ari. "Go to the Great Library, there is something of use for you there. Start at the *beginning.*"

Her eyes slid to Fallon, "Go *home.* You will be greatly needed in the coming days. Hunter, study the *stories of Amyntas.*"

She paused, taking a breath and centering herself. I watched the rise and fall of her chest, trying not to overlay it with the bloody version of my vision. "Sapphira, train with your magic *and* your body. And learn all that you can from the memories you took from others. Only when you know all that they *did,* will you stand a chance to stop what they will *do.*" She should have been finished, having repeated what I had seen. That should have been all. But Lyra wasn't finished, her eyes as surprised as mine. "Trust yourself and your abilities. Your visions are a great asset. Your magic must become like a second skin, as second nature to you as breathing. Abhijay, you must gather your allies. The entirety of the Moroi and Dhampir. The Lycanthropes too, which will be harder. There is to be a final standoff between Strigoi and your people. You must prevail, or I see no future for your country but teeth and blood."

I shuddered, goosebumps along my skin, as her prophecy sunk in. Colte looked just as shaken.

Abhijay bowed low, face grim. "Thank you, Seer, for the forewarning."

"Come, let us go inside out of the chill," Lyra said, standing, vision completed. "I'm sure you would all be more comfortable talking in the café. Hunter, you can get everyone fresh coffee – that *you* will pay for."

"Of course." The Nephilim grinned, winking at her.

Lyra took my arm, leaning in conspiratorially. "A few years ago, he burned down half of my café, and now he must repay the cost of repairs. One coffee at a time."

"It was an *accident*, Love," Hunter exclaimed, a hand over his heart, eyebrows up, and eyes wide.

"So you say." Lyra retorted, rolling her eyes and shaking her head. "I still do not believe you."

The others trailed behind us quietly as we made our way inside, lost in thought, or making plans for what was to come.

Hunter went straight to the counter and got to work, the heavenly scent of freshly ground coffee soon filling the air.

Lyra ushered the group to the biggest table, telling them firmly to sit and wait for the coffee. "Sapphira, will you help an old woman for a moment?"

I smiled. "If you find one, I'll gladly help her."

"Oh, you grub." She laughed. "I'm older than I look."

"What do you need?"

"Come with me." She led me by the arm, heading towards the door at the back. "I have something that belongs to you."

It was strange seeing her house neat and tidy, all of her belongings in their correct places. In my mind, the last time I saw her home, everything was destroyed – broken and bloody, strewn around, and discarded. It must have shown on my face because Lyra patted my arm reassuringly. "It's alright, everything is fine here."

"Why did Hadrian and his people destroy the place, if you knew what was coming. Why bother making it look like you had fought him off?"

"To throw off other prying eyes," Lyra replied, closing the door behind us. "Our friend must be cautious right now. The Queen mustn't see what he is really up to. Not yet."

Lyra's little cat rose from its place by the fire, mewing a greeting as it stretched.

"You know where it is." The Seer gestured to the mantle before removing the apron she wore. The clothes underneath, ocean blue shirt, and white pants were spotless, even after a full day working in the café.

I *did* know. I could feel it calling to my blood, wrist tingling in response.

The bracelet felt warm in my hands when I picked it up. "Thank you, Lyra," I said softly, heartfelt and appreciative.

I put it on my wrist carefully, taking the time to run my finger over each of the charms. An apple, a crown, a heart, a conch shell, a sword, a rosebud, a harp, a crescent moon, a mountain, the sun, a star. And the little angel wings.

"Thank you for what you did for me at the end," Lyra said, just as softly, eyes on the charm. "That meant a lot to an old woman like me – Hunter too. You've made friends in the both of us for as long as we live," Lyra vowed, moving to embrace me. "Hunter and I will never forget what you did for us."

"I may not have known you for very long, but it was the least I could do for someone I care about." I smiled sadly, eyes meeting hers. "You and Hunter deserve every happiness, Lyra."

Silent tears ran down her cheeks, a mirror of mine. "Right, enough of that." She sniffed, pulling away from the embrace, looking down at the cat rubbing against her leg. "I'll feed this monster, and you go back out there. Hadrian will be here shortly. And your friends need to depart soon after."

I returned to the group, who were all sitting in silence, joining them at the table as Hunter handed out freshly brewed coffee.

I loved Lyra's coffee. It was like a magic elixir, a cup of pure rejuvenation and peace. Anger leveled out, energy was restored, and left my soul feeling light and free.

Lyra appeared after half of my cup had vanished, and Hunter laid a hand on Lyra's shoulder and gave a gentle squeeze as he placed hers in front of her. She smiled up at him, raising her hand to pat his.

I am here for you. Hunter's action seemed to say.

I know. Lyra's replied.

The love between them was apparent to anyone who looked and again made me wonder what had happened between them. Why weren't they off somewhere together, sitting on the porch swing of their little cottage and enjoying each other's company?

I knew to bring it up, to draw attention to it was the wrong move, both Hunter and Lyra had shut my questions down before, and I had to bite my tongue to stop myself from doing it again. Lyra saw me watching their exchange and turned her smile to me, though the brightness had dimmed a little. "Some things are best left unshared."

Hadrian and Valdis chose that moment to make their entrance, the darkness of their door like a mini black hole, drawing the undivided attention of everyone present. I could feel my friends building their walls, power pulsating around them, guarding against possible hostilities. Lyra's energy remained calm, almost amused, as did mine.

They had all seen my vision, knew that the new arrivals posed no immediate threat. Still, years of fighting and protection duty had their instincts stuck in overdrive. Better to be prepared than dead, I guess.

Valdis wore the same outfit she had been earlier, her dark skin like decadent chocolate against the red leather. There were little throwing knives in sheaths across her thighs and arms, their silver blades shining menacingly. Fast, deadly, and terrifying. I knew her aim was near perfect, having watched her work with them before.

Her sharp eyes took in every inch of the café and its patrons before stepping aside for her King to pass, seeing no apparent signs of a threat.

Hadrian wore a suit – the same navy blue one he had worn in the throne room visit of my vision. He oozed a calmness that *had* to be faked. He came across as almost disinterested. Bored even. How long had it taken him to master what I assumed was his Court face?

I got to my feet as the door to his realm closed behind him. Lyra did the same, moving with surprising speed and grace to embrace him.

"It is good to see you, old friend." He told her, smiling as best he could with what was left of his face. His voice was as gravelly as I remembered, like stones being ground together.

"And you, you old coot." She told him playfully, brushing one of her hairs off the front of his suit gently as she retreated out of the embrace. "Will you tell the Hag Mora I said that a trip to the springs was overdue?"

He nodded once in assent, before turning to the rest of us. The Soul Eater bowed his head in sober greeting to the others, and I watched as they returned it uncertainly. The walls were still tightly in place, but I could see a sort of calmness beginning to filter through too.

"Hello again, Sapphira Dawn." He said, leaving me to last. My eyes, which had been taking in the others, returned to the King as he spoke.

"Hadrian. It's good to see you." I smiled, the greeting genuine, enjoying the spark surprise in his remaining eye.

"So it is true then," He ground out, eyebrow raised. "You have had a vision revealing we are to be allies?"

"I did." It was my turn to nod, a sly grin sliding into place. "Would you like to *see* what you told me?"

Not only was I now a firm believer in magic and monsters, but I was also gaining confidence in my own abilities. Actually *wanting* to show them off.

Oh, how things had changed.

Twenty minutes later, Colte was shaking his head, lips pressed together, eyes full of incredulity and outrage. "This is a bad plan. Like *colossally* bad."

"As bad as leaving you to die?" I asked, raising my eyebrows quizzically. "*Your* plan was suicide."

"I'd rather it be me than you!" He retorted angrily, slapping the table, causing the cups to rattle. I felt the table shudder under the force of it. "We can find a better way!"

"There *isn't* one. I *saw* that-"

"I don't care!" He cut me off with a snarl. Colte took in an angry breath, eyes blazing as he glared at me, ready to combat my reasoning with his own pigheadedness.

Abhijay cleared his throat, throwing Colte a warning look. "Control yourself, or I will have you stationed elsewhere."

Colte's eyes flashed, but he wisely kept his mouth shut. I threw A.J a grateful smile.

"As I was saying," Valdis said, turning our attention back to the strategy at hand. "Sapphira's vision gave us a snapshot on what could work to convince the Fae, for now anyway. It gives us more time to organize our next move – *and* frees Sapphira from the debts. If we follow along with it, and I don't see a valid reason why we shouldn't," She added, frowning at Colte, "We are already a step ahead in this game. And trust me when I say, *we are going to need it.*"

"And what then? What happens after Saph is free?" Ari wanted to know. "She'll still be in your realm while we run around out here, trying to find anything that will help you. What happens if your plan doesn't work – or we can't find anything? I'm not putting much faith in *visions* when her life is on the line."

"Apparently, my life has always been on the line, Ari." I reminded her calmly. "And I'd rather go into the coming fight without the debts hanging over my head. I have faith that this *will* work."

She scoffed, rolling her eyes. "A few months ago, you had no idea that any of this was real. You were full of rage and disbelief when you found out – doing all you could to deny it. Now you want to throw all sense and caution aside and put yourself in danger. You are insane if you think that you can go into this with nothing but *faith*." She spat the last word, lip curled in distaste.

The plan wasn't *that* bad.

I would go with Hadrian and Valdis, playing out the scenes from my vision. Fallon would go to the *Modena Al-Djinn* and deal with whatever Lyra had seen happening there. As well as ask the historians to look into what else I could be if not the Goddess Incarnate. However, I was still outnumbered in thinking that they would find anything useful. Everyone else seemed to believe that I was who they had always said I was, the Goddess of Reincarnation. I believed – hoped – that they were all wrong. The Fae seemed to firmly believe that I wasn't.

Colte and Abhijay would prepare their people for a battle against the Strigoi, bargaining for as many allies as they could get along the way.

Hunter would keep up his research on the *stories of Amyntas*, while Ari hunted through the Great Library. For the information that would lead us to victory, I suppose.

Lyra would stay here, keeping her eyes open – so to speak – searching for clues through visions – hers and those of her Seer contacts around the world.

I looked to Fallon, who had remained quiet through all of the planning. She was watching me speculatively, hands clasped in front of her.

"What do you think?" I asked, hoping that she would back me – could see the benefit of splitting up.

"I've spent many years protecting you, sheltering you from this world and its dangers." She started slowly. "My mistake was leaving you completely in the dark. I know that you have had a little training, but what you're talking about is huge. There is too much risk. You aren't ready."

"Without risk, there is no reward," Hadrian argued quietly before I could, the voice of a King waiting for his allies to come around to his point of view. "You have seen what Sapphira is capable of now, saw too that she is perfectly safe in my home. Can you say the same if she remains here?"

Abhijay nodded his agreement, Ruler, to Ruler. "I agree with the Soul Eater. If this plan is going to work, we cannot be distracted. Our parts must be played out perfectly, and her presence will only cause our attention to be split. I will not risk the lives of any more of my people because my focus is in the wrong place at the wrong time. Our only hope of coming out of this alive is the plan we have now."

You don't need their permission. A voice whispered in the back of my head. *You're not a child, make your voice heard, and take ownership of your own life.*

"I'm doing this," I told the people gathered around the table firmly. "And I'd appreciate your belief in *me*, even if you don't have any in the plan. We don't have time to bicker about it anymore, there is a lot to do if we are going to take out the Strigoi *and* the Sidhe Queen." I got to my feet, glancing at Hadrian and Valdis. "I think its time to go."

Hadrian conjured the door while I said goodbye to my friends.

Lyra smiled from her place at the table, a look of pride mixed with worry all over her weathered face. Hunter, with a goofy grin, winked and waved. "Good luck, little thief."

I stuck my tongue out at him. "You too."

"I still think you are making a mistake," Colte whispered as he pulled me into a bone-crushing hug. "Can I convince you to change your mind?"

"Not a chance." I shook my head into his shoulder. "You just focus on staying alive and kicking Strigoi ass. I don't want to lose you again."

I stepped out of his arms and into Fallon's.

"Stay alert, keep your guard up." She told me softly. "If you need help, call me, and I will come." I nodded my agreement, and she let me go.

Ari was watching me from across the table, "Don't die." She ordered eyes narrowed, daring me to disobey.

I snorted. "Yeah, that's pretty low on the list of things I want to do."

"Good." She nodded, turning to Hunter and murmuring something I couldn't hear.

"I wish you luck, Sapphira," Abhijay said from beside me. I fought the urge to jump or let out a little squeal of surprise. The mountain of a man could sure move silently. Undoubtedly a Moroi superpower. I definitely had to start paying more attention to my surroundings.

"You too, A.J." I smiled at him, throwing a fake punch in the air between us. "Show the Strigoi whos boss."

Abhijay chuckled a deep masculine sound that made my heart flutter, patting me on the back. "I will."

Valdis cleared her throat. "Time to go."

I took one last look at my friends, not knowing if we would ever all be in the same room again, committing every inch of them as they were now to my memory.

Hadrian stepped through his door, disappearing as I made my way over to Valdis. She grinned at me and gestured the way her King had gone. "After you."

"Be safe, Sapphira. No stupid risks." Ari called as I stepped out of Athens and into the Dark.

A single step, and I was back in the City of Darkness. Magical transportation kicked ass.

Hadrian conjured a golden pendant from thin air and held it out for me to take as soon as the door had closed. I noticed the sigil of his realm carved into the pendant face, a detail that had escaped my notice in my vision encounter. I knew what was going to happen when I accepted the pendant from him, but couldn't help the jolt of shock that fired through my body as the gold liquified at my touch and sank into my palm. The magical liquid swirled around inside of my hand, flowing down into my wrist. It settled there, quiet and waiting until it was needed—a magical bracelet on my left wrist, and the enchanted sigil in the other. I was starting to collect magic and magical objects like the little figurines I used to have in my house. Soon, I'd probably begin jingling like a cat with a bell collar—no canary dinners for me.

"That is my mark, a sign to all that you are a guest here. And as such, are under my protection and bound by my rules. You may come and go as you please, so long as your intentions are free from ill-will against any who dwell here." Hadrian declared before turning to his Second. "Valdis, summon Mora. We have plans to make, her and I."

The Necromancer grinned wickedly, eyes sparkling in anticipation. "At once, my King."

Chapter Fifteen

H adrian ordered Valdis to help me remove the old tourniquets put in place to limit me over the years. Limitations placed on me by Fallon.

The Necromancer explained that, like she and Hadrian had told me in my vision, those tourniquets had limited my emotions and responses. They had allowed Fallon to change the way I reacted to emotional stimuli, calming me when I was angry or upset, making me sleep instead of exploding.

"I'm sure the Djinn thought she was helping," Valdis said to my scowling face. "If you remembered – and felt – every magical interaction in full, especially the deaths of your family, you'd probably be an utter mess. In fact, your whole life you believed you were human, correct?"

I nodded, still scowling at the world. "Yes. Up until your King tried to take my soul anyway."

A slow grin crawled across her face at my words, and Valdis winked, making me turn my scowl on her.

"Right, and if a *human* had experienced that – not to mention a Strigoi attack and the revelation that her whole life was a lie. Or that the world was full of monsters and she had no magic to defend against them, do you think that particular human would be able to cope?" Valdis asked, eyebrows raised. "Or would that human be driven insane by the knowledge?"

"I see your point, I do," I sulked. "But I'm not entirely human, am I? At least I would have known about all of this stuff. I wouldn't feel like a fool – or that things are moving so fast that I can't keep up. No one even gave me the option of knowing; I never had the chance to *try*. How could Fallon and the others know how I would have reacted to this world naturally?" I know I sounded like a petulant child, but I couldn't stop it. "They all just decided that it was easier to keep me in the dark."

Valdis smirked, red lips shining in the lamp-light as she looked around the room pointedly. "There is nothing wrong with being in darkness."

I groaned, shaking my head at her in exasperation, eyes drawn to the throwing knives in her deft fingers. She was flicking them into the air in front of her, quick and precise little movements that had them spinning from one hand to the other, almost too fast for my eyes to keep up.

"I do," She confirmed, catching the knives and effortlessly stashing them in the wrist sheaths she wore. "But I'm tired of your 'woe is me, my friends lied to protect me' routine. Woman up – get over it and move on. We have work to do."

Removing a magic build-up, I hadn't known was there, was difficult. Fallon had been layering it on for *years*. It was hard to differentiate her put in place responses and my own natural ones.

Valdis explained that she would be my escort through the jumbled mess inside of me, like a spirit guide leading me on a spiritualistic inner quest. I would be able to hear her voice and feel her presence while I had to do all of the actual work myself.

She sat on the floor of my suite opposite me, legs crossed and knees touching mine. Her hands were placed in her lap, palms resting against her thighs – the exact same pose she had ordered me into.

"You should be able to feel out the tourniquets, now that you know they are there. The magic that created, and holds them there, will feel foreign and out of place within you." Valdis said, closing her eyes and breathing deeply. "When we find it, you will need to remove it. I like to visualize burning it out – like setting paper alight and watching as the flames turn it to ash. But whatever works for you."

I sighed, closing my eyes, wondering if I was ever going to think conversations like this were ordinary.

It was like I just got used to the idea of one type of power, and another one would throw itself at me, leaving me baffled and horribly behind in the skill department. Everyone else seemed at home with it all, were expecting me to be as good as they were – *better* even. How many times would I feel inadequate and out of place before I could just *woman up*, as Valdis had put it?

"Breathe deep and clear your mind," Valdis instructed calmly. "Let me in so that I can be by your side to guide you."

I took a few deep breaths, trying to clear my head of all sulky thoughts. I could do this – I had to do it. My part of the plan required me to be in complete control of myself. I needed to be free of all outside influences, there could be nothing of anyone else in my magic that they could grab hold of and use against me.

I felt Valdis' presence at the edge of my mind. She felt like a dark, yet playful and sturdy energy full of restlessness and not so hidden sharp bits. I visualized a door in the walls I had built there, and let her in.

"Good," She murmured. Her voice somehow sounding both far off in the distance, and inside of my head all at once. "Let's go hunting."

My mind was like a maze; tunnels, twists, and turns, as well as dead ends and deep, seemingly bottomless caverns. There were patches of dull color mixed through the vivid and bright places, Valdis commenting that doubt, fear, anger, and depression are what would leave my mindscape dark or dreary.

"That isn't what we are looking for, those are all you. Look for patches of color that seem out of place next to the rest." Valdis guided softly.

My inner eye roamed, not entirely sure that I would notice something like what Valdis was asking. I saw large patches of blues and greens, layers upon layers of shades and textures, like blankets folded in a cupboard. The darkest hues were at the bottom, leading all the way up to almost white.

The moment the thought entered my mind, my mindscape rearranged itself so that I was standing in front of the linen cupboard of my old house. The closet itself was distinct, in focus, but the surrounding spaces were blurred – details unclear.

"Nice," Valdis commented, tone more than a little surprised. "It's good that you can control details here. It will make your job so much easier."

A dark patch appeared in the closet, messing up the perfect blue shade variant—doubt making an appearance.

I heard Valdis sigh, could almost see her rolling her eyes in exasperation. She nudged me with her knee. "Focus. Can you see that?"

"The smudge?"

"No, the shades out of order."

I didn't, not at first. But then there it was, hidden in the back—the second pile of blue blankets, gradient all wrong. Once my inner eye saw it, it was impossible to miss, and it drove me crazy.

I worked to fix it, taking my time to get it right. The darkest shades at the bottom were harder to differentiate than the lighter ones, the palest blue felt like air, transcendent, joyful, and carefree. But it was the shade with the least amount of blankets, and I knew that it meant that I rarely ever felt that way in my life.

When I was happy that it was correct, the same as the front row, I still had some blankets left over. They felt more cumbersome than the others, and kind of scratchy to the touch. Valdis didn't interject, letting me work it out for myself. I felt her there with me, a comforting and mischievous presence at my side.

"These don't belong." She declared, stating what my mind was already telling me. "They are not yours, so remove them. You will need to *push* them out as they burn, make your intentions clear."

We watched the blankets burn until there was nothing left, only ash. I imagined a strong wind blowing them away, out the door of my mind, and into nothingness.

"On to the next," Valdis told me, her previous surprise replaced with satisfaction. "You're doing great."

Green, yellow, red – on and on it went. Every color and hue imaginable. I hadn't thought that emotions could be distinguished into so many colors, but Valdis informed me that it wasn't only emotion in this place.

"Anything that makes you who you are is kept in here. Thoughts, beliefs, and convictions. Memories, magic, and the soul – all the good stuff."

"Why did it look different when I..." I paused, remembering what I had done to the Fae in my vision. I could see it all playing out nearby, like a television show. Only, the people were translucent as they acted out their scenes around me.

"The difference is that you *invaded* their mindscape. It looked and felt different to you because it wasn't your space, and Raine and Darragh were fighting to keep you out." Valdis answered calmly. "Even though you had them under your siren-song, the mindscape will always try and keep out intruders – like an internal failsafe."

"So how did Fallon manage to do this to me?"

"You must have let her in at some stage. She couldn't have gotten so deep if you hadn't. And strong emotional states lower the defenses, creating a slightly easier way in – but they would have to be *insanely* strong."

My mindscape was looking better, everything where it should be, and yet, Valdis didn't seem ready for us to leave.

"One more thing before we go," She said, and this time her voice held a tinge of regret. "You aren't going to enjoy this, but it needs to be done."

Panic rose, a dull russet with sparks of the brightest yellow shooting through my mindscape.

"There is a block holding something back, can you see it?" Valdis asked carefully, fully aware of how I was feeling, the sudden flare of anxiety added to the panic at her words. "For your mind to be healthy – for you to be in control of yourself – you need to break it and let whatever is behind there out. It will probably hurt, mentally, *and* physically." She warned.

As she spoke, I could feel it, that build up and pressure. It reminded me of a dam, the water pushing up against a wall. As I thought it, like with the blankets, it appeared.

A gigantic stone wall was almost bursting with the pressure from whatever it was holding back. It rose up above my head – I couldn't see the top – and ran further in both directions than I could even guess at.

Whatever was behind the stones *wanted* to be released, had been trying to get free for a long time. The wall had minute cracks, the stone beginning to degrade in places, a sign that the wall was losing the battle.

"What's behind there?" I breathed, eyes wide as I stood before it.

"Can't you sense it?" Valdis replied, her voice gentle. "It's your fear. The hopelessness and pain you've buried since you lost your family is there too."

"How do I bring it down – what will happen when I do?"

Valdis was silent, her presence fading until I almost couldn't feel her there at all.

"Valdis?"

I reached out my hand, my fingers brushing against the stone softly. The wall groaned, sharp sounding cracks echoing through my mindscape. It started under my fingers, quickly spreading out along the wall in its entirety. I could hear the cracking and rumbling as the stone gave up, crumbling apart and beginning to fall.

A grey liquid began pouring out – slow little trickles at first, but as more and more of the stone gave way, those trickles turned into streams. And then rivers.

"Valdis!" I yelled, heart racing as the wall buckled, in the distance, falling completely. "What do I do?"

The grey liquid, like dirty bathwater, was gushing out now, a giant wave helping to destroy the remaining parts of the wall as it rushed towards me.

"You have to face this part alone." Her voice whispered through my head. "I'll be waiting for you here when you are done."

The water hit me then, knocking me off my feet and dragging me along as it continued its rampage through my mind.

"Valdis!" I screamed or begged – both, I think.

I was drowning in it, the tidal wave of fear and pain.

It filled my lungs, broke my bones, and my heart as it tossed me around. It forced me to replay every single interaction and experience of my life up to now, making me face them all. I couldn't scream, couldn't see anything other than pain and fear and hopelessness.

You have to face this part alone, Valdis had said. But how was I supposed to do that – what was I supposed to do with all of the misery?

My therapist would have told me that I had to face it, too. That I needed to work through it. *To heal is to accept and move forward.* I am who I am because of my past and everything that had happened to me. I had survived so much already – I could deal with this too.

I pictured the water entering an open space, like a large flat field, and leveling out. The wave began to lose momentum as the path it followed widened. It spat me out, leaving me gasping and dizzy.

Water lapped at the edges of the field, —no more raging wave crashing through my mind – more like a placid lake instead.

I could see the worst events of my life playing out below the surface, like evil little fish lurking there. But the urgency and aggression had dimmed, was more manageable now.

And of course, now that I had pictured them that way, there were *actual little fish* in my stupid lake of fear and pain.

Reflections in their scales showed the scenes that they had previously been, making them *terrifying* evil little fish.

Even knowing that everything was happening inside of my head, I still felt shocked when my thoughts altered the course of events.

What now? Was I supposed to get rid of it altogether – like I had with the tourniquets? Or was acknowledging it enough?

"Swim, Sapphira." Valdis' whisper caressed my mind.

I didn't give myself time to think about it, knowing that I would definitely talk myself out of doing it.

"Those damned fish better not eat me," I muttered, walking into the water. "Or I'm going to haunt you forever, Valdis."

"Make it out of there alive, or I'll use your body for one of my creatures." She retorted.

Shit.

My mindscape shuddered alongside me, like an earthquake, creating ripples and little waves in the water and scattered the fish closest to me. The colors around me changed – panic again.

If Valdis' threat didn't make me move, nothing would. I had seen her creatures, and that was not a fate I ever wanted to share.

The lake was freezing, and deeper than I had thought it would be, the cold infiltrating my bones almost instantly. Teeth chattering, I pushed myself to swim, to keep my body moving as fast as I could.

I could see the other side of the lake, and the door that awaited me there. *When had that appeared?*

Something bumped my foot, but I didn't stop, even as my heart raced in my chest. My mindscape body was going numb from the cold, movement getting harder as my energy was sapped away. Each stroke, every *inch* I pushed myself forward, was a marathon of effort.

Another bump, quickly followed by a sharp bite and release. I screamed, kicking my legs wildly, losing momentum and sinking below the surface. The murky water, mixed with my fear, made it almost impossible to see what had grabbed at me. I *hoped* that the fish were the worst things in the lake, and tried as hard as I could, not to picture giant, hungry reptiles lurking under the surface.

I fought to get my head back above water, but those sharp teeth grabbed at my leg again. This time they didn't let go, dragging me down, deeper into the murky depths.

I knew that I had to get my leg free, that I had to get the hell out of the lake. But the teeth were wedged in deep, the creature full of energy, while mine had all but dissipated.

I wondered what would happen to the real me if my mindscape body died here.

Valdis would use it to create a zombie version, and everything would be lost.

Nope. Nope, nope, nope. Not going to happen.

I twisted my body so that I was facing whatever it was that had attached itself to my leg, the thing that had thought I'd make a tasty treat.

Not a crocodile, but one of the evil fish, I was relieved to see through the murk. Using my free leg, I kicked at its head, repeating the movement until the pressure lessened. My lungs were burning, begging for air, as the fish let me go, retreating to a safer distance.

I pushed myself up, aiming for the surface, as more fish swam closer, interested in the commotion and bloodied water.

Voices – and terrifying screams and growls – began murmuring, the sound muffled by the water, but still surprisingly clear.

"Run, baby!"

"It's all your fault."

"...worthless."

"…powerless to stop it."

"You're pathetic."

"Picana, or Maiden?"

The voices were getting louder, more frenzied as I neared the surface, urgency rising to a crescendo. I risked a look beneath me, and instantly wished that I hadn't. A massive school of fish had amassed and were surging up, straight at me, sinister churning shadows rising from the gloom.

I struggled to break the surface, adrenaline pushing me forward. But the fish were faster, teeth cutting into flesh, pain searing through the wounds all over my body.

Finally, air filled my lungs, the lake's shore tantalizingly close. Hope exploded through my core at the sight of it. *So close!*

And then it was gone—the water surrounding me as I was dragged under again.

I could do this, the damned fish would not be the end of me. I would not be afraid, would not let my fear – because that was all the creatures were – drag me down again.

I stopped struggling against them, ignoring the pain and the burning in my lungs and focused instead on the pressure building in my core. It detonated out like a bomb exploding, the water around me pulsating out with such force, the fish thrust backward, stunned.

I surged to the surface again, propelled by the blast, and dragged myself into the shallows, gasping as my lungs tried to fill with the air they craved.

I collapsed onto the bank, lying on my back, staring up at nothing, arm resting across my chest.

I don't know how long I stayed like that before a hand appeared in front of my face—dark, flawless skin, with long blood-red nails.

"About time." Valdis grinned in the way of greeting.

I took her offered hand, and she pulled me to my feet. "Let's get out of here."

Coming back to myself, finding Valdis still sitting across from me in the suite, allowed the adrenaline to fade – leaving behind exhaustion, pain, and deep sadness.

Tears pricked my eyes, and I hurriedly tried to hide my face.

Valdis crawled over to sit beside me, her back against the wall.

"There are many places in our world that you will need to hide your feelings. They will be seen as a weakness, a weapon to use against you." She said, voice soft with understanding and compassion. "But this is not one of them."

I sniffed, wiping away my tears with the back of my hand.

Valdis patted my leg gently. "I can stay with you while you work through this if you like?"

"Why are you so nice to me?" I asked miserably.

How was it that a near-stranger was here with me, showing empathy and understanding, and all of my friends weren't?

Flashes of Fallon, Colte, and Ari crossed my mind, memories of my friends in times that I'd been upset.

Colte's awkward hugs, and pats on the back. His palpable relief when I'd stopped crying.

Ari's tough-love approach, the *suck it up – everything is* okay lectures.

And Fallon. She'd let me talk it out, secretly flooding my system with magical calm.

Valdis sat beside me, offering support, but letting me deal with my issues in my own way.

"What happened to the *woman-up* approach?" I asked, watching as she sighed and rested her head back against the wall, eyes closed.

"This isn't some childish reaction, Sapphira. You're unpacking a literal lifetime of baggage here; the death of your family, monsters and magic, torture, and deception. You literally swam through your fears and made it out the other side. It's a lot to deal with. But you are doing it wonderfully."

I rested my head against her shoulder, feeling her tense for a moment before relaxing again.

"Thank you for being here, Valdis." I murmured, letting the tears fall. "It means a lot."

"I know." She replied. "I never had anyone to help me through – before I came here, that is."

"Will you tell me about it?" I asked gently, sniffling. "I mean if you want to."

Valdis sighed again. "This had better not bite me in the ass."

Her stomach chose that moment to growl in hunger, mine answering just as fiercely. The Necromancer got to her feet, a swift, graceful movement that I doubted I'd ever be able to replicate, and offered me a hand up. "Let's at least eat while I tell you my pitiful story." She said.

I let her help me to my feet, needing to use her arm for balance as I wobbled dizzily. My stomach growled again as we made our way out of the suite and into the stone hall.

"My mother was a Necromancer, like me. She was born in a small village in Africa. Her people were peaceful, considering the magic ability they possessed." Valdis began as we strode towards the kitchen, arm in arm. "She grew up learning to control the power inside of her, learning to release it into animals that had died. Those creatures that she created would protect the village from hungry predators and enemies alike."

Her voice was full of pride but dampened by sadness too. I knew that her mother must be dead, by that tone alone.

"One day, the village was attacked, and most of the villagers were slaughtered. My mother's creatures held off the warriors so that she could escape. She never saw any of her people again."

We'd made it to the kitchen, Valdis pausing her story to rummage through the pantry.

For such a medieval palace, the kitchen was surprisingly modern. It wasn't as fancy or shiny as Hunter's, but it was perfection compared to anything I had ever had. The room itself was small, considering it was in a damned castle.

"Hadrian had this built for me." Valdis smiled, seeing the question on my face before I even asked it. "I'm the only one of his subjects that eats human food, and he quickly tired of having to get it for me. Hence," She spread her arms, gesturing to the space around her. "all mine. Do you want some stew?"

I nodded, taking a seat on the stone island to watch her deft fingers at work. Carrot, celery, pumpkin, potato, and many other vegetables that I didn't recognize, were diced in minutes, added to a pot of water with peanuts, onion, garlic, and chili.

Valdis moved on to chopping chicken as I breathed in the already amazing scents filling the kitchen.

"What happened to your mother?" I asked after the chicken entered the pot too.

"She ran," Valdis said, joining me on the counter. "For weeks she was alone, her creatures all destroyed. My mother knew that she had to get as far from her village as she could – it was the only chance she had to stay alive. Eventually, she was found by my father's people, dazed and almost dead. They took her in and raised her into adulthood as one of their own. They were all Shamans – healers. But somehow never discovered what she was. But my mother was always careful to never reveal where she came from, or what she was, even after she married my father."

"That must have been hard, keeping so much of herself from those around her."

Valdis nodded. "She once told me that she struggled with the decision, but knew that it was for the best – even though she felt like her life was a lie."

"What did she do about her abilities, if she had to keep them hidden?" I asked, watching as Valdis jumped off the counter to stir the stew and add a few spices I didn't recognize.

I knew, even from my limited experience, that the magic inside of you built up until it was unbearable. Power, like energy, always needed release.

"My mother released her magic into the ants and other bugs around the village. Tiny, little releases every day that went unnoticed for years." Valdis informed me, lips tilted upwards. "The villagers had no idea that there was a Necromancer in their midst."

My stomach growled, and my mouth was watering. Valdis' stew smelled heavenly.

"My mother never wanted children, had never wanted to pass on her abilities with the dead to another person. She tried to keep herself from falling pregnant in all of the ways she could think of. But I came along anyway. She was terrified that I would be like her, that my father and his village of healers would discover us. In the end, it was my father who saw when my magic manifested. I was only very young, unaware that what I was doing was meant to be hidden away. I brought back a village child that I had loved after she had died and been buried. This was in a time where Shamans still ate the important organs of the dead, you see, so it was a shocking sight for the villagers to see her risen again. My mother tried to cover for me, admitting what she was to save me. But my father had seen me. There was no hiding the fact that I was a Necromancer like my mother."

Valdis paused, lost in the memory, wooden spoon frozen over the pot of stew. When she resumed the story, her voice was dimmed, void of emotion. "They threw us in the well, hoping that we would drown. My father didn't even try to stop them, even as my mother begged for my life – not her own. The well was shallow, though, so she could stand. She made me sit on her shoulders, keeping me out of the water. They burned the girl, my own skin aflame as her body was destroyed. The villagers cursed us, crying in despair as the girl's soul was lost to them forever.

Mother's bugs brought us tiny scraps of food that kept us alive for the weeks that we were down there, even though each day saw her energy flagging."

The woman before me shook herself, glancing down at the stew as it bubbled on the stove. She narrowed her eyes at it, the wooden spoon stirred through the pot vigorously, as though she could see the villagers in it.

Once, I would have been horrified – *terrified* of what the woman before me had done, what she *could* do. But all I could feel was anguish at what she had gone through at such a young age.

As Valdis gathered bowls from a cupboard below the stove and dished out two of them, I sat quietly, waiting for her to continue. She handed me a spoon and one of the bowls, turned off the stove, and rejoined me on the counter.

"We didn't know that the village elders had sent for the Fae. We didn't know that the Fae had been wiping out all traces of the Necromancers in Africa." Valdis continued as we began eating. The stew was incredible, so full of flavor, but my focus was on the story being told. "When they arrived – an entire legion of Fae warriors – my mother and I were raised from the well and placed in chains. She was given an ultimatum: go with the Fae and produce creatures for their armies, or die in the dirt right there. My mother, defiantly, told them that she would never create anything that would be used for war. So they slit her throat and left her to die in a puddle of blood and dirt, the villagers cheering as she died.

They never gave me a choice. I was dragged behind the Fae warriors, and taken into Faerie, and given over to a young Kamilla. I grew up under the care of Darragh and Raine."

We both shuddered, the stew was forgotten in the horror of the revelation given. And the memories that came with it.

"It was decades before Hadrian was called to court – his realm having recently fallen under Kamilla's might. But he didn't come alone. The previous *Goddess Incarnate* was with him." Valdis paused, smiling at me. "Your suite was hers once, did you know?"

I shook my head in amazement.

"Hadrian and Theresa informed the Fae Queen that my magic belonged in the City of Darkness, where it would be more substantial in strength and of more value to her goals. She reluctantly let me go, the biggest mistake she could ever have made, and I came with them here. I've been here ever since, grateful to my King, and plotting my revenge on the Fae." Valdis finished her story matter of factly, getting off the bench and placing her now empty bowl in the sink. "And now we are even, you know all about me and my pitiful life, and I know yours."

I was in awe of this woman, I realized. She had survived everything that had been thrown at her and was still functional.

"How did you manage to get past all of that?" I asked, placing my bowl in her waiting hands.

Valdis shrugged, turning back to the sink. "I worked through all of my baggage with Theresa and Hadrian. They became the family I needed, and I would have done anything for them – I still would."

"What happened to your father and his people?"

"Hadrian and Theresa took me back there, and I killed them all. They were my creatures for many years before I destroyed them." Another emotionless reply. "Shamans are as rare now as Necromancers are. It is their turn to hide."

Oh my.

"And Theresa?" I wanted to know. "What happened to her?"

"Died in battle," Valdis stated, continuing to clean up after our meal. "We've been waiting for her return – and now here you are."

"I'm not her," I said softly. "I'm not Theresa."

"Obviously." Valdis snorted, turning to face me again. "But you could probably help Hadrian and the other Soul Eaters like she did."

"What do you mean?" I frowned. "I've already agreed to help you all."

"With the Fae problem, yes," Valdis said, nodding. "But, there is something that Hadrian hasn't asked you, no matter how much I pester him about it."

I stared at her, waiting for her to continue.

"Theresa could limit the effects of the geas placed on Hadrian by the Queen. The Goddess' magic allowed him to bypass the geas's limitations and gain more sustenance from the souls he ate, slowed the rot in him, giving him back the majority of his power. Without her, he has been unable to stand against Kamilla as he should."

"How did she do it?" I breathed, eyes wide. The amount of power and knowledge that Theresa must have possessed was awe-inspiring. Even with the memories from the Fae – one of which was a master healer – I had no idea where I could even *start* to do what Theresa had done.

"I don't know," Valdis replied sadly. "Hadrian doesn't even know the full extent of it. I've been scouring the libraries in search of answers, but nothing so far. Theresa used to keep journals, but no one has seen them since she died." She added. "I think they were hidden in the suite, but I've torn that place apart countless times, and couldn't find them."

I'd find them. I vowed silently. And I'd do whatever it was that Theresa had done to give Hadrian the strength he needed

– the *advantage* he needed to defeat the bitch Fae Queen. I felt something settle inside of me, a conviction – a feeling of *truth* to my vow. The type of magical pact that could not be undone or withdrawn. It held me to my word, whispering of the consequences of trying to back out now. But I had no intention of turning away from this vow, not with so much at stake. I didn't fight it as it settled in; instead, I welcomed it, offered it a place over my heart.

Valdis seemed to see the decision I'd made on my face, to feel the truth in the air. She grinned wickedly, eyes losing the haunted glaze her story had given them. "Kamilla won't know what hit her with you on our side. How can she have even a *chance* now that you have so much power?"

I returned the smile, a mirror of the one the Necromancer still held on her red lips. "She *never* stood a chance."

I left Valdis in her kitchen and wandered back to the suite to start my search. I was supposed to be training with Mora, but she hadn't summoned me – she was probably still busy planning with Hadrian.

I'd use my free time to find Theresa's journals and work with Valdis learning how to fight with knives. She'd agreed to teach me when I'd asked her, claiming that it was a skill everyone should have. The Necromancer would join me in the suite after checking on her latest group of creatures.

I was determined to have something to show her by the time she arrived, whether that was the journals themselves, or a place to search that she hadn't already done so.

Looking around the spacious rooms, though, I had to admit that there weren't that many places that they could be.

The bedroom was furnished in a minimalistic fashion – a king-sized bed, and two nightstands. The walls were stone, like the rest of the palace, and were painted in a deep blue. The floors, too, were stone and covered with rugs to keep the chill down.

I could see no prominent place there that books could be hidden. I checked the nightstands anyway, the mattress too. I felt along the walls, searching for loose stones, but came up empty.

The balcony had the same results, as did the bathroom. And the sitting room.

The only room left was the gigantic walk-in closet, and that was where Valdis found me, digging through the jackets left behind by Theresa.

"What are you doing?" She asked me from the doorway, hands on her hips.

"Looking for a hidey-hole," I stated, trying to unwrap myself from the fur coat that had grabbed me from its hook. "But this monstrous thing is trying to kill me."

Valdis laughed, stepping into the closet to join me. "That was Theresa's favorite coat. She told me that she thought it had a mind of its own."

"I can believe that." I huffed, managing to extract myself and step away from it. "It is beautiful, but I don't do fur."

I tried to push it back into place, between two similar coats, and my hand fell on something unyielding in the liner around the collar.

"What is that?" I wondered out loud. My fingers ran over the spot again, feeling something out of place.

Valdis moved closer, looking over my shoulder. "There's something sewn in there." She breathed. "Look at the stitching."

I stepped back, gesturing her forward at the same time. "You should do it."

Valdis' eyes never left the coat, even as she smiled her thanks. "I've searched this room countless times, and not once did I see this."

She ran her fingers over the collar of her friend's favorite coat, finding the hidden treasure. Quick as a flash, she tore the lining open, whispering *Sorry* to the coat – or her dead friend, I couldn't be sure.

"It's a key." She told me, holding it up in the flickering candlelight.

We stared at it as if it would reveal all of its secrets if only we would keep our gaze on it.

It was old, even I could see that—an intricately designed bronze key, what looked like vines creeping up the sides.

"What does it unlock?" I asked, taking it from her hand as Valdis passed it to me. It was heavy – surprisingly so for something as small as it was. It sat in the palm of my hand, the same length as my pinky finger.

"I have no idea," Valdis replied, eyes still intent on our find. "But it has to be important, or why would Theresa have hidden it there?"

I couldn't imagine wearing the coat with the key stitched into the collar. It must have been utterly uncomfortable. But Valdis had said that it was the Goddess' favorite. Perhaps we had just discovered why.

"That key belongs in the greenhouse." The gravelly voice made both Valdis and I jump and look around guiltily as if we had been caught doing something wrong.

Hadrian was leaning against the door, eye on the key, and lips compressed. "Valdis put it back where it belongs, and get to work. Sapphira, Mora is waiting for you. I suggest you don't keep her waiting."

Valdis took the key back, doing as her King said without another word, throwing me a regretful look over her shoulder before she disappeared.

Hadrian moved to let her pass and turned back to me, eyebrows raised when I didn't move.

"You're not even curious to know why that key was there?" I asked.

"It seems trivial in comparison to what else is going on, wouldn't you agree?" The Soul Eater's tone was reproachful, and he gestured for me to exit the closet.

I did, turning to him as he gently closed the door. "What if whatever that key unlocks can help us?"

"Doubtful, Sapphira." He said. "The only thing that can help us is *us*. Follow the plan. Go see Mora, before she sends you nightmares to curdle your blood."

I sighed, resigned to doing as I was told. I only hoped that Valdis was curious enough to investigate the greenhouse – hopefully, the key led her to find the answer to where the journals had gone.

In the meantime, I'd go to Mora and learn control over fear – and I hoped that my time swimming through it had taught me something useful.

The Night Hag looked different in person, less of a ghost, and more like a physical being. Her patience – or lack of – was the same as it had been in my vision.

"You're late."

"Sorry, Mora." I started, smiling apologetically. "I got held up."

"I don't care, my time is precious, Sapphira. Be here on time, or I will no longer be at your service – no matter what the King says, or who you claim to be."

"You don't believe that I'm the Goddess?" I asked, eyes wide in surprise as she shook her head.

"Of course not!" She exclaimed indignantly. "Theresa was my friend, and I would know her soul anywhere – as should Hadrian. I do not sense her in you at all – similar magic, perhaps, but you are not her. Therefore, you must be nothing but a pretender."

"What am I, if not the Goddess?"

The Night Hag grunted, waving the question away. "Enough chatter, you've wasted enough of my time. Get to work."

Without any more warning than that, Mora thrust herself into my head, creating the nightmare that I would need to escape.

Raine's image shimmered into being, his knife in hand.

And I ran.

Chapter Sixteen

I ended up on the floor at Mora's feet, panting and dripping in sweat.

"Well…"She started, staring down at me in surprise."That's a first."

A giggle escaped my lips, a desperate sound, and I grabbed at my side as it cramped. I'd done it. I faced my worst fear, and I'd killed him… *eventually*. I'd been surprised that it had been *Raine* again, and not Darragh honestly.

"It seems as though you don't really require my talents after all," Mora added, motioning for me to get to my feet. "You can tell the King that I'm done with you."

"Are you serious?" I stammered. "That's it?"

"What did you expect?" She snapped, turning to her workstation. "I work in fear and doubt, and you have managed to master the worst of yours."

"This seems too easy," I muttered, shaking my head. Was I in another vision? Was this part of Mora's test?

"Too easy?" She exclaimed, spinning to face me again, her eyes flashing with outrage. "You think my work is *too easy*?"

"No!" I cried desperately, hands out in front of me in a non-aggressive gesture, as the lights flickered, and the Night Hag grew in size. She was towering above me, black fog whirling around her. The transformation happened in the blink of an eye. "I didn't mean that your work is easy – just that it seemed unreal that I could have mastered my fear so soon!"

"I smell the Necromancer on you. Has our Valdis been playing in your head, Pretender?"

"She helped me remove outside magic, as your King commanded, nothing more."

In another blink of an eye, the Night Hag was back to her original size, the fog gone, as if it had never existed.

Mora clicked her tongue, shaking her head. "*Nothing more*, you say. A foolish girl you are, Sapphira. Valdis helped you master yourself quicker than I ever could."

I shook my head, unable to stop the smile that wormed its way across my face. At least things were starting to go my way – I wasn't as hopeless as I was before, and my new friend was to thank for it.

"Go, get out of my face." Mora ushered me out of her training room. "There are plenty of other people in this city that you can annoy, go find one of them."

"Like who?" I asked, letting her push me towards the door. "What am I supposed to learn now?"

"Learn something you don't already know – like combat skills. You can't fight for shit." She said matter of factly, before slamming the door in my face.

"She said that to me once, almost word for word."

I spun to face the owner of the voice that carried across the street.

Valdis sat with her back against the building there – a skyscraper made of glass, surrounded by wooden hut-like buildings.

She had changed into a white tank top and black pants as if she was going jogging. Her hair was pulled back, and she wore no makeup – not that she needed any, her dark skin was flawless.

I joined her, barely noticing that the street was empty of all other inhabitants, and raised my eyebrows. "I can't imagine you being bad at anything."

"I was young and untrained once too, Sapphira." The Necromancer replied, getting to her feet. "I'm supposed to train you in all things battle-related. But, I thought we could go for a jog via the greenhouse first, since you had shown an interest in it earlier?"

I grinned, taking her hint. "Well, I do need to work on my stamina. A run sounds great, and I do love plants and all things greenhouse related."

"Excellent!" She exclaimed, a pile of clothes appearing in her hands. "Change into this, and we can get started. The view there is definitely *journal-worthy*."

It took me longer than I cared to admit to get into any sort of rhythm while we ran. And I do mean *ran* – Valdis set a pace that was in no way the relaxed jog I had envisioned.

I was glad that she had given me the tank top and tracksuit pants to change into, the skirt I had been wearing before would have been horrid to run in.

Once I had found my groove, though, I found that I enjoyed it. I had never been a runner before, but it was a release that I could definitely get used to.

We didn't talk as we made our way through the seemingly deserted city, snaking our way through the streets. The only sounds were our feet pounding the cobblestones, and our breathing.

I let my mind wander, putting myself on autopilot as I followed Valdis. I thought about what my friends would think of the City of Darkness. And of what they were all doing now. I knew that I would have to check in with them soon, but I found myself putting it off for as long as I could.

I actually enjoyed being here, having time to slow down and discover myself. I didn't want to rush back into the fray – always on the move, always in danger.

The City of Darkness, and Hunter's Villa – vision or not – had been the only two places where time seemed to slow since all of this had started. Valdis and Hunter had fast become my two favorite people to be around. Their fun, calming nature was soothing to the soul.

"We're here," Valdis announced, coming to a stop in front of a large, nondescript brown warehouse, and pulling me back to reality. "Come on, I'll show you my favorite plants."

She opened a roller door, wincing as it shrieked from lack of use, and ushered me inside.

I looked around curiously as another shriek echoed around, Valdis closing the door behind us.

The entire warehouse was full to the brim with all kinds of trees, vines, and flowers. They covered the countless shelves that ran in rows across the floor and climbed the walls all the way to the roof.

"This was Theresa's domain while she was alive," Valdis informed me softly as she came to stand beside me. "She loved this stuff more than anything. I couldn't bear to see it die after she did."

I wondered at how many years Valdis had been coming here, tending to her dead friend's garden. Did Hadrian know?

I wondered, too, at the relationship between the King and the previous Goddess. The way that everyone spoke of her here, I knew that she was adored. But Valdis made it sound like there was more to it – more to *Hadrian and Theresa* than just friendship and strategic alliance.

Valdis held out her hand, the key we had found earlier sat in her palm. She didn't look at me, her eyes roaming the expanse before us. "Hadrian said that the key belongs here, let's find out *where* exactly." She pointed down the center row of the jungle. "I'll take the right side, you take the left. Holler if you find anything."

We got to work, carefully moving the pots and looking underneath them, scouring the floor and walls for any sign of a lock, in which the little key would fit.

It seemed to take hours just to reach the end of one *side* of the first *row*. We could be here for days and still not find anything.

I could tell that Valdis was just as frustrated, it seemed to pour out of her in waves.

"There has to be something here!" She screamed, slamming down the pot she had been looking under. "Why would she have taken the time to hide the damned key so well if it didn't mean anything!"

"You're right, Valdis," I said, continuing the search. "We'll keep searching until we've found whatever it was she was hiding here. It had to have been important, so we won't give up."

She grunted but kept looking. I could hear that the frustration had turned into something else just by the sounds that made their way over to me – a pot slam, and a sniff. Slam, sob. Slam, sniff. On and on it went.

There had to be an easier way to do this, though, I thought, turning slowly and letting my eyes wander. *If I was Theresa, where would I hide something important?*

"Valdis?" I called softly. "What abilities did Theresa have?"

"She could open portals and travel through the realms, and turn her emotions into weapons. She could revive the recently dead – oh, and *she could fly as though she had wings*." As she spoke, realization dawned on Valdis' face. Her eyes were drawn upwards towards the ceiling, towards what I had already discovered.

There, in the center of the roof, was a hive of spiky vines. They wrapped themselves tightly around something that glowed faintly. I'd mistaken it as a light source at first, but something about it kept drawing my attention.

"How the hell do we get up there?" She asked. "I can't see a way up – unless you, too, can fly?"

I shook my head, searching for something that could help, but coming up empty. "Can you make out what it is?"

Valdis clambered up onto the top of one of the shelves, head tilted back to look at the vines and their guarded prize. "I think it's a chest. Sapphira, it could be the journals."

Her excitement was evident – and catching.

We tried climbing the walls, but couldn't get high enough to swing across.

We tried throwing pots at the vines in the hope that they would drop the chest, but they only tightened around it whenever the pots got close enough.

Valdis even tried finding the source of the vines and hacking at them with her knives. The thorns cut through more of her skin than she managed to cut through them.

I attempted throwing my emotional daggers, but they disintegrated on contact.

We couldn't get near the chest, much to the chagrin of Valdis, but we made a plan to return tomorrow and try again.

In the meantime, Valdis wanted to blow off some steam – and that was supposed to involve sparring. With me. And no magic.

I was so screwed.

Hadrian found us in my suite hours later, lying on the floor in a sweaty heap.

"I came to check on you, since you both failed to make the meeting earlier." He reprimanded softly. "Where have you been?"

"Valdis called it sparring," I groaned, unable to move my limbs to place the last word in quotation marks with my fingers where they belonged. "Hadrian, I think your Second tried to kill me."

"If I had, you'd be dead." Valdis retorted, sitting up and wrapping her arms around her knees as she pulled them to her chest.

"You missed a briefing about the impending battle for our realm… because you were *sparring*?" Hadrian repeated slowly, tone deceptively calm.

Valdis shrugged, flipping her black braid over her shoulder. "I thought that you wanted Sapphira to be able to take care of herself in a fight. She has a better chance now than she had a few hours ago."

I froze, waiting for the explosion I was sure was about to happen. But Hadrian only smiled, the hole in his cheek warping around the rotting tissue as he did.

"The time for your defiant games is over, little one." He told her, something akin to love in his gravelly voice. "The False Queen comes tomorrow. Get rid of your new pets before she arrives."

"I haven't even started on them yet, Hadrian. It would be a waste to end them so quickly."

"That wasn't a request, Valdis."

My gaze shot from the King as I sat up, eyes searching Valdis' face in surprise and apprehension. I knew who they were talking about, there was no doubt in my mind.

Raine and Darragh were here, and they were *still alive*.

"What happened to your hair, Sapphira?" Hadrian asked before I could lose my mind over the fact that the Fae weren't dead.

"There was a little accident involving a sword," Valdis smirked as I ran my fingers through my now shorter blonde hair. Before the sparring match, it had reached below my waist, and now it sat just below my shoulders.

"I like it." Valdis put in, seeing the uncertainty in my eyes. "Very battle chic."

I made a rude gesture with my hand that Valdis laughed off.

Hadrian cleared his throat, impatiently demanding attention.

"I will do as you command, my King." She told him. "Sapphira and I will be ready for when she arrives. Just send a messenger for us, and we will make our entrance and get *your* games started."

The Soul Eater nodded, leaving as quietly as he had arrived.

I opened my mouth – to say *what* I had no idea, probably something prissy or whiny. But Valdis jumped to her feet, suddenly full of energy as she smiled down at me.

"Do you want to kill a Fae?" She sang, eyes alight with sadistic joy. "You can choose which one…"

She let the question hang in the air, seeing the indecision in my face. I knew that I had already faced what had happened to me, had healed what I could. But the thought of seeing Raine and Darragh again made my skin prickle with dread. My heart pounded in my chest, and I felt those evil little fish under the murky lake in my mindscape, sending ripples across the surface.

I swallowed the lump in my throat.

I'd already killed them once. Granted, it had been in a vision and not real, but still. It totally counted. Valdis had spent years with the vile things, I couldn't even imagine the treatments she had to have endured.

I could have found out if I really wanted to. I knew that the Fae's time with Valdis was locked inside the filing cabinets full of their memories in my head. But I wouldn't look. She deserved the respect of not having those moments dragged out for others to see.

"They were my gift to you," I reminded her, forcing a smile. "You have some fun, make them suffer."

She grinned, her whole face lighting up, even as her eyes gleamed with mischief. "Oh, I plan on it."

"I'm going to bed, wake me up when it's time to get ready for the visit."

Valdis nodded, all but skipping out of the suite, like a kid on the way to the candy store.

I had hoped that I would fall asleep as soon as my head hit the pillows. But my mind was racing, going over not only what I had learned since coming back here, but what I had to help Hadrian and Valdis accomplish when Kamilla came too. It seemed that my pause, the downtime I had been enjoying, was coming to an end.

My body – cooled now after the sparring I had done, and the running before that, was beginning to ache. And stunk of stale sweat, which filled my nose every time I moved. I needed a bath. Badly.

I sighed, got off the bed, and headed to the bathroom.

While I ran the bath, I stared at myself in the large mirror that adorned the wall.

I'd lost weight – I was still curvy, and my body was toned in a way it had never been before. My eyes were sharper, more cynical of the world.

I ran my fingers through my hair, surprised at how straight the cut was, considering it had been hacked off with a sword.

I had no one to blame but myself for that little accident. I'd had my hair in a braid, and being an absolute beginner, had swung the blade right through it while trying to follow along with the movements Valdis had instructed I do. The whole bottom half of my hair had landed on the floor to the sound of her laughter.

I removed my clothes, turning to the bath, which was half full of steaming water. I stepped in, and sighed with contentment, aches already improving.

As I turned off the taps, lowering myself so that everything below my neck was underwater, the bracelet on my wrist caught my eye. One of the twelve charms, the little silver conch shell, seemed to be glowing faintly.

"Hello, little guy," I murmured, lifting my arm closer so that I could get a better look at the shell. "What are you doing?"

I felt silly, talking to a charm, especially since it wasn't doing anything anymore. It was the same little shell that had sat against my skin since Lyra had given it to me. No more glow.

I shrugged, lowering my arm again, chalking it up to being tired.

But once the bracelet was underwater again, the shell resumed it's faint glowing.

Fascinating.

The longer I looked at it, the brighter the glow became, until it was so bright I had to look away. I lifted my arm out of the water for good measure, glad to see that the glowing had ceased again.

"What are you trying to tell me?" I asked it, blinking the afterglow away.

"Do you really expect a piece of silver to answer you?"

I thought I was above squealing and acting like an idiot, but apparently, I was wrong. I flopped around like a fish, water displaced and splashing onto the floor as I reacted to the voice floating through the air.

"Calm, Sapphira. I mean you no harm." It was a female voice, her tone sweet and unassuming. But, as I searched the bathroom, I could see no one.

"Who are you?" I demanded. "*Where* are you?"

The conch shell charm burned bright again – not just with luminosity, but heat as well. I cursed, thrusting my wrist back into the water to keep it from burning. The light exploded outwards, filling the bathroom like it held a sun inside it.

As the light extinguished, gone as quickly as it had appeared, and my eyesight returned, I saw a woman sitting on the edge of the bath, delicate fingers playing in the water near my feet.

She was blonde, hair almost pure white that curled around her face and over her shoulders in soft waves. When she leaned down, closer to the water, the ends of that hair stopped inches from the surface. If she's been standing, it would have come to a stop below her waist.

The woman was skinny, almost painfully so. The slip of a dress she wore did nothing to hide the smallness of her. I felt that if I reached out to touch her, she would break.

The dress itself reminded me of the long, flowing Grecian style, material so thin it was almost translucent.

Large blue eyes dominated her petite face, pink lips smiled softly as she waited for me to finish my assessment.

I tried to cover myself, embarrassed by my nakedness in another's presence.

"I am Enyo." She said. "And I was wondering how long it would take you to summon me, Sapphira Dawn."

"I didn't summon you," I stated, eyes darting towards the pile of towels on the basin behind her. "I wouldn't even know *how*."

"You did, indeed, summon me here. The charm you wear calls to me when submerged." Enyo calmly replied, removing her fingers from the water and standing up. She took the few steps from the bath to the basin and returned with the towels. "I have worked alongside those of your bloodline many times throughout history, and now it is your turn."

"What are you talking about?" I snapped, snatching a towel and awkwardly standing in the bath while trying to wrap it around myself. Was she delusional?

I felt my rage stirring inside of me, why was it that I couldn't have any alone time? Why did people think that it was okay to invade my space all of the time?

The woman let out a long-suffering sigh. "Mortals." She muttered. She watched as I shuffled towards the bathroom door, towel tightly wound around my still dripping body. "You were supposed to be preparing for the war, and instead,

I find you unprepared and wasting time. Did you not take your grandmother's words to heart?"

"My *grandmother*?" I froze in the doorway, eyes narrowed. "Are you sure you're talking to the right person here, Lady? I don't have a grandmother."

"We don't have much time left, and honestly, I'm disappointed in your progress." She continued as if I hadn't spoken. "You have mere days left before the first battle, and at this rate, you will not live to see the second."

"Woah, time out," I demanded, palms up in front of me. "You need to explain yourself here – start at the beginning. *What the hell are you talking about?*"

She was instantly in front of me, inches from my face, her delicate hands covering my ears. "See, hear, and *know* the truth."

I was pulled from my body, thrown through space and time. I watched scenes flash around me – images of battles and people long past.

Enyo was there – a muscular warrior Goddess in armor, standing proudly beside a God, looking down on a human village.

"*These savages could never topple us – we were born to rule them all.*" The male sneered.

"*They have the right to decide for themselves.*" Enyo disagreed. "*A chance to live their lives in peace. I'm tired of war, aren't you?*"

"*A wager then, Sister, a new game between us.*" The God laughed coldly. "*I will work on warping and destroying them, and you endeavor to get them to be more than the sniveling worms they are. Beat me, and your precious creatures can endure. Lose, and I will wage such destruction their like has never seen – a war I will revel in for eternity.*"

A push forward in time – And Enyo, in her armor, full of savage bloodlust. She tore through army after army on battlefields thick with blood, eyes blazing as she drew closer to her shining brother.

The scene changed – a later period in time, another battlefield. Enyo's brother was standing above her, sword at her throat. *"You cannot win this game, Enyo. It will destroy you. Admit defeat, or die."*

Another flash forward – a young Lyra, frowning down at a scroll in her hands. *"If I do this, my bloodline is cursed."*

"If you don't," Enyo told her sadly. *"The realms are lost. Ares will tear them apart."*

Flash forward again – Hadrian, before his face was destroyed, and a beautiful woman – Theresa – standing together before the diminished Enyo. *"It has to be now, we cannot wait any longer. I am sorry, Theresa, but it must be you."*

"I will do it. I am sorry for what this means for you, Hadrian. I only hope that she works it out quickly. Promise me that you will help her."

"I promise, My love. I will do what is needed when the time comes."

Flash – Ari kneeling at Enyo's feet, tears in her eyes. Hunter beside his sister. *"Please, don't make me do this. There has to be another way."*

"You must, Ari. Put your personal feelings aside, they cannot get in the way. The balance must be restored – and we will need them before the end. We will need them all."

Enyo released me, taking a step back as I was flung back to my own body. We were both panting at the exertion of what she had shown me.

"You've been using us all like pieces in a game?" I hissed, furious that the Gods – actual gods! – thought so little of mortals. How many lives had they toyed with for their own amusement? How much torment and misery inflicted throughout history was because of them?

Enyo's eyes were full of sadness and defeat. "I am losing the game, Sapphira. And I cannot allow that. You are my final play at victory against my brother. You must be ready."

"I am not a pawn in your game!" I screamed, my rage exploding out of me, swirling angrily through the air, sharp as knives.

"You are the result of eons of careful manoeuvering on a gameboard made by the Gods, Sapphira, *my final gambit*. You are the world's last hope of surviving Ares and his insatiable appetite for death and destruction." Enyo opposed sorrowfully. "I do not have the strength in me to keep playing."

"What was your plan here?" I sneered. "What was all your *manoeuvering* for me supposed to accomplish? What do you expect me to be able to do?"

I was screaming again, but I didn't care. The swirling vortex of rage kept growing in size and speed. Enyo stood against it, seemingly unbothered.

"You're the key to victory. Without you, all realms fall." She stated, eyes on mine. "You will lead your allies in battle, and diminish Ares and his players."

"No."

"You don't have a choice." Enyo was beginning to fade out, leaving me when I'd just learned the truth. What little strength she'd had before, now sapped. "Work harder while you still can, Sapphira. Or millions of lives ended for nothing – *billions* more will end because you weren't good enough."

I was left alone in the bathroom, shivering from both the cold and her departing comment.

"Fuck the Gods." I hissed, daring them to strike me down.

I dressed, pulling my rage back inside of me, and went searching for Valdis, hoping she hadn't finished with the Fae before I got there.

I felt the sparks of her magic before I'd even reached the door to her dungeons. I sent out a little pulse of my own as if to say *Can I play too?*

The Necromancer opened the door with a grin. "I knew you'd change your mind."

Her hair was pulled back in a top knot, the leathers she wore covered in blood. Valdis' smile faded as she took me in. "What is it, what's wrong?"

I offered her my hands, offered to show her what had put me in such a foul mood.

Frowning, she placed her face between them, eyes finding mine.

I let the memories flow over to her, watching those beautifully mischievous eyes fill with disbelief.

"No, it isn't possible." She whispered, shaking her head slowly when it was over. "We need to talk to Hadrian – make him tell us what the hell is really going on." She made to leave, to confront her King.

"Wait." I grabbed her arm, stopping her before she could go any further.

I could see that she was hurt by his secrecy. The fact that both Hadrian and Theresa had kept this from her. I could see too, some of the same questions running through her mind. How much did Hadrian and Theresa know? What, exactly, had been their parts to play in where things had ended up?

She yanked out of my grasp, hissing. "Why?"

I gestured into the room behind her, to the Fae waiting to die. "Their lives are yours, but I need their magic. Then, we can talk to Hadrian about Gods and deception."

We found Hadrian in the throne room, preparing for Kamilla's visit. Which, by the harried movements of the people scurrying around, was imminent.

His eye narrowed, seeing our disheveled, blood-splattered selves. "Tell me you discarded your playthings properly – no traces left?"

"Of course." Valdis snapped. "I know how to do my job."

Technically, *we* had disposed of the bodies. We'd left them in the woods near the *Banríon Cruach,* an anonymous present – and warning to the Queen.

"Good, then you should be getting ready. The game will start soon."

"We need to talk about another *game* first." Valdis spat, arms crossed over her chest. "Sapphira show him."

Hadrian's eye widened. Whether, at the Necromancer's tone, my waiting hands, or the knowledge of what she was hinting at, I wasn't sure.

"I beg your pardon?" Hadrian's voice was deceptively calm, but even I could sense the undercurrent of anger there. "Are you defying an order from your King?"

The room seemed to grow colder as the people close enough to overhear her froze. I doubted that anyone spoke to the King like that, not even his Second.

Hadrian was not someone that you defied. Not if you were one of his subjects, and definitely not in his own domain.

"Show him!" Valdis snarled at me, eyes flashing. "Now!"

"I will not indulge your tantrum, Valdis. You will do as I command, or face the punishment." His words were like ice, a King that allowed no dispute to his power. There was an almost imploring look in his eye as he stared her down, though. A private, silent plea to just *wait*, to have this conversation somewhere more secluded.

Short of jumping him, I could do nothing. So I just stood there, waiting for them to sort it out themselves.

Valdis was a seething storm, ready to explode and flatten everything in her path. She wasn't thinking clearly enough to pick up on the supplication Hadrian was offering her.

She opened her mouth to speak, but Hadrian was there, hand on her throat. He had moved so fast, I hadn't seen it. Judging by the looks from his people, they hadn't either.

"Speak against my orders again, and I will snap your neck." He growled through gritted teeth.

Some of the fight left her then, the realization of how close she had come to doing something utterly foolish. Hadrian, who had been looking for it, released her.

"You will take Sapphira to her suite and get ready as I have ordered."

"Yes, my King." Valdis murmured, bowing her head in deference. "I am yours to command."

His gaze didn't leave her until we had left the room.

I didn't think I had taken a single breath through the entire conflict, and gratefully did so as we walked through the halls towards the suite. Valdis was silent the whole way, seething.

"I'm sorry, Valdis," I said, sincerity clear in my tone, as she slammed the door to the suite behind her.

"I almost lost control of my creatures, Sapphira." She admitted in horror, hugging herself. "I was that angry, my magic raised them all. I've never been that close to ruining everything before. Never."

I swallowed the lump in my throat, afraid to speak in case I said the wrong thing.

Valdis shook herself, blinking to clear the tears that threatened to fall. "It's what happened to Theresa." She continued. "She meant the world to me, and he told me she had died in battle. Now, I think that was a lie. *And he knew about it.*"

Valdis moved into the bedroom, her magic calling for her creatures as she did.

Between one step and the next, Valdis changed from the bloodied leathers into a long silver dress. The one I'd *seen* her wear for this meeting, with material that rippled around her body like liquid mercury.

"Let's just get through this," I said finally, a little jealous of that dress. "And then he can explain himself."

The horrid red gown from my vision appeared in Valdis' hands, and she smirked at me. "I spent a few days looking for this dress. Thanks for the inspiration."

I glared at her. And then at the dress. "You know, I think I hate you today."

She laughed. "I know, that was what inspired me."

"Glad I could be of service to your amusement." I sighed, reaching for the dress.

The meeting with Kamilla went almost identically to the one I'd already *seen*.

The only difference was that this time, I felt sorry for the Fae that would suffer at her hand in her search for the magic I held within myself.

Hadrian met me in the dining room, looking resigned to the argument he would no doubt be having with Valdis soon.

I shared the memories of my encounter with Enyo with him, feeling him tense as he realized why his Second had been so furious.

"I see." He said slowly after I had released him. "I was wondering when this would come to light. Where is Valdis now?"

I shrugged, adjusting the dress and taking my seat. "She told me that she had to collect something and would meet us here."

"How did she seem when she left you?"

"She feels betrayed, Hadrian. I don't think she understands why you kept all of this from her." I shrugged again. "I don't blame her. I think it's time you came clean, don't you?"

"Are you chastising me?" He demanded, tone full of reproach. "You think you know better than I?"

I held my hands up in surrender. "I don't want to fight. I just want the truth. To understand, that's all."

Valdis breezed in then, skin covered in scratches and blood. Her dress was in tatters, but it was what she held in her hands that caused Hadrian to rise from the table, his chair falling backward and hitting the floor with a bang.

My heart hammered in my throat as she slammed her treasure onto the table, eyes triumphant.

The chest from the Greenhouse.

It was still faintly glowing, the wood covered in intricate carvings of strange symbols and patterns.

"How did you get that down?" I breathed, my eyes wide as I took it in.

"I climbed onto the roof from the outside and sent my creatures in to distract the vines. I broke one of the skylights and swung across to cut the chest loose, and brought it straight here."

Hadrian and I watched as Valdis pulled the key from her cleavage and placed it in the lock on the front of the box.

It clicked open, and Hadrian held his breath as Valdis opened the lid. I leaned forward to see inside, hoping that whatever was in there would give Valdis the answers she sought. Hoping that the contents of the chest would be the answer to the questions we *all* sought.

Valdis let out a little laugh in victory, reached inside, and pulled out a journal.

It was thick, bound in leather, and tied closed with purple ribbon.

It's treasure no longer inside, the chest stopped glowing, the patterns shifting – morphing together until only one carving remained.

A single word, a name. Theresa.

"That journal will answer all of your questions about what happened to her, but it will not bring you any comfort," Hadrian warned Valdis. "It can never bring her back to you."

Valdis ignored him, placing the journal on the table, running her hands over the leather softly, reverently.

This was a moment that I didn't need to be a part of, I decided suddenly, Valdis needed this for herself.

And if she found anything that would be useful to me, she could let me know.

I didn't even think she noticed when I got up and left the room, so intent on the journal.

Hadrian joined me moments later, frowning. "Why did she go after it?"

"For you. And for Theresa."

"So now you know that the last *Goddess* was mine." He said, changing the subject a little. "Does that make you uncomfortable?"

"Why would it?" I asked, eyebrows raised. "I'd guessed at it a while ago, but it has nothing to do with me. Who you love is your business."

"Fair enough."

"Tell me what your part to play in all of this is." I smiled to lessen the demand in my voice. "How did you and Theresa get mixed up with Enyo?"

"Theresa was a Goddess – same as Enyo. Though the game is between Ares and Enyo, all other Gods and Goddesses in existence have parts to play – the outcome will affect them too.

Theresa's part was more significant than some, having power over reincarnation, and the magic of her latest incarnate.

She had to halt the cycle, keeping the mortal players Ares favored from coming back for the final battle. But it didn't work the way it should have, her magic was already stretched thin because she was helping me." Hadrian paused, taking a few deep breaths to steady himself. "In her final moments, she had to choose – her part in the game, or the life of the one she loved."

"She chose you." I breathed, taken in by the story, *knowing* that it must have been the way things had gone.

"She chose wrong." Hadrian corrected. "Theresa should have done her job. She would still be here if she had."

"But you wouldn't be," I argued.

"You don't understand yet, do you?" The Soul Eater asked softly. "She failed in stopping Ares' favorite players from returning to this cycle. His strongest allies – the ones that *you* now have to face – are all here, preparing to wipe us all from existence. And without Theresa, I cannot fight the geas. I will not be able to reach the depths of my power to stand against them. The only good thing to come out of her choice was the magic she transferred to you the day you were born."

"*What did you just say?*"

Enyo knew, *somehow* she knew that Theresa would fail. She made Theresa agree that in the moment of her death, her incarnate's magic would be taken and held until Enyo's final player arrived. I felt the return of Theresa's magic the day you were born, and knew that the final battle was upon us."

"It must be hard for you, having me around," I said, tears threatening to fall. "Sensing Theresa every time I use the magic, being reminded of what you lost."

"It was in the beginning." He admitted honestly. "But I know you are not Theresa, and I promised her that I would do anything that I could to help you play your part. I promise *you* now, Sapphira Dawn, that I will be your ally until the very end." I felt the vow winding around us, tightening as he continued to speak. "Not just because I swore to Theresa that I would. Your kindness, your innate sense of right and wrong, your willingness to help an entire realm of monsters gain their freedom. And your love for Valdis. All of these reasons would have made me make this vow to you now."

The tears were falling now, running down my face in silent streams.

"I am grateful for the person that you are, for what you are willing to do for the ones you care about," Hadrian continued, his voice shaking unevenly as he spoke. "That was an unexpected windfall for me, I had not planned on feeling this way about you. You will always have a place here if you need it. No strings attached, no reason to earn it. It is yours."

It still surprised me – especially in moments like this – that people, *beings* that were, from the outside, dark and monstrous, were, in fact, full of light and love. I had more positive, heartfelt interactions with the monsters of the dark places than I had with those in the light.

Hadrian and Valdis had shown me more understanding and empathy than many of the other people in my life. They had no hidden agendas, no secret pacts about *how* and *who* interacted with me. It was simply *I am here for you, I understand.*

"I know how she did it!" Valdis called from the dining room, breaking the heaviness of the moment. "I know how Theresa held the geas at bay!"

Chapter Seventeen

"T hink of magic like a muscle," Valdis told us as Hadrian, and I sat at the dining room table again. She stood, bouncing on the balls of her feet, the journal opened in front of her. We ignored her tear-streaked face and focused on her words instead. "The more you use it, the stronger it gets, right?"

"Right," I confirmed, as Hadrian nodded at her to continue.

"Using your muscles – magic – takes up energy, no one is exempt from that. But the more you use that muscle, and the stronger it gets, the less energy you use in flexing it."

"That is why the older we get, the stronger our magic is," Hadrian said as if Valdis should have already known all of this. Or maybe it was or my benefit.

"Yes, yes. But it worked a little differently with Theresa's magic." Valdis replied impatiently. "Theresa could bypass all of the waiting and slow build-up by *taking the energy from others*. That is how she kept you stronger than the limitations of the geas. She was siphoning energy from others, and sharing it with you!"

"I know, Valdis," Hadrian said softly, sadly. "And it was one of the reasons she wasn't strong enough to keep going. She was using her own life force to keep *me* strong, not just that of her donors. The geas was fighting back, and it took more energy and magic than she could spare just to hold it in check at the end."

Valdis deflated a little, shoulders drawn in.

"I promised that I would do whatever I could," I said into the heavy silence. "And I will. Does Theresa's journal say *how* to do it?"

"Sapphira, no." Hadrian's tone was firm, his eye piercing as he stared at me. "You need all of the strength you can get for yourself."

"Bullshit!" Valdis interjected angrily. "She can help you, I know she can!"

I reached across the table, sliding the journal closer to me as they stared each other down.

Theresa's handwriting was neat, intricate swirls of words organized over the pages, detailed hand-drawn illustrations mixed in with the text.

Valdis had left it open on the relevant page, Theresa's instructions on the power exchange. It seemed pretty straight forward – just touch the recipient and will the magic and energy into them.

The geas was a hiccup, a problem that needed a creative solution. Theresa had written that she pictured the geas like a rope snaking around inside of Hadrian. The power she sent for him had to both hold the geas in place to stop it tightening its control, and tunnel into Hadrian – giving him strength and deeper access to his own power.

She noted that there was a slight disadvantage, a moment after the exchange that left the giver weak and unable to draw any magic for themselves. Theresa warned that the transfer could not occur while the giver was low on energy, or if death was imminent for either person involved.

Hadrian and Valdis were arguing, neither had noticed that I had taken the journal, or read the instructions laid down by the Goddess Incarnate.

They didn't pay any attention as I got to my feet, walked around the table, and placed my hands on Hadrian's shoulders.

He jumped at the contact, and then went extremely still. "What are you doing, Sapphira?"

I focused on the energy swimming through my system, the magic I'd taken from the Fae. Before Hadrian could jerk out of my grasp, I pushed some of that magic into him, feeling the geas perk up in interest.

I sent most of the magic straight at it, willing it to hold the geas still, to force it to unravel a little, giving the rest of the magic a gap to fall through.

That magic tunneled down, finding a deep well of trapped energy – of power, unlike anything I had ever seen. It broke the traps when it hit them, freeing the power and joined it as it surged upwards, back towards the geas.

I felt Valdis sending some of her energy too, sensing it swirling around the geas, testing for weaknesses.

Hadrian gasped as he felt what was happening inside of him, could sense what I was planning to do next.

I willed the rest of the Fae magic, the power I had kept for myself, forward, into Hadrian to attack the geas.

Together, we fought Kamilla's hold over him, pushing harder and harder against her magic.

Energy flagged, I let him go, sagging to the floor.

Hadrian was panting, hands over his face, slumped low in the chair.

Valdis was staring at us, mouth open, eyes wide in shock, body shaking.

I couldn't blame her, I felt similarly. I thought that I could do what Theresa had done – shared energy to get Hadrian through a little longer.

Never could I have imagined myself working with the Necromancer and the Soul Eater to do what we had just done.

From the reactions from Valdis and Hadrian, I didn't think that they thought it possible either.

Together, we had *burned the geas out*.

Valdis was crying, a smile of pure joy on her lips. "It worked…I can't believe it, *it actually worked!*"

"You have to go – now!" Hadrian hissed urgently, removing his hands from his face and spinning in the chair to look down at me.

His face was perfect. No more rot, the hole had healed – his missing eye too. The Soul Eater looked as he had in Enyo's memories, young and whole. "You cannot be here when Kamilla comes looking for what happened here. You must *run!*"

I struggled to my feet, using the back of his chair as support. Valdis rushed over to grab my arm as I wobbled, holding me up firmly.

"I want to stay," I told them. "I can't leave you to face her alone."

"Of course you can!" The Soul Eater snapped. "It would be senseless for her to discover that you were still alive – our long term plan would fail. Valdis, go with her – keep her protected. I will call for you when it is safe for you to return home."

Valdis opened her mouth to argue, but Hadrian's power lashed out, holding her tongue. "I am your King, and my *orders will be obeyed*." He growled.

Valdis stiffened, expression hurt.

"It will ease my mind knowing that you are *both* away," He said, softer, but still leaving no room for argument. "I cannot lose you too, Valdis."

They shared an embrace, murmured goodbyes between family. Hadrian bowed his head to me, a sign of his gratitude and respect. "Thank you for all you have done." He said with a smile that brightened the room.

I returned it, eyes welling with tears at the love in the room. "Anytime, it was a pleasure," I told him, meaning each word with all of my heart.

And then, it was time to go.

Athens again, and that enchanting aroma of coffee filling the air.

Lyra's café was packed, tourists and locals alike crammed into the tiny space, and the courtyard outside.

Valdis and I had changed into clothes less conspicuous and were weaving our way through the crowd when Hunter's cheerful face popped up in front of mine. "Hello, Little Thief."

I chuckled at the surprised look on his face as I threw myself at him, squeezing him in a hug. "How do you always materialize wherever it is that I am?"

"It's my hot girl radar," He confided conspiratorially when I released him, winking at Valdis, who snorted and rolled her eyes.

"Yeah, okay, Casanova." I laughed, clapping him on the back playfully. "Whatever you say."

"We were expecting you earlier," He added. "Been busy, Little Thief?"

"Not really," I told him, following close behind as he wound through the crowd towards the Café entrance. "I've been on vacation."

"Not a very good time for it," Hunter commented, holding the door open for us. "You've missed a lot."

"It's a good thing you can catch us up then, isn't it?" I returned. "You, being the gossip you are and all."

The Nephilim led us into Lyra's house, gesturing for us to sit on the couch by the fire. "Lyra will be out in a minute." He said.

The little cat, awakened by our entrance, meowed in annoyance and jumped up onto Valdis' lap.

"Hello, little guy." She purred, stroking its fur slowly. "Aren't you handsome?"

"Hunter, you keep that mouth of yours shut, before I stitch it closed for you." Lyra gruffed, closing the door between the café and her home.

Hunter, who had been posed to make a flirty comment at Valdis, snapped his mouth shut, miming locking his lips and throwing away the key.

The old Seer made her way to the armchair and sat down with a sigh. "Tourist season is intense."

She took us in, sharp eyes not missing a thing. "You've discovered something important."

I nodded. "It would seem that way."

"How much do you know?" She prodded, glancing at the bracelet on my wrist.

Hunter sat on the arm of the chair, eyes focused on my face.

"I met an old friend of yours," I told them, finger on the conch shell charm. "I have to say, I'm not a fan."

"Ah, yes," Lyra agreed, nodding slowly, eyes a mix of understanding and calculation. "Enyo has that effect on people sometimes."

Valdis snorted, startling the cat that had fallen asleep in her arms. "Understatement."

Hunter grunted his agreement.

"What did you do?" I asked, leaning forward. "What was it that you did to curse our bloodline?"

Lyra smiled sadly, her eyes full of remorse, and sank lower in her chair. "I signed our lives and magic over to Enyo's cause. All who share my blood must take part in her game, must help to cloak her player's movements from Ares and his allies."

"And in return?" I asked. "What did you get out of it?"

"Long life – enough to see it through." She told me flatly. "I'm to guide them all to the end - I will live long enough to watch my entire family die."

"Not much of a trade-off," Valdis muttered.

"It was the best I could do at the time." Lyra snapped. "At least those of my blood have had guidance."

The cat jumped from Valdis' lap, joining Lyra on the armchair.

"I meant no offense, Old One." The Necromancer amended. "I can see that there was no easy choice. I only meant that the Gods don't play fair with others."

"No one in our world plays fair." Hunter put in, shrugging. "That is why the Gods found it so easy to get us to this point."

"True enough," Lyra agreed, patting his thigh lightly. "No creature trusts another kind, all think they are mightier. It is rare to see two varieties working together."

"But we have allies – Ares does too," I argued. "I've seen Moroi working alongside Djinn and Nephilim – Seers too. I have allies in the City of Darkness."

"Yes, but that has taken generations and extenuating circumstances. *You* were the reason for it all. Without *you*, none of *that* would have been possible."

"Not true," I disagreed, shaking my head. "The possibility of a better life for everyone made that possible."

"You are young and naive and don't fully understand creature politics," Lyra said gently. "This world is not a fairytale, there are rarely any happy endings."

As she spoke, I could feel something brewing in the air, a sense of urgency – demanding my attention. I narrowed my eyes, trying to focus on it, wondering what it was – where it was coming from.

An image pierced my mind, forcing my eyes closed.

The café was burning, people screaming and running for their lives. Monsters – terrifying creatures with twisted skin, sharp claws, and razor-like teeth, ran between the terrified humans, tearing into them with relish. Blood ran through the cobblestones, a torrent so thick and fast that it made me gag. Body parts floated in the fountain, the water there running red too.

"The Seer's line must end." A cold, calculating male voice hissed. "Start with the Matriarch, and the rest will fall."

"Yes, Ares." A familiar female voice answered. "Your will be done."

"See that it is, Fae Queen."

I came out of the vision, heart pounding with panic. My eyes found Lyra, her eyes clouded as she experienced the same vision. "Kamilla is coming for you."

"Not just me," the Seer corrected, her eyes clearing. "Ares is after our bloodline."

"Can you warn them all?" Valdis wanted to know, tense on the couch now. "Tell them to run?"

"My family is vast, and not all of them have the Sight," Lyra informed her, getting to her feet. " But I will do what I can."

Hunter got to his feet too, staying close to the Seer. "What do you need from me?"

"Can you take Valdis and close up for me?" She asked. "We can limit the carnage by removing the mortals, at least."

Hunter nodded, gesturing to the Necromancer to follow him.

Lyra moved to the mantle, fingers tapping the wooden edge until the door had closed behind the others. "Sapphira, come here." She said firmly. "Hurry."

I was at her side in seconds, brows furrowed. "What is it?"

"Give me your hand."

I held it out for her, and she took it, running her fingers over the bracelet. It seemed to respond to her, causing my skin beneath it to tingle as the charms hummed.

"I bequeath to you, blood of my blood, all of the gratuities that have been given to me. All that I have is yours. I do this freely and of my own accord." She let me take my hand back, turning her eyes back to the mantle.

"What did you do that for?" I asked breathlessly. "Why *me*?"

Lyra didn't answer, attention on the items sitting in front of her – items that I could now see.

A crystal, and a cat statue, made from what looked like marble, sat in the middle of the wooden mantle. A photo of a young Lyra holding a child in her arms sat to the left. And a jewelry box filled the space to the right.

"If anything happens to me, it is *you* that will have to lead the Seers. Now, at least, you will have everything that you need."

"Lead the Seers?" I repeated, frowning again.

The old woman sighed. "Our bloodline is the only one left with the full advantages of the Sight. It is obvious now that Ares and his people are behind the decline in others. I had wondered at the decline in Seer numbers over the years."

As she spoke, she took a large crystal from the mantle and held it to her chest. "Now, they have focused in on us. I have kept those with the strongest gifts close, have had them out in the world keeping an eye on things. We have found a way to communicate visions directly – mind to mind across vast distances. Now, I need you to join our hive so that you, too, can *see* as we do."

I shook my head, equal parts amazed and creeped out. I opened my mouth to decline, to ask her to think of something else – anything else. I didn't want another responsibility, another job. The ones I had already were too much for me.

But Lyra had been expecting that response and shoved the crystal into my hand. She forced my palm closed, with more strength than I had thought possible.

"You must do this, Sapphira." She affirmed sternly. "It is the only way you can stay ahead of them. You need all the pre-warning you can get."

The crystal in my hand shattered, the shards digging into my skin. I cried out in pain, seeing my blood dripping onto Lyra's floor.

"Blood of my blood has spilled, joining the ancestral enclave of Seers." Many voices joined Lyra's whispering across vast distances, merging together as one. "*Let her mind be open to the visions sent her way by those in the Hive. Welcome, Daughter of the Dawn.*"

Hunter and Valdis returned, chatting amongst themselves.

Lyra opened my hand, carefully plucking shards of crystal out of my palm, as I stood frozen, staring at her wide-eyed.

"What has happened now?" Valdis asked, taking in the scene before her. "Sapphira, are you alright?"

I managed to nod, eyes not leaving the Seer as she calmly began wiping the blood from my hand, the shards dropped into her apron.

"Did you warn your people, Seer?" Valdis turned her attention to Lyra.

"I've told them all of what has happened here, they know to be careful now."

"The café is all locked up, Love," Hunter announced, sprawling out on the couch. "But I think that you should come to the Villa for a while."

Lyra sighed sadly and glanced around her home, having finished with my hand. "I think you're right."

Hunter sat up, surprised. He glanced between us, trying to figure out what had changed, I assumed.

"Great, it's settled." He said carefully. "Shall we gather your things?"

"My clothes and the cat." She told him. "Everything else can stay."

"Are you sure, Love?"

"I am." Lyra nodded. "Hurry, I want to see the ocean before sunset."

Together, they disappeared into the bedroom, murmuring softly as they packed.

Valdis joined me in front of the fireplace.

"What do *we* do now?" I asked her softly.

"I don't know," she replied smirking. "You're the one that needs a plan. I'm only here to look good."

A laugh escaped my lips despite my mood. "Okay, Valdis."

We waited until Hunter and Lyra returned, and all left the café together.

"Hey, Hunter?" I asked as they were preparing to leave. "Did you ever figure out what you were supposed to learn about the Stories of Amyntas?"

"Maybe." He smiled, shrugging his shoulders. "I found records of some amazing battles from wars long ago. I thought that the tactics were what I was looking for, but Lyra won't tell me if I'm right. I passed them on to Ari and the others anyway."

"What was it that you were going to tell me earlier – about what I had missed?"

"We should go, Hunter," Lyra said. "And you should go to see your Dhampir friend, Sapphira. He can tell you what has been happening."

Hunter took the old Seer's bag in one arm and hugged her to him with the other. The little cat purred against her chest as Lyra waved goodbye, and they vanished – heading to paradise on the safest place left on Earth.

"To Australia then," Valdis commented, arms folded over her chest. "Hopefully, the Strigoi are ready to die – my knives have been silent too long, and I'm *itching* for a fight."

We landed in my old home town, and while Valdis found us some food, I sent my mental probes out, searching for Colte. It was a long shot, but I got lucky. I felt him right on the edge of my limits. I think I woke him up because he went from calm to surprised and confused in two seconds flat.

Valdis returned with some sandwiches she'd purchased from a bakery – I had no idea where she got the money from, and we jumped to Colte's location.

He was in a tent, lying on a stretcher bed in his underwear.

"Hi!" I chirped, mouth full of sandwich.

"What the - " he yelled, jumping to his feet and lunging for his pants.

"Why are you in a tent, Colte?" I asked, looking around.

With the two new bodies inside – plus Colte and the stretcher, it was super cramped. My head almost touched the roof – Valdis' did. She was munching away on her food, eyes sparkling as she watched Colte fumble with his pants.

"It's uh…" he started, wiggling the jeans over his hips hurriedly. "It's the war camp. The *Maharishi* says that the fighting will begin soon, and this is the spot he picked for the army to gather. What are you doing here, Saph – does Abhijay know?"

"Should he?" I answered his question with another question, eyebrows raised. "Can't I visit a friend before he goes off to battle monsters?"

"Well, yeah!" Colte replied. "It's bad form for unannounced guests to appear in a war camp – I'm happy to see you, though, for sure!"

I didn't think I had ever seen him so flustered. I'd never seen him in his underwear before, though, so maybe that was the reason.

I offered him the last half of my sandwich, seeing him eyeing it off, and he took it gratefully, digging in.

"You should go to see Abhijay." He told me, crumbs escaping his mouth as he talked. "I'll take you both now if you like?"

The last comment was directed to Valdis, who guarded her remaining bit of sandwich close to her chest as he eyed it hopefully.

"Lead the way!" I exclaimed cheerfully, stepping aside and gesturing to the exit. "Is it also bad form to appear in a war camp empty-handed?" I wondered out loud as he led Valdis and me out and into a sea of identical tents.

"Nah, I'm sure you'll be okay."

I followed Colte as he navigated through the maze around us, taking in the vast amount of Moroi and Dhampir that hustled throughout the camp.

I'd never been in a place with so many people before, and it surprised me that it smelled so bad. The smells – sweat, urine, and god knows what else, was like a punch to the face.

"How long have you been camped here?" Valdis asked, seemingly at home as she followed along calmly.

"About a week," Colte replied, glancing back at us. "We were the first ones here, but we've had people turning up fairly consistently the closer we get to go-time."

"How does the Australian government not see all of this and come investigate?" I pondered. "How can you fight a battle here unnoticed?"

"No one outside of this camp can see anything inside of it. And, once the fighting starts, the entire battlefield will be shrouded."

"*How?*"

"Have you ever been on a long car trip and kind of zoned out along the way?" Valdis asked. "Like, you got to your destination, but couldn't quite remember parts of it?"

I nodded. "I suppose so."

"*Shrouding.*" She shrugged as if it all made perfect sense. "Magic users have been using it to hide things from mortals for centuries. Most likely, those moments that you couldn't remember clearly were you passing through a shroud in place to hide something, like a battlefield."

"Or the compound," Colte added, wiggling his fingers at me, grinning like a fool. "It's magic, baby!"

He stopped in front of another tent, more significant in size than the others. He nodded to the two Moroi standing guard as they gestured us through with bored expressions.

Inside, a group of men and women stood around a table, talking amongst themselves. I didn't recognize many of them, but knew that they were all Moroi, Dhampir... and *Lycanthropes*!

Abhijay had managed to recruit them after all. For that, I was glad.

The Maharishi himself lifted his gaze from a stack of papers in his hand to take us in. He gestured for the others to leave, and I stepped aside as they did without question, passing by me to exit the tent.

He was wearing what looked to be black leather armor and chainmail across his broad chest, and a dhoti below them. The image of an ancient warrior was quashed, though, with the military boots he wore.

"Welcome, Sapphira, Valdis," he said when we were alone, his deep voice rumbling. "What can I do for you both?"

"Lyra said that we should be here," I said lamely, "So here we are."

Valdis snorted from beside me.

"Would you care to give your allies an update, *Maharishi*?" She asked Abhijay.

"Of course," he inclined his head, motioning us closer. "Has Hadrian sent you with his stratagem?" He asked her politely. "It would allow for a more in-depth overall plan if we had his numbers and tactics to add to ours."

"Unfortunately not at this stage. I am not an emissary for my King, but a companion and guard for Sapphira." Valdis informed him as she looked over the map laid out on the table. "One of his Generals should be along shortly with all that you require."

"I see." Abhijay turned to me, leaving Valdis to investigate. "How are you faring in all of this?"

I shrugged. "I've never been to war before," I said, smiling and trying to make a joke.

"For that, you should be grateful." He told me sorrowfully. "Wars are terrible things."

I nodded, smile gone. "Is your daughter here?"

It was Abhijay's turn to nod. "She is. Although, if I could have sent her anywhere else, I would have."

"There is a flaw here." Valdis cut in, pointing to something I couldn't see.

Abhijay joined her, and they began talking strategy. I couldn't keep up, having no idea what things like *Triplex Acies, Oblique Order*, and *Double Envelopment* meant.

Colte, who had been hanging out by the tent entrance, grinned as I approached him. "Done?" He asked.

"I guess so. Valdis and Abhijay are talking battle jibberish."

"Want to take a walk?"

I remembered the horrid smells in the camp and shook my head. "Can we just go back to your tent and hang out for a bit?"

Colte nodded, offering me his arm. "Of course, *Goddess*."

"Don't call me that," I said hurriedly. "Please, never call me that."

"Sorry, Saph. I was just trying to be funny. My bad." I could tell by the creases on his forehead, the way his eyes searched mine, the downward slope of his mouth that he didn't understand my reaction. But he knew me well enough not to press the issue.

I took his offered arm, leaning into him, and sighed. "It's alright, Colte. These last few months have just been a lot to take in, you know?"

"Yeah, I know."

We walked back to his tent, me trying to subtly block out the smells along the way, Colte telling me a story about digging latrines that ended with him covered in less than pleasant things, that had me in stitches.

"I've missed that." He said when we had reached his tent.

"What?" I asked, following him in.

"Your laugh." He admitted, sitting on his stretcher. "It's been so long since we've just hung out – had any fun."

"I know." I hugged myself, looking at my friend, who was about to fight against the Strigoi. I refused to entertain the idea of Colte not making it through the next few weeks but had no idea what life would look like for us after all of it. "Do you think we'll ever have normal lives again?"

"Depends on what you class as *normal*," he replied carefully. "I don't think we could ever go back to living in your place and drinking every weekend. We could never go back to pretending to be human either."

"No, I guess not." I sighed. "It was wishful thinking, I suppose."

"Nah, those were good times." Colte winked, eyes full of forced humor. "The most fun I ever had was winning against you in poker. And video games. Oh, and that time I beat you in the cook-off."

"That was a rigged competition – and you know it!" I groaned, letting his familiar playfulness wash over us. I hadn't realized just how much I had missed him, and the natural teasing that we had shared until we'd started again.

"Who forgets to put *eggs* in a *cake*?" Colte laughed. "It was *not* rigged, you just can't bake."

"Lots of cakes don't have eggs," I grumbled, sticking my tongue out at him.

"Okay, Saph." Colte rolled his eyes, smirking. "If you say so."

Pain speared through my head, causing me to stagger backward.

Colte was there, holding me up. I could see his mouth moving, but his words were swallowed by the voices in my mind.

I could hear screaming – fear and panic-filled voices tearing my head in two. So many voices were crying out at once – it was hard to separate them, to make any of them out clearly.

"The Fae are leaving the mounds."

"…warriors…"

"They are here!"

"…end the Seer lines."

"…dead!"

"Help us!"

"…looking for Grandmother."

"What do we do?"

"Hide – they are coming for you all!"

Just as quickly as it had started, the voices and the pain stopped, like a door had been slammed.

My vision was blurred, the tent – and Colte's worried face spinning.

"Valdis!" I gasped, hands digging into his arm. "Take me to Valdis and Abhijay, Colte – *now!*"

The Dhampir all but dragged me back through the camp, pushing Moroi out of the way as we raced by.

"Saph, what the *hell* was that?" Colte hissed. He had heard it too, I realized. He's been holding onto me as I was lost in the panicked warnings.

"Seer telephone," I told him, words a little slurred. "I think I'm the new switchboard."

He swore, picking up the pace. "This is not good."

We stumbled into Abhijay's tent, disrupting the intense conversation taking place there. Valdis and Abhijay looked up, concern filling their faces at the sorry sight of us.

"What is it?" The Moroi demanded.

"What's wrong?" Valdis asked at the same time.

"I have to get back to Athens," I told them both. "Kamilla is hunting Seers."

There was a round of frowns thrown my way, not entirely disbelieving, but something close.

"The Fae are making a move. The Legions have left the mounds." Colte added, reporting to Abhijay. "The Seers reported it moments ago."

"I cannot move an entire army to Ireland – or Scotland in time to make a difference there," Abhijay growled. "And any message I could send would be too late."

Valdis was watching me closely. "We were told to come *here.*"

"I know, but I have to go. I need to make sure that Lyra is safe."

The memory of her café in flames echoed through my mind. I knew that she had left Athens, had gone to Thira with Hunter, but still, I had to see her for myself.

"You'd have to leave now," Abhijay stated as the earth beneath our feet began to rumble, and inhuman screams pierced the air. Calls to arms and the sound of boots thumping in the dirt sounded outside the tent. The ringing of metal being released from leather as Abhijay drew a sword from the belt on his hip brought my attention back to him. "It seems the Strigoi are attacking in tandem with the Fae."

Kamilla and Ares had finally made their move – one that was intended to divide the armies Abhijay had worked hard to assemble – and remove the only people that could see their plans, all in one fell swoop.

War was here.

Colte spared a minute to hug me, telling me to go, before he vanished into the chaos of the camp. I sent up a silent prayer to Enyo, to the mortal's god, and to anyone else who would listen, to keep him safe. I couldn't lose him.

Abhijay was shouting orders, calm and commanding as he strode into the din, barely sparing a backward glance at Valdis and me. A General to the core – no time for sentimentality in battle.

Valdis grabbed my arm, turning me to face her. "I haven't heard from Hadrian yet." She told me, worry lacing her words. "If Kamilla is on the move, I should have *heard* something by now."

My eyes widened, guilt and worry swirling through me, I hadn't even thought of him in all of this.

"Go, I'll be fine," I assured her. "I'm not staying here, I'm going to check in with Lyra and Hunter – and I haven't seen Fallon here yet, I'll see if I can find her too."

"By the sound of things, the Strigoi numbers are massive. Hopefully, I can get to Hadrian and return with reinforcements to help here." We shared a quick embrace, and as she pulled back, Valdis grabbed my face, forcing me to look her in the eyes. "Be safe, keep out of the conflict for as long as you can, Sapphira. I mean it," she added as I opened my mouth to reply. "Don't be stupid. Don't play the hero – *we* need you to play *your* part, not the part *they* expect you to." Valdis let me go, still holding my gaze as she stepped away. "Go."

I went, disappearing as the sounds of conflict and painful death rose in the camp around me, a finger on the angel wing charm to help guide me where I needed to go.

The last thing I saw was Valdis spinning to face something coming through the tent, her knives out, and a snarl on her face.

Chapter Eighteen

I t was jarring, the difference in noise, jumping from a war zone, into the peace and quiet that Thira offered.

I appeared on the balcony of Hunter's villa, eyes instantly searching for the Nephilim and the Seer.

I found them sitting in the lounge room, a hushed conversation between them, the little cat curled up on Lyra's lap.

"Lyra!" I breathed in relief, all but running to her. "You're okay!"

"Of course I am." She replied, voice a little shaky. "Thira is a safe haven. I am in no danger here."

"Did you hear -"

"How could I not?" She cut me off, eyes welling with tears, Hunter's reassuring hand on her back. "They called out so loudly. *My poor family.*"

"The Strigoi attacked at the same time, Abhijay and Colte are fighting them now," I said, tears in my eyes too.

Hunter sat up straighter, alarm on his face.

"But I ran. I couldn't have helped there, I don't know the first thing about war. I thought I had to come here to help you – to do *something* for the Seers." I continued, wringing my hands together.

"They knew the risks." Lyra sniffed, wiping her eyes. "I hate this, but they knew what could happen. There is nothing that you *can* do now, Sapphira – not for them."

"The survivors have all gone underground, hiding. We need to be smart with the assets we have left." Hunter added. "Let Ares and Kamilla think that there are no Seers left. Use what we know against them. We *have* to gain the upper hand as quickly as we can."

"Where are Fallon and Ari?" I asked him, *hoping* that they could be of assistance somehow, *wishing* that they had the answers to stop all of this.

"Fallon is at the *Modena Al-Djinn*, trying to convince her people to join the war, and Ari is…" Hunter paused, eyes darting between Lyra and me. "Ari is with Enyo."

I growled at the mention of the Goddess, my rage bursting out of me. The vortex whirled violently through the air, sharp as blades.

Lyra's cat hissed at it, back arched and teeth bared.

"This is all their fault!" I snarled to no one in particular. "Those *fucking Gods and their games!*"

I wanted to kill them – the Gods who thought so little of us. I wanted to make them suffer like *they* had made so many suffer. I wanted to tear them apart and burn them all to ash.

Let them *see* what mere mortals could do – let them *know* that we were more than expendable playthings.

How dare they think that we were any less than them. How dare they assume that *they* were more worthy of life.

All life mattered – not just those that thought themselves superior or more powerful – or more deserving. *All* life had the right to exist, to thrive and grow.

Gods or not, they could not dictate the existence of others anymore – enough was enough. If they thought that they had the right to extinguish others, *then I would show them all how that felt.*

I wasn't going to play by their rules. I was going to tear them up and spit them out.

And then, I was going to take their war to them.

The Seer's eyes were wide as she watched my magic grow darker, swirling faster and faster as my temper got worse, my rage responding to my thoughts.

Hunter, too, seemed surprised at how much my power had grown. He had positioned himself between Lyra and the threat my magic posed her – protective of his Love always.

"Breathe," Hunter called softly, reassuringly. "We are not your enemy, Little Thief."

My eyes shot to him, seeing the worry in his face. I could see myself reflected back at me through his eyes, a dark and vengeful being, full of hate and anger standing alone in the middle of a storm. I faltered then and slumped to the floor as I pulled my rage back within me, pushing it down.

Hunter relaxed, letting out a little sigh.

"You are fast becoming a powerhouse." He grinned. "I fear for those that you would turn that power on."

"As you should," Lyra said firmly. "When Sapphira's magical potential is realized, there will be nothing that can stand in her way."

"Who would have thought." Ari's voice sang from the balcony.

The Nephilim strolled in, calm and collected – as though she hadn't played a part in all of this. "After all that time fighting the truth, look at what you're becoming."

"What truth?" I hissed, eyes narrowed. "You all told me that I was the *Goddess Incarnate* – none of you said *anything* about *truth*." I spat the last word in her face, rage building inside of me again.

Ari was unperturbed by my anger, smiling sweetly as she sat on the edge of the coffee table, adjusting the miniskirt she wore as she did.

"Why didn't you tell me about Enyo and your lies?" I asked her, hands clenched into fists at my side.

"My lies?" She asked, head tilted to the side as she took me in. "Sapphira, my whole existence has been a lie – a punishment because I chose to help you."

"What are you talking about?" I snapped. Ari was a fallen angel. She'd been around for millennia before I was born. How could I be at fault for her life?

"I fell because our God wouldn't take a side. I thought it was unfair, that He should have stepped in to help Enyo against Ares. But he was young – compared to the other gods, and was sure that they could work it out. I changed my entire essence, my divine programming, to step down from heaven and work here, living with those… *creatures*." Her lip curled, nose screwed in disgust. "Getting them ready for *you*, for the parts they had to play."

She paused, glaring at me. "Do you know what my job was before all of this? I hunted those things down, I fought against them for my God."

"Ari, cool it," Hunter warned softly. "It isn't her fault, *you* chose this. You chose for both of us."

"*She needs to play her fucking part!*" Ari hissed at him. "Or it was all for nothing!"

I was shaking my head, in denial or outrage, I wasn't sure. Ari's words were a shock, yes. But kind of made sense of her behavior around the others. The reason she was so cold and distant, but something still didn't make sense to me.

"Why would you pretend to be my friend, if all of this was true? Why not treat me as coldly as you did the others? Aren't I just another creature to you?"

Ari huffed a laugh, running a hand through her dark curls. "That's the bitch of a thing, Saph. You frustrate the hell out of me, but I can't hate you – and I've tried to. Somehow you make those around you love you."

"I can't do this right now," I said to the room. "Colte and Abhijay are fighting for their lives, and we need to help them. I need to go."

"Saph, you can't fight the Strigoi." Ari rolled her eyes, getting to her feet. "You don't know how."

"Watch me." I snarled, vanishing into thin air.

As I landed back in the camp, I built a shield from my rage, covering my entire body, and imagined it was solid, not the ethereal smoke-like substance it usually was.

My magic responded, the shield becoming a forcefield that hugged my body, and made it feel like I'd put on a few pounds. But now, at least, I felt a little safer. Nothing could touch me unless I wanted it to.

I'd suffered through enough war movies with Colte – mainly cartoon ones – to know that armor and shields were crucial.

I'd seen, too, what the Strigoi could do to an unprotected body. I liked my body parts where they were, thank you very much.

I tried to block out the memories of my broken family, and the bodies of the fallen at the compound. Fear would not be an asset now.

I had no weapons, save for my magic, and I felt it building inside of me, ready to be of use.

I could hear the sounds of battle – clashing steel, shouts, grunts, and moans. I listened to the occasional gunshot, the bangs echoing above the other sounds, terrifying and somehow out of place at the same time.

My heart pounded, so fast it felt like my entire chest was shaking. I jerked each time a gun went off, half expecting a bullet to fly past or hit my shield.

From where I stood, I couldn't *see* any of the fighting, broken tents obstructing the larger view. It worried me that the Strigoi had gotten this close to the camp. Shouldn't the actual battlefield be further away? In Colte's movies, the camp had remained safe, a place for the wounded to retreat to.

I turned, heading towards the loudest sounds of confrontation, hoping that Ari was wrong and that I did know how to do this.

I met with a group of wounded Dhampir, retreating from the fight. They were surprised to see me there, instantly on alert.

"Friendly," I told them, palms up, forcing a smile and trying to look inoffensive. "Have you seen Colte?"

The oldest of the group, a man of about thirty, was being supported by two younger men. He had a deep gash in the side of his leg and a nasty-looking bite on his neck. He managed to point in the direction that they had come from. "That way."

I nodded my thanks and hurried past them, apprehension for my friend intensifying as I saw how easy it was for his people to be hurt. *That could have been him.*

I reached the last row of ruined tents, the noise levels almost unbearable now.

Blood pooled in the dirt, splattered over the tents. Chunks of meat that had once been *people* lay where they were thrown. The smell was putrid – blood, sweat, fear, and the unmistakable scent of death clung to everything.

A body flew past, snarling and spitting blood. Strigoi.

My blood ran cold at the sight of it, my magic clamping down, coiling around me like a snake, ready to strike.

A Moroi warrior was not far behind, panting and gripping a sword that flashed in the sunlight.

The Strigoi turned, lunging back at the Moroi in the blink of an eye. The two Vampires came together, a gnashing, snarling ball of energy and fury. The Moroi was trying to swing the sword, to make contact with the Strigoi's body, but the beast was too close. Teeth and claws ripping into the armor the Moroi wore, trying to get at the skin beneath.

Even someone as untrained as I could see that the Moroi was in trouble, he needed more space between himself and his opponent. His sword was useless in such close confines.

Knowing that it was stupid, but needing to something, I whistled, drawing the Strigoi's attention. Adrenaline pumped through my veins as I eyed the monster, waiting for it to attack.

It hissed at me, and using the Moroi as a springboard, leaped towards me, teeth bared and claws outstretched. The Moroi fell to the ground, winded.

I fought the urge to scream, aware that if I did, the sound would draw attention from other Strigoi nearby. I conjured blades made from my rage, made them hard and sharp, and hurled them at it, watching with grim satisfaction as they cleaved into the skin.

But it kept coming.

My blades, the ones that had been lodged inside the Strigoi's skin, evaporated, leaving behind bloodied holes.

I conjured more, throwing those ones too. The monster was close enough that my panicked throw didn't matter; the knives found hold anyway. The Moroi, having been granted more space to swing his sword, did so, taking the Strigoi in the back.

It fell to the ground, spinning so that it could see us both, inhuman eyes darting between both opponents. It snarled, rancid breath reaching my nose, making me gag.

I pinned it down with my magic, hands shaking, as the Moroi raised his sword, bringing it down in an arc with such a penetrating force, the Strigoi's head separated from the body in one, clean cut.

The Moroi bowed his appreciation and turned to find another adversary. I followed suit, drawn into the almost frantic speed of the battle, eyes searching for Colte in the swarming mass of bodies fighting around me. He had to be there – alive and still fighting. None of the blood or body parts belonged to my friend, I had to believe that.

I didn't see him, or anyone that I knew, but I *did* see that the Strigoi were winning.

And, they had brought their spine-chilling friends with them.

My eyes widened, and breathing became impossible, as I watched a retinue of the grotesque Vârcolac tearing through the Moroi lines.

Other, equally hideous monsters were picking off the wounded, beaks and talons ripping into them with relish. I shuddered, goosebumps crawling across my skin. I knew that I'd found the culprits behind the body parts strewn across the camp.

A horn sounded somewhere in the distance, a signal – or a warning.

"Saph!" Colte's voice, tired and panicked, from somewhere to my left. "Get out of there!" My head snapped around, eyes searching. He was running towards me, arms gesturing frantically. The leather armor and dulled chainmail that he wore was slick with blood and gore. His exposed skin – face and forearms were too. "Run!"

I didn't question his orders, sprinting towards him as fast as my shaking legs, and the added weight of my shields would carry me. I was overwhelmingly relieved to see that he was alright, but it was dampened by the fear his eyes were filled with. What did he know that I didn't?

I leaped into his arms, pushing all of my feelings into the embrace. Colte's arms tightened around my waist, and he spun, throwing us both to the ground. We ended with him on top of me, pinning me down into the dirt.

I could feel his heart, the rhythm like the beating wings of a hummingbird. His brown eyes wide and staring into mine.

My breaths matched his, fast and shallow. I tried to push myself up, to get him off of me so that I could stand.

"Don't move." He told me urgently, full of terror. "Not yet."

Before I could ask why, the world exploded around us, with fire and pain, and Colte was screaming in agony.

It seemed that hours passed like that, me; frozen in place, doing nothing, him; holding me down while he screamed as he burned.

My ears were ringing, but I could still hear the roaring of fire as it burned everything around us. It seemed far off, though, background noise against the sound in my head.

Colte's eyes were glazed with pain, his mouth still open – but silent now.

I was screaming his name, I think, panic blurring my reality. My voice lost in the chaos around us. He didn't seem to hear me, and I could no longer feel his heart beating against my chest.

The heat in the air dissipated, flames snuffing out, like magic.

Magic had done this.

Hands appeared above me, grabbing at Colte. I panicked, remembering the creatures that had been tearing apart the wounded.

Fear swarmed my senses, making me dizzy. It took me a minute to process that they were humanoid hands, *not* claws or talons. Colte was pulled up, off my body by a familiar Moroi, his name escaped me, but I'd seen him at the compound working as a guard. A friend of Colte's.

"It's alright, you are safe," a male voice said, somewhere in the distance. "The Strigoi have fallen back for now."

Another face swam in front of mine, blocking my view of my friend as he was taken from me.

"Can you move, Sapphira?" Abhijay asked, his deep voice muffled. "Do you need help to stand?"

I thought about it, assessing my body for any sign of injury. I was numb, more from shock than damage – like a bird who had crashed into a window, stunned, but okay. Colte had taken the brunt of the impact and flames when he had used his body to shield mine. He hadn't known that I already had a shield, that he should have protected himself. I hadn't known what was going to happen, or I could have prevented the pain he was feeling right now.

I nodded, taking a shaky breath, and held my hand out for Abhijay to take.

The Moroi took it gently, pulling me to my feet, keeping a hold of me until he was sure I wouldn't fall.

"We need to get Colte to a healer." He said, nodding to the group of Moroi and Dhampir that had surrounded us, a shield – a wall of flesh between us and any danger.

Abhijay turned back to me, eyes full of concern. "We didn't know that you had returned, or we would not have set off the blast until you were clear."

I couldn't talk, I had nothing to say to him anyway. My eyes sought out Colte, being carried away. Right then, he was all that mattered.

"He will be taken care of," Abhijay assured me, having followed my gaze with his own. "He needs blood and time to heal. Do *you* have any injuries that need taking care of?" He prodded as if speaking to a child.

I shook my head, willing my legs to move, to follow after Colte. I didn't want to leave him, I needed to see for myself that he was still alive, that he would be okay.

I managed a grand total of five steps before I tripped on the smoldering remains of a monster, and fell flat on my face.

Abhijay was there, picking me up and placing me on my feet again, hands strong and sure.

Moroi, Dhampir, and Lycanthropes were gathering, falling back to the relative safety of the burned zone. We walked by them, a slow and silent procession, as we followed Colte to wherever the healers were.

They picked their way through the rubble and ash, keeping their eyes on the Strigoi amassing across the grassland that had served as a killing field.

We didn't make it far, though, before the tireless Strigoi's warcry sounded, and the ground shook as they began another charge.

"*Form the lines!*" Abhijay shouted, and his people, worn from the previous incursion, hurried to do as he instructed.

Their Maharishi took in the enclosing enemy, the way they were grouped, and yelled again. "First-lines *Triplex Acies*– watch the flanks! Second-lines *double envelopment*! Guerrillas, get around them, *Hit and Run* – watch your exit!"

Utter gibberish to me, but his people and the Lycanthropes seemed to understand, faces grim as they moved to face their enemy.

Abhijay turned to me, eyes full of an emotion I couldn't place. His mouth was set, brows turned down. "The Strigoi cannot leave here today. If my lines fail, Sapphira, Australia will fall to their insatiable appetite. We won't have the numbers left to keep them in check anymore."

I heard his words, could feel the urgency of them. I sensed too, what he wasn't saying – that this was his final stand.

He was warning me of what he thought was coming. He didn't expect to win, and he wanted me to prepare myself.

The unflagging Strigoi numbers – their ferocity and unpredictability – were too much for the Moroi as they were. He needed more warriors, more magic. More teeth and claws to add to the fight - an advantage to turn the odds in our favor.

Where were Valdis and Hadrian and their people? Where were *Fallon* and *her* people?

The Strigoi had reached the Moroi frontlines, and the sounds of battle tore through the air again.

Jarring booms added to the clamor, the Moroi were setting off more bombs, these ones thrown like grenades – explosions resonating through the onslaught of monsters.

It didn't make much of a difference to their morale, though. The Strigoi and their allies didn't so much as pause to check on their fallen.

They just kept coming.

Abhijay dragged me backward, further from the chaos, the way that Colte had been taken. I spun in his arms so that I could watch the fight, concerned for a large number of Moroi and Dhampir that would cease to exist in the next few minutes if help didn't come.

The front lines had arranged themselves into three groups, thirty Dhampir per group, opening their ranks to let the Strigoi pass deep into their numbers, closing in on them again – cutting them off from the primary host. They fought with swords and guns, teeth, and claws. It was violent and loud, both sides suffering.

The second line, made up of Moroi were in groups too, a long line that spanned the expansive battleground, ten bodies thick. They pushed forward, the center becoming the flank of the front line, the wings pushing further ahead, and slowly taking ground, started to fold in around the Strigoi lines. I could see, in the distance, the flanks of the Strigoi host fighting against surprise attacks – the Lycanthropes hitting a point in the line, and disappearing – only to clash again somewhere else. The strigoi and their allies spent more time chasing the Lycanthropes than actually fighting.

Abhijay's tactics seemed to be working, the Strigoi host split in countless places. But still, it wouldn't be enough.

"You shouldn't be here, Sapphira. We cannot lose you." Abhijay said, drawing my attention back to him.

We'd stopped, back in the mess of ruined tents. Wounded Vampires lay on stretchers – and the ground. Harried healers moved about, trying to bring comfort and relief to an ever-growing number of injured. Groans and screams dominated here, mixed with the sound and smell of vomit and blood.

"I can't just leave," I murmured, still a little stunned by everything that was happening around me. "You need all the help you can get. And this is my fight too, I can't expect others to fight them for me forever."

"I can't afford to have my focus split, I'd be too worried about you to give the battle my full attention. Please," he added, eyes pleading. "You need to go somewhere safer."

"You lose here, there will be nowhere safe anymore!" I argued, pulling out of his grip, rage bubbling up inside of me.

"Stay with Colte then," Abhijay said, sighing in defeat, eyes darting to the battle behind me. "Keep him and the other wounded safe for as long as you can. Promise you will leave if the camp is overrun again."

I nodded, and he made to leave, pausing to squeeze my shoulder. "It was an honor meeting you, Sapphira."

It sounded so much like a final goodbye, that I pulled him into a hug, holding on tightly for as long as I could.

"Don't die, AJ," I ordered, voice shaking as I let him go.

He smiled sadly but didn't say anything, not willing to make promises he knew he couldn't keep.

I watched him go, waiting until he had reached the edge of the camp before turning to find where the healers had put Colte.

I found a healer that knew where my friend was, and she took me there, grumbling under her breath as she did.

"Thank you," I told her retreating back as she disappeared out of the tent and back into the fray. She didn't reply, already gone.

Colte lay on a stretcher in the middle of the tent, on his stomach, back exposed. Strips of bloodied cloth were strewn on the floor around him, the remains of his armor there too.

I sobbed, stepping closer to him, hands out to touch my friend, to give comfort. But they stopped inches from his charred and blistered skin, unwilling to go further in case I inflicted more pain.

There were deep lacerations there, among the burns and blisters, where shrapnel from the blast had punctured him.

His eyes were closed, and I had to genuinely look close to see the rise and fall of his body that told me he was still breathing.

"I'm so sorry, Colte," I whispered, kneeling beside him.

"Not...your... fault." He groaned out, eyes opening slowly. The pain he held there was intense, tugging at my heart. "Glad you're... alright."

I felt the tears on my cheeks, my eyes blurry with them, but I managed a smile for him. "It'll take more than a bomb to take me out."

He laughed, the sound ending abruptly with a groan of pain.

"Are you going to be alright?" I whispered, afraid of the answer. His body was in bad shape, a twisted wreck. I knew that he had told me Dhampir heal faster than humans, could survive a lot. But this just seemed... too much to come back from.

I hated seeing him laid out like that, so hurt and flat. I missed the playful, sarcastic party boy – the tease and the philosopher.

I missed the cheeky glint in his eyes and easy smile: his smugness and steadfast loyalty.

I wanted him back.

I sent up another prayer that he would be okay, that the people I cared about would survive this.

Whoever was listening to my pleas right then, and chose to ignore them, could get fucked.

Chapter Nineteen

I stayed, talking nonsense at him, recounting favorite memories of our time together, as he slowly faded away.

As he took his last breath, I found that I couldn't breathe either, the sobs that wracked my body painfully deep and full of despair. My hand shook as I stroked his face, trying to find the words to say goodbye. But nothing I could say was good enough, nothing *meant* enough.

He was supposed to survive.

Sounds from the battle were louder now, coming closer. Had the Moroi lines failed – as Abhijay had feared they would?

A healer rushed into the tent, coming to check on Colte.

He noticed me kneeling beside the stretcher, face a mess of tears and snot, and his eyes slid to his patient, understanding, and resignation all over his face.

"You need to go." He told me, reaching for something in the satchel he wore at his hip. "The Fae are here in immense numbers. We stand no chance against them. The Maharishi has ordered the healers to burn the dead and run."

"You can't burn him." I gasped, eyes wide. "He's my friend. You *can't* burn him."

"I know it is a hard thing to see, but it must be done. Do you know what will happen to his body if I don't do this before the Bitch Queen – or the Strigoi find him?" The healer shuddered, mind no doubt going down that path. "It has to be now, there are still so many to get to."

I nodded, seeing in my mind the horrors that would befall him if the Healer didn't burn Colte – being torn apart and eaten, or his skin being worn by a Skin Walker – things much worse too.

He was my friend, he should have survived, but he was gone. Even in death, he deserved better than this – than any of this. But the healer was right: this fate was the best option available. At least this way, Colte would be at peace.

"Quickly now." The healer prodded. "Decide."

I wiped my tears, looking at my friend's face for the last time, silently saying goodbye."Do it," I said.

He pulled out a vial, wasting no time, and rushed to the stretcher.

I watched, in frozen horror, as he poured the contents over Colte – a vile smell emanated from the blue powder as it hit the skin, sparking cobalt flames. They danced along the surface of Colte's ruined flesh for a moment, before exploding in on themselves, pushing into his body and setting it alight from the inside.

The healer dragged me to my feet, moving me back, out of reach of the flames as they expanded outwards, intense heat, and azure light filling the tent.

In a matter of seconds, my friend was nothing more than a pile of ash, the healer already gone to find the next body.

The Strigoi and their monsters were winning.

The Fae had joined the fight.

Colte was dead.

Kamilla was here.

Rage replaced the sorrow, mixing with magic as it threatened to tear me apart. The pressure built in my chest, breathing became difficult as those facts swirled through my mind.

Colte was dead, and Kamilla was *here*.

My hands were clenched at my sides, teeth gritted, and eyes narrowed. I gave myself over to the fury, and it took the reigns gleefully, tampering down everything else.

Raw power reverberated, exploding out of my body, jade light humming with deadly intent.

I'd make them all pay for what they had done, and I'd enjoy every minute of it.

Shields in place again, my body glowing with a jade light, I walked through the camp, eyes focused on the fight ahead.

Moroi, Dhampir, and Lycanthropes all moved out of my way when they saw what my deadly light did to the Strigoi stupid enough to get near it.

Nothing got through my shields.

Not even the mists of blood, all that was left of the creatures touched by my power, reached me.

More and more Strigoi attempted to breach, to take me out as I made my way toward the front lines.

Abhijay's people swelled behind me, closing the ranks that their enemies had opened, dealing with the monsters that tried to run from the death I offered.

They were exhausted from the fight that had lasted all day, from seeing their friends and families slaughtered. Many were injured, barely able to wield their weapons.

But still, they fought, rallying at the sudden balance shift, adrenaline and hope filling the air alongside their battle cries.

Warriors on the front line noticed the shift before we reached them, pushing the Vârcolac, and the taloned monsters toward us, surrounding them, and giving them no escape.

A vampiric smile curled my lips as they met their bitter end.

My magic was starting to slow and weaken, energy expenditure too high to keep this attack up forever. I had taken out dozens, if not more, of the monsters, but there were still so many. And I had yet to see Abhijay or any of the Fae among the fight.

I took a minute to scan the battlefield, trusting that my magic would hold, and the Moroi and Dhampir around me could manage without me for a few moments.

The Fae armies were engaging the Lycanthropes further off, behind what was left of the Strigoi host – the latter attempting to return to the Moroi lines.

I spotted Abhijay leading a large group of his people toward them, an attempt to open a gap to lead the Lycanthropes to safety.

It was suicide – the arrival of the Fae had more than tripled the enemy's remaining numbers – and the Fae were fresh, the Moroi were not.

We needed more people. And we needed them *now*.

I sent a sliver of my magic out, hoping to find Valdis, Hadrian, Fallon, or Hunter. Even Ari would have been welcomed. But, wherever they were, it was too far. I could sense no one that could come to our aid.

I pictured them in my head, their faces floating behind my eyes. *I need you.* I pushed the thought out with as much force as I could muster, hoping beyond all hope that *someone* heard it.

Returning my attention back to the conflict happening around me, I noted that the Strigoi were beginning to retreat, pulling back to the Fae lines as they suffered from the renewed Moroi onslaught.

A quick glance in Abhijay's direction caused me to curse. His attempt to open the ranks around the Lycanthropes was failing. The Fae were too strong – using magic as well as weapons against them.

My own devastating magic petered out, expended, though my shields remained in place, granted, it was a weakened version.

"We need to help Abhijay," I muttered. "He won't last much longer without it."

"You heard her – *move!*" Someone shouted – a Moroi male with a wicked-looking double-edged sword slick with blood. "To the *Maharishi!*"

The call went up, echoing down the line. "To the *Maharishi!*"

The look in his eyes told me that he, like me, knew they wouldn't make it there in time.

But *I* could.

"Go," he said firmly, thrusting his chin in the direction of his Leader. "Save him."

"I'll meet you there," I told him.

"Leave some for me." He said, a wicked spark in his eyes, lifting his sword.

I nodded, grinning viciously in anticipation of killing the Fae. "Don't take too long, then," I warned, vanishing into thin air.

I reappeared beside Abhijay, almost catching a sword to the throat. Had my shields been down entirely, and AJ's reflexes been slower, I wouldn't have had a head anymore.

The Moroi's eyes widened, and he snapped something in another language – I assumed it was a curse. I would have been swearing like a sailor.

"What are you *doing?*" He growled in my face. I barely heard him over the blaring of battle. "You need to go!"

"Backup is coming, hold on," I yelled to him, ducking under a volley of arrows. I added some choice words under my breath, legs shaking.

He pulled me to him, dragging me backward, covering us both from immediate danger by placing us behind his people. *"Get out of here!"*

"Who's leading the Lycanthropes?"

"What?" He looked at me as though I had lost my mind, grip tightening at my elbow.

"Who is leading them?" I repeated. "Who is it that I need to be looking for over there?"

As it dawned on him what I had planned to do, his expression changed - his mouth drawn down, eyes narrowed and full of thunder. *Oh my, this man was not used to being disobeyed.*

I couldn't stop the smirk that tilted my lips, or that my eyes narrowed in a challenge. "Don't make me go over there blind, AJ."

An explosion knocked me off my feet, sending me flying.

I landed in the dirt *hard*, surrounded by fallen Moroi and Dhampir. A cheer rose from the ranks of the Fae, vicious snarls and howls joining in, loud enough that I could hear it over the ringing in my ears.

The ground shook with the rumble of marching feet as I realized my shields were gone. I was unprotected, unarmed, and my magic hadn't regenerated.

"Reform the line!" Someone shouted urgently. *"Incoming!"*

Shit.

Abhijay reached me then, crawling on hands and knees through the dirt. "Get up, Sapphira. Look for a woman – Freyja. She's in charge. *Go!*"

I'd never seen him so unnerved before, so out of control. Whatever was coming had to be terrible – genuinely horrifying for Abhijay to be acting this way.

He forced himself to his feet, bringing me with him, screaming desperately in my face. *"Go, Sapphira!"*

He pushed me away, spinning to pick up his fallen blade.

And then the full force of the Fae army bared down on us, and I lost him in the tumultuous sea of blood and death.

I couldn't use my magic to jump, so instead, I ran.

Dodging blades and teeth, arrows, magic, and claws – as well as falling bodies.

Something caught my arm, stinging as though I had been bitten. I cried out in pain but didn't stop.

Time itself blurred, so focused on making it to where I was supposed to go, precise details escaped me. For that, I was glad. I'd be having enough nightmares over what I had seen already, that adding *more* would find me never sleeping again.

Too soon, I was gasping for air.

I was tired and lacking energy, and still had so much distance to cover. Adrenaline had left me not long after my magic had, and I was running on empty.

Body shaking, I forced myself to keep moving, cursing myself for getting into this mess.

I could feel the smallest of slivers of the magic inside of me, building itself back up sluggishly.

It wasn't enough to conjure my shields again or use it as a weapon, so I left it there, letting it grow.

I felt a slight pressure in my head, like the beginnings of a headache, and heard the faintest of whispers, voice caressing my mind like a lover.

We are coming.

My heart soared, hearing those three simple words. Someone had heard me after all, and *help was finally coming!*

A surge of hope had me picking up speed, hurtling through the warzone with renewed enthusiasm. I barked a laugh, grinning like a fool, my mood lifting joyously despite the horrors that surrounded me.

They were coming, the Lycanthropes were close now, and I was still alive – things were looking up!

That was, until Kamilla stepped out in front of me, and punched me in the throat.

I was dead – or dying, at least. I had to be after that.

The pain was incredible, and not in a good way. Kamilla sure knew how to throw a punch.

I was making friends with the dirt again, mouth gaping like a fish as I tried to get air through, what felt like, a crushed windpipe.

The Fae bitch stood over me, a snarling smile on her perfect face, eyes ablaze with bloodlust. She wore the same armored dress that she had the last time I saw her, adding deadly but delicate-looking gauntlets on her hands, and from my vantage point, she looked like a War Goddess. The battle raged on behind her, devastatingly violent and bloody. The whole image was quite cinematic if I was being honest.

"You're supposed to be dead," the Queen mused. "Imagine my surprise when I saw you just now, running around like an idiot."

I stayed where I was, sprawled in the dirt, looking up at her while I struggled to breathe, unable to speak.

Kamilla bent down, getting closer to my head. "It's fascinating really, that someone as pathetic as you could ever be confused with a *Goddess*. How you escaped my home, killed my men, and hid your presence from me is baffling. Oh," She added, smiling condescendingly. "And I know what you did to Hadrian." She shook her head, tutting her tongue as if reprimanding a child. "*Naughty* little mortal."

An explosion erupted to our left, throwing chunks of dirt and people all around us. Kamilla didn't even flinch, her cold gaze focused on my face.

The chunks didn't touch her, disintegrating in little bursts of crimson light in a wide arc around her.

Magical forcefield, I realized jealously. *My own magic would be a nice asset right now*, I thought, But it still hadn't regenerated enough.

Kamilla flexed her fingers, long silver blades sprung from the gauntlets, effectively giving her claws.

She smirked as I flinched, trying to raise myself up onto my elbows and scoot backward, away from her.

"Look at you, crawling in the dirt, where you belong." She crooned, standing again to follow me leisurely. "You will die there, like the rest of your kind."

I struggled to my feet, watching her face as a predatory look entered her eyes. *Weapon* – I needed some sort of defense against her since magic was out of the question.

I risked looking around, searching for anything that could help me.

It was a mistake.

Kamilla lunged at me, claws aimed at my throat. She hissed as I ducked under them, spinning to keep my eyes on her.

She came at me again, feigning to the left, and swiping out to the right. The claws brushed my cheek, pain exploding as I moved too slowly.

I backpedaled, my foot catching on a body, and fell.

Kamilla laughed, closing the gap between us in the blink of an eye. She brought her knee down onto my chest, claws piercing through my shoulders, pinning me to the ground.

She hissed in my face, eyes triumphant. "Goodbye, little *bailitheoir draíochta*."

Raising her right hand, the claws releasing that side, she made to bring them down again, aiming this time for my throat.

Survival instinct kicked in, forcing my arm up, catching her wrist before the claws could reach my exposed neck.

That tiny sliver of magic inside of me flared, racing to the surface, ready to be of use at last.

I flung it at the Queen, watching as her eyes widened in surprise, my magic finding hers, and pulled it out, back into me.

My own eyes were wide, as shocked as Kamilla was.

"*No.*" It was a whisper, unsure, and afraid. "He said you wouldn't be able to do that."

As her magic poured inside of me, and my body gained energy, it was my turn to smile. I knew who she was talking about – it could only have been one person – or more correctly, God. Ares.

I pulled her other hand away, the claws tearing at flesh as I mistook the angle on the way out. I ignored the pain, pushing her away, relishing in the sight of her in the dirt, backpedaling like I had done moments before, as I got to my feet.

"He lied," I told her callously.

She was almost empty now, power depleted. Her pride wouldn't allow her to stay down, though, and she sprang to her feet, snarling. "You bitch!"

"You're right, I am." I laughed, drunk on magic – *giddy* with it.

I rebuilt my shields, more robust than they had ever been, crafting a sword from the power I had taken from Kamilla, and pointed it at the Queen. "I learned it all from you."

She saw, then, that there was no way she could defeat me without her magic. She saw no empathy or salvation in my face.

Kamilla saw only her coming death, and that realization reflected in her eyes.

The swirling luminescent jade magic, the young mortal woman with blazing green eyes, that would end her life.

And she ran from it.

My mind told me to go after her, to end her before she could regenerate her magic and cause more problems, but the magic inside of me was content to let her go. It wanted to merge and mutate – to grow into something bigger, *better*. I was inclined to agree, to bask in the pleasure of it.

I was full to bursting with power, *swimming* in it, as I watched her go.

I felt as though I could tear the world apart – felt as though I could do anything at all.

The rush was addicting, and I could sense what I craved all over the battlefield – there were thousands of Fae fighting there, *thousands* of different sources of magic.

I wanted *more*, and I was going to take it all.

I spotted Valdis and Hadrian at the far end of the battlefield, tearing their former oppressors to pieces.

The Necromancer had brought her own army – creatures that she had made from the dead. As she moved through the Fae warriors, dealing death blow after death blow, her movements like a deadly dance, her creatures threw themselves at their enemy with reckless abandon.

Hadrian fed on the souls of his victims, building strength even as his enemies weakened.

The whip in his hands was a hypnotic weapon. Long leather straps connected to a bone handle lashed out, the hooks on the ends efficiently catching prey and dragging them to the ground.

The magic he used to defeat them was unlike anything I had ever seen. Russet shadows that jumped from him and eviscerated flesh and snapped bones of the Fae he faced.

I made it to the Lycanthropes, eating magic and killing monsters along the way.

Freyja grinned at me after I had found her, exhausted but grateful for the help. "You took your time." She said, returning to face her adversary, ripping out his throat with her teeth. "Get us out of here, would you?"

Using Kamilla's magic, I reinvented the shields from earlier, the ones that left nothing of the enemy. This time, though, I made it an offensive weapon, not a defensive one.

I pictured the magic like battering rams, thrusting it out at the enemy between the Moroi and me.

Everything my creations touched exploded, the boosted power causing considerably more damage.

When the Fae realized that the Queen had vanished, and their enemy had gained the upper hand, they began to retreat, leaving their dead with the remaining Strigoi. They, too, began their retreat, seeing that their allies had left them.

A resounding cheer went up among the Moroi, Dhampir, and Lycanthrope survivors as they realized that the fight was over.

We had won.

Chapter Twenty

T he Pretender Queen is still out there?" Valdis asked, brows furrowed, voice incredulous. She slammed her palms on the table between us, almost splintering the wood with the force she inflicted. *"You let her go?"*

The last words were delivered with an animalistic snarl, her teeth bared, and brown eyes molten fury.

"Lapse in judgment," I shrugged, cleaning the filth from under my nails. I was sitting in the only chair in sight, seemingly the only one of us that could no longer control their legs.

I was trying hard not to lose control of my emotions, the aftershocks of the day were catching up with me.

And I was *not* okay.

Most of my energy and focus was used in keeping my body from shaking, and not falling into a weeping mess on the floor.

"I'm not going to apologize, but I know it was a mistake," I told her, adding somewhat nonchalantly, "and I plan on hunting her down anyway. Kamilla won't be a problem for much longer."

Valdis scoffed, rolling her eyes. "How exactly do you plan on doing that? She's going to go underground now – you should have taken her out while you had the chance!"

"Enough, Valdis," Hadrian said calmly from beside me.

Valdis, full of anger, hissed but didn't say another word.

"If there is nothing else you need me for, I need to focus on the clean-up," Abhijay informed the room – the *tent* – pushing himself off the edge of the table before the argument could continue. When no one opposed, he smiled, gratitude shining in his tired eyes. "Thank you for your help today, all of you. Without you, we would have surely lost."

He bowed, hand on his chest, and left.

The clean-up would involve removing all traces of the battle, moving the wounded, scouring for Strigoi nearby, and then – using magic similar to what the healer had used on Colte – burn the battlefield to ash.

Or so Abhijay had told me as we'd limped back to the camp after the fighting had ended.

Valdis was still glaring at me. I should have been able to see steam coming from her ears.

I sighed, getting to my feet, grimacing as my muscles protested.

Overused, and cut up, my shoulders and arms cried out the loudest, bleeding again every time I moved too much.

One of Abhijay's healers had been called to patch me up, but I'd refused, telling them to help the other wounded first.

There were that many injured Moroi, Dhampir, and Lycanthropes, that the healers hadn't returned, too busy fixing up the deserving men and women that had fought and lived through the day. I was more than okay with that.

But now all I wanted was a few painkillers, a hot bath, and about a week of uninterrupted sleep.

I'd worry about Kamilla, the Gods, and why my other friends hadn't come to help when I woke up.

"Look, I know that you're mad, I am too. But right now, I'm tired, I stink, and I'm coming off a major power high. Can we put a pin in this argument for now and just go home?"

Both Hadrian and Valdis startled at the last word, surprise, and pleasure on their faces.

"Home?" Valdis asked carefully, face surprisingly hopeful. Like she'd just found out she was going to have a sister.

I snorted, eyebrow raised but turned to the Soul Eater. "Your offer still stands, doesn't it Hadrian?"

He nodded, a smile playing at his perfectly sculpted mouth. "Of course it does; the suite is yours."

Valdis, letting the argument drop, for now, grinned, brown eyes sparkling in wicked pleasure. "You're going to live in Darkness?"

"I don't think there's anything left for me in Australia – my family is gone, my house is gone, and my friend is dead."

The smile on the Necromancer's face faltered.

"And besides," I paused, shrugging and smiling through the pain in my shoulders, the one in my heart, too. *That* pain would last longer and be harder to heal. But, the vengeance and wrath that I had planned for those responsible would be an excellent place to start. Kamilla had better stay in hiding because if she ever popped her head out, I'd rip it from her shoulders with a smile.

"I've found that Darkness suits me just fine."

The Gods

Y ou underestimated her, Brother." The Goddess stated
plainly, feeling power flow through her body for the
first time in centuries.

Her skin darkened, no longer pale but closer to her original
bronzed complexion. Her hair color, too, deepened. She
smiled, sighing in pleasure.

"It is only the beginning, Sister. One battle does not the war make." The God replied coldly, staunching the flow of magic he'd given, the cost of his defeat. "Let us see how your chosen one fares with what comes next."

A word from the author.

Thank you for reading! I hope you enjoyed the beginning of Sapphira's story.

If you *did* enjoy it and have a moment, I would appreciate it if you would think of leaving a review on Amazon, Goodreads – or anywhere you would typically do so.

Reviews are vital to an author's success for many reasons, and I, for one, love reading them!

Thank you so much – your support means the world to me, and I know for a fact that I would not be the author I am today without readers like you.

Acknowledgments

I'd like to thank Gary - Husband. Partner in crime. Bringer of food. Thank you for putting up with me and all of my crazy mood swings while writing this. Thank you for watching every single *Bluey* and *Paw Patrol* episode ever made with the kids. I'm sorry (but not really) You know I love you, right?

Thank you to my kiddies, who kept dad on his toes while I was doing my 'homework' – yes, just like you have to! (*Have* you done your homework today?!)

I love you guys, for real life.

Thank you to my mum, Lyn. I am who I am because of you. I love you always and forever. I'm totally your favorite, right? You can admit, I won't tell anyone. (Blink twice if it's yes!)

Thank you to my reading team: Shana, Toni, Rebecca, Evan, Tamara, Laura, and Ena.

Your support, time, and honesty are what made this possible. Thank you for being avid booklovers and readers of my favorite genres. And, of course, for letting me bug you at all hours. Are you up to do another one?

Thank YOU, dear reader, for taking a chance on my book.

There are literally *billions* of books out there, and yet you still chose mine!

Your support means so much.

About the author.

B.L. Callaghan is an Australian Foster Carer and Early years Educator with over a decade of industry experience.

B.L. is the author of the Kids in Care series, a children's picture book series for, and about, children in Foster Care.

She runs the Facebook page "More Than A Foster Carer", where she shares her experience working with the foster system.

B.L. lives in rural New South Wales with her husband, a changing number of children, a dog and some chickens.

As a self proclaimed creative soul, she has had a passion for writing fiction from an early age. When not wrangling chickens, children, or dogs, B.L. loves tagging along on epic quests, and being whisked off on magical adventures.

www.ingramcontent.com/pod-product-compliance
Lightning Source LLC
Chambersburg PA
CBHW020255120726
47904CB00001B/213